# Keep Your Hands
on the Wheel

KATHRYN HEYMAN

PHŒNIX

A PHOENIX PAPERBACK

First published in Great Britain by Phoenix House in 1999
This paperback edition published in 2000 by Phoenix,
an imprint of Orion Books Ltd,
Orion House, 5 Upper St Martin's Lane,
London WC2H 9EA

A CIP catalogue record for this book
is available from the British Library.

ISBN: 0 75381 086 7

Printed in Great Britain by
The Guernsey Press Co. Ltd, Guernsey, C.I.

*For Kym Heyman, with love and infinite respect.*
*Also, as always, for Richard Griffiths – beloved kindred,*
*beloved flesh.*

# *Order of Service*

The Entrance of the Bride

The Declaration of Purpose

The Confession

The Objections

The Vows

The Giving of the Ring

The Kiss

The Sermon

The Blessing

The Wedding Procession

*Prelude*

# Charis

This is me when I was thin. The hair isn't mine. Bright blue Cleopatra wig. Three bucks at the Royal Darwin Easter Show. We got one each: Marah's is bright red – they called it Fire Engine Passion. That one on Jethro's head is supposed to be rainbow. And mine was blue. It was the last time we went anywhere with Dad, so I must be – what, eleven? No. Twelve. Definitely twelve. I've got boobs. It's the last time I was ever thin. I keep it here on the fridge, to remind me. About being thin. That I can be. Have been. Mum's idea. She sent it to me with a note:

> Dear Charis,
>    Hope all is 'smashing and brill' ha, ha, as it certainly is for me. Dingo and I are off to the 'Snowies' for a week, which should be beaut – same old white stuff for you, hey? Anyway, dug this 'pic' up of you, look how thin you are!!! Thought it might help with your 'weight battle'. Stick it on the fridge as a reminder and when you go to eat anything, look at it and think: That's what I can be. Good idea? Always works for me! See you 'soon', still looking forward to the day you come home!
>    Lots and lots of love,
>    Mum.

And that was it. So I stuck it up, in case the spirit of my witch-mother is floating around this kitchen. Which wouldn't surprise me – if there's a chance I'll be caught eating something, my mother will be there, calorie-counter in hand. With lotsandlots of love, though, which is nice. Anyway, so that's what I can be. A

3

pubescent girl in a blue wig too scared to open her mouth. It's great to have ambition.

# *Marah*

Someone down the hall is playing 'Bridge over Troubled Water', do you believe it? I don't mean to, but I start to feel all soft. When you look through a window and there's music playing loud and there's mist and grey and falling leaves outside and there's warm tea inside you, somehow – have you noticed this? – somehow then Lloyd Webber, Cole Porter, even Simon and Garfunkel start to sound important. Emotive. You feel like you're in a movie, you let yourself be dictated to. I know for a fact that it isn't just me that this happens to, although not everyone is game enough to admit it. Game. I love that word, it's so fresh. Like a little bantam hen, isn't it? Strutting about, ready to take on the world. About to be eaten by a huge fat rooster. Do bantam roosters eat their hens? Actually, are they called bantam roosters? I should look it up in the bird book downstairs in the common-room. It probably wouldn't be there, though, not exotic enough. I'd best not look, I'd only be disappointed. It's not important anyway, not really.

They used to say that about Charis – game. Game for a laugh, game for a go. Who said that? Jethro, I think. I think I'm game, actually, more game than Charis. Because I'm here, I was game to get here, game to make my future. Mother calls it sensibly making choices, but it's gameness. It's fall outside. Fall. I'm trying to use the right words, to make myself sound less like an Australian. Fall. Sidewalk. Nickle. I'm not trying to pick up an accent, not really, but I think a slight twang would be nice. I wouldn't complain is what I mean. I bought two sweaters the first week of semester, with a big Y on the front. One blue and one white. You can buy postcards with a picture of the campus on the front, they're very discreet. I bought twenty and I've made a list of who to send them to. Not to make a big deal of it, just to, you know, say here I am: I got here. Absolutely got here.

Mother gave me a self-timing camera before I left, so I'm snapping all over the place, just for the fun of it. Here's me kicking leaves outside the halls. Jethro gave me the mittens. This is me in front of the Chrysler Building – I asked an old woman to take it for me, I thought she wouldn't steal the camera, but I was still nervous. It's a good camera. I don't like that one so much, I look a bit fat in it, if the truth be told. Maybe it's because I was worried about her taking the camera. Silly, silly me. I'm collecting them all on my wall, and I think I'll send some home as well. I want to have one of me ice skating, maybe doing a turn with my arms out in the air. That's for when winter comes. Maybe it would be nice to have someone else in that photo. And to be a size eight when it's taken.

# The Entrance
## of the Bride

# All Dressed in White

The light zebras down the car. Charis, dozy in the dark-light-dark of it, walks her fingers along the edge of the window, a line of glass barely squeezing out from the rubber. Her fingers walk and dance, keeping time with the shadows and with the radio songs. Up the coast they drive, upup and up, then in, heading for the centre. They started out way before dawn. Noeline was still in bed, Charis and Marah had peeped in at her, spread across the huge bed, her arm thrown out. She always opened her mouth when she slept. Once, Jethro stuck an apple in her mouth while she was asleep like that, mouth wide open, arms spread out. She walloped him when she woke up that time. Really walloped him, which wasn't like her at all, she said so herself. 'Mum.' Marah whispered it from the door, just to see what would happen, just wanting her to wake up and say, Oh, what the hell, why don't I come too? But she hadn't. No sound from that mother, not even a flicker of an eye. Still, it was an adventure, having breakfast in the dark, hearing no sound from the road outside. Jethro ate his Weetbix with his eyes closed while Joe carried all the bags out to the car. They'd driven for hours before there was even a slash of pink, knifing across the sky.

Joe is alone in the front, his hands big and brown on the wheel. The front seat is strange and empty without Noeline beside him, her hand on his knee. Charis, Marah and Jethro are tucked in the back, skin sticking to the vinyl seat. Now and then, Joe says, 'Climb over the front,' to Jethro, and Charis says, 'Can't I climb over the front, Dad? I'm the eldest,' because she calls him that even though he's not her dad, not really, not her real one, and he says, 'No, only Jethro, because Jethro gets sick.' The road winds out endlessly before them, the shadows stretching for miles, the tar bubbling below them. The day grows white with the heat and houses stop flashing past them on the side of the road, replaced by tall eucalypts. Then the trees stop, replaced by thick scrub. And then, the scrub stops. Just dust and the occasional dead tree stump.

When another car drives past, they yell and wave at each other like old, old mates. Play 'I Spy'. Run out of things to spy. Something beginning with D. Dirt. Something beginning with D. Dust. Something beginning with D. Dead wombat. Joe starts singing an old song, bunging on a girl's voice specially: '*Keep your mind on the drivin' and your hands on the wheel, keep your snoopy eyes on the road ahead. We're havin' fun, sittin' in the back seat, huggin' and a-kissin' with Fred.*' When he finishes each bit he does a high-pitched giggle and Charis leans over the seat and hits him and tells him not to be so silly.

They make it all the way to Eucka on the first night. Unfold themselves from the Land Rover, bones creaking, noses full of the smell of burning vinyl. Heads full of heat and country music and long shadows. Red dust dances around their feet, catching clothes, dipping into mouths. Jethro chucks his guts up, as soon as his feet touch the dust. Joe says, 'No more Minties for you, my boy,' and Jethro sticks his tongue out all covered in spew. Loads of trucks are parked in the dusty car-park. A big sign is stuck up outside: EUCKA MARIGOLD TRUCK STOP CAFÉ – BEDS. EATS. GAS, painted on in red. Joe blows his lips out when he sees the sign. 'Gas, ha. Do they think we're in bloody America?' and Marah mouths the word 'America', all dreamy.

There is a line of demountable rooms out the back of the service station, three of them lined up next to each other, and divided inside by partitions as thin as cardboard. One room for the four of them: four single beds, one desk, one lamp, one tiny electric fan whirring like crazy. Yellow curtains, covered with dust. The shower is outside, in another demountable. Bore water it is, stinking of the deep earth. Marah ties a hankie over her nose while she showers, but then she gets dust all over her legs as soon as she is dry. Charis just holds her nose and Jethro says

10

he doesn't want a shower anyway, he'd rather stink of his own smell. Inside the café, three men in blue singlets are huddled around one red table. The waitress has a name badge – Trudi – but when Joe says, 'Give us three burgers, two Fantas, one Cherry Cheer and a pot of coffee, wouldya, Trudi?' she gives him the filthiest look ever. Joe whispers that probably Trudi pinched the name badge from someone else and her real name is actually Fredarina. Jethro laughs so much that the Cherry Cheer spurts out of his nose and then Charis has to put her head on the table until her guts stop hurting from laughing. Even after they turn out the light in the stuffy little room, Joe keeps saying, 'Fredarina,' and, 'Oh, my darling Fredarina, please may I have a spot of burger in my burger?' in a really posh voice and then they laugh so much that the beds squeak.

There are two bright orange nylon tents in the back of the Land Rover. One for Charis and Marah, one for Jethro and Joe. They leave the Eucka truck stop when the sun comes up, and Jethro hangs out the window yelling, 'Bye, Fredarina, we love you,' as they drive away, laughing their heads off. Now and then, Joe goes all quiet in the front, stops singing suddenly and stares ahead at the road, with his lips pulled together the way he does sometimes. Outside the window, the tree stumps start to look taller, whiter, and thicker. Anthills, Joe says. Giant buildings made of sand and dust and full of whopping great white ants. They pull over and Marah takes a photo with her new Polaroid: Joe, Charis and Jethro, standing next to one of the anthills, grinning into the blaze of sun. The anthill towers over all of them. It sounds hollow when you put your ear to it, but there are zillions of billions of lives going on in there.

They pass Ungudara and Walla-walla before they see a big green sign pointing the way to the Manchester Arms Hotel. Hang a left and go straight for eighty miles and there it is. Surrounded by the red dirt of the Territory, but with a fake green lawn, a metal arch over the entrance, and a garden of dry-looking roses. The skinny woman behind the bar has sweat pouring out of her. There is a picture of the queen when she was young and beautiful and a row of trophies for something or other, all lined up and polished on the high mantelpiece. A round blue neon light buzzes behind bars, now and then sizzling with the sound of electrocuted fly. The lemonade comes in a jug and the woman says no, they can't have a glass of iced water – they like to keep the water for the roses. Joe raises his eyebrows high up near his hair, says, 'What's bloody wrong with wattle or kangaroo paw?' but he says it so quiet that no one would notice anyway. They take the jug outside, sit at a wooden table shaded by a huge jacaranda.

'Aaaaaah. That's hit the right spot. Bloody oath.' Joe stretches his arms above his head, his belly poking out between his shorts and his singlet.

'Giss some chips, Dad, I'm starvin.' Jethro pokes his father's arm.

'Shoulda eaten yer eggs at brekky, then.'

'Garn, Dad.'

'Yair orright, piss off, then. Get some for all of us, willya? Here's two bucks – I'll have salt and vinegar.'

Jethro takes the dust inside with him.

'Da-aad.' It is Charis who starts it, kicking her heels against the wooden bench, flicking jacaranda leaves away with her fingers.

'Wha-aat?' He does the whining voice back at her.

'It's a good holiday.'

He blows a loud breath out of his lips, like a lazy laugh. 'Giss a chance, we've only just begun.'

'It's good but.'

'Yair, really good.' Marah does her special super-grin at him.

'Why wouldn't Mum come with us?' Charis, trying the Marah-grin, but ending with a face that seems lopsided. 'She'd have a good time with us.'

'Yair.' Joe's face goes heavy. 'Sure she would, love. She just needs a break at the moment.'

'From us?' The super-grin slips from Marah's face.

'From everything, I think. You know yer mother, she works too hard for her own bloody good, she reckons she's got to do all the lesson plans for next term and sort all the rosters out. Problem with being head-teacher. Anyway, I wanted some time with you on me own, isn't that allowed?' He tilts back on his

12

chair, calls over his shoulder. 'Hurry up with those chips, Jethro, ya great bludger.'

They scoff the chips, wiping salty fingers on clothes. The sun burns down in dapples, makes black and white patches across the dry lawn. They fall dreamily silent, lulled by the heat and light. Big sighs fall from them. Charis's eyes start to close, her head tipped back, warm and moist. Sweat trickles down her face, a bead of it drips from her chin. When the lemonade is gone, Joe says if they don't get a move on they'll never get to Kakadu, let alone bloody Darwin. When they walk through the bar, stumbling a bit from the sudden darkness, he turns the picture of the queen around to face the wall. Charis turns it back again, so that Her smiling face can be seen. Charis thinks the queen is lovely, just lovely.

They only mention Noeline once more, just before they reach the gates of Kakadu and Jethro says, 'I wish Mum was here, why isn't she?' and no one answers. After a while, trees appear again, but real trees not scrub. Thick and ripe with green, and green earth as well. The sun is sinking behind the trees, an orange fireball dive-bombing the land – smooth as smooth – and the dark begins to rise up and swallow the ground.

They drive to the end of a wide dirt road while the light still hovers around the trees and they pitch the orange tents by a gorge, a series of falls. Joe tears up mosquito net and wraps them each up, one at a time, Jethro first. Makes them turn around and around while he douses them with the chemical cold smell of Aeroguard. There's no mozzie net left for him, so he holds a burning mosquito coil and rubs the rest of the Aeroguard into his face. Charis and Jethro pretend to be mummies from Egypt, jumping out and scaring Marah, who is a bride coming down the aisle, all dressed in white. Dum dum da da. Joe is the bride's husband, waiting at the end of the aisle with a mosquito coil in his hand instead of a ring. They have to run screaming when Jethro and Charis jump out from behind the Land Rover going, 'Who disturbs the mummies, wooooooo.' They do it six times, the marriage never quite coming off because of the mummies, until Marah trips on her mozzie net and starts crying. Joe lights four mozzie coils in a square outside the tents, one for each corner of

13

the earth. Marah sleeps like Noeline, her arm spread out, flung over Charis's chest.

They wake to the smell of bacon and the sound of the waterfall. Joe has tied a bit of the mozzie net around his head and dances around the gas ring singing, 'Burn, baby, burn, disco inferno,' pointing his arms all over the place. Charis says, 'You're such a dag, Dad,' and hugs him hard. They eat the bacon straight from the pan, holding the rashers on bits of paper towel. Marah eats only one piece, which is good, it leaves more for Jethro and Charis. When they finish up, Joe says, 'Right, who's for a morning dip?' and everyone says, 'Me, me.'

They race through the trees, playing Catchies under the dark wet of the rainforest, with the whuuuuush of waterfall getting bigger, even bigger. Jethro is It, he whacks his hand on Charis's arm and yells, 'You're It.' A mosquito bites her nose and she slaps herself on the face. She's laughing so much she trips on the root of a bougainvillaea. Joe puts his foot on top of her and says, 'We claim this Charis in the name of the republic,' and Jethro and Marah cheer while Charis pretends to cry big sobbing tears. Joe hoiks her to her feet and points at the very next tree – huge, a huge bloody thing it is. Wide as the whole place and its leaves making the place where they stand dark as dark. There is a hole in the ground – just a hole, like God has poked a finger through – and the roots, thick as the branches of a redgum, run down through the hole. Down and down the roots, making a kind of ladder, the haired roughness of the roots sanding fists and faces. Joe climbs down first, then Jethro, then Charis, and Marah last. She almost stops breathing, the hole is so tight. The hole gets smaller and even smaller, the earth coming close and pressing on the edges of her back. She scrunches her eyes tight shut then – somehow this is easier with dark inside as well as out – and feels the rub of Joe's hands on her waist, feels the whoosh of his breath, lifting her down, feet on squelch of solid mudground.

The light hits her eyes like a bomb. She snaps them shut again, lets the light ease into her face, woo the lids apart. It was the same for everyone; it's so bright when you get to the bottom you just have to hold your breath. They have climbed down to a heaven. The roots settle and dig on the edge of a spring, bubbling and only just warm. All around is green, with little diamonds and crosses of light jumping through. They step into the water in a line, Joe holding hands with Marah holding hands with Jethro holding hands with Charis. Soft sand sinks under their feet while they run, screeching like parrots, into the water. Warm and soft, like the sand. Even a waterfall, blasting its way down the rock on the far side of the pool. Marah says, 'This is the best, Dad. The best thing ever,' and Charis lies on her back with the water just over her ears. Water slips over her cheeks like skin and her hair floats up around her. She closes her eyes. Listens to the splashing as if it's far away. She knows her face won't stop smiling. Not ever. By the time they get out of the water the sun is high up overhead and all the shadows have disappeared.

They eat white bread rolls filled with sweaty cheese for lunch. The milk has spilt in the esky, so everything smells a bit cow-like. After lunch, Joe wraps left-over mozzie net over their eyes and walks with them in a line. All holding hands again, but this time with Joe leading. His voice is strong and clear, calling out in among the kurrajongs, 'Not far, that's the way, no, don't take it off, Jethro, it's meant to be a surprise.'

Jethro tugs and rubs at the rough blindfold. 'It itches, Dad. It's scratching at my head.'

'Orright, take it off if it's really truly scratching. If you really can't stand it. But you have to keep your eyes shut, or it will spoil the surprise. Well, ya don't have to, I spose – it's up to you, but I reckon it'll be better if it's a surprise.'

Jethro leaves the blindfold on and lets himself be pulled along in this human chain, lets himself be pushed by Joe on to something solid and yet swaying beneath this feet. He can hear water, but still opens his mouth in a loud gasp when the netting is finally pulled off him. 'We're on a boat. Excellent.' He swings his head about like a bird, watching everything, everywhere.

There is a solid engine chug and they start moving, slowly, into the sun. The woman in the big hat – Nora Yoreguide – speaking into a little microphone, tells them that there are hundreds of plant and animal species. Charis and Marah lean over the edge – the gunnel, Nora calls it – counting types of plant. Near the water's edge, there's a fallen tree, brown and dry-looking. As the ripples from the boat ease across the river, the tree opens its mouth wide, wider than a river. Marah screams and Charis feels a trickle of wet seep into her knickers. Joe puts his arm around each of them, his mouth wide and happy on his brown face. 'Don't ever be sucked in by a crocodile, my girls. They're cunning bastards. Really bloody cunning.' Jethro runs across and all over the boat, looking for more crocs. Each time he sees one he swings his arms up high and sings out, 'Hello crocodile, you cunning bastard.' Not one crocodile responds.

By the time they pack up the tent the next morning, Joe has skin peeling all across his shoulders. Jethro is pink except for the stripe across his nose where he remembered to put Zinc cream. They drive up the dusty road again, playing Spot-O and Twenty Questions. Jethro wins each time. When they get to Darwin, the sun is setting and they can just see a Ferris wheel in the distance, twirling away on the casuarina spit. Red and orange fire across the sky, lighting the wheel up. It looks as bright as fairy floss, but Joe says it's shutting down for the night soon and anyway better to be there first thing, bright and early after a good rest, tomorrow. Tomorrow, when everything is bright and good. This is a memory. Memory can be that way.

# *Charis*

There's a huge man with a sword in front of me. I have to cut him open before I can get to the prize, but he's got the sword and he's waving it right in my face, right up close, and saying he doesn't want to hurt me, he won't hurt me if I promise not to tell. I wake up when I scream, the same as I always do, a strangled little sound which wouldn't get me saved in a dark alley. But anyway. My pillow is wet with sweat and spit. I've been doing that dribble thing that I hate but can't seem to stop doing. My room stinks, there's probably a mouldy apple core under the piles of clothes. I lie in bed holding on to my skin, tucking my hands under the small fold of fat on my gut. It's warm there. Familiar. I keep my eyes open for hours, not wanting to sleep again, not wanting the man with the sword to come, and not trusting him to stay away.

I must fall asleep some time, though, cause I wake up to the sound of Janey and John screwing really loudly. John's shouting, 'Oh, do it, baby, baby,' and Janey is barking like a bloody poodle, for God's sake. I wait until the noises have stopped before I get up. My whole self is aching like I've been in a fight. I must've slept with my head tucked under my wing, cause my neck feels like it's bent in two. Bloody bloody. Janey's left two pineapple danishes in the bread-box, so I eat them both, to get back at her for making the poodle noises and also to give me strength to face the Fat Controller. I sit and stare out of the window for a while, with bits of danish sticking to my fingers and around my mouth. It's one of those mornings when everything is slow, maybe a hangover from the dream. Even after rubbing my face hard with

17

the stinking grey face-cloth, I still feel like my body isn't with me. Like I'm only half here.

Downstairs, the street is wide awake. Heat from the launderette seeps up through the floorboards. Launderette. If I say to people that I live above a laundromat, they look at me, like: a what? How bright do you have to be before you work it out? Laundromat equals launderette. Bottle-o equals off-licence. In the end, it's easier to use their language than to try to explain and explain and explain. Like it's so difficult to get. Either way: I'm speaking like a yank or a pom, that's my choice, always. When it's grey outside, like this, I forget what I came here for. Forget that I chose it, to be a pom, to be here. Where it all happens. Where the opportunities are. Where the culture is. Culture being me dressing up in half-torn costumes and singing snazzy little anniversary/birthday/wedding songs to public servants. Still, better than South Windsor, Western Sydney, New South Bloody Wales. Better than suffocation. Or than a slap around the chops with a wet mullet, for that matter.

By the time I get outside, the sun is almost blaring and the launderette is full of bodies and the smell of other people's washing. My moped starts on the second go, which is something of a record, and I almost convince myself that if the lights are with me, I won't be late. Or, more ridiculously, that the Fat Controller won't notice whether I'm on time or not.

'Take ya bleedin time, Big Gracie.' He's standing on the steps when I get there, holding the preggy-bride costume out as if I'm half an hour late instead of a measly bloody twenty minutes. Wanker. I wish he wouldn't call me Big Gracie, but I've given up trying to tell him, because I can see he loves it when I get annoyed, so I just imagine myself decking him instead, while I smile with my lips closed. It's my own fault, I suppose, for telling him about me name. Charis. Charis means grace. I was laughing at the time, a bit pissed, I think, goin, 'Me mum thought I was gunna be full of grace, anyway that's what she wanted.' The Fat Controller had laughed. 'She got that dead wrong, didn't she? Have ya gotta sister?'

None of his bloody business is what I said, and it isn't.

18

I stay sat on the moped, just staring at him.

'Getya skates on darlin' I hate it even more when he calls me darlin and you can see the spit trickling down his chin. What I hate the most is when he calls me Little Ozzie, as if I'm his pet. He blows his nose, makes a loud snort. 'Hadda call for a Betty Bondage in Hackney. Do 'er first, then pop up to Islington for the preggy bride. KO?'

I say OK, and get changed inside, in the office. There's a big JANGLE'S JINGLES sign leaning against the desk and a pile of telegrams. Donny a.k.a. Fat Controller writes all the telegrams, doesn't trust it to anyone else. It's very sensitive, he says, a very important occasion in people's lives, they need it to be special. I look at the song for this one:

> When Bobby lies down in the boardroom
> Anne from accounts is there too
> it's lucky the missus missed the meeting . . .
> or else she'd be screamin' screw you (boom, boom).

I mean, for God's sake. This is for the guy's leaving do in some office. I have to storm in, all dressed in my preggy-bride costume (bride dress, veil under my moped helmet, plastic cushion – nothing new or blue) and throw my bouquet at him, accusing him of leaving me at the altar, sing him the telegram (they're all to the tune of 'My Bonnie Lies over the Ocean') and then storm off, sobbing. Glamorous work indeed. Betty Bondage, as you can imagine, is even better. A German accent, fishnets and stilettos, a big black cape and a nice assortment of whips. I put a collar on the birthday boy and drag him around the room in front of his mates. Big belly laugh. In the words of the witch-mother: ha ha. I whipped a guy really hard once, and drew blood, because he'd tried to grope at me under my leotard. Give me half a chance and I'll rip out the next guy's fingernails.

I have to squeeze myself into a size-fourteen leotard and bride dress (also the black dress for – you guessed it – the French Maid, ooh la la, Messieurs), cause Donny doesn't like his girls to be over size fourteen for the straight singing telegrams. He'll have them up to a size twenty for the Fat-o-rama Strip-o-grams.

Anything over a size twelve can be a Fat-o-rama, which is handy to know, isn't it? The first telegram I did, I was so nervous I thought I was going to be sick all over the guy. Donny came with me, stood at the back of the room watching me, giving me the thumbs up when I started shaking. It was a Valentine one, with me as the gift. Fancy that, hey, some girl giving her boyfriend a French Maid singing telegram for some romantic gift on Valentine's Day. I couldn't work that one out, still can't. But then, I can't work Valentine's Day out at all, I can't work romance out, or sex, or anything. It seems like a waste of time to me, even though I can't think of anything else to be doing with my time. It's true, Janey and John always seem busier or less bored than me. They don't seem happier, though.

Janey got me this job. At least, she saw the ad, saw me being miserable being a waitress and said, 'Go on, go for it, you've got a great voice.' When I was a kid, before Dad left, we went up to the Territory and stayed for ages in some hotel. Marah and Jethro and I made up musicals and performed them around the pool and everyone in the hotel told us how wonderful and clever and talented we were. I couldn't get enough of it. Marah spent most of the holiday being sick, throwing up for any old reason: too much fairy floss, too many somersaults, too much bumping in the car. She was always like that: fragile. Jethro and I were hardier, stronger. Like Dad. Or like I thought Dad was, until he didn't bother coming back.

Anyway, blah blah blah and all that. I put Betty Bondage on first – it's gunna be a bit tricky, I can see that, cause for Betty I paint black swastikas on my face (black lips and barbed-wire lines on my eyebrows – it's all very tasteful) and the blushing-bride look doesn't go with swastikas. So I'm gunna need to find a ladies somewhere, whack some Ponds Deep Clean on to the face and paint some rosy lips on before I stick the cushion up my gillet. It's OK, though – I'm going over it all in me head while I get into me suspenders and stuff. Donny's still standing outside on the stairs when I walk out, starin at nothin. He goes, 'Careful with the dress, my girl,' like he always does and I stick my finger up at him and say, 'No wucking furries,' like I always do and then I ride off into the sunset. Ha ha again.

My *A to Z* is falling apart in my rucksack. Page twenty-three, the one page which happens to have the street I need, is torn in two. One half of the page is creased up and covered with what appears to be orange juice. The other half is fine, apart from a splodge of chewing gum covering what was once Mare Road. I throw both halves away and head off in the direction of the Hackney Empire, pull over, run into a chip shop and ask where J & E Services is. The shop smells of dead cat. The woman behind the counter says, 'Services for what?' I'm like: How the hell am I supposed to know? Services, it's just services. Could be personal services, motor services, bloody farmyard services for all I know. Still, there's no point in getting her off side, so I just ask where the nearest minicab office is and run out of the shop yelling, 'Thanks anyway.' The cab office (smashed cashier window, cigarette buts on the floor, smells of stale beer – could be my place) is devoid of any handy smart-ass cab drivers, but a bloke waiting for a taxi to King's Cross tells me that Sinclair Street is literally around the corner. If it weren't for the fact that he adds, 'Sexy outfit, baby' (he does, he says 'baby'), I would want to kiss him.

The birthday do is happening right in the poor bloke's bloody office, a huge room with his secretary sitting outside like a guard dog. She knows about it, because she stands up when she sees me coming and shows her teeth in what I think is meant to be a smile rather than a growl. She says she'll buzz him, so that he can come out and everyone can see. There's a whole corridor with offices off either side, so I start to make a racket and tap on all the doors. 'Come on out, Betty Bondage is about.' I didn't pretend it was classy. Eventually I get a bit of an audience, standing about in the corridor, not sure what to make of it all. Laughing, but most of them – the blokes especially – are pink around the ears as well. Seems to be mostly men, in crumpled white shirts and ties. There's a couple of bewildered-looking women in floral dresses. Birthday Boy is grey-haired and even more bewildered than the women. I drag him about in front of them for a few minutes, make him lift his leg against the secretary, sit up and beg, that sort of thing.

The way everyone laughs when I call the bloke Betty's naughty little pooper scooper, I get the idea that he's the boss, so

I whack him really lightly with my whip, don't even ask him to take his shirt off. I'm flat as a bagpipe when I sing, but they all seem to think it's marvellous anyway. Outrageous. I can hear them in the pub later, telling each other and their mates, 'Absolutely outrageous, hey, we're mad at work, we are. Stark bloody mad.' One of the white shirts stuffs an extra twenty quid in my hand, goes, 'We must keep the mistress happy,' really, really slimy.

I get changed in this teensy cubicle that they call a loo, and it stinks as well. Beautiful bride I make, though. I get the usual honks and cars stopping to let me cross the road and all that and I give em all big waves or fingers, depending. It's best at the lights, when I stop and put me feet down to balance myself on the moped, I get that double-take thing from whoever's in a car next to me. They kind of glance out the corner of their eye, see the white dress, the preggy belly – then their heads swing around for real. I try to pull the dress up so I don't get stuck on the take off. It's good when I'm doin Betty Bondage or the French Maid as well, cause they get an eyeful of fishnets and stilettos under the wedding dress. People have weird ideas about brides, I reckon. Like, they shouldn't be able to even walk on their own, let alone ride a moped. (OK, it's no Harley but it's tougher than a Volvo. Isn't it?) Mum had some old uncle give her away when she married Dad. Should have been my real father, I suppose – whoever he is – but I can't see him being willing. Given the circumstances. So it was a smelly old uncle whose name I don't even know. She said he had to because her father was dead and anyway she hated him, so what other man was there to do it? That's what she says, whenever I ask. Which isn't often these days, obviously.

It takes me ages to find the right building for the preggy bride. I just grin at the people who stare at me on the street. Mostly wankers, but some grin back. The office turns out to be some paper supplier's or something, stuck up on the tenth floor in this huge posh white building, which means I have to go through two lots of reception and no one knows anything about the telegram. Security blokes snigger as I walk off, so I give em a flash of me bum, complete with red fishnets. That shuts em up. I find the place eventually and the guy stands around looking awkward, like they always do. During the song, I look around for Anne from Accounts, but I can't spot her. I throw the bouquet at him, storm out, and get stuck in the elevator with some doddering old bloke who keeps asking me where the wedding is. Altogether now: ahhhhh, sweet.

So, I'm zooming along Islington High Street – i.e. zooming at twenty miles an hour, putputput – thinking about the coffee éclair I'm gunna get from Delifrance once I drop the dress back to Donny. I've got a left-over scrap of halva in me bike pack, so I reach behind me when the lights turn red. It's covered in fluff where the plastic wrapper has come undone, but I'm not too bothered, I scoff it anyway. I'm starving. Or at least very hungry. I shouldn't really say I'm starving, because according to Janey if I live in the Western world, the likelihood of me starving is a quazillion to one. Or something. She's always coming out with figures like that, numbers that don't mean anything. I expect the lights to take ages to change back, the way they usually do in stinking bloody London (I like moaning about London, it makes me feel really European and well travelled), so I lean back against the bike pack, close my eyes and chew, just for a second. And in that second the lights turn green. Surprise bloody surprise.

Some yobbo in a blue Merc starts honking at me before I've even got a chance to swallow the halva, let alone kick the starter. He gets a finger from me as I vroom off, get about twelve feet across the intersection and sort of stutter to a stop. The glorious Oxfam wedding dress is caught in the wheels, so either the moped stops or I come flying off. In terms of humiliation it doesn't make much difference either way, cause by the time I get off the shitting bloody bike, the back half of the wedding dress is completely torn away and wrapped like a bandage around the back wheel. Being a total grown-up, I kick the bike and scream at it before I start unravelling the poor bloody dress. Glamour glamour glamour, that's me.

Cars are banked up behind me, tooting horns madly while I wiggle my big fishnetted bum in their faces. When I get the dress unravelled and turn around to wheel the moped to the side of the road, the guy behind me stops hooting and leans out the window, says, 'Oh dear, I'm sorry, love, would you like a hand?' like he's just realized I'm pregnant. I say, 'No, thanks, I'm fine,' and then shudder as if I'm having contractions. I keep pushing the bike, but stopping every couple of steps to double over. I'm panting and pushing for all I'm worth and hanging on to my belly. He yells, 'Hang on,' and, pulls over to the side of the road and gets out of his car. I go, 'Oh no, oh no, my waters've broken, it's gunna come, me baby, me baby,' really loud and half-hysterical, pushing like mad. Bloke pulls his mobile phone out of his pocket – wanker – and starts dialling, while I push harder and make loud grunts, till I pull the inflatable cushion out and go, 'My baby, my baby.'

Bloke has no sense of humour, honestly. He just stands there, looks at me like I'm piece of poo, then walks off back to his car. Slams the door.

The gutter's cold on me bum, but at least I get to sit down. My lips are shaking like I'm about to start laughing me head off, and I think I am, I can feel that trembly laugh feeling building up down in me chest. I feel it come up through my throat and I open my mouth, ready for the laugh to dive out. My chest keeps shaking, but I realize I'm crying, not laughing at all. If Donny sacks me, I'll have to go home. I hate London, but at least it's not home.

# Marah

The room is too cold, I can practically feel nodes developing on my vocal cords just from the strain of waking up, taking a breath, walking across the floor. Really, and winter is supposed to be ending. Every morning, the sun makes a stripe across my face and wakes me up. No matter how cold it is, you still get the bright sun. I could pull the curtains shut I suppose, but I don't. I like it, being woken up like that, with that stripe of sun shining into my eyes. The cold doesn't actually hit me until my feet touch the floor. The boards are bare and dark. The whole room is dark. Actually, the whole of the hall is like this, dark, boarded, held in. Why it should be worse for graduates, I don't know, but the truth is that it is. Is worse. And I don't think it's just me. All the grad students look dark like the hall, full of gloomy wood. It's the cold that makes me think like this, bleak and old.

I sat outside Sterling Library yesterday, going over the libretto. Everyone else seemed to be in little clusters of people, all amazingly bright and excited. Little huddles, giggling. I don't believe the giggling for a moment, though, I know it's a trick. When you walk past Davenport it looks all ancient and stone; they call it mock-Tudor or something. But if you get in through the gate, look behind you or look around the quad, you see it's not stone at all, it's all red brick, with shabby shutters that don't even close. The giggling is like that, that's what I think. If you get through the gate of the giggler, I believe it would be a whole different picture. Because it always is. And that's what I need to get, in the audition. I need to get not just the voice but the intention. Intention behind the action – I've got that underlined in my notes from Supplementary Drama on Friday. Everyone

25

moans about having to do it, including me, but actually I like it. Collette said she thought it was really a bit much expecting us to do that on top of everything else, and what's the point, it's the voice that counts. Lenherr says versatility, that's what counts, and he's right. Callas was a magnificent voice, but it was her performances that brought everything to life. Action and intention, anyway, that's what I'm going for.

This is the darkest of all the colleges, and the coldest, it must be. Nodes, nodes, nodes: do not think about nodes. Apparently you're five times more likely to get cancer if you think about it once a day than if you never think about it, that's the truth. Nodes are the same, I'm sure, although no research has been done on it yet. There are three things I have to do when I wake up; they fight over which comes first. At the moment, this is the order:

1. Toilet and wash face. I think these can count as one, because I do them both in the same space, more or less. Same space being the triangle of floor which sits in between my room and Wilma's. Instead of a mirror, there's a whole wall of reflective metal, so you feel like you're in an industrial fridge.
2. One hundred sit-ups, a combination of crunches, stretches, pulses and twists, and I'm always careful with my back.
3. Dressing-gown on and vocal warm-up.

Again, I know they could count as two things, two separate actions, but the truth is it takes hardly any time to whip my dressing-gown on and then just a second to get myself by the window. Also, they are one intention. So, I think it would be silly to count them twice, because then I might as well count everything. Pulling back the sheets. Sitting up in bed. Swinging legs out from bed. Placing feet on floor. Taking steps into bathroom. You see? It would go on for ever and obviously I haven't got time to spend the whole of my life putting everything into order, only some things. Only the important things. I know standing by the window is a bad place to warm up, the cold comes straight through the glass and I could easily get distracted by looking down at Cross Campus and wishing I was on the grass with a little huddle of friends. But I don't, I just don't do that. I'm more in control than that. Anyway, it's not a proper warm-up, it's not like I'm stretching my cords or anything, because actually I'm not. All it is, I'm opening my throat, loosening it enough for the day not to be a shock.

Lenherr's wife had nodes and she'll never sing again, not properly. I've got no intention of ending up like that. She was a lovely soprano. Beautiful. Very florid, I suppose, but amazing control. Lenherr played me a recording of her as Mimi in *La Bohème* – a New York Opera version. Absolutely lovely. Even in the recording you could tell it wasn't just words and voice for her, that she loved Rodolfo madly. The thing is to get them both, the vocal control and the character belief. Lenherr said I try to coast on the physical performance and it's a waste and I have to get my voice *out* and *up* and it doesn't come from my throat and I sound like a straining fishwife and how can I get an Australian accent even into the Italian? Tapping me on the diaphragm the whole time. Because I told him I did drama-school before I switched to the Con., he's decided I need to work sixty billion times harder on aural and vocal skills. As if I would have got a scholarship if I wasn't up to scratch. Not that I said that to him, I never open my mouth to him except to sing. Anyway, Lenherr: I don't want you in my head right now.

Thing is, I need to be warm and soft for the audition, but I need to hold something back. That's a drama-school trick and they thought I was mad at the Con., but who got the only K. G. DeGado Yale School of Music Scholarship for International Students of Outstanding Promise? Me. Mother was so puffed up with pride she could barely speak. Breathing is the best thing to concentrate on, holding and controlling the breath so that my diaphragm is as warm as my throat. Breathe first for eight beats, then for sixteen, and then twenty-four. Everything, but everything comes from the breath. Then vowel sounds: mae, meee, my, moh, mooo. Soft and easy. I'm as prepared as I can be, of course I am, and there's no point in exhausting myself beforehand. Wilma calls out from her room, asks if I'm coming down to breakfast. Yes, I say, I'll be down in a minute.

She's nice, Wilma, cool but nice. Divinity or theology or

biochemistry or something like that. Leaves dental floss lying on the floor of the bathroom which I pick up every morning and every night, and hair in the sink. Has been known to leave wet towels on the floor, which I have never commented on. Reminds me when meal times are, as if I'll forget. Smiles at me if we pass on the street and occasionally sits by me in the dining hall, passing condiments and wondering how I'm getting on. How it's all going, is what she says. Apart from that, I wouldn't know her from Adam. Very strange indeed, sharing a bathroom with someone who doesn't know that I prefer Argento to Puccini. If it weren't for the bathroom slitting between our rooms, I would be able to hear her munching on every chocolate bar or apple that she takes into her room. She's a bit fat, actually, if the truth be told, but I don't know her well enough to suggest a diet.

I've got my clothes laid out, across the chair by the towel rail. Everything looks old in this place, even the chair looks like it was built hundreds of years ago. I love it, absolutely love it, really. All the sense of real history every time I move or eat or breathe, you don't have to look for it, it's just there. Not like Australia, where it's all pretend history. Oh, here's a building which has been here for one hundred years, ooooh, how exciting. Or: here's a rock which has been here for ever. Well, of course, I mean every country has rocks. Big deal. Vanderbilt studied here. That makes a difference.

I'm wearing my green pinafore dress for the audition; it's casual but professional-looking. Hair back, but not too tight. Just foundation, mascara and lipstick. I think it's better to look quite natural. It's even colder on the stairs than it is in my room. No surprise there, then. Warm in the dining room, though. As soon as I push the door open I get hit by a rush of heat. It's all the food, and the bodies, and dishwater. Wilma is sitting next to two girls who I don't recognize, but that doesn't mean I haven't seen them before. I just haven't noticed. She smiles and waves, big and cheery, so I go over to her table. Looking around, to see who else is about. Anyone interesting. She introduces me to the other two: Molly and Someone – Dolly or Susie or Anna. Molly says she's met me before and I go, Oh, have we? But I think she's making it up, I'm sure I'd remember. She's loud, but friendly

28

enough. Wilma says, Big day today, then? and I wonder how she does that, remembers what people tell her. Instead of asking that, I say yes and that I'm all warmed up. Dolly or Susie or whatever she's called chips in and asks what big day. I tell her I'm doing an audition for the major production for the year, *Dido and Aeneas*, and that I'd love to get Dido, of course, wouldn't everyone, but then I'd settle for Belinda.

Wilma laughs and says she didn't realize there was a Belinda, it's certainly not in the original and the truth is I don't have a clue what original she's talking about. It must show on my face because she says, You do know the story, don't you? Well, I've read the libretto and studied the score and thought about character motivation and subtext and intention, so I think I know the story as well as the next person. Better. So I smile and say, Well, of course, how could I expect to understand the character otherwise?

Molly sits forward and in a little giggle girl voice, goes, How amazing, I didn't realize opera singers thought about characters, I thought they only cared about the singing. She says 'opera singer' as if she's saying 'opera star' and I'm not sure if she's being sarcastic or genuine, even though she's smiling at me and sitting practically on top of my chair, nodding her head away, nod, nod.

Not wanting to risk it either way, I tell her that not everyone does, not every singer, it's just that I did a bit of drama before. Although we're expected to understand the basics. Before I can explain what the basics are, the server asks me if I want coffee, juice, jam, hash browns, what?

The problem with being in halls is that they feed you all the time. Absolutely non-stop. Cooked breakfasts, huge slabs of pie and potatoes for dinner, giant desserts every night. Hard to say no to, and sometimes I don't. There is a chocolate roulade now and again, I usually have seconds of that. It's like I can't help it, although I'm always a bit embarrassed afterwards. Embarrassed and bit sick. Because it's not good to fill yourself too much, it really isn't. I know that, obviously I do, but I don't always remind myself when it matters. Everything echoes in the dining hall, every mouthful you take, every time you ask for a second serving. Everyone else hears it. The server slams the plates down and the echo travels around for absolutely ever. Honestly. She's got a grey apron on, but you can still see the gravy stains.

Wilma has got a half-full plate in front of her, but even so she asks for a serve of hash browns and a fried tomato and, really, I have to hold my mouth shut, because I know it isn't my place to tell her what to eat and what not to eat. The hash browns smell fantastic, my mouth is watering so that I can hardly speak. Wilma waves her plate under my nose and says, These are fantastic, you really should try them, you need energy. I tell her I have plenty of energy and barely manage to stop myself telling her the truth: that eating hash browns will give you cellulite, heart disease, cancer, pimples, and possibly varicose veins. Eating a big fat-filled cooked breakfast every day will give you all these things, but it will not give you energy. That's what I don't tell her.

Fruit salad is what I have, with a scoop of yoghurt. Because that's at the cold buffet, I have to walk across the hall and collect it myself. Half-way across the room, I suddenly get this feeling like everyone is looking at me, the whole room. Especially the boys. Men. My legs feel shaky and my hands are heavy on the end of my arms, flapping around like great useless bits of meat. Fried smells stick in the air and the buffet table gets further and further away, my footsteps louder and louder. When I get to the buffet I hold the table edge for a moment, and then I take a bowl of fruit salad, just one scoop. It's full-fat yoghurt and I don't know whether I can make it back to the table without spilling it, or someone saying, What a greedy pig, as I walk past. Molly and Wilma are jabbering away at each other while Wilma shovels the hash browns into her mouth. Watch them, watch them and then I can get back: I keep that going through my head until I get to my seat. Smile, relax, chew. Everything is fine. Just fine.

Somehow, there's always noise here. It looks so quiet when you first arrive, all the old brick and these thick windows. Bits of noise float around me, little splashes of laughing and talking. That noise I like, actually. It's the all-night noise I can't bear. Moray's is right next door and the music and yelling goes on all night. And in the day as well, someone yelling outside my door,

30

someone else laughing, Wilma munching. When I come back from the dining room, almost waddling from four cups of coffee swishing about inside me, I lie on the bed trying to sing scales. Partly just for fun and partly to see if I can get my diaphragm to push out under the coffee. I can't, not really. My diaphragm is heavy and my breath feels hard so that there's no tightness in my voice, it's full of air. Lenherr says I should sing walking, running, lying, flying. You have to on stage, you see. It's all very well producing perfect adagios whilst standing next to your accompanist, but the test is doing it in action. Not with a full stomach, though, it's not good with a full stomach, so I try to avoid that.

I walk across the green, keeping my focus on my breathing and letting the final aria play itself in my ears. My chin is lowering to my chest, climbing down the octave. Even when you're not actually letting the voice out, if you imagine it vividly enough, your body will produce the physical sensation of singing. Amazing, isn't it? The sun is so bright in my eyes that I have to squint to see where I'm going. I'm half-way up the stair of Stoeckel Hall, I look up at the carved circles above the balcony and think: circle, it's a circular lament. I'm thinking somehow that might help me be easy with it, the sense of the aria being circular rather than a simple descent down the chromatic scale, when I think: Circle-balcony-stalls-circle, ohNOOHNOoh. My face literally goes cold, I swear it, and I actually feel my heart stop thumping and I start running. Sprague Hall – where I remember the audition actually is happening – is on College Street, just a couple of blocks away. Still, when I get to the door, I've got coffee swishing back up to my mouth and a damp, damp face. Breathe, relax, wipe face dry, be calm. Because I can do this, and they know I can and it's a simple test of how well we do in this situation and a way of making it fair and professional at the same time. Calm, cool, I can do this. Absolutely. Wipe the sweat.

No one's in the foyer when I go inside, half-blinded from the darkness after the bright of the sun. Circle shoulders, drop head forward, walk the length of the foyer. Walk to the auditorium door, listen: no piano, no voice. Some soft murmuring and then a voice – Margrette? – says something like Mumblemumbleonce more, Elisabeth. I walk to the other end of the foyer then, because I don't want to hear, although I do, of course. Elisabeth has a magnificent voice, but she is usually reedy on the lower end of her range. Not today, though, not by the sounds filtering through the heavy door. Relax, breathe, think: Intention. By the time the door opens and Lenherr calls me in, I'm sitting like a stiff board on the red velvet bench. Elisabeth gives me a grin on the way out, touches my arm and says, Go for it, Marah. Which is nice of her, I think. You know, she could have been a witch about it. Some people are. Witches about these things. Auditions, competition, these things.

Lenherr squeezes my hand before I go up to the stage and smiles at me, a first. Margrette says, Hello, Marah, what have you got for us today? as if I'm a fish-seller with a basket of nice cod on my arm. In fact, I think I can smell fish and it makes me feel sick. My stomach lurches and my throat goes tight, and for a moment I think I won't be able to answer her at all. When I do speak, it comes out sounding tight and tinny. I say I've chosen Dido's final aria. Lenherr nods as if this is some sort of surprise to him, even though he's heard me working on it over and over. Margrette says, Lovely, lovely, are you ready Raymond? Raymond is hunched over the piano, his skin looks green in the dark of the theatre. He tips his head sideways and simpers out at Margrette, gives a nod. For just a second, not even that – a millisecond – my stomach turns. But I watch the wall at the back, the spot in the middle, keeping my eyes above Lenherr's head. I let the breath run through me and imagine my diaphragm filling with solid light. When I let the diaphragm rise, the lightsound makes a stream and swims upwards, up into my chest. It's warm and full in my chest and I let it cover all the inside of my ribs, all the inside of my shoulders until it is so solid and strong that it will burst forward, smashing right through my skin. Instead, I coax it up again, into my throat, into the cave of my mouth. Control. When the light gets to my teeth, I open my lips. Strangely, my eyes close at the same time. Sound shoots from my head, my fingers, my pores. Silence when I finish. Lenherr clears his throat and says, That was fine, Marah, could we have the initial aria but – and he clears his throat again – we would like it *piano*. I close my eyes, breathe, relax. I can do this, I know I can. Whatever else, I know I will not think about nodes. I just won't. I won't.

*The Declaration*
*of Purpose*

# We are Gathered Here Today

Even from the shape of his back, you can tell that Joe is not happy. His shoulders are hunched forward, so that all you can see from behind is the round of his back. His head is tucked in tight like a broken bird. He taps at the glass of the phone box with a coin. Clink clink, scrape scrape. His foot is scrabbling in the dust as well, making letters or shapes. Now and then his hand – the hand with the coin in it – is raised to his head, rubs away at his forehead. Even from far away, even with the noise of the tinkling Ferris wheel and some bloke calling on a loud-speaker to roll up roll up for the pumpkin prize, even if you had no eyes to see, you would know he isn't happy. Blind Freddy would know that. So it seems stupid, like he's just pretending, when he lifts his hand up and waves and turns around and does a big cheesy grin at Jethro and Marah. Or perhaps he doesn't do the cheesy grin, perhaps this is added in after, for effect. Perhaps memory conjures the grin up later, the way it conjures smells of vanilla and freesias when there was really only tar and dirt. Either way, Joe does come out of the phone box, that much is sure. He leaves the phone box and Jethro and Marah stand up and walk across the dusty path of people swarming to the fairy-floss stand. Jethro is nearly knocked for six by a gaggle of teenage girls walking arm in arm. His eyes are so fixed on Joe, and Joe's pretend grin, that he doesn't notice – not even when Marah grabs his hand and yanks him out of the way, across the path to Joe.

'Where's Charis?' Joe's hands are back in his pockets. He shifts foot to foot.

'Gone to have a wee.'

37

'Don't be disgusting Jethro.' Marah slaps at him.

'Wee is not disgusting. It's natural. Anyway, who was it who weed right next the tent and got it all over your foot? You, wee-foot.'

'Liar.'

Jethro does a smirky smile at her, then taps on Joe's arm. 'Didn't Mum want to speak to us?'

'Yair, she did, love – but me money ran out. Sends her love. Hopes it's fun. Said to win her somethin on the clowns.' Joe's head is down, looking at the ground.

Marah does not look at Joe, does not say, 'What about the fifty cents? I saw it in your hand, I know you didn't put it in.' Later, she will be sure that she had a sick feeling in her stomach and knew it was better to be silent. It's not impossible that this is true, but more likely, this: she sees Charis hopping down the path with an armful of fairy floss. There is indeed a feeling in her stomach, a growling for fairy floss, and her silence is because her mouth is full of the promise of sticky sugarsweetness.

'Wherejaget the money for that?' Her voice is indignant.

'Dunno, just had it.' Charis already has a mouthful of pink floss.

'Giss us some.' Jethro reaches his hand out.

'Rack off.'

'Dad. Tell her to share.'

Joe half-jumps, woken from some dreaming. 'Share with them, Charis.'

'I was gunna anyway, if you'd just waited for one half second and not been so greedy.' Pulling the big-sister, she likes to do that.

It drives Marah mad, every time. 'You're the greedy one, fat pig.'

Charis oinks contentedly and hands a parcel of pink fluff to each of them, even one for Joe.

Marah says, 'Don't be so smarty-pants next time,' as if it is a threat, as if it is she who has delivered the fairy floss like a godmother. Jethro says nothing, though, his face is buried in the bag, bits of sugar are sticking to his face and you would swear you could hear him oinking. Sugar dissolves in his mouth warm and fresh. Each crystal stays for a moment on his tongue, he can feel the edge of the sugar, can imagine the inside of the white crystal. This is how it must be, how it must have been. Joe doesn't eat his, just picks at the threads, so Jethro scoffs Joe's bag as well. Oink oink. The phone call is forgotten, Charis is so pleased with herself she forgets to ask what Noeline said or did. Anyway, you can bet that she has heard the silences and wonders what more could be said on the telephone than those gaping silences have already said.

Joe pulls himself back from the far place he's in and claps his hands together. Ringmaster Joe. 'Right-o. Who's for the Ferris wheel, then?'

Jethro says no, not the Ferris wheel, the Matterhorn, and promises he's got both the stomach and the nerve. Sugar crystals are still shivering on his tongue, making him invincible. They all queue up for the Matterhorn, even Marah, who's usually so chicken about rides. The line stretches up as far as the Largest Vegetables tent. Sometimes, people get right to the end of the queue and then turn around, saying they've just remembered they have to meet someone. The Matterhorn rises above their heads, blotting out the sky. Screaming bundles of people are tossed right near them, then tossed away. Sometimes you can hear the words that people scream and it feels kind of embarrassing. Names, mostly, calling to each other, or, 'Oh no,' 'Help.' Someone in the red swinging container yells, 'I can't do this.' Charis jumps up and down the closer they get. She likes to think she's a daredevil and she calls Marah a big fat chicken when Marah even looks over at the Ferris wheel. Once they all load into the metal container and the guy with the 'Darwin Beer-can Regatta' T-shirt switches the switch, though, it is Charis who starts screaming her head off. Yelling that he hasn't strapped her in properly, really he hasn't. She's grabbing at Joe and yelling out, 'Tell him to wait, I'm not strapped in, I'll fall out,' and Joe's saying no, no it's OK, everyone's strapped like that and you can just tell he's trying not to laugh. She's convinced, though, and she yells so hard that the ride operator has to hold off flicking the 'on' button until he's checked Charis's strap.

Once the button is flicked, they start twirling in their little tin, rising and falling at the same time. Spinning faster and faster. When it's so fast you think your head might blow off, it tilts sideways and it absolutely truly feels like you'll fall off and slide down into the Darwin ocean. Then it tilts the other way, spins faster-slower-faster. You can feel the metal, digging in, rubbing against your skin, and one of Joe's shoes flies off and smacks Marah right in the face. Each time they tilt this way or that, a big scream goes up. Each person on the ride is part of every other person then – they are all together, all one family yelling about something or everything or nothing. Jethro begins to wonder if the switch is broken, if they don't know how to switch it off, right about the time he feels the fairy floss rising to his throat. He doesn't even have time to yell 'watch out' before his mouth opens like it's going to be a scream but what comes out is a big line of sick. Although he might imagine it fanning out and covering the whole of the showground, maybe even the whole of Darwin, really it spills out mainly on to himself. Charis and Marah yell, 'Oh, yuck,' and Joe reaches out his hand, touches Jethro on the arm in amongst the twirling.

When the ride stops they all smell a bit of sick and the woman in the booth asks if Jethro's all right. He doesn't want to go back to the hotel, he swears he doesn't, but Joe insists. Really, who wants to wander around ponging like sick? That's what Joe says and the answer is no one. Calls are coming over the loudspeakers for last-minute entries in the beer-can regatta as they walk through the showground gates. Jethro swears, really swears, that he'll be OK and he'd rather watch the regatta, but he's bundled into the car like a bag of shopping. Joe drives extra carefully, slowing down around bends, trying to avoid red lights, and Jethro, still fairy-floss queasy, is grateful for it, although he keeps complaining. He is grateful, even, for the sight of the hotel, Lameroo Lodge, with its twelve-foot-high fibreglass boxing kangaroo perched on the roof. They'd laughed like mad when they first arrived and moaned out loud about tourists until Joe said, 'Oops, we're tourists,' and asked if what they all meant (including himself, because he had moaned as well) by 'tourists' wasn't really 'foreigner', and they had better remember that if you had pale skin, chances were you were a foreigner. Especially if you spoke English. There had been a silence then, a small flame of embarrassment burning away between them. At least, that's how it is to be remembered.

Lameroo Lodge is empty, everyone is at the show. Jethro stops complaining when he sees the empty pool, the water flat and inviting and blue. He doesn't even wait to go inside and change into his bathers – just strips down to his undies and says he'll get the sick off him in the water. Cool blue grabs him, closes in over his head and swallows up the noise in his head. He would stay there for ever if he could, under the water, with the cold wet against his eyes. Who wouldn't? Who wouldn't want to be a fish-animal, if that were possible? Jethro holds his breath and stays under until his whole body will burst with the quiet. Joe bundles up the sick-covered clothes by the side of the pool and pads down to the laundry. Charis yells, 'I'm comin in,' and jumps in right next to Jethro's head, clothes and all. After Marah changes into her yellow bathers and covers herself in sunblock, she spreads herself out on the wooden banana chair. She bends one leg and puts her Woolworth's sunglasses on the top of her head so that she looks like a movie-star, or someone on the cover of a glossy magazine. When Joe comes back from the laundry, Jethro swims to the edge of the pool and says, 'Let's just stay here for the rest of the time, Dad,' and Joe says, 'Yair, why not?' as if that's what he's been thinking of all along. Which he has. They watch the sun fly down to the ocean and listen to cicadas singing while the dark comes up. The lights shine on the pool so hard you can't see the stars and Charis says, 'This is magic, the best thing ever.' They stay up till midnight, having hold-your-breath-under-water races until their faces are pink.

Three days of lying by the pool later, they are each chlorinated and sun-bleached. Joe still looks crumpled, but there is at least the fleck of gold in his hair and the red on his shoulders has turned rich brown. His teeth are white against his face and, strangely, this makes him look happy. Other tourists – some Americans, a pommie couple, two girls from Melbourne – come and go around the pool, but deferentially, knowing they were not there first and have no right. Jethro and Marah stretch themselves along the only two sunbeds, grinning like hosts at the

41

strangers who have to make do with their towels. Joe chucks Charis from his shoulders and then races her up and down the pool. On the third day, Marah looks down at the pool and at her own brown legs and thinks she will have to prick herself she is so full of it. Full of herself, the sun, the chlorine, everything. She even wants to hug Jethro, lying in the chair next to her, looking smug with an *Archie* comic. On the fourth day, Joe says they have to go home tomorrow and he isn't smiling. He makes another phone call after the sun goes down. This time Charis, Jethro and Marah line up to have a minute of Noeline's voice. It crackles and is distant, she doesn't sound like their mother but just some woman who has not been in the sun enough.

Charis is first, that's the rule for the eldest. 'Mum?' She is hesitant, far away from the morning – just eight mornings ago – when she stood with Marah at the door of Noeline's room, willing her to wake up.

'Is that you, Charis? How's it goin? Are you having a good time?'

'Yair. OK. I mean, yair it's good.' Shyness sneaks its way into her mouth.

'Yair? Dad all right?'

'Spose.'

'Jethro all right?'

'Yair. He's OK.'

'You OK?' Noeline seems to have lost the ability to speak without a question mark in her voice. 'No problems?'

'Not really. We saw a crocodile, but.'

'You don't say "but" at the end of a sentence, Charis, do you? Can you put your brother on?'

'OK, bye.'

'Charis?'

'Yair.'

'You know I love you very much, don't you? I love you all very much – you do know that?'

Noeline has never sounded so strange: miles away – which, of course, she is – but also anxious and unsure. When Jethro takes his turn grunting down the phone at her, she asks if Charis is all right, how Marah is, is Joe OK. And so on, and so forth. Marah relates the story of the waterfall, and of the boat-trip and of Jethro being sick and doesn't wait for Noeline to ask questions. Joe takes the phone again after they each have had their minute. He turns his back, folds his arm over his body, speaks quietly, says: 'Oh, I see; Can we talk about it? Don't say that; How am I supposed to tell them?' and, 'Oh, god, Noeline, please.' These are words that only he and Noeline can hear, but they are no less real for that. We can take it on trust that they are said, these words, and Noeline's words jab at him, whatever they are. Some things, after all, have to be guessed at. By the time he hangs up (although Noeline has already put the phone down and he is listening to his own breath bouncing back to him), the hotel lobby is full of families and young backpackers peering at the Where to Eat in Sunny Darwin poster. It takes him almost five minutes to find Jethro sitting behind a potted palm tree counting to one hundred, ready-or-not. Together, they hunt down Charis and Marah, who have broken all the rules of Hide and Seek by 1) hiding together when this is expressly forbidden on the grounds of collusion and cheating, and 2) hiding in the pool, which is outside of the game area and also (this is Joe's point) potentially dangerous. They eat chips for tea, sitting on the steps by Diamond Beach and no one mentions the phone call or going home.

Joe sits up listening to his three children breathe, until two in the morning. At about midnight, Marah opens her eyes and watches her father standing at the window, staring out. She murmurs and rolls over, back to sleep. They are each short-tempered in the morning. Clothes are squashed into cases and half-hearted showers are taken. Breakfast is a mournful farewell by the pool. Charis insists on the front seat on the grounds of eldest and tries to start a game of I Spy. No one jumps in, though, so she plays alone for a while and then falls into the silence. They stop for lunch by the Daly Falls and Joe says, 'No swimming, we have to get a move on.' He is far away and doesn't speak and by the time they arrive at Longreach, the four of them are bound up in the quiet. It stays that way all through the next day's driving, too, all the way to Cunnamulla: sleepy and silent. They stop for toilet or sick breaks and the heat has stuck their lips together so that they cannot speak. Cunnamulla has a proper hotel with a proper restaurant. Table-cloths and everything.

It's there, in the Cunnamulla Hotel Bistro, that the cat gives Joe his tongue back. He asks Jethro what his favourite day of the holiday was and Marah what her favourite meal of the holiday was. Charis says, 'Ask me, ask me,' and he says, 'What was your favourite hour?' Jethro says, 'What was yours, Dad?' and Joe says he can't answer because he loves every second he spends with each of them, really he does. He looks like he's going to cry, so Jethro stands up and gives him a hug across the table. Joe pats Jethro on the back then and makes him sit back down so that they can all hold hands around the table. And it's then, while the waiter takes away the plates and asks if they want more lemonade, that he says things will be a bit different from now on. That he loves them all very much. Very much. That he loves them and so does their mother, but – and there isn't an easy way to say it – their mother needs a little time on her own. That is, without him. Which is partly why she couldn't take the holiday with them all, and they had hoped that might be enough. Enough time on her own. But it wasn't. Isn't. Because she needs some time to know how much she loves him. And, he doesn't know really, doesn't really understand it himself, but it will be all right – he promises that. Promises that it will be all right and that he will still be with them all the time. Really, nothing will change, nothing.

Listening to the stream of words flooding across the table, Charis sits up straight and puts her concentrating face on. She's careful not to look at either Jethro or Marah but anyway they are looking away, down at the table. No one speaks for a very long time.

# Charis

The clunk of the letter-box opening. Hand comes through, right into the hall, and three letters drop on to the carpet. It seems just wrong, just dead wrong, not having to go outside in your PJs, hopping over bindis on the lawn (they're a bastard when they get stuck in the soles of your feet) to get to the letter-box. Wake up, and there they are, letters on yer welcome mat. If we had a welcome mat here. We've got half a piece of carpet, though. Green with brown vomit pattern swirled through. Very classy. Landlord Mr ThingyBadBreath – no, really, really bad breath – I thought he had dog poop on his shoes the first time he came round to collect the rent. It was a huge shock when I realized the smell was coming from his mouth. The worst thing about bad breath, though, is it always makes you think it's your own, doesn't it? I mean, even now, even though I know it's him, whenever I meet him, I do that thing where you breathe into yer hand and then smell it. Which only really proves whether or not you've got smelly hands. Which I have. I can't remember his name, truly. I don't know if I ever knew it. I just go, 'Yair, hi, here it is, the gas is leaking, the bathroom's mouldy, the oven needs fixing, yer breath smells like dog crap, blah blah blah, etcetera.' So anyways, he says we're lucky, dead lucky to have fitted carpets. Fitted my big bum. I'd hate to go clothes shopping with him if he thinks these carpets fit anything except the bin.

Three letters on the hall carpet. Something from the Dole Office for John, a To the Owner of the House thing, which I open (*You*, yes, *you* are entitled as a *special privileged person* to *win* blah blah blah). I read the whole thing, just in case I really can win something, cause you just never know, and Jethro went to school with some bloke who used to win those competitions, so sometimes it really is worth a try, even though you don't think so at the time. In this case, I could be a *number one winner* if I take out a mortgage. Very likely, I don't think. Something with an airmail sticker on it which makes my heart pop up for a minute, because I think it might just be Marah. It's for John, as it turns out, so my heart does a little sigh and settles back down. Good heart, down heart, heel heart.

She only writes when she's happy, I know that about her for sure, so I worry when I don't hear anything. But then, who knows when Marah's happy and when she's not? Maybe not even her. Maybe she can't write cause she can't decide what state she's in. Sometimes I think I carry everything, all the feelings and all the truth for my whole family. My breath is dry and I suspect I might smell like Landlord. Truth be told, the whole flat smells like something has died and is quietly rotting in the fridge. We had a cleaning rota once. Once being the operative word, of course. Kitchen: me; bathroom: John; vacuuming: Janey. Lasted half a week. I don't know who let it slide first. Me, probably. Basically it's clean, though, if you ignore the rotting smell. Which is, frankly, getting harder to do. Puts me off the idea of breakfast, so I head back up to the bathroom and wait for Janey to finish flossing her teeth or curling her hair or whatever it is she does in there for so long.

When the phone rings I'm in what we laughingly refer to as the shower. I turn the pathetic drizzle off and bounce downstairs in a towel too small to cover me. Not that it matters, there's no way John will be up before afternoon and Janey's seen it all before. I've got huge amounts of water dripping off me, soaking into the green and brown vomit swirls, makes it even more lifelike. Yum. I grunt into the phone, in case it's the DHSS asking questions about John. They rang up once, some woman who didn't say where she was calling from. Asked a load of questions about John looking for work, was he or wasn't he, did he do it every day, did he go for interviews for every job no matter how far, wide or bloody unsuitable. I'd gone, 'I dunno, I dunno, I dunno, and who the hell is this?' Gave me the creeps. I always do the grunt now, so I can pretend I don't speak English if I need to.

Fat Controller grunts back at me. 'Whatya do that for? Ya sound like a sow on 'eat. Puts me right off ringing ya.'

'Whaddaya want?'

He starts humming the theme tune to *Love Story*, the really annoying one that no one can ever remember the words to. Barely recognizable, though, in Donny's arsey little whine. At least I recognize when I'm singing flat: he genuinely thinks he has the potential to be a fat version of Paul Weller. He's having a lovely bloody time, humming away. Ethel Merman on steroids, more like. I let him get on with it for a while then yell into the mouthpiece (which is covered in hair and smells of John's cigarette breath), 'Shuuuuut uuuup.' He stops humming and there's a little pause. I put on my dead calm voice and go, 'Look, Donny, I'm standin here in the nuddy dripping all over the floor and I'm freezing my tits off. Is there anything you phoned to say, or are you just being generally annoying?'

'In the nuddy? Cor, I feel all hot an' horny'

'You're making me feel sick in me gut. Whaddaya want?'

'You've won yourself an 'art.'

'Great. Can I go now?'

'Some bloke from your last gig. Phoned this morning in a right lather. Wanted yer number an' all sorts. Said I'd phone you, give you 'is number and leave it wiff you. Safer that way.'

'No thanks.'

'Give 'im a chance, you don't even know which one he is.'

'I don't care. I'm not interested. If he phones you back, tell him I'm becoming a nun.'

'Bloody hell, Gracie. What is it wiff you?'

'Don't call me Gracie. My name's Charis.'

Just before I hang up, he squeaks down the phone, 'I got ya a new preggy-bride dress,' but I don't answer. I don't care. Donny thinks I'm frigid. He's told me about four times. He tried coming on to me once, after a late gig when I brought the French Maid costume back. He was like: Oh you're gorgeous, and I was like: Get your hands off me. Now I keep the costumes overnight and take them back in the morning. Some bloke phoned up once before, after a Betty Bondage gig, said he just wanted to get to know me, blah, blah blah, the usual story. If they get turned on by whips and German accents and big tits, that's their problem. I just can't be arsed myself. What's the point? Mum doesn't give a toss what else is happening. I could win the Nobel Prize for Telegram Singing and she wouldn't care, but if I turned up with a boyfriend, she'd think I'd arrived. Especially if I'd got miraculously thin. When Marah got her scholarship, Mum's only response was: 'What about Daniel?' This poxy skinny weasel that Marah was with. Is with still, I think, if you count being in completely different parts of the world as 'being with'. Anyway, I don't give a pink poo what Donny thinks of me.

I've got this dirty nappy feeling in my gut from talking to Donny. I dunno what it is, but I feel slimy, like I've been involved in something dirty. When I was fourteen, after Mum and Dingo got together, I kissed some boy from up the road. Lying down, with tongues. We found this bit of grass out the back of the house and lay down, I think it was his idea, I can't remember. Must have been the middle of summer, cause I had sweat all under me arms and at the back of me legs. Rodney James, his name was. He had to take his glasses off to kiss me. He polished them and laid them down really carefully next to him and then said, 'Where were we?' in a film-star kind of voice. I felt incredibly embarrassed for him, bunging that voice on. Instead of laughing at him, though, I looked up and simpered. Tried to do it through me eyelashes. Couldn't think of anything film-star to say in return, so I grabbed him and pulled his face down to mine. Bumped noses if I remember correctly and – this I remember vividly – he dribbled into my mouth and down my chin. Not that I minded, I found the whole thing interesting. Pleasant even.

Must have been the middle of the day, the sun right overhead. That's why the shadow seemed so long. We both looked up at the same time. Dingo was standing there looking absobloody-lutely huge. The poor boy got yanked off me dead hard, had red marks on his arms, and tripped on his glasses. I got dragged inside. Neighbours coming out to hear what the fuss was, the works. Dingo called me a slag and I had that feeling in my gut, sickdirtysick. When Jethro yelled at Dingo to mind his own business cause he wasn't even our dad, I told him to shut up and mind his own business. No one knew where Dad was by then. Or if they did, they weren't telling. I just couldn't be bothered with it all. It comes back now and then, only sometimes, that grubby-around-the-edges feeling. It always comes back when I think of Dingo.

I've still got shampoo foamed up in my hair, so I put myself under the shower again. Water's gone cold, which I have to say is not unusual. When I get out of the shower – goosebumps marking me legs – Janey starts banging on the door. She has a knack, that girl, of making everything loud. Walking downstairs is an exercise in earth-shaking for her; she does not tap on doors, she bangs. Even opening and shutting the refrigerator door involves squeaking and slamming. Sex: well, you know, the poodle noises and all that. And that's on a mild day. Bang, bang, bang on the door – and I was having such a lovely quiet moment in here on my own.

'Charis, are you in there?' Janey can be remarkably bright sometimes. It's not likely that a burglar would break in and use our shower when they could stand under a tap on the high street and get a better wash.

'No, Janey, I'm not. I'm in your room reading your journal.'

'Ha.' Her voice is shaky, even through the door I can hear that.

'What do you want?'

'John's got to go down the DSS. Wondered if you fancied coming out for breakfast with me. There's no food in.'

Here's something else about Janey: she doesn't like to be alone. John wasn't on the scene when I moved in, wasn't even a twinkle in Janey's eye. She had the lease on the flat, lost a flatmate, advertised, and – here I am. All lovely chubbley. She got me a waitressing job at All Seasons, we sometimes ate lunch together, spent the odd night in watching *EastEnders* and drinking Scrumpy Jack. She was always – is still always – eyeing blokes up, checking out their bums, their pecs, their this and that. One morning I woke up to find my milk emptied, the toilet seat up and John sprawled on the floor with a paper. And that was it, he never left. Janey calls on me when he's busy, which is rare. It's not that she's being a witch, it's priorities, that's all. Blokes always come before non-blokes, it's understood. Except by me, because I appear to have some vital thing missing. Missing some gene that would make me think male sweat is sweet and that I'd be happy if I had someone else's toe-nail clippings to worry about.

I don't say any of this to Janey, though. The other thing is, what she means by 'let's go out to eat together' is, 'I'm skint and can you buy me brekky?' I still owe her for the pineapple danishes, so I open the door, tell her to get out of me way so I can get dressed and where does she want to eat? She's in the hall in a pink stained dressing-gown which I have never seen before and her eyes are red-rimmed. This is unusual. Particularly the dressing-gown. Clothes are important to Janey: more important than food. She works more shifts than anyone else at All Seasons and never, never has money for food or electricity bills. Always has money for River Island, Miss Selfridge, Monsoon. Shopping therapy, she calls it; she's a real believer. This is not the time to challenge her on these points, however. She's looking like an unset jelly, quivering and slightly green. Obviously, I'm meant to notice: how could I not?

'What's the matter?' I've got an I'm-your-best-mate voice I keep especially for these occasions. 'What's up? Carn – tell Auntie Charis all about it.'

'Nothing. I'm fine.' She says it in a high-pitched voice, almost a squeak, and she puts on some strange approximation of a smile.

'Is it John?' As if it would be anything else.

Jancy's slightly distorted smile up-ends itself and she does this series of little whimpers, a cross between failing brakes and a puppy with distemper.

'Janey?' I want to tap on her forehead, go: Hello? What's the problem? John's a wanker anyway. Instead, I go, 'Do you need a hug?' as if I'm an Oprah Winfrey fan.

She nods and does the whimper again and I'm still no closer to knowing what on earth is going on. Janey seems to have lost the ability to put words together in anything like a coherent form, so I tell her to get herself dressed and we'll go to Camden, have breakfast at Harry's, my shout. It's only when we're walking out the door, Janey still red-rimmed but gorgeous in black bell-bottoms, that I wonder whether this is an elaborate con of hers to get me to buy breakfast. Uncharitable thought: I wipe it out immediately and replace it with something nice about cream cakes.

She keeps the visor up on her helmet, keeps turning her head left to right, right to left. Looking at the magnificent view of the London traffic. Every time she turns her head, the peak of the visor bangs me on the back of my head. When we go around corners, she squeals and hugs me tightly as if I'm her protector. By the time we putter to a stop around the corner from Harry's, I'm ready to toss her under the wheels of the scooter and put us both out of our misery. Still, she'd be there for me. I suppose. If I needed it. But that's the thing, the difference. I wouldn't need it.

Harry's is full of glass and steel and noise, the kind of noise I like: slices of words, clink crack of glasses and cups, waiters yelling at each other in the kitchen, a cappuccino machine. The noise makes it feel warm, in spite of the glass and steel, which, frankly, I can't bear. Janey likes it, though, and that's the whole point of this exercise, isn't it? To cheer her up, jolly her along. I'm good at this, I know the score, even though it bores me. Before I left, Marah broke up with Weasel-skin once or twice a month. Before Weasel, it was someone called Jacob, and before him, someone else. Always break-ups every month, always me dropping my hat, or my life, to come round, take her out, listen-chat-listen-chat. You see? I do know the score. Never say he's an arsehole, even if he is, because she'll be back with him that week and she won't thank you at all. Believe me.

'John wants to break up.' Janey starts before we've even got the brioche. Her voice has dropped back to its normal pitch, but now she sounds Valiumed-out.

'No. Since when? Do you want brioche and coffee?' I'm trying to sound concerned, but I am also concerned for my stomach. Which isn't unreasonable, given that I've been up for almost three hours and still haven't eaten, and a waitress with two schoolgirl pigtails is heading towards us.

Her mouth tilts downside-up. 'Just coffee. Since last night, I suppose, but then who knows? He never tells me what he's thinking, so how the hell am I supposed to know?'

I smile at the pigtailed waitress. 'Two coffees and one brioche and jam. Thanks.'

Janey grabs at the white laminated menu. 'And cheese omelette.' She looks at me. 'Is that OK? Have you got enough money? Toast as well. Could I have bacon with that?' She smiles at me. 'I'm hungry after all.'

'When did he tell you he wanted to end it?' I know this role, the coaxer, the gentle ear.

'He said he wanted some space. Last night. That he needed a bit more time on his own. To find out what he wants to be doing with his life.' She puts her hand up to her mouth, looks away from me.

'Fair enough. Don't you as well?'

'As well what?'

'Need time from him. You're together whenever you're not working. It must get a bit suffocating.'

'We're not together now. We're not together when I'm working. He's got lots of time on his own, it's just an excuse, I'm not stupid. Not completely. He thinks I'm cramping his style.'

'He hasn't got any style.'

'Thanks, Charis.'

I suddenly feel impatient with it, with her, with him. I know how it goes: he wants his space, wants to find himself, or his path or his whatever; and she hangs about waiting for him. I know how it'll go: we'll sit here half the afternoon, Janey and I; we'll talk about him and eventually we'll move off the subject and talk about other stuff, just stuff – what we want, the taste of the coffee. Emma Thompson. We'll sit a while, maybe get some cake and Janey will say how wicked we are and I'll tell her not to be so silly. Then we'll go off to the pub and spend until evening drinking cider and playing snooker. Eventually, it will be fun and we'll start giggling and I'll remember why I liked Janey in the first place and we'll both say, 'Men, ha, what a bunch of wankers.' Except I will believe it and she will not. Even though she will say, 'It's so good to spend time together, we should do this more often.' Because when we get home he will not be there and she will wilt by the window, watching for him. For days she will stand there, wilting. Or he will be there and she will run to him and disappear for weeks, months, into him. I know all this, because I've been here before.

The coffee comes, smelling fresh and good. Janey grins at me, says, 'It's so good to do this, to spend time together, just us. We should do it more often. Don't you think?'

# *Marah*

Spring. There are buds all over the place, small yellow flowers – crocuses? – coming up on the green. A little pocket of sweet-smelling flowers has sprung up in front of Connecticut Hall, gathered around the gate. Each morning, the smell gets stronger. Yesterday, I nearly stopped, knelt down and smelt them. There were people around, though, as there always are, and, really, I don't have all day to do things like that. Although obviously I'd like to, and it would be nice, and possibly even helpful. Probably if there weren't people hanging about, I would. What I'd like to do is pick some. At night. It's only a small pocket, there's barely enough to make up a bunch at the moment, although I'm sure a whole lot more will grow up over the summer. They must have planted more, surely. Someone must have thought ahead enough to realize that a whole bunch of undergraduates would want to have some of those flowers in their rooms. You would expect someone to do that, think ahead like that. Although, in my experience, not everyone does. It's surprising, I think, the number of people who don't. For instance, this morning two girls picked several of the scented flowers and also at least three crocuses. While I was walking past, watching them. The thing is, I understand why you would do it. Obviously I do. They smell like spring and you want that, you want that smell, that feeling, in your room. But the point is, if everyone did it, none of us would have the smell of freesias as we walked past, would we?

There are no flowers outside Stoeckel, but I only have to make a slight detour to walk down Temple Street, past three churches, one after the other. All lined up in a row, like sisters, and surrounded by flower-beds. It's not because of the flower-beds

54

that I walk past, though. I'm not sure what the reason is. Last term – fall term – I walked past one of those churches on the morning of Thanksgiving. Everyone was fussing about Thanksgiving, fussed about it for weeks. Posters were everywhere, invites to parties and feasts and vigils. I couldn't understand why there was a church service going on when it wasn't even Sunday. Fortunately, I didn't tell anyone that, which would have been embarrassing. Colette asked in class what I was doing for Thanksgiving and I said, Oh, probably go to the HGS Thanksgiving, and she said she was going home to her folks and this was the first Thanksgiving with real snow that she could ever remember and wasn't it great? I didn't really get what was so great about it being snowy, especially when I kept slipping over, but I said, It is, it is great, isn't it? It looked beautiful, the snow, I could see that.

I mean, I get what's great about Thanksgiving, sure I do. What has Australia got like that? When do they ever get together and have a feast and celebrate all that's good? Never, that's when. Oh, maybe Christmas, I suppose, but there's Christmas here as well. There's Christmas everywhere. You know, it's nothing special, nothing unique.

So this morning of Thanksgiving, I went out for a run. I was going to go up to East Rock and back but I got just as far as the green, as far as the row of churches. It was the singing that stopped me. Amazing, really, that a hall full of untrained voices could sound so good. I sat on the steps of the United Church and closed my eyes and listened. Nearly went in as well, but I thought: What would I do in there? I'd have nothing to say. So I didn't. I sat outside on the steps and listened to the singing. Songs I didn't know, and then speaking. I listened to a group of strangers giving a catalogue of things to be thankful for and I had to squeeze my fingers right into my eye sockets to stop myself crying. Don't know why that was. Snow was everywhere, it was thick and cold. That was one of the things they gave thanks for, would you believe it? Maybe it made me weepy because I missed Daniel. Although I didn't want to give thanks for him, I can't actually imagine doing that. I did miss him. Do. I do miss him. It's always been rock-solid with us, we've never been shaky like some people are. Never a problem. Strange, isn't it, because we are different. Daniel actually does not like opera, although he has tried, for me. I mean, I do miss him. It's just that he seems so far away and I can't really remember what he looks like or what he sounds like.

Skinny. He's skinny, but solid. He works out and everything, he's not puny at all. I'm not sure if I remember this, though – his wiriness, the curve of muscle on his arm and the taper of his waist – or if it's from the photos. There's one of him above my bed, smiling down on me. Like God, I suppose. That's who would normally be there, above your bed, looking down on you. That's who the picture would be of. But I have Daniel, whose voice I can't seem to hear in my head at the moment, even when I try. If I had a ring on my finger, on my ring finger, it would be better. Clearer. It would be clearer to me and to, well, to everyone, that I was attached. We talked about getting engaged before I left and I still think it was the best idea. In the circumstances. Not that the circumstances were bad, you know, it just seemed that it would be easier to not forget. If there was something official. Also – and I don't think I realized how important this would be until now – it makes quite a difference to other boys. Men. Guys. I can never find a word that suits. Daniel is not a man, I don't think of him as a man. Technically, he is a man, he's twenty-five years old and male. That would make him a man, wouldn't it? But in my head, I think: boy. It's different with girls, you can be called a girl all your life and it's nice, it's not insulting in the way it is with men. Men do not like to be called boys. And the truth is that if I had an engagement ring on my finger, things would be a lot easier around here. Saying, Oh, no, I'm fine, I don't need a date because I've got a boyfriend at home, is not the same as saying, Everything's fine with me, you can see, here, on my finger, I'm engaged. Daniel isn't great on letters, actually, if I'm being honest. Three this term, and one of them was a postcard from Coff's Harbour. We could have called it a day when I left, but why would we? Everything's fine, has always been fine.

I always walk past the churches now. I stop and listen. Even on weekdays. Even when I have to detour. I don't know why, I really don't.

I'm supposed to meet Elisabeth at College Street, in the lounge, to go over the understudy role. Thing is, I know she'll be late and I am running early. As always. I don't say this to Elisabeth, but I think if she's serious about understudying me, she should work a little bit harder. Punctuality is an asset in any profession. Actually, I'm going to be at least an hour early if I don't slow down. Also, we're supposed to read the original story, to give us some context. Margrette is all for context, as long as it doesn't interfere. She has been heard to suggest that we are spread too thinly, too wide. Now, I would agree with that, even though I am someone who likes to be spread quite thin. It's important to know what the real focus is, that's what I think. It's what I say as well, if I'm asked. Although in this situation, these specific circumstances, I don't mind. Actually, I agree. The libretto doesn't give a whole lot away, and it's harder to invest it with resonance somehow than it is with, say, a German piece. Obviously that is not always the case, certainly not with Bernstein or Copland, for instance. Americans know how to make the language exciting, they always did. More than the English, anyway: *Fate your wishes does allow, Empire growing, pleasures flowing.* What is it supposed to mean? Mostly it's Belinda's part which makes the least sense: *Grief increases by concealing.* Makes no sense at all. It goes on like that. Gibberish and nonsense, a lot of it. Even though I don't have to sing Belinda, I need to understand it. All of it. Elisabeth said she hadn't realized that I was Australian until this week; she thought I was maybe from Boston or Vermont or something. That was nice. Even though Collette laughed and said You have to be crazy, Elisabeth, don't you ever listen to what's going on? Which wasn't so nice. I don't think I sound so Australian. Less than I did, anyhow. Collette's from New Orleans. Really. I love the way she speaks.

I've got the book in my bag, it's thinner than you might expect, and quite different from the libretto. There's no reason for that to surprise me, but somehow it does. Not completely different, I suppose, it's just that Dido burns herself in the book. Burns herself right up. That surprised me and I didn't entirely like it. Even though it's spring, even though the air is warm and soft on my skin, I have this desire to take the book into the library. The light in there is so secret, it feels like you're huddled into the quiet. Partly it's that I think there are proper places to read, and a library is one. Sitting on the steps of a church is not. Hanging about in the student lounge probably is one, but I don't like the colour of the floors in there, or the noise. There are always little groups and it's not that I feel excluded or that I couldn't just walk up and join in – because I don't feel like that, I know I can join in any time I want – it's just that it's so loud and if you want quiet it's not the place to be. Quiet enough to talk, sure, quiet enough to sit at one of the small tables with Elisabeth and go over the schedule, but not quiet enough to read and make notes. And obviously if I'm going to read, I'm going to make notes. Besides, I like the library, what's wrong with that?

I go to the manuscript library, not Sterling, because it's like being underwater. Everyone holds their breath, and skin gets a blue-green tinge to it. On the outside, you'd swear it was a normal building. A nice blue colour, nice but not completely unusual. Then you get inside, and the whole place is different. Squares within squares. With the skeleton on the outside. Squares don't have skeletons, obviously, but if they did. It's so that the air can't get to the books. They're so precious nothing is allowed to touch them. I love that idea, I just love it, the idea that something might be so precious, so special, that it shouldn't be touched. Shouldn't be polluted. People should be like that. We should think of people like that.

You can go in and sit at the desks with your own book, but most people don't. Most people go in for no other reason than to look at a rare manuscript. That's strange, as well, because I'm simply not interested at all in the old books. I just like being in the blue light. Each wall is made of marble so thin that the light shines through. Marble polished and honed and rubbed away until it is almost transparent. The care in that, the love – that amazes me, it really does. And on the outside, you'd never guess it, you'd never guess that everything inside was so fragile and precious and secret.

I leave my bag at the desk downstairs but take the book with me, up to the first floor. There's a table by a corner, tucked in quiet and safe. Waiting for me, it's my table with my name practically written on it. What I like about corner tables is the way you can lean in to the wall, it feels so solid. Tucked in, like a child, I always go for them. Not in the dining hall, obviously, because there aren't any corners. Anyway, it only works if you're at the table on your own, and I wouldn't sit at a table in the dining hall on my own. That would be, I don't know, sad. I have this memory of Jethro sitting at a playground table one lunchtime. Completely alone. He was so small as well. Sitting with his sandwiches, kicking his legs against the legs of the bench. He didn't care really, I mean he was fine. I was being very Big Sister about it, worrying for him, I don't know why – why I would have worried like that, when I didn't need to. Probably, if I asked him now, Jethro wouldn't remember it at all. Anyway, my guess is that he wanted to be alone. Where did that come from? I don't carry this picture around with me, I'm sure I don't – but it just swam up like water. Vivid and cold. Funny.

Actually, I don't remember very much from when I was a kid. Not that I've forgotten; I suppose it doesn't seem important, that's all. Little things, I do sometimes remember little things. Charis having her first kiss and all of us having a laugh about it – Dingo found her kissing some boy and it was a great joke, we all laughed, even Jethro. What else? The smell of the lemon tree in the garden. Things like that I remember. Basically, life's too short to get swallowed up in history, isn't it?

While I'm walking towards the corner table, I'm clenching my stomach muscles in, out, in, out. Then my bottom muscles, clench, hold, squeeze. Callanetics. Small movements in each muscle that tone and trim. They really do make a difference, even though you wouldn't think it. There's no sweat and you can do it anywhere, that's the advantage. Personally, I prefer to use them as an addition to more traditional cardio-vascular exercise. A few years ago, Mother broke up with Dingo. Lasted about a year, I think. When Mother first introduced me to his replacement, he said, But you're too tiny, I can't believe you're an opera singer – look at you, you're lovely and slim.

Mother said, Disappear if she turned sideways, wish I had her figure.

And he stroked her hips and said, Nonsense, Noeline, you've got the best legs this side of the Atlantic, and you'll soon lose that bit of tummy if you come out on the boat with me.

She has got marvellous legs, my mother. For her age. Dingo came back, begging to be with her, after a year, promising to do better, to buy a new boat and take her out on it. It's not true any more, the all-singers-are-fat line. Callas was at her best when she was thin, I believe that, I really do. Abdominal muscles support the diaphragm and the stronger the stomach is, the stronger the voice. Anyone who says otherwise is lying, or doesn't have a clue about technique. Lenherr says that Callas lost her voice when she lost her fat, but he's as round as a potato, so he's going to want to believe that, isn't he?

Perhaps it's because I'm concentrating on my abdominal and bottom squeezes that I don't notice him. We must head for the table at almost the same pace, but from opposite angles and directions. Because at the exact moment that I throw my copy of the *Aeneid* on to the table, he puts his hand on the back of a chair and pulls it out. Corner tables are simply too small, too cosy, for two people who are strangers, so I look across the table and glare at him. Trying to indicate with a polite but cold glare that this is my table, that I have had my eye on it and have been approaching it with the express purpose of sitting at it alone, with my book. Instead of backing off, or glaring back, he smiles. His eyes are the most amazing blue. Pale, almost as pale as ice, but bright with it. American teeth are always so beautiful, and he has a square jaw as well. Truly, he's so beautiful that I hold my breath and wonder if my hands look big. Sometimes they do seem very big, too big for my arms, or my body. Holding things, or picking small objects up, or waving – any of these things – suddenly seems difficult. My hands get in the way of everything.

The reason I know that he has such beautiful teeth is that he smiles at me. Quizzically, I suppose. I would think that might be the right word for the sort of smile he offers me. Quite quick across his face, with a half-raised eyebrow accompaniment. A sort of Oh-we've-both-landed-the-same-table-and-here-we-are look. Glaring at him has suddenly left my mind. I can't think why I would want to do that, why I ever would have wanted to.

Daniel has left my mind as well. This happens sometimes; it doesn't really concern me, it's not like I don't love Daniel, it's not like I ever run off with anyone else. Once I did. Not with Daniel. Before him, with Adrian. That's how I started being with Daniel, I suppose. Or how I ended being with Adrian. I sorted of started being with Adrian when I ended with Jacob. Not in the same way. Not with any of what you might call cross-over. None of that. But it's not likely to happen now, because it's different. Because I love Daniel, I actually do, and all that I'm doing here is noticing that Americans have nice teeth generally and this one has a nice smile in particular.

It's not easy to read, the book, and I notice my mind wandering a lot. If I turn myself almost sideways, sit not quite facing the table and not quite facing away from it, then I can see him. He's got a grey book in front of him, he looks absorbed. I imagine what it would be like if we were both reading the same book, and how we'd laugh in a quizzical way, to match the smile. Instead of thinking about the book, I'm thinking about what his name might be, and waiting for him to look up and say something funny or clever. My watch is heavy on my arm, digging into me. Elisabeth will not be on time, but I will be. I read a page, check my watch, go back to the beginning of the page, tingle. I really am tingling now, and I don't mean to. He's got a ring on, a solid one, not on a wedding finger or anything like that, though. Silver, with some pattern carved in. He puts his hand up to his head quite a lot, runs his hand through his hair. Beautiful hair, shiny, dark.

The table is quite small, it's quite a tight fit with the two of us here. Our knees touch. He has canvas jeans on. Black. Even though I've got lace-up shoes on, I wonder what would happen if I slipped them off, then accidentally stretched my legs out and touched his thigh. Accidentally. Or if I forgot he was there somehow and slipped my feet on to his chair, just to ease the weight on my bones, to change my positioning. The tremble is right up me now. It's a bit like singing, your whole body squeezed tight and full. Vibrations touching every edge of every cell. Too tight with trembling, I stretch out, cross one leg over the other. My foot touches his leg, brushes the inside of his calf. He

61

jumps as if I've hit him or split hot coffee down his back. His head jerks up, and he says, What?

Before he's got the word out of his mouth, I'm saying, My legs, I was crossing my legs, sorry, ha, sorry.

It all comes out very fast and too loud for a library and I just know that my neck has gone pink. He looks back down, annoyed, if his face is anything to go by. Which it is, because it's all I've got to assess the situation with. My mouth is dry with embarrassment.

I check the watch, then sigh as if I don't want to go. I'm still going to be too early for Elisabeth, but I have to get out of the library. Humiliation is hanging close in the air and I don't want to be around when it lands. I've been there too many times before.

*The Confession*

# In Word, Thought and Deed

There it is again, the bang bang bang right on the wall, right there in Jethro's ear. Bang bang bang. He can hear Noeline's voice jumbled up with the banging. Small spurts of laughter and odd words, he can't make them out, only the sounds. Sharp and savage, they are sounds like trees breaking in winter. Or perhaps he makes it like this, imagines it so, pretends later to himself, relates the story in which it happens that this is what came to him when the laughter cracked through the wall: winter, hailstones, branches snapping suddenly from trees, gale-force winds. Dingo's voice punches through the wall, a thud of a word: *damn*, as fast as the hammering. Soothing cluck-cluck sounds then, Noeline making soft hushing words: 'There-there, are you all right? Ooooh, let me see.' Or perhaps: 'Silly you, oh, well, give it another go.' For Jethro, it is only the rhythm of the words which makes any sense, any impact. This is what he says later, much later. He rolls on to his back, stretches his hands above his head, tries to creak himself out to the length of the bed.

Outside Jethro's window, a frangipani tree is swaying, dropping petals to the ground. He can see the branches of the tree if he props himself up on one arm and tilts his head slightly to the left. He doesn't do that though, not this morning, with the hammering coming through the wall and Noeline laughing like a girl right there near his bedroom so that it almost makes him sick. Whether he does or not, whether he sits straight up in bed to get a proper look at the tree, it is still there, petals slipping easily from the branches and parachuting down. You don't have to see something for it to be true. Noeline could see the tree – if she looked, if she wanted to – from her bed, without even sitting up. Joe planted it for her, as a birthday present, or Mother's Day – one or the other. Only this is sure: Joe planted it in the night, so that it would be a surprise. Positioned it so that Noeline wouldn't even have to raise her head. In summer and spring, the whole garden is rich with the sugarsweet smell.

Sometimes Marah picks the stemless flowers and floats them in a green glass bowl. Green, deep green as an ocean. The bowl is shaped like a flower itself, and small bubbles of air are trapped in the green glass. The frangipani flowers bump against each other if there is a breeze. The bowl sits on the small table in the lounge until the yellow on the petal-ends starts to turn brown and the smell turns to rot. Noeline throws them into the red plastic bin on the back porch and scrubs the slime from the bowl with Mr White's Super Household Bleach.

'Jethro? Are you awake?' Noeline's voice has stopped giggling behind the wall, has moved to his door, is accompanied by a small taptap. 'Jethro?'

'No. I'm not awake. Go away. Witch.' He says the words so quietly they are barely heard. Are not heard, in fact, by anyone other than himself. Perhaps are not said but only thought.

'Jethro?' The door opens a crack, Noeline's face peeps in. 'Come and give a hand to Dingo, love. We're finally gunna have some shelves in the lounge. He needs a hand, though.'

'What's wrong with Charis? She can help him. She's older.'

'Dingo wants you to help him. Be good practice. Dingo can help you with your woodwork. We thought you'd like that.' Noeline has edged right into the room, is standing over Jethro, ruffling his hair. She sits on the bed, pushing his legs aside to make room. 'Don't you want to learn about woodwork?'

'Spose.' He sits up, tilts his head so that he can see the frangipani.

'Good boy.' She pats his leg, as if he is a pet. Stands up, brushes herself down.

'Is Dad coming back soon?'

Noeline pauses, looks at the smallness of Jethro lying there in his bed. He is still swallowed up by the mattress, still tiny against the pillow. Dark hair sticks up in small tufts. Tufty: they used to call him that. No one's sure when they stopped, or why. One day, just like that, no one called him Tufty. Or Jeddy. They called him Jethro. But his hands are still small on the sheets. He can scowl and screw his face up and call her a witch – yes, she's heard him say it, more than once as well – he can do all that as much as he likes, but he's still a boy when you get down to it. She smiles at him and says, 'Yes, perhaps, we'll see.' Or words which sound like that. She shuts the door behind her and for a moment rests her head against the wall. She can hear the vibrations from the hammering. Dingo starting up again. Someone ought to give him a hand. Noeline is so quiet walking into the lounge, walking up to Dingo, that he doesn't hear her, doesn't notice through the hammering.

'Thanks, Dingo. We really owe you for this one, don't we, Marah?' Noeline's hand brushes Dingo's shirt.

Marah has wound herself into a small ball, squeezed to the back of the armchair. She is listening, watching, storing things up to remember, things to tuck away somewhere secret. She pulls her shoulders in tight, as if she is a bird, and draws the book in her hands closer to her face: *Hollywood Babylon*. She turns a page, does not glance up. There is a photograph of Jayne Mansfield, lying across a rug. She has a leopard-skin bikini. On the opposite page, a picture of a wrecked car, the car she died in. Decapitated. Marah traces her finger around the outline of Jayne Mansfield's chest, wonders where she was chopped off and whether it was a clean cut or not. See Jayne crash. Crash, Jayne, crash.

'Marah? Hello? Please excuse my daughter, Dingo. She disappears when she's got a book in her hand, or a record on the turntable. Marah, please don't be rude in front of our guest, he's doing us a favour.'

'Why? We don't need shelves, we never had them before.' Marah looks at the page number – nineteen – and shuts the book, snap. Looks up at Dingo, at his cotton cap, his checked shirt, his belt full of screwdrivers, small hammers, tape-measures.

'We did need them. Your dad and I have been saying for years that we needed them in this room. He just never got round to it. Like lots of things. He has a problem with getting around to things, your dad. Dingo just happened to be in the area today and has very kindly offered to put them up for us. I think the least we can do is be a bit polite. Would you like a cuppa, Dingo?'

'That'd be a dream, Noeline. Thanks, love.' Dingo pulls a hankie from his pocket, blows his nose.

'Jethro's just getting out of bed. He wants to give you a hand, so don't get too far on with them.' Noeline smiles at Dingo, eyes looking up at him, as if he is taller than he is. 'It's very sweet of you to do this, Dingo. Honestly, I was on at Joe for years to put them up. Would've done them myself, so it must have been desperate – I didn't have a clue where to start, though, would've ended up with the books sliding down on to the floor, I swear.'

'Don't underestimate yourself, Noeline.'

'Honestly, I wouldn't know what to do with a spirit-level. Anyway, Joe always said – you know what he's like – he'd get around to it in just a second. Story of our lives, I tell you. That car was a time bomb until I finally took it in to get fixed. After months of him saying he was going do it, wasn't it, Marah?'

'Why can't Dad come round now and do it? I know he would.'

Noeline looks across at Dingo. Frowns. 'Darling, you know we're having a little bit of space, your dad and I. Don't worry, he'll be visiting. And it's lovely of Dingo to put the shelves up for us now, isn't it?'

Marah shrugs, opens the book again, reads that Jayne Mansfield had a seventeen-inch waist and one hundred and twelve lovers. At least. One hundred and twelve men who loved her. Marah tingles, squeezes the muscles on the inside of her legs together. Sometimes, she squeezes her bum tight and it makes a tingle too, up and down her body. She has whispered in the night that she will be a star, with a tiny waist and long eyelashes and men who love her. Not like Jayne Mansfield, though, because Jayne Mansfield had drunken parties which went on for days and people got arrested all the time and then she got her head chopped off. Hollywood is not the place, anyway, not for Marah. She opens books, watches out for the place which will be the place, but it is not Hollywood and it is not here, not South Windsor.

Jethro shuffles through the door, his Scooby Doo slippers

scraping the carpet so that he seems like an old man. When he speaks, his voice croaks with lack of sleep. 'Where's Charis?'

'Dunno. Outside or somewhere.' Marah does not look up from her book. 'How come yer up so late?'

'Dunno. Feel sick.'

'What's up, matey?' Dingo stops hammering, looks at Jethro like he cares, like it's any of his business.

'Nothin.'

'You sick?'

'Dunno.'

Noeline ruffles Jethro's hair so that his head wobbles. 'He's catching Charis's disease. Can't use a sentence when a grunt will do. At least Charis has got an excuse.' She looks at Dingo, laughing. 'Teenagers, what can you do with them? But this one, he's not even eight and he reckons he's hit puberty.'

Jethro wriggles away from her. 'I don't. I'm homesick for Dad.'

Marah closes the book on James Dean, looks at Dingo, standing there as if he owns the place, as if he is Noeline's best friend, when he's supposed to be Joe's. 'Me too.'

There's no mistaking the raising of the eyebrows between Noeline and Dingo. No mistaking what it says, either: See? What did I tell you? What can you expect? That's what they say to each other without opening their mouths. It's obvious.

'I want to phone Dad, why can't we?' Marah has joined forces, has got the special whine in her voice. 'When's he coming back?'

'Is he staying at your house, Dingo? Can we phone him there?'

'Of course he's not staying at Dingo's, you dork. What made you think that? Otherwise he'd be here, wouldn't he?' The words come out from her even though Marah must know without a doubt – because she has heard it said hundreds and hundreds of times – that Dingo is Joe's best mate. It's clear that Joe is not there. Not at Dingo's. Something in the way Noeline looks up at Dingo, laughing, passing tools. It would make you feel cold, that's the truth of it. 'You're stupid sometimes, Jethro.'

'Marah, there's no need for that. We don't speak like that in this house, do we?' Noeline sounds for all the world like she never yelled at Joe that he was stupid, ridiculous, a laughing-stock. 'We don't have an address for your father, he's obviously not interested at the moment. I'm sorry, darling, I don't want you to feel hurt, but he doesn't want to speak to you right now. I'm sure it will settle down soon.'

Dingo turns his head fast away from Noeline, bends down and picks up a bracket. Keeps his whole body turned away so that Marah wants to say, 'What? What are you pretending?' She doesn't though, she keeps silent, gulps her questions down. Opens her book at Fatty Arbuckle, tucks her head in so that her ears are covered.

Jethro says, 'I don't feel like helping with the shelves. I'm goin outside to find Charis. I don't want shelves anyway.'

'Suit yourself. If you find Charis, tell her we're expecting her here for lunch, if she can drag herself away from her friends. Be careful on the road, Jethro.'

Jethro shuts the door, does not say, Yes-Mum-Certainly-Mum. Says nothing. Not even: You're a liar.

It takes Dingo nearly the whole day to get the shelves up. When they're done, they cover the entire wall, with cross-sections of wood dividing them lengthways. So that Charis can have a section, and there's a square for Marah, and one for Jethro, and a place to put the telly and a place for the stereo and everything. Noeline fusses, wiping a cloth across the wood, collecting up the small seeds of sawdust. She says it's beautiful, the most beautiful shelves, she couldn't have possibly imagined that they'd be so good. They are beautiful, there's no denying it. Although when Charis finally shows her face at tea-time, she looks at the shelves, rolls her eyes and asks what on earth happened to the wall. Noeline is arranging some dried honesty and baby's breath in a blue pottery jug. She puts the last stem in, shifts it just so, and instead of answering the question, says, 'What happened to Jethro?'

'Whaddaya mean? I haven't seen him all day.'

'You. What do *you* mean?' Noeline blows the small petals from her hands.

'I mean I haven't seen him.' Charis is being deliberately smart, just asking for it.

'Don't be smart, Charis, and don't say "ya". You sound like a yobbo. Jethro went out to find you, I thought you would have been looking after him.'

'He might have gone down to the Bay Scrub. There was a gang of them building a cubbie.'

'Right. Go down and see if you can find him. Try the Wilsons' if he's not there. Tea will be on the table in forty-five minutes and if it's not too much to ask, I'd like to have a nice family dinner.'

Charis does the trick with her eyes again – she's been practising – and pulls the door hard behind her, just enough to avoid it being a slam.

There is an apron behind the kitchen door, which has never been seen on any living person. It has plastic breasts sticking out at the top. A gift from someone to – who? – perhaps Noeline, perhaps Joe. Whatever: it hangs there collecting dust, its plastic breasts hanging shrivelled and unfilled. When Noeline takes it off the hook and puts it on her own body – which is what she does just after Charis pulls the door hard behind her – the breasts perk up, pop themselves out. Although designed, probably, as a joke for a man to wear when sizzling chops on the barbie, the apron is at its best on a woman's body. The breasts seem happier that way, they point upwards. Beneath the breasts (very pink), the apron is a sensible blue, not too dark, not too light. Noeline wraps it around herself, ties the straps at the back (she does a simple granny knot, easy to do without sight), prods at the plastic, says, 'Buggered if I know where this came from, but it's the only one we've got.'

Dingo, sitting at the kitchen table, a white cup full of milky tea in front of him, laughs. 'You don't need them, love.'

'Whaddaya need an apron for, anyway? Ya never normally wear one.' Marah has barely shifted all day. Has opened and shut books, has once or twice risen for orange juice, hot chocolate or crisps, but returned always to the curled up comfort of the chair. Joe's chair, really, if you want to know.

'I'm cooking steak-and-kidney pie. Don't want to get flour on myself.'

Steak-and-kidney pies come from the box in the freezer, everyone knows that. Not from flour and bowls and Noeline

71

humming in the kitchen and rolling pastry out with an empty milk bottle. Things sizzle in a pan. Slicing and chopping noises have come from the kitchen all afternoon, but still, it's a mystery, this sudden arrival of smells and sizzling.

'Mum –' Marah sniffs the air like a rabbit – 'what are ya doin?'

'I told you, I'm cooking steak-and-kidney pie.'

'Why?'

'Because we need to eat. Because it's dinner time. Because, just because. Why not?'

'But,' – Marah hesitates – 'you never cook pies. Except from SuperSave.'

'Don't be silly, of course I do. Apple pies. Chicken pies. And I do that cheese and vegetable pie that Jethro likes. You've got a short memory, Marah.'

Noeline has never cooked a pie in front of Marah. Nor has she ever baked a cake, or made bread, or created biscuits. Cooking is not what Noeline does. Except that now, apparently, she does. She makes pies. She is Noeline Dell, pie-maker extraordinaire. Marah puts *Hollywood Babylon* on her own special shelf of the new bookcase, and takes another book down. *Too Young to Die: Stars Killed in Their Prime*. When Charis comes back through the door an hour later, dragging Jethro behind her like an unwilling stray, Marah has worked her way alphabetically through to 'R' – Otis Redding. There is an Otis Redding album on the record shelf. Joe's records and tapes are still scattered about the house. Dingo says there's no point in records, better off getting the new compact discs. He's got some, Marah has seen them: *Midnight Oil, Cold Chisel, Linda Ronstadt*. He's got a CD Walkman, used to show it off to Joe. Before Joe moved out and left his records behind.

When the pie comes out of the oven – Noeline balancing it delicately, a red oven glove on each hand – Charis and Jethro applaud and yell, 'Food, finally.' Noeline tells them to shush, but it's easy to see that she's pleased with it. Brown crust, risen up high, with a pastry leaf sitting on top. Better than shop-bought, everyone says so. Noeline bangs a spoon on the table as if she's calling a load of farmers in to dinner, not just three kids. Three kids and a big bloke, as it turns out, because Dingo sits down to eat as well, even though it's supposed to be a family dinner. And

Dingo might be Joe's best friend, but he's not family, not really, or he wasn't the last time anyone checked. There's mashed potatoes to go with the pie, and baby carrots cooked in honey. Charis starts eating before everyone has sat down and Noeline gives her a look.

Dingo eats fast, shovelling food in as if he's not eaten for days, in between asking Noeline questions, questions, questions. What does she like about being a headmistress, has she ever been white-water rafting, would she like to go some time, could he have some more pie? Ignoring anyone else at the table. Noeline doesn't seem to notice, doesn't seem to mind that it's bad maners to talk over the top of other people and ignore them. Really, she does it herself. Offers carrots and wine to Dingo, says nothing about Jethro not touching his vegetables, says nothing about Family Dinners. She's made rhubarb crumble for dessert, and there's ice-cream as well. Jethro screws his face up, he hates rhubarb because it smells like wee and tastes like sick. Noeline is serving the crumble into plates (just ice-cream for Jethro) when the phone breaks through like an alarm.

'Dingo, will you grab that? I'm gunna drop this if I move.' Three plates are beside her, one in her hand. Rhubarb drips red on to the white floor.

Dingo is already out of his chair, clumping across to the phone, grabbing at the receiver as if it is more pie. 'City Morgue, can I help you?'

Charis giggles into her hand, thinking of someone phoning a dead person.

Dingo clicks the phone down: hot potato. Noeline stops serving the rhubarb, puts a plate of ice-cream down in front of Jethro and looks over his head at Dingo. Eyebrows raised.

'Wrong number.' Dingo smiles around the table, notices Jethro and Marah and Charis for the first time. 'Anyone fancy a drive to the river?'

They do, they do fancy a drive to the river. With the moon shining on the waves and the heat wrapping around in the darkness, it's the best. They're allowed to take the frisbee and they stay on the shore until after Jethro should be in bed. Even though it's the end of the weekend and there's school the next day. When they come back, laughing and full of sand and dust, Dingo says he'll give Noeline a hand with the dishes. Marah, lying in bed watching the moon outside, hears no clinking of other dishes, but she hears sighing and wonders if it's the wind. Just before she falls asleep, she could swear that she hears Noeline crying. She's forgotten it in the morning, her memory is short and the day is bright. She has to wait for the bathroom and she bangs on the door yelling, 'Hurry up, Jethro, I need a wee. I'm gunna be late if ya don't get out of there.' When the door opens she steps back, ready to run in and maybe kick Jethro on the way. It's Dingo, though, not Jethro, who comes out, drying his hair with one of the good blue towels.

Marah's face turns pink and she slams the bathroom door behind her. She does not say 'good morning', but then neither does Dingo. She splashes her cheeks with cold water until the heat has gone.

# Charis

Buck's night. Stag evening. Women get to be hens. Hen parties. Cluck-cluck. While the blokes are out doing whatever it is stags do (locking horns or being shot by fat men with gout and ridiculous voices), the girls are pecking at the crumbs. Which is why stag nights get singing telegrams being French Maids, and hen nights get the Blobendales. Obviously, the average stag night is not my favourite gig. But a girl's gotta eat. When Donny phones and says, 'Stag night in Willesden,' as if he's a spy delivering the secret, I tell him to rack off and get someone else. Then I say I'll pick up the costume at eight-thirty. My French Maid is more Boris Yeltsin than Juliet Binoche. It's basically the same accent that I use for Betty Bondage, who's supposed to be German. No national stereotyping going on here at all. There's an English nanny-o-gram as well. Mary Poppins with a cleavage and a cane. All in the best possible taste, and just for a laugh. Ha ha. My sides are splitting. Donny reckons he should bring in an Aussiegram, who'd turn up, sing a song and then move into your house for six months with fifteen mates. High art. Very cutting edge.

It's dark and cold when I get to Donny's. Put-putting through the centre of London with the wind whistling through my fishnets, so that by the time I arrive I've got goosebumps sticking up through the net. After the cold of the bike, the inside of Donny's house feels ridiculously warm and cosy. Makes me sleepy and almost weepy as well. Something to do with the sticky sweet smell coming from the corner of the room. Pot-pourri. In a little silver bowl. I pick it up, sniff until I'm ready to sneeze, but I still want more. Familiar, it's a smell I know and sends me somewhere I'm not sure I want to be.

'What's this supposed to be? Are you turning soft in your old age?' I shake the bowl at Donny. He's never been big on smells. At least, not while I've been around.

His face turns pink, or maybe I imagine it does, maybe it's just the heat. He certainly looks flushed. 'Nothin wrong with making things nice, Gracie. It's Scent of Summer. Frangipani and lily of the valley. Makes it feel fresh. Besides, I've had a rat problem and there's something dead under the floor. Surprised you hadn't noticed.'

'I did. I thought it was you. And it's fran*ja*pani, not frang-ee pan-ee.' Between a sudden queasiness at the thought of dead rats beneath my feet, I have a flash of a frangipani bush in our yard. Mum planted it for Dad, before she was witch-mother. A birthday present, I think, so he'd smell it always outside his window. Nice thought. Shame she kicked him out a year later. I smelt it, though. It's in almost everything I remember, that sweet smell, marking the turn of the seasons. Getting sweeter and more sickly each year. Even the faked-up, melted-down version of the smell in the pot-pourri jar makes the spit swim up to my mouth, as if I'm about to be sick.

Donny really is blushing now, I've never noticed him change colour before and it's a bit disconcerting. He gets the map for the stag night and the song sheet from his office, and asks if I want a drink before I go. With dead rats under my feet, that's the last thing I want, so I say I'll just change and head straight off. Plenty of time to find the place, and blah blah blah. My flat is bad, there's no question of that, but at least all the bugs are alive. When I strip off in the office, I have to keep brushing myself down, I'm imagining all sorts of things crawling up and down my body. Imagining flesh being eaten off me by enthusiastic rodents. The skirt of the French Maid costume appears to have a small nibble out of it, but then that may always have been there. The teensy-weensy white apron will be crushed and marked by the time I get to Willesden, but if these guys wanted glamour, they would have paid for it. When I come out of the office, Donny is sitting on the floor with a map spread out in front of him. From the back, I can see the bald patch, smooth and shiny as a clean baby's bum. I shake my feather duster on the hairless bit and make what I imagine to be a ratty squeaking noise. Donny yells and slumps forward so that, for a moment, I think I've given him a heart attack. Bloody hell. He sits up, though, and tells me to get out and get French Maiding. I say, 'Ooh, Fifi eez soo, ow you say, le sad, to make Monsieur scared.' Donny doesn't laugh at all; I didn't expect him to, given his terminal lack of humour. Even in that tiny moment when I thought, really thought, that his heart had gone pop, the main thing I felt was relief. Relief at the possibility that I wouldn't have to go out and wave my feather duster around the crotch area of a pissed man about to marry some stupid, stupid girl.

The pub is called the Mad Hound, which worries me slightly. To get to the downstairs 'private party' room, I have to walk through the main bar. Yahoo. Yes, sir, I am here to tickle your fancy/clean up your act/dust your desires. Even the barman gets in on the act, calls out a request for room service. I'm tempted to stick the duster down his gob and tell him to sing Frère Jacques. He's skinny and pimply and not enough of a challenge, so I flash my bum instead. That'll teach him. Things can only get better. At least, that's the theory. Rapidly disproved when I push open the door to the private bar. At least sixty rugby players, jugs of beer on every table, the Spice Girls on the juke-box. Great. Classy, just what I expected. One of the rugby players sticks his face up to mine and starts licking his lips. After four tries, I manage to yell loudly enough in his ear to get him to turn the juke-box off. Thumbs up and more licking of lips. I'm in a room with the men who killed Pete Bog. Pre-neanderthal. When the juke-box stops, the yelling keeps on keeping on, until I jump up on to the nearest table and stamp my pretty feet. I know, French girls don't flamenco, but this is fusion. My hair flicks and my skirt snaps and I almost break my neck, but they stop.

I've got no idea who the lucky man is, so when I've got their attention, I wave my duster in the air and say, 'Ello Messieurs, where eez ze my petit Monsieur ooo eez leaving me for zis woman?' The scrum yells and pushes forward a captainy-looking bloke. Fair hair, fat square face. Lucky woman. Beer has been

sloshed on the table and I know I'm gunna go bum over tit if I
don't get down, so I tell Fatface to stay still for Fifi, so that I can
come down and check his linen. Ooo là là. Wobbling delicately
on my ridiculous heels (French girls do the dusting in stilettos for
some reason), I back myself down on to the vinyl chair. Left foot
first, while I'm still telling Fatface that he 'eez ze sweetest
monsieur in ze, ow you say, pole, no, silly Fifi, eet eez le bar.' I'm
supposed to get him to sing 'Voulez-vous coucher avec moi, ce
soir' while I dust him, but I'm feeling a bit unsure about his
ability to take it as a joke rather than an invitation. Something in
the way he moves – hands out, ready to grope anything with
breasts within a fifty-metre radius. Both feet manage to touch
the ground, which is slippery with beer and something sticky-
brown. Bourbon, perhaps. Plan B: improvise.

'Now I vant all ze boys to line up, yes, like zees, quickly now,
like good petit Messieurs. Some on zees side, some on zees side.'
I prod and poke with my duster, organizing and leading. Should
be a primary-school teacher. Really, I missed my calling. When
I've got them in two groups, with an aisle down the middle, I
grab a white tea-towel from the bar and stick it on Fatface's head.
'Voilà, ze lovely bride. But where eez ze groom? Ooo, ee eez
here.' I grab the tallest bloke and drag him next to Fatface. So far,
so manageable. They walk down the aisle together, with
everyone singing 'Here Comes the Bride'. It's only when I say,
'You may kiss ze bride,' that things go wobbly. Fatface shoves his
groom out of the way and puts his hands out for me. I smack him
with the feather duster, but he's not having any of it.

'Orright darling, giss a kiss, then.' His face looms in at me.

'Oh, no, Monsieur, Fifi is not ze groom.' I shake the duster in
his face and try to push him away.

He pushes my hand aside, and before I can step back, his hands
have come out like pincers and tweaked my nipples. Although
I'm ready to slap him, I tell him he's a 'notty boy' and pretend to
laugh. Forgetting the golden rule: don't laugh, it only encourages
him. While the scrum cheers as if he's going for a goal, he steps
forward, grabs me by the waist and sticks his hand up under my
skirt. Right up to my knickers. Hands groping about, squeezing
my flesh. And he'd go further, try to get in as well, if it weren't

for me turning the duster around so that the sharp end faces him, and shoving it hard into his crotch. I know it's hard because he doubles over and yells, 'Bitch,' as if I care. I stamp on his foot for good measure. Stilettos can be useful. Rugby players aren't known for letting women kick their mates about, so I hold the duster out in front of me like a sword and run fast through the crowd. Fortunately, they're still parted down the middle and I manage to get through before they realize what's happening. Ooh là là inbloodydeed.

When I walk-run back through the bar, my duster still poking in front of me, the barman calls out, asks me if it went OK. Trying to be friendly, not having a go, but I tell him to shut his face or I'll cripple him. Then I get out of there as quickly as I can, so that he can't prove me wrong. Kebab smells hit me when I get out the door. Makes me feel queasy, although I love kebabs and it's not like me to be off my food. When I kick-start the bike, I notice that my foot is shaking. I didn't even collect the fee. No fee, no food. Choices, choices, choices: I could go back in there and demand full payment and a written apology; or I could invite a rat to chew my fingers off one by one while water drips on to my eyeballs. No competition. I head for Donny's, for the rats. Thinking of excuses all the way across London. Because he is not going to be happy. Storming out without the money, it's just not done. By the time I get to Acton, I've decided to quit if Donny hassles me. I've got the speech worked out in my head, I rehearse it while I'm waiting at a pelican crossing. I'm concentrating so hard that I nearly run over a woman with a pram.

Donny is sitting in his favourite spot, outside on the high steps. He likes to see his little telegrams heading up the road towards him, even in the dark. He plays guessing games with himself – which headlight belongs to whom. Anna is getting into her tiny Renault, her Carmen Miranda hat under her arm. An orange falls off as she slides into the seat. She toots her horn as she drives away and flashes her headlights at me. I give her a wave. Donny whistles at me as I swing myself off the bike and I give him my usual finger in the air. Ready for a fight. My stilettos leave little indents in the lawn; I can feel the dirt coming up with my heel with each step I take.

'Bit early, aincha? Mustn't have taken long.' Donny is a dark patch on the steps, a vague fat shape. He lifts his hand and I can see light reflecting on a beer bottle. 'How'd it go?'

'Haven't they called ya?' I click-click up the stairs, my stupid shoes tapping out anxious rhythms on the cement.

Donny's voice goes wary. 'Why would they have? What av ya done, Gracie?' He takes a big gulp of beer. Doesn't offer me a bottle, even though I'd kill for one.

'Don't call me bloody Gracie. All I've done is protect myself from a bunch of wankers. They owe you the money, I didn't get it. None for me, none for you.'

'Bloody hell.'

'Bloody hell yaself. You go back and get it and let some poo-for-brains rugby player grope you. Go on, have a go.'

'Just tell me what happened.'

'I got there. Started the telegram and he seemed to think it was a free-for-all-o-gram, stuck his mits up me skirt, grabbed me tits, blah blah blah. So I stuck the duster in his knackers. Hope I crippled him. Anyway, I've had it. I'd rather waitress for wankers than dress up for em.'

'Oh, Gracie.'

'Get stuffed, Donny. He was out of order.'

'I know. Here.' He shuffles around on the steps and pulls his wallet out. 'You did the gig, you get paid.' He shoves thirty quid into my hands.

My resignation speech slips out the back of my mind and leaves the door swinging. 'Thanks.'

'You shouldn't have to go through that. I'll take care of it. Bastard.' Donny's voice is loud beside me. 'You need a body-guard.'

'I don't need your sarcasm.'

'I'll come out with you. I'm bigger than most of the punters.'

'No, Donny, really. I'm fine. I can handle it. I handled it this time, I'll handle it next time. Anyway, if you come out with me, who'd go out with the others? You can't do it for me and not for anyone else.' The last thing I want is Donny standing up the back of my gigs, keeping an eye out. Hanging on the back of my bike with his arms around my waist. I don't think so.

Donny lets out a big breath. I can almost smell his breakfast. 'Charis.'

It's a shock to hear him use my name. He makes a point of being the only person in the world to call me Gracie, or Big Gracie, or Little Ozzie. It's not just me he does it with. He had a Jangle's Jingles Christmas party not long after I started. Everyone there had a nickname which only Donny used. Anna is called Twiggy. Sue is called Barbie. Because of Barbra Streisand, not Barbie doll. And Donny is called the Fat Controller. But only by me and never to his face.

He does the big breath again. 'Charis. I don't want anything to happen to you.'

The night is cool on my skin, but suddenly I'm hot. Prickles of heat jump up and down me arms and I have to put both hands on the stair beneath me. 'No, me neither. But I'm sure I'll be fine.'

'Let me come out with you. If anything happens, you know, I'll be there.' Donny's voice has gone all puppy-dog and it worries me.

'I'll think about it. Anyway, I'd better go. Thanks for the cash.' I go to get up but Donny grabs me arm and pulls me back beside him.

'I need to talk to you, Gracie.'

I'm desperate to run down the stairs, get on my bike and zoom away, but I nod as if I'm willing to talk.

'I think you know what about.' Donny moves closer to me, so that I have to shuffle right to the stair edge to avoid touching him.

Truthfully, I don't have a clue, and I don't want to get into any sort of deep and meaningful with Donny. But I think maybe he wants to talk money and it really is time I got more than thirty pounds for a telegram. OK, I'm being optimistic. 'Money?'

'Money? Is there a problem with the money?'

'Just that when I started, you said I'd be on thirty quid a telegram for the trial period and then it would go up to forty. That's all. And I'm still on thirty.'

He takes ten pounds from his wallet. 'OK. But listen, that's not it. I still think about you. All the time. Since that night.'

I should have taken the money and run. I should run now, but I don't. Curiosity gets there first and I open my mouth: 'What night?'

'The night we, you know. I know it's a long time ago, but, I think about you. I've been waiting and waiting to talk to you, but it's never the right time.'

My head has gone soft. Although I have no clue what night he is talking about, something is stirring uncomfortably way back there in the rear end of my brain. 'Sorry?'

'After the Christmas party.'

'I'm sorry, Donny, I don't remember.' And it's true, I don't remember, but still, that shifting, lumbering something, waking up. I get a dim image of Donny's face diving in close to me and then – oh, no – his lips clamping on to mine. Hands everywhere. Mine and his. No, surely not.

'Really?' His voice is disappointed. 'It was just an accident, I suppose. We were both very drunk.'

'Must have been.'

'But I would have wanted to even if I was sober.'

I want to stop Donny talking, because I know what's coming and I don't want any moonlight confessions of undying anything. When I was a kid we had a huge bookcase covering one whole wall. Dad built it for us, I think. I seem to remember him hammering away for days. My shelf had a brass frame with a picture of Simon le Bon in it. Now that was undying love. Nothing has touched it since. Dingo must have moved in some time around then, because I seem to remember him saying that Simon looked like a girl. Later, he threw the frame out. Said he hadn't, but the picture was gone and he'd wanted to punish me. Don't think about Dingo. Just don't.

'Donny, before you say anything, I think you should know that I'm a lesbian.'

Donny splutters into his bottle and a bit of beer sprays on to my leg. 'But, that night, you, we – you never said.'

'I know. It just happened, I'm sorry.' Where have I heard those words before? They almost choke me on the way out of my mouth.

'Oh. Sorry. I should have guessed. OK. Well. Never mind, hey? Are you sure, though? Really sure?'

'Really sure.' I want to ask him what he means by 'I should have guessed' and I try not to be offended. Should have guessed what? 'Anyway, I'd better be off, Donny. I've got that gig tomorrow.'

He nods and lifts his bottle in salute. My lie hangs in the air between us and it follows me down the stairs like a bad smell. When I get on my bike, I look up to wave at Donny, but he's gone inside. His beer bottle glints in the light. My bike stalls three times before I get home and I lie awake all night imagining throwing a Simon le Bon statue in Dingo's face. The last thing my imagination shows me before I finally drift off is blood trickling down on to Dingo's shirt, making fingers right across his chest. I'm not sure, but I think I fall asleep smiling.

# Marah

I've got the morning off. Leisha is working with the cherubs and the tenors all morning and the leads have been told to rest. Usually, I'd have to go to Hendrie Hall for Counterpoint with Magrette, but she's on sabbatical and anyway Leisha says we need to spend the next three weeks putting everything into rehearsal. First full run this afternoon, and I have to start croaking in the middle of the night. Wilma leaves taps dripping all the time in the bathroom and I'm sure the damp gets into my chest and throat. All night I dreamt about being strangled, being held down and unable to scream. Having no voice, all night. Sweat covered my face when I woke up and my legs were sticky as well. I could feel that my throat was tight, but when I started to do my breathing exercises, I felt like a knife was being pushed through my cords. Perfect timing. It's only a rehearsal, not even a dress, but they'll all have their eyes on me, waiting to see if I trip up. Leisha has been working with us all separately, chorus as well, since she arrived.

Leisha Degrant. She's in the Hall of Fame of American Opera Singers, how about that? I looked her up before she arrived, I wanted to be informed. If it weren't for Magrette going on sabbatical, we probably wouldn't have got to work with a guest director. Leisha expects us to behave as professionally as any company, and so she should. She's directed *Dido and Aeneas* four times. She's done the *Fairy Queen* and *Dioclesian* as well, one for the Met. Purcell is her big passion, that's what she says. Then she says passion is the wrong word to use for Purcell, respect is the word he would prefer. Purcell was big on respect, duty, that sort of thing. Loyalty, fidelity.

Daniel has sent me a photo of him sailing. You can see the edge of the bridge behind him, just the small point of the curve, before it hits the shore. He's got mirror glasses on; he says it's retro-chic, but I think he looks embarrassing. The camera is reflected in the glasses, and a pair of hands. Dingo's hands. Dingo is teaching Daniel to sail. I think that was Mother's idea and I should feel happy about it, it should be a nice thing, but the truth is that it makes me feel a bit seasick. Queasy. I suppose it's just the thought of Daniel having a nice time without me, maybe that's it. Anyway, I've put the photo in my wallet. To remind myself, when I need reminding. Which, of course, isn't very often. There was a letter with the photo. Half a page. Eighteen lines. Mostly about sailing and the hospital, and then a few lines at the bottom saying he hopes the course is going well and he can't wait to see me and he sends all his love. That should be enough for me, I should be happy with that, and I am; I am happy. Sometimes it feels like there's a little gap, that's all. But I'm happy, and Daniel's lovely. He's very kind.

One day, I want someone to create an opera for me. They used to think that *Dido and Aeneas* was written for a bunch of schoolgirls. Young gentlewomen. There's actually a whole section missing. The libretto is there, but there's no music. Imagine, a whole thread buried somewhere, a missing link. So we just have to guess, to fill in the gaps, or leave it blank. A new opera, created for me. That's what I want. Not like the young gentlewomen of Josias Priest's school, not created to keep me quiet or teach me a lesson. Created for me, to stretch me and show me off. It's not a lot to ask. Sometimes I wish Daniel was a composer, or I imagine myself being married to a composer rather than a doctor. If I'm going to get married, and I certainly hope I am, I'd better be fast. Before I get a name for myself. Some people have a professional name and a private name, but I don't think I'd like that. It might get confusing. Never knowing what's what or who's who.

My throat is tight even after a glass of warm water. It's tension, I'm sure. Tension and Wilma's dripping tap. She seems so nice, Wilma, but she's as inconsiderate as they come. Last week, she left a bucket in the bathroom full of soaking underpants. Really.

Which has probably also affected my voice. Mind you, Gladys Moncrieff never warmed her voice, never bothered herself about anything. And I know that because my mother's grandmother sang with her, how about that? Actually, I would guess that I inherited my voice from her. It certainly didn't come from my mother. She's tone deaf, and she doesn't think she is. She belts out jazz standards and tries to sing along with *La Traviata* all the time, changing key every bar. Embarrassing. And she tells people I got my talent from her, do you believe it? I wouldn't know if it came from my father. He didn't bother with me, so I'm not bothered with him. Fair's fair. He just took off when it got too difficult to keep seeing us. He went in one direction, I went in another. Like modal counterpoint. Passing each other but in opposition, not touching. It doesn't hurt me, it's fine. His choice. Charis won't hear a wrong word said against him, honestly. And then she has this big thing about Dingo, how she can't stand Dingo. Charis doesn't look forward enough. If she were to ask me what her major problem was, I would tell her that it was her backward-lookingness. Looking back to the past, to things that are over. She has this idea, Charis does, of the way things are, and she harps on and on about the way things used to be.

After I've gargled and stretched, I've still got the edges of the dream in my mind and still got the traces of croak. I open my mouth wide, stretch my lips, stretch my tongue, loosen the whole mouth and roll my neck. Head is passive, neck is active, that's the trick. Loosens and warms the inside of the throat. Sweat is the best thing, that's what I believe. I know it's unconventional, but it really does get rid of germs. Which is why I put my shorts and sneakers on and power-walk down on to the sidewalk, and up past College Street. Once I get past Sprague Hall, I start running. The road rolls underneath my feet, one-two-one-two. As always, I start with a jog, I let my body ease into itself. There's a big long patch of road leading right up to East Rock where I run. East Rock sits up there, a goal, while my feet go pounding. Sometimes, I get a headache from the concrete beneath me, but not today. Today, I concentrate on the muscles in my thighs. I imagine myself thin and fit. I imagine my voice strong and supple. Sweat pours down my chest, warms my throat. Faster, stronger, better. That's the rhythm in my brain while I run. Beneath that rhythm, I go over theory notes in my head: Pavane is duple metre, Galliard is triple metre. I keep it going, triple-metre chants sifting over the ground bass of my footsteps. Like patting the head and rubbing the belly. Look at me, I can do everything at once.

Before Mrs James discovered my voice – helped me discover my voice – I couldn't do anything at once. That's how it felt. All through primary school, there was Charis: madame popular. Loud-mouthed and bossy in the playground, and that's why no one picked on me. Karla Simpson nearly hit me once, and some other kid said, Don't do that, Charis will get you; and Karla said, Sorry. Just like that. Sorry, Marah. Actually, I didn't really want lots of people around me, didn't need lots of friends. Before Mrs James, all I wanted to do was get an A for maths. Not that I ever did. B plus was the best I ever did. See? Mother says, Oh, Marah was always the high-achiever. But it's just not true. She doesn't remember, but I do, I was there. High school was the thing that changed it all for me.

In my first music lesson, we had to each stand up and sing four bars of some folk song, 'Donna Donna', I think it was. Some kids didn't want to do it, didn't want to sing on their own, but I had a solo in the primary-school end-of-year concert and even though Karla Simpson said it was because I was a suck-up crawler, I knew it was because I could sing. Even then, I knew. Without any evidence at all. So I couldn't wait to open my mouth for Mrs James and sing my little bit. *On a wagon, bound for market, here's a calf with a mournful eye. Why don't you have wings to fly with, like the swallow so proud and free?* That's the bit we had to sing. Poor stupid calf.

After I finished she smiled and said, Very good, would you stay back please, Marah?

I was the only one who stayed back, and she asked me if I would like to take voice as my instrument, would I like to have voice coaching with her? She was a choral singer, worked for years with Sydney Opera. Desperate to find a protégée, as it turned out, and that was me. Poor Mrs James. She's still there, still stuck in West Sydney, still teaching. Always said she loved it, and maybe she does, but I'm here in New Haven, Connecticut, USA, and I feel sorry for her. I really do. Because I know she'd love to be me.

Mrs James advised me against drama school, told me I should go for music theory before I was old enough for the Con., but I wanted that something extra to mark me out, to make me special. University of Western Sydney let me do both, actually, so I was lucky. Made my own luck, really, if the truth be known. Because I had to fight very, very hard to do a double degree, but I knew I could do it. Youngest in my year, as well. Youngest at the Con., too. But I'm not the youngest here, or the best. I'm way behind on theory, and everyone gets a chance at a lead during the two years, so I have to make the most of it. To stand out. If I want to be the best, I have to think about it all the time, and that's what I do. Eyes on the goal, all the time. Know where you're heading and you'll get there. I believe that, I really do. That's the other problem with Charis: no goals. Happy to just drift along. Jethro's the same. Since he dropped out of uni, all he's done is drift about doing odd jobs. He worked as a jackaroo, for goodness sakes – what's the point of that? And now he wants to go off to Thailand or somewhere ridiculous, apparently. Wants to volunteer to build houses. Jethro's only three years younger than me, but you'd swear he was still a teenager. It's only my opinion, but I do think that at twenty-one, you should be settling into things a little bit. Idealism is all very well, but we all have to grow up some time.

When I get to the bottom of East Rock, I let myself go. Pelt up to the top, pushing as hard as I can. Always hold something back until the end. I can hardly breathe by the time I get to the top and my heart feels like it will burst out of my chest, or up through my ears. Hair is stuck to my neck and my face, I can feel sweat running down my chest. It's a bit grubby, but actually I love this feeling. Face hot, breath hard, legs sore. I slow to a walk and lean against a smooth-barked tree to do my stretches. It's pale, almost as pale as a gum tree, but without that grey, sickly look. Hands against the trunk, I lean down, and then up. I stretch my back so that I'm like a snake, looking up to the canopy. It's not a high tree, and only a few leaves, but it feels solid. I press my face against the trunk and wrap my arms around it. Not to do any tree-hugging or anything ridiculous – just to stretch my biceps. My hands don't touch solid bark on the other side of the tree, they touch sharp wood and absence. Air. It's an empty tree.

When I move around to look at where my hands were, what I see is a skeleton, the inside is black and charred. Amazing, really – it looks so green and healthy and solid, but it's had lightning strike out its whole middle. Still growing as well. Determined little tree. For some reason, it makes me want to weep. It's all right, I sometimes feel a bit emotional after running, that's all. There's nothing wrong with me or anything like that. I'm remembering the calf in 'Donna Donna' and how I thought it was the calf's fault that it was going to be slaughtered. Because it hadn't got itself some wings. It's an accusation. But this tree, it's organized wings for itself. Struck by lightning, but it keeps growing. And if you only looked at it from one side, you would never know that anything had happened. It should make me feel inspired, but it makes me feel sad. I walk back to the halls so slowly that I miss lunch and I don't even have time to shower before rehearsals and my throat still feels tight.

Red is still on my face by the time I get to the hall; I can feel the tingle in my cheeks which means I'm flushed. Elisabeth is waiting on the steps, she grins at me as I walk up. She has dressed up, put red lipstick on and everything. Usually, she wears a pale colour, I've noticed that it makes her look a bit washed-out. Red suits her, brings colour to her face. Although I don't understand why she's put dark lipstick on for a rehearsal. We'll be lucky if we're working with props, let alone lighting. I've pulled my hair back and put a black hairband on. Neat and workable, and perhaps just a little bit preppy, that's what I'm going for.

Elisabeth says, How are you doing, Marah? Friendly as anything. She asks me if I'm excited about playing Dido. I say – truthfully – that I am but that it will be more exciting for her when she has a lead in a full opera rather than just a miniature. Although the melodic development in *Dido* is equal to any baroque opera, definitely. Elisabeth says she's going to Quebec at the end of term, and do I want to come along? I'm so surprised I almost cry. I don't know what's the matter with me, tears popping out every five minutes. It's unusual for me, really. I'm very happy, as a person. People say that to me all the time: Marah, you're so happy, so positive. Everyone should be positive.

When Leisha comes out and calls us in, Elisabeth says, Well, how about it? I nod my head and say I'd love to go. As long as I don't have any extra preparation to do, of course. The auditorium, where we're all gathered, is dark after the sun on the steps. Spots wriggle back and forth in front of my eyes and I almost feel dizzy from the darkness. Gerald Cotes – graduate of Yale College, boy wonder, son of *the* Madeline Cotes – calls out, Hail the arrival of Queen Dido, and even though I feel stupid, I do a royal wave. Laughter rumbles about until Leisha says, OK, let's settle down, I want to say a few things.

Elisabeth sits down right where she is, just on the floor. I stay standing until Leisha waves me into an empty seat next to Gerald.

Now, Leisha says, first things first, you've all worked very hard so far, I'm very pleased with the effort you've put in, thank you – but the hard work is just about to begin. I expect each of you to read at least one paper on the opera, you need as much background information as possible. Yes, Gerald, I know it's tedious, but we are trying to train intelligent singers.

I look around as she's speaking, at the dark auditorium, the shadowy faces half-lit, and I am full of being here. Full of myself, that's what Jethro says. But I'm not, I'm definitely not that. Full of something, some anticipation. Leisha keeps talking, starts thanking the undergraduates who will be crewing for us, telling us to remember to respect everyone who works on the production. We're all nodding, dark shapes of heads bob bob bobbing along. Although this is the smallest of all the works we'll do, it's the first, so you can feel everyone tingling with excitement.

Leisha gets out of her seat and walks up on to the stage. She says, See how powerful I am from here? But see how small I am as well. You each must be powerful here, must fill this space. It's your choice, how you are on this stage, whether or not you are swallowed by it. And, as I said this morning, that's as true for the cherubs as it is for the soloists. Not just the leads. Everyone. Now – she sits down on the edge of the stage, kicking her legs – I know some of you think this is an insignificant work. That we're giving you a baby piece to start off with. Firstly, remember that a singer's career is built on what you don't sing. You should be singing off your interest, not your capital. What do I mean by that?

Gerald says, It means that you're quoting from Callas, and Elisabeth asks, so quietly that I'm surprised anyone hears her, When did Callas say that?

Someone behind me – I can't make out the voice, but it's a male one – says, Before she died, and everyone laughs, including Leisha.

Then she says, No, it means this is a perfect work for your first season. But it's not a baby step. Absolutely not. *Dido and Aeneas* is a complex work, more so because it is so compact. I know you've been discovering the challenge of the vocal score individually. Dido's final recitative, 'Thy hand, Belinda,' is in my humble and biased opinion an amazing piece of vocal writing. In the space of nine measures it makes a draining descent through an entire octave, hitting almost all twelve tones of the chromatic scale along the way, *and* in the process preparing the descending chromatic *ostinato* bass of Dido's great lament. Clever. But it's more than clever composition, it echoes the emotional state of our heroine. Echoes and illuminates. Every, I repeat, *every* one of you, is contributing to the illumination. Each person in this opera – each person singing, each person on stage – is part of the tragedy. Each one plays a part in the distress of Dido, in the calling of Aeneas. Remember that this is deceptively simple, that such complexity, such tragedy, is there underneath the surface, hiding away. Work together to dig it out. Now, Allan, can you play us through for warm-up?

I'm practically vibrating when she finishes speaking. I'm leaning far forward in my seat, waiting for every word. If I was a louder sort of person, I would shout, Bravo! or something like that. But I'm not that sort of person, I'm the sort of person who stands up and gets up on to the stage for warm-up with everybody else. So that's what I do. We warm up together, and fairly quickly. Just a few scale runs, some loosening and enunciation exercises. The run starts easily. We really do work as a whole, each moment of individual and choral rehearsal comes into play. Only one stop during the first scene, everything's fine. When I open up for the first aria, I feel everyone hold their breath, there's a pause across the entire stage. My voice rushes out and up, splatters the walls of the auditorium and drips down. When I finish, a collective breath is let out, like a sigh. But by the final recitative, I'm flagging, my throat is tight again and I strain. On the final note, I almost crack. Just a demi-croak, but still, it's there, under the surface. When we finish the run, Leisha says, Marvellous work, Marah, marvellous. Elisabeth says it too, and Alex – my Aeneas – says, Fantastic. I smile and say thank you to each of them, but as I sit down for Leisha's notes, I'm thinking: Who saw? Who heard? When Gerald Cotes says, Marah, you should come up and stay with my folks some time, I just know he's trying to trip me up. So I smile and say nothing, not even, Thank you Gerald, that's very kind. Gerald says, You know, you must be missing home. Yes, I say, Of course I am.

But I don't know if it's true. I am missing something, but I don't know if it's home.

# How to Wish for Your Fate:
## Cathartic Identification with Dido

*A paper delivered at Yale School of Music
by Dr George Psalter*

## Abstract

The elusive performance history of Purcell's *Dido and Aeneas* has
been the cause of much musicological debate, in which the
question of the original cast has come to dominate. The
majority of scholarly opinion remains that this is indeed a work
first 'Perform'd at Mr Josias Priest's Boarding School at
Chelsey. By Young Gentlewomen' in 1689. Yet given the
sketchy documentary traces of the opera's early career, it is
unsurprising that this view has been both challenged and
defended with equal passion, along with an equal paucity of
corroborating evidence. Often the ideological positions, or
simply prejudices, of the critics are all too easily seen in the
clarity of the documentary vacuum.

This paper reviews such evidence as does exist and examines
the arguments on both sides of the debate. Is there sufficient
evidence to claim *Dido and Aeneas* was first performed by pupils
at a girls' boarding school, or is there another plausible
explanation? Was this performance rather a revival of some
earlier (male, professional) première? In recent years, those
critics who deny or are disappointed by the boarding-school
première hypothesis have been accused by feminists of mini-
mizing the validity of such an obviously female context.

This paper argues that the feminists are correct to assert that
the opera was first performed by schoolgirls. However, the

ideology behind this assertion is challenged. Far from providing thinly veiled role models of women who experience physical rapture on account of one another, as one writer has argued, the opera teaches young women the virtues of womanhood and in particular the supreme, albeit tragic, value of self-sacrifice for the sake of male destiny.

A cathartic identification is indeed invited with Dido, but she is to be identified with as an exemplar of feminine duty. When Dido realizes she cannot have Aeneas, that his destiny precludes her, she sacrifices herself on a self-built funeral pyre. It is whilst the flames devour her that she watches her Aeneas sail off to his noble destiny, a destiny she has in fact helped him win through her own willingness to sacrifice herself.

Belinda is ultimately right to sing 'Fate your wishes does allow.' The opera teaches young women not to selfishly seek their own wishes, but to learn to wish for the fate their gender ordains for them. If Dido can finally sing, 'Death is now a welcome guest,' how much more could the girls of Josias Priest's Boarding School learn to love their own socially ordained futures?

*The Objections*

# Or For Ever Hold Your Peace

The car is outside each morning for a week. Parked across the road, near the palm tree on the Martins' lawn, across from Dingo's car. No one has said anything, but Marah and Charis, on their way to school, have both seen it. There's frost under their feet now, and breath comes from them in bunches of steam. Jethro leaves while it's still half-dark, for footie training. He has seen the car, a blue Honda, as well, but has no opinion about it. Perhaps assumes that it belongs to the new people down the street. Charis is quiet in the mornings, walking alongside Marah in silence until the cold and the noise of the primary-school playground wakes her up. She says goodbye to Marah then, and walks the rest of the way to the high school. Lords it over Marah, too – that she is the one to put the high-school blazer on, while Marah is still dressed in the baby uniform of South Windsor Heights Primary School. Each morning, for a week, they walk past the car.

At the end of the week, rain hits. Too late for Jethro, who is already running around the footie field in his white shorts and South Windsor Heights Primary sports top. Covered in mud, no doubt, because he goes for every possible tackle, even when there's no chance at all. Charis and Marah are half-way up the drive – barely out the door, in fact – when the spitting starts. Marah puts her hand out, flat, palm up to the sky, and feels the wet drop on to it. 'Better getta raincoat.' She grabs at Charis's hand, trying to slow her, to pause her.

'Nah, it's no worries. Look.' Charis dances about, arms out, face up. 'It's only spittin'.'

'It's gunna pour, but.' And Marah is right, for as she speaks, the sky opens and rain falls down.

Charis stops dancing, stops her silly larking about, and says, yes, they must get raincoats. Inside, Noeline yells at them to get a move on and suggests they should have thought of the rain earlier. Protected by their yellow rain-hail-or-shine-coats, Charis and Marah storm back outside, just on the edge of running late. When they run past the car this time, there's a man in it. Sitting in the driver's seat. When he sees the two of them, all yellow and rain-proof, his head moves as if to bob down, and then bobs up again. Red red robin, bob bob bobbin along. It's true, too, that he is a red-haired man. It's Charis who notices him first, Charis who turns her head, looks right at him and lets out a yell. 'Dad.'

'Hello, darlin. Jump in.'

Marah looks around, checks that no Dingo or Noeline is lurking anywhere close, nosing around, minding everybody else's business. Charis doesn't check at all, doesn't even look to see what Marah thinks. No, she just jumps straight on in, wraps her arms around Joe.

'Marah? Wanna ride to school?' Joe leans across the car, with Charis's arms still wrapped about him. 'Sweetheart?'

Marah looks once more over her shoulder, then slides into the car. She says 'hi' so quietly that Joe doesn't hear her and has to ask if that old cat has got her tongue, or is she just feeling shy. It is Charis who says: 'She wants to know where you've been and why you went away.'

Joe clicks his seat-belt in, starts the car. 'Sweetheart, I didn't go away. Yer mother, well, I told you what yer mother wanted. Space. Or somethin like that. Anyway. I've tried ringin, lots of times. I think, well, I dunno really, but maybe there's been problems with the phone. Dunno. Last time, I got a disconnected signal.'

'Mum changed the number, we were getting so many calls from Mr Nobody.' Marah shifts so that her face is pressed against the cold window. 'No one ever said you called. Why didn't you come round?'

'I did. I'm here now. I'm sorry, sweetheart, it should be simple but it just isn't, and yer mother needs to sort some things out, apparently. You know that's got nothin to do with whether or not I still love youse.' A big breath comes out of him, in a lump. 'I dunno. It's complicated. I've missed ya. I called a lot, love.'

Charis puts a deep cold fury into her voice, you could hear it a mile off. 'That means they lied to us. Liars.'

'Is Dingo livin in our house?' Joe stares straight ahead, at the road, the way he should.

Marah shifts against the window, turns to look at Charis. Shifts again. 'Sort of.'

'Sort of? Nah, leave it. I don't wanna know after all.' Joe zooms into the primary-school car-park, right through a puddle. 'How's school? Orright? Jethro still playin footie? Tell him he's gotta stop goin for every tackle, he has to pick his moments, OK? Will ya remember to tell him that? Pick his moments.'

'Yair. When are we gunna see ya again?' Marah turns her head for the first time.

'Soon, darlin. We'll get it sorted out, ay? Maybe we could have weekends, somethin like that?'

Charis puts her hand on his shoulder. 'I wanna live with you, Dad. I don't want Dingo around all the time.'

'Is he around all the time, then?'

'Yair. We don't like it.'

'Nah. Me neither.' Joe doesn't look at either of them as he says it. Just stares at the water dribbling down the windscreen. 'We'll see what we can sort out, ay?'

The siren for school starts yelping out, and Marah says she has to go, has to get to class on time. Joe nearly squishes Charis into the back of the seat, leaning right across her to hug Marah close. He says he loves her, she has to remember that, and she says, yes, she will. She'll always remember that. She promises. Marah steps in the puddle as she steps down from the car, and black mud is up her legs as she waves the car off down the road. Charis stays in the car, driving on to the high school, and hangs half out the window, waving to Marah as if this is it, the last time she'll ever see her. At playtime, Marah pulls Jethro over to the corner of the playground and says that Joe came to see them and not to tell Dingo or Noeline. Jethro zips across his lips, hush up boy. Or says, no, he will not shush up, no way. One or the other, who can be sure which he says and which he means?

Since Dingo's been around, Noeline's been cooking all sorts of fancy meals. Pesto sauce, tabouleh salad, lemon chicken. Tonight, it's chicken satay, and she's bought crème caramel from the deli. Only for her and Dingo, the crème caramel. Ice-cream for the kids, with tinned peaches. Jethro says he doesn't want stupid old ice-cream, he wants crème caramel and why can't he have it, and anyway the satay just tasted like peanuts. When Dingo says, 'I think you owe yer mother an apology,' Jethro says, 'Shut up, you're not the boss of me,' and has to go to his room. There is silence around the table then, except for the scraping of Charis's spoon, tracing up every squeeze of ice-cream. Dingo's hand is resting on the table, a fist next to his plate. Noeline reaches over and squeezes his hand, it would almost make you sick she does it so sugar sugar sweetly. She calls him 'love' as well. 'Thanks, love. He'll be all right.' Charis and Marah make sick-up faces at each other across the table.

'Right, clear the table, please, Charis. Marah, you're on washing-up.' Noeline leans back in her chair and points at the sink, as if no one knows where it is. 'Have you got homework?'

Charis sticks her finger in Marah's bowl and licks the ice-cream up. 'Nah, I'm cool.'

'Please don't speak like that, Charis. You've got no homework at all? No assignments due?'

'Nup.'

'Then you can study for your maths test.'

'That's not for ages.'

'All the better.'

'All the better to what? Eat you with?'

Before Noeline can speak, before she can let the steam out of her ears, Dingo is on his feet. 'It's OK, Noel. I'll give you a hand with the dishes, ay, Charis? We can both clear up and it will only take a second. Then you can study while I help Marah wash up. Or whatever.'

No one sees Marah puff her cheeks up and make goggle eyes at Dingo behind his back. Not even Charis knows that it happened, that Marah is getting ready to spit on Dingo's back. Except she doesn't, she just says, 'Gee, thanks, you're so kind' – exactly like a movie star who learned how to get sarcastic. Noeline smiles and says, 'Goodness me, why does it always have to be such an ordeal?' She gives a little laugh after she says it, to show that she is good-humoured about it all, about everything. This is a trick Noeline has, and you wouldn't even notice if you hadn't lived with her all your life, if you hadn't been listening to her little digs and her little laughs ever since you were born. Dingo doesn't notice that it's a trick, that's a fact. He ruffles her hair, as if she is a baby, and says, 'Oh, you're too good-natured, Noel.' Joe would have noticed, that's another fact. Joe would have said, 'Give it a rest, love.' But Joe is not here, so he says nothing.

'I wonder when Jethro will come down to join us. His sulks don't usually last long. Do they, Charis?' Noeline taps her fingers on the table, the nails making a light clicking sound which accompanies the scrape and rattle of dishes.

Dingo balances cups, plates, two jars, in his hands. 'He'll be fine, Noel. Hope you don't mind me giving him a bit of discipline. Kids need it. Where does the chutney go?'

Charis is silent, telling nothing about Jethro's sulks or correct places for chutney. Marah piles the dishes up next to her, making a high tower at the sink. Steam covers the window when she runs the hot tap. She draws a line through it, just marking it, just because. The lemon-fresh detergent makes a yellow line, like honey, on the water. She turns the tap on harder, watching the steam come out with the water and the froth bubble up. Instead of putting the dishes in, she pokes her fingers through the bubbles, drawing eyes, nose, a mouth. There's a hole in one of the pink rubber gloves, so that when she slides her hands into the slippery warmth, water comes in through the thumb and eases its way up to her wrist. Only when Dingo arrives with his tea-towel at her side does she get a move on and plonk the dishes into the water. Glasses first, because Noeline likes them clean and sparkling. Then cups and crockery. Pans and cutlery are always last, getting scrubbed up in water the colour of baby poo. Dingo winds his tea-towel up, ready to flick her on the legs, as if he is the old Dingo, Joe's mate, just having a laugh. Marah doesn't laugh or squeal or move away. She lets him get on with it, while she stares out of the window, at the darkness flat against the glass and the dim shapes of the trees outside. Perhaps she sings a song to herself until Dingo gets bored and does the wiping up in silence. The plates seem loud, banging on the counter beside him. Not as loud, though, as the doorbell, zinging, ringing through the clatter and the clump and all the unspokens.

Dingo slings the tea-towel over his shoulder, calls out, 'I'll get it,' even though Jethro has run down the stairs, wondering, wondering, wondering. Even though Marah is right now pulling her gloves off, ready to open the door and greet whoever it will be standing there. Even though Charis is falling from her chair, trying to be the first to the door. Dingo ignores all this, or does not see it, and stomps off to the front door as if he is the king of the castle. Which he is not.

Noeline leans her elbows on the table, the way she tells Charis not to, and says, 'I wonder who that'll be at this time.'

Dingo has the door open, only a fraction, though, as if he is trying to stop a Mormon coming inside. All you can see is red hair and a bit of denim.

'Dad.' Jethro makes a yelp with his voice and a leap with his body, aiming past Dingo. Aiming for Joe, leaning against the door frame with his big hand raised to the bell. Joe's arms are open, ready to grab Jethro into his arms and squeeze his head off. 'Gidday, mate. Giss a cuddle.'

Dingo folds his arms across his chest, pushes the door even more nearly shut. 'Go back inside, Jethro, it's cold out there. You can see yer dad in a second.'

'Jethro. Come and wipe up, please. Now.' Noeline's voice carries like a shriek.

'Whaddaya doin here, Joe?' Dingo's voice is low, but not so low that Charis and Marah, standing in the hall, can't hear him.

'Could ask the same of you, mate. Not that I'd want to use that term with you any more. Ya friggin bastard.'

'Speak like that in front of the kids and you won't be welcome, mate.'

'Doesn't look like I am anyway. I want to see me bloody kids. Let me in.'

'Yair, well, didn't seem like you wanted to see them for the last five weeks. Noel isn't too happy about that, Joe. I'm just here helpin out. Listen, nothin happened until after you moved out, nothin.'

'Well, you've been bloody quick about it. I've barely been out of the house a month and you're stuck in like a mullet up a bloody drainpipe. Now let me see me bloody kids and get out of me face, I can't stand the sight of yer ugly bloody mug a minute longer.'

'Noel wants you to phone and make an appointment to see the kids. She says that's what ya should do. When it's convenient. Ya can discuss access then. When ya make an appointment. Not just barge in like this, any time of the night or day.'

'Strangely enough, Mr Cuckolder, I couldn't bear to ring this doorbell in case you answered it. Funny that. And I did bloody phone to discuss friggin access, didn't I? And you bloody hung up as soon as I said, "Who the bloody hell's that?" How many times, Dingo? Eight? Ten? So it's a bit friggin difficult to ring friggin well up when ya *don't let me speak on the friggin phone.'*

'Keep yellin and you'll be out, Joe, I'm warnin ya. We don't want any trouble. I mean it.'

'Just let me see the kids.'

'You've had yer chance, Joe. You'll have to phone, mate. Ya don't live here anymore.' Dingo pushes the door forward, so that Joe's hand is pink beneath the edge.

'Don't you shut the door on me, ya friggin, friggin arsehole.' Joe pushes his hand against the door, pushing forward while Dingo pushes back.

'Just go, Joe. Go on, get out. We don't want ya here.'

Marah, standing by the newly built book shelves, calls out, 'I do. I want you here, Dad.'

'Me kids want to see me, now get out of the way.' Joe pushes again at the door, so that Dingo does a half-stagger back.

Joe's leg is inside, his blue denim knee hard against the edge of the door. His face appears, red and sweaty. He makes the same sort of grunt as he makes when he's lifting Charis over his shoulder, and shoves, shoves, shoves against the door. Noeline is like a dream on the sidelines, calling out that she'll call the police, she really will. Dingo steps back suddenly, so that Joe falls into the hallway, almost bangs against the wall before he stops. And it's Dingo who steps back in, right near Joe, and buts him with his elbow, buts him hard so that Joe staggers back. Only for a second, though, it's only a second before Joe has lifted his arm and only a breath before his fist has formed and smashes through the air right on to Dingo's face. They are a lump then, the two of them, bouncing from wall to wall, blood on Dingo's face smearing across Joe's shirt. The gilt mirror falls off the wall and Charis screams out, 'Stop it, stop it.' Noeline picks up the phone and dials fast. She crouches over the mouthpiece, shapes herself around it like a bass clef, curved and sorry.

Joe slams Dingo against the wall, right near Marah, and his blood streaks near Marah's hand. Her shoulders are shaking from the crying that she's doing. It's as if she's invisible, no one hears it. She puts her hand out to Joe, touches his arm and he slows down like a toy. He goes soft, looks at his hands, looks at Dingo, at Marah. Says, 'Oh, god, I'm sorry, kids,' and backs himself out the door. Jethro puts his head under a cushion.

The police arrive without the siren flashing, without any lights, camera, action. There's two of them: a round-faced girl and a tall man. Neither wears their hat and both agree that domestics happen all the time, even in the best neighbourhoods, you'd be surprised, you really would. They take statements from Dingo and from Noeline. Marah says, 'Dingo shoved Dad, he shoved him first,' but she must say it quietly, because no one even blinks. Charis drives Jethro mad sometimes, pretending he's not there, pretending he's invisible. Marah plays it, too, stepping over him, ignoring anything he says. You wouldn't think police officers would play that game, you would think they'd be too old. Charis sits on the floor, her legs pulled right up to her chest and her head on her knees. She puts her arm out for Jethro, as if she's his mum, and he snuggles next to her. Voices are droning on and on, full of 'Then he pushed himself in?' and 'So he slammed you against the wall?' Noeline and Dingo nod and hold hands and the policewoman reads their statements back to them.

'How would you like to proceed with this?' The policeman is grey-haired, gruff-voiced.

Noeline shifts closer to Dingo. Or seems to. 'I'm sorry?'

'Would you like to press charges or have an injunction out against him?'

The girl leans forward and adds her soft, sympathetic voice. 'An injunction means he can't come within a certain radius of the property. Given what's happened here tonight, I'd recommend that you do.'

Noeline looks small, shrinking into herself on the couch. 'I don't know. I just don't know. We're all very shaken.' It's a whisper. 'He's never, well, this is unexpected. Really our marriage has broken down because of his lack of action. You know –' she smiles at the girl – 'never settling to anything, never finishing anything he started. A drifter. But never violent. I would never have thought that of him. Not really.'

'I'd encourage you to think seriously about it, Mrs Dell. For your own peace of mind.'

'She's right, Noel.' Dingo's voice is like the girl's, hushed and tip-toeing.

Charis says, 'Does an injunction mean we won't see our dad? Does it mean he'll go away?'

The girl says, 'No, no, of course it doesn't mean that, it would just be under better circumstances. More desirable circumstances.' Jethro stays huddled under Charis's arm while she says, 'We want to see our dad, we don't want him to be gone.'

But Marah says nothing. Nothing about the new rules which will mean Joe will be away, far away and never to be seen. She says nothing, doesn't open her mouth, barely even opens her eyes. If you look closely, you can see her getting ready to disappear and never be seen again.

# Charis

I can hear the phone ringing as I slam the door, but I'll be damned if I'm going back in there. Bad smells are everywhere in my life, following me around like a, well, like a bad smell. For some completely unfathomable reason, Janey has decided that she needs a cat. She thinks it will keep her and John together if the worst comes to the worst. That they'll stay together for the sake of Fluffy. Apparently he came with that name, and she thinks it would be just too cruel to diddums to change it. Point is, he stinks. Spraying his testosterone everywhere, or whatever it is that male cats spray.

Heat and dampness rise up as I walk through the launderette, so heavy that I can barely breathe. Fresh air is a rare treat, although the term 'fresh' is probably a heresy in Shoreditch. Except in connection with dog poo, as in fresh and steaming and smeared across my shoe. Which is, of course, the first thing I encounter once I get on to the street. The usual crowd of grannies are sifting through their knickers in the launderette and one of them taps on the glass window at me. Smiles and waves, pointing at the poo as if it's great entertainment and any of her business. Business, ha ha. After ten minutes of scraping my foot against the gutter and growling at the huddle of pensioners gathering by the window, I still smell but don't seem to leave a brown trail behind me when I walk. What's a collective noun for grannies, I wonder? A knit? A blue-rinse? A bingo?

There's a half-rusted tap near my bike, so I turn it on and stick my foot under the brown stream which, I presume, is supposed to be water. Mud splatters up both legs, and now I stink of rust. Oh, happy day. The good news is that all the stepping/washing/

splattering takes up time, fills in minutes that I now won't have to fill in either sitting in the flat with the smell of randy cat, or spending money I don't have drinking coffee I don't particularly want. If I'm lucky, the lights will get stuck on red, there might even be an accident blocking the road. Which will mean that without loitering in an off-licence for twenty minutes, I don't have to have a conversation with Donny. About what I do or do not remember, about whether I do or do not genuinely fancy women, about anything at all. Memory's a funny thing, and so's deceit. If I lie to make it better, is it still a lie? And there's a thing: maybe I forgot because I needed to, maybe I made it better for myself. Even so, when I look at him now, the memory is unplugged and I can see his face looming at me and my hands groping him as much as his are groping me. Beyond 'Here's your costume/have a load of money' I'd prefer not to speak to Mr Controller at all. Pity's got the better of me and I can barely bring meself to call him Fat Controller these days. Now that really is pathetic.

Unfortunately the lights are glowing green all the way to Donny's and, for once, there're no bombs, no traffic jams, no mindless - exercises - in - diverting - cars - around - London - just-because-it-would-make-a-pretty-pattern. So the traffic's against me. I'm fairly late but if I don't fall off my bike or something, there will still be time to have some kind of conversation. Here's the truth: singing telegrams is not where I saw my life going when I dreamed my life up. If I ever did that, which I'm not convinced I had the chance to do. Fame, fortune, blah blah blah, oh, yes, but not grotty pubs and torn costumes. But I'm not going down that path, wanting more. Wanting success. I'm not taking anything away from Marah, I can't be arsed with that. I drive around the block four times. On the second trip round I see a red Honda with a big red-haired bloke in it. Like Dad. Like Dad outside our house, when? The last time, the last time I remember. On the fourth trip round I look at me watch and panic ever-so-slightly. It's a fine art, this timing thing. Late enough and I miss the smoochiness, too late and I miss the job.

As it turns out, I'm right on the edge of losing it, although not as badly as Donny. He's standing on the steps yelling at Susie when I get there. She's looking impressed, arms across her body, lips curled. She does that well, Susie, the lip-curling thing. My helmet gets stuck on me head somehow, so I have to walk up the steps still tugging at it and no doubt looking like an *X-Files* extra. Up close, I can see that Donny practically has little bits of spit flecking his mouth.

'Where the hell have ya been, Gracie? I've had to call Susie in, poor girl's had to cancel a date.'

'I didn't cancel it, Donny. It collapsed. It's OK, Charis, I needed to pop in and pick up some money anyway.'

'Well, still, fact remains. Where the bloody hell ya been?'

'Sorry, Donny, I had an accident at home. Dogs.'

Both Donny and Susie look at me blankly but I don't want to get into a total fabrication – I think I've got enough of that on my plate, or conscience, or whatever – so I run the rest of the way up the stairs, finally hauling the helmet off me head as I get to the door. 'Anyway, sorry. I'd better just grab the cossie and get over there. Have ya got the song, Donny?'

Donny puts on a junior train inspector's voice – it's the most officious he can get. 'No. No, I'm sorry, Gracie, but Susie has come all the way over here and in all fairness the gig is hers. You should have been here early. I'm sorry, but there it is.'

'No, really, Donny. Give it to Charis. It's her gig. I've got stuff to do.'

'No, it's only fair.'

'No, really. I'm fine. It's Charis's gig.'

'No, it's not. It was her gig and now it's yours.'

Susie pulls the song sheet out of her bag and hands it to me. She's already backing down the stairs. 'There you go, Charis. Thanks anyway, Donny. I don't want it. I was only going to do it as a favour, but it's the last thing on my list of things I want to do today. Can I be any clearer? I want Charis to do it, I'm delighted she's here and now I'm going. Bye.'

As she backs her way down the stairs and turns to jog across the lawn, I can see that Donny is ready to try one last time, and for a moment I think he'll cancel the gig just to spite me. But, broken heart or not, he is a greedy man and the thought of losing money must pull him back from the brink. 'Right, get yer arse into gear. You've got half a second to get changed. And I want to talk to you afterwards. I mean it. This is the third time you've been this late and I'll be honest with ya, it just ain't good enough, Gracie.'

'Yair, righto, Donny, whatever ya reckon. I'm sorry and I'm a truly evil person, whaddaya want me to say?'

'Don't say nothin, you haven't got time. Go on, get.' He's like an old dog-shooter, standing on the steps, shooing me down the path.

It's preggy bride again, this time for an engagement party. Why do people find the idea of another woman bursting into your wedding or engagement remotely entertaining? Booked by 'mother-of-bride-to-be' it says on the bottom of the booking form. What a delightful gift from yer mother. Better than anything I could imagine the witch-mother ever coming up with, though. Not that she'd come up with anything. Ooh, she'd love to describe herself as 'mother-of-the-bride-to-be'. Poor Marah. She's the only one likely to go down that path. Witch-mother bought me a bride doll, once. Waited patiently for me to march it down the living-room aisle, but it was never gunna happen. Jethro got the doll in the end. He used it as a test dummy for his remote cars. Even though she was too big and far too stupid-looking. So, she didn't do the trick for any of us. Marah wasn't interested in those days, not in dolls or brides or being the good girl. She was different then. That was before. Before Dad got kicked out of our lives, before Dingo took over. Before everything.

Somewhere, I saw a photo of Mum marrying my father. My blood father, the one I never met. Not Joe. Green ivy is under her feet and she's got a little white mini on, with a white cocktail hat. Net drips over eyes. He's almost invisible, I can barely remember him in the photo. You know, the usual, black suit, white tie, short hair. Well, it's not about him, is it? The whole wedding thing, the whole let's-dress-up-for-the-camera game. It's about her. Only chance to be the star, maybe. She hid the photo away after I saw it. For all I know, she burnt it on one of her cauldron fires. It was in a blue photo album, in the back of the china cabinet. She looked beautiful. I can remember looking at it, at her long eyelashes and her dark hair all down to her waist and knowing I could never be like her. She knew it too. When I asked her what it was, why Dad wasn't in the photo, she said, 'That's a very old photo. It was way before you were born and I was young and silly.' When I asked if the man was my real father, she said Joe was my dad and don't ever say about my real father in front of him and it wasn't her fault if my other father didn't want any contact and would I please go away and stop going on about it. Or words to that effect. When she married Joe, I was in a bouncinette in the house of a teacher from Mum's school. Marah and Jethro weren't even twinkles in Joe's eyes. They stopped on the way and picked me up. Took me on honeymoon, rumour has it. But I remember nothing, I might as well have not been there. Might as well have been a twinkle.

The engagement party is in Maida Vale, in a garden. There are complicated instructions on the booking sheet: I have to park around the block (why? I don't exactly have a sign on the bike which says 'preggy bride come to wreck your party'), go to side gate and tap, *not ring*, on the wall. Synchronize watches: the tapping is supposed to happen at 2.10 p.m. By the time I've parked, tugged off my helmet, kicked a cat which is trying to claw my wedding dress, neatened my hair and tottered up the drive, it's nearly half-past. When I tap on the fence, I'm greeted by a cross between a hiss and a snarl. The gate opens and a tiny woman in one of those smart grey trouser suits squeezes herself out on to the path. Military operation, code name: OTT. The poor woman is red under her eyes and around her lips, and her whole face seems to be held together by the force of her lips sucking the skin in.

She's very, very cross. Or so she tells me. Without waiting to find out whether or not I had an accident, or have dragged myself from death's door. What she tells me is that she has been waiting at that door for eighteen, *eighteen* minutes, do I hear her? I tell her that I do hear her and where would she like the telegram to happen and perhaps I should do it first and then we could sort it out. Oh, no. Mrs Mother-of-the-bride-to-be has different ideas. She is not paying for such shoddy service and she certainly will not be recommending us to friends, and, frankly, it's just not good enough. This feels too familiar, me not being good enough, not being up to it, and I'm amazed that I manage to restrain myself from sticking her miniature rose bush up her bum. Somehow, though, I find calm, I find a quiet voice. Quiet enough to tell her that I do, indeed, understand where she is coming from and how upset she must be but that there were unavoidable and actually tragic problems on the Kilburn Road and I'd be happy to do the telegram at a reduced price, twenty pounds off. You'd swear that she's planned the whole thing, the way her pinched little face lights up. She bears an uncanny resemblance to a sick poodle.

She takes me through to the garden, where about twenty people are huddled, looking pissed rather than joyous. She calls out to the 'groom-to-be' and, whammo, I'm on. Groom-to-be looks quite startled, more than they usually do, so I can't help wondering whether there's some secret message that Poodle Woman is trying to jab into him. The whole garden – not that it's very big – is full of couples clutching at each other, hanging around each other's waists, necks, arms. Any protruding limb gets covered by the other person, if you're part of a couple. And that's it, it always is part-of-a-couple, it's never you, yourself, from then on. I have known grown women who have lost the ability to count or press buttons once they've become part-of-a-couple. Sadly, some even forget how to stand up without clutching the man's arm or hand. Tragic, viewers, but true. Send donations now, while there's time. All the nice couples applaud nicely when I finish me song, but they're not impressed enough to give tips. Poodle Woman isn't impressed enough to add the twenty quid back in. If I only pay myself twenty quid, I'll never have to tell Donny what happened.

Except, of course, that when I get to Donny's, he's worn a little worry path in his tatty rug. Pacing up, down, up, down. He's gnawing at his fingers as if they're cigarettes. 'How late were you, Charis?'

'Barely at all. Caught good lights on the way over and managed to get there in the nick of time.'

'How much of a nick?'

'I dunno, geez. A nick. A nick's a nick, how much more information can I give ya?'

'No problems, then?'

I should be wary, I should know this trick by now, but I don't shut up, I don't confess. I go: 'Nah. No worries at all.'

Donny stops pacing, stops gnawing and a look which I can only describe as triumph flashes over his beady face. 'That's not what Mrs Wyatt said.'

'Who's Mrs Wyatt when she's at home, then?' Although I don't need to ask this question because I know exactly who Mrs Wyatt is. She is Poodle Woman.

'She booked the telegram. It was very important for her. She had to wait by the fence for almost half an hour. Trying to keep all her other guests away, trying not to spoil the surprise. It was very carefully planned, Charis, and she's not impressed. Neither am I.'

I skipped two weeks of school when I was fifteen. Couldn't bring myself to face the teachers and, well, everyone. Spent two weeks sitting in Cole's cafeteria eating chips and gravy. Came home on the second Friday and Mum asked how school was, I said fine and she hit the roof. School had phoned her, 'concerned at my recent bad attitude, wondered if there was a problem'. She grounded me for a month, drove me to school in the mornings, not talking, and never, ever asking what the problem was. No problem. I've got the same feeling now, that I've been conned, tricked into a bear-trap. All I can do is growl.

'Oh get off it, Donny. There's no way she was waiting for half an hour. If she was, it's her own fault. I was about eighteen minutes late. If that.'

'Twenty minutes is far too late for my professional reputation. It's not the first time we've had problems and I'm beginning to feel that it's just not worth my while keeping you on. Just because we've had a personal relationship doesn't mean that you can walk all over me as an employer. And I am actually your employer.'

I'm so busy thinking, Personal relationship? When did I blink and miss it? that I almost entirely miss the 'I'll have to let you go' speech. Words leave my head and I nod at Donny, doll-like.

'Well, if you have nothing to say to that, I think it's best all round if you find some other job.'

'Donny, don't do that. I'm sorry, it won't happen again, really.'

'I've heard it all before, Charis. You say it again and again. I can't take the risk of you offending clients and affecting future work. This is my livelihood, after all.'

'And what do you think it is for me?'

'I don't know. A joke, I think.'

'What, you don't think I take it seriously enough? My career doing Betty Bondage grams?'

'Now that's exactly what I mean.'

Thoughts – sensible thoughts – of 'what will I live on without this job?' disappear. I'd like to smack Donny and his smart fat face. He sounds more and more like my mother, preaching and smug and pleased I've been caught out. 'Stick yer bloody telegrams up yer fat arse, Donny. Yer only pissed off because I turned ya down.'

'That's not fair, Charis.'

'Oh, right, and dumping me with no job is. Get stuffed.' I attempt to storm out and slam the door behind me, but I trip on his stupid rug, half-turned-up in the corner. 'And I'm not a lesbian.' I'm ready to add: 'I just don't fancy you, fat-arse,' but he might change his mind and I know I need the money. Anyway, my arse is fatter than his.

My hands shake on the throttle all the way home and the last thing I want to be greeted by is the sight of Janey and John wriggling all over the living-room carpet, squealing ickle endearments to an indifferent cat. Janey breaks off as I step over her and says, 'Your mum phoned about three times today. I told her to phone after five, what time is it now?'

'Quarter past.' John never speaks in more than a grunt, so I'm always honoured when he uses a word. Or, sometimes, two.

'Oh, bugger. She's the last person in the universe I want to speak to.'

'She said she's got important news.'

'Big whoop. Tell her I'm not here.'

Janey nods, tickling the spraying-furred-one under the chin at the same time and going, 'Ooooh, he's sooooo darling.' She's so

113

absorbed in her tickling that she doesn't move when the phone rings. John climbs over her, picks up the phone, grunts into it. Listens, grunts again and holds the receiver out. 'It's for you, Charis.' I shake my head, make cutting motions across my neck but he says, 'She won't be a sec, she's just coming,' and holds the phone out for me.

I snatch the receiver and kick him close enough to the groin area to give him a good fright. 'Hi, Mum.' I don't even try to stop my voice sounding annoyed.

'Hello, darling. Are you well?'

'Fine.'

'Good. Well, we've got some incredibly exciting news. Are you sitting down?'

'Yes, Mum.' It's easier to lie than to explain that we don't have any chairs anywhere near the phone and the cord won't reach to the floor and, yes, I really should get a mobile and join the world.

'Dingo and I have decided to get married. Isn't that funny? After all this time? Haha.'

My stomach goes dead and I can feel the fingers of my free hand already starting to scratch at my palm. I hate that, when I do that.

'Excited? We've been planning it for a long time but we wanted it to be a surprise. We wanted it to be just at the end of the Sydney-to-Hobart – did I tell you Dingo's racing with Clark Shrivers this year? So, you've got three weeks to get packed. I've chosen dresses for you and Marah, but you'll have to check them when you get here. I've left a little bit of time for all of that. So. What do you think?'

'Mum, I can't afford to come back right now. Sorry. I hope you have a good wedding.'

'Don't be so silly, darling. You girls are as much a part of our lives as Jethro is, even if you're far away. We've sent the ticket to you International ExpressPost.'

'I can't, Mum. I've got things here. My job and, you know, my life.'

'Darling, it's only for a few weeks, you can come back to your life. We'll only be getting married once. And the ticket's non-refundable. We couldn't not have you there, could we?'

114

'I spose not.'

'OK, darling. See you in three weeks. Kisses.'

'Yair, OK, you too.' I get this little flash, of Joe coming round, banging on the door. Mum saying, 'We don't want you here.' And me, in the corner, saying, 'Yes, we do, I want you here,' but too quietly. I always open my mouth even when I should stay quiet and stay quiet when I should open my mouth.

By the time I put the phone down, my stomach is lying on the floor and I'm ready to scratch myself until I bleed. Even now, after all this time, my head swirls and I want to be sick, want to smash her face through the phone. I said yes, I said OK, but I didn't mean it. Even after all this time, whatever else she does, she can't marry Dingo. She just can't.

# *Marah*

Cold travels up and down my spine, it's right in my bones. Birds are outside, though, carrying on as if it's the height of summer, the height of joy. It should be the height of joy, I should be waking up, rejoicing at my good fortune. Gratitude is the attitude; Be pleased to be pleased. Truthfully, I don't feel grateful at all, I don't feel anything. Cold, that's all, just cold in my bones and right down in what feels like my liver or spleen. I am not going to think about Elisabeth on opening night, I am not. There are too many other concerns, too many equally important matters my head needs to attend to. Shivers start at my feet and move up my body until I'm lying under the sheets shaking. The bathroom door bangs from Wilma's side, so I know it's safe to get up and get into the shower. Hot water down my spine, that will take the shaking away. It's probably the cold that's making me feel prickly around my nose and eyes, a kind of stinging for no reason.

When I swing the bathroom door open, ready to have heat pouring down me, Wilma drops her hairbrush and her towel. Honestly. She's laughing, saying, Oops, I forgot to lock the door, but I'm so embarrassed I stare at the hairbrush on the floor. Eventually I say, You've dropped your hairbrush, sorry, I thought you'd finished in here. Wilma pulls the towel up and says, Well, not a problem, I'm done anyway. Then she does that smile, lean-in-close thing she does, and asks if I'm excited about the show, because it must be coming up for the opening. I say, Well, yes, it is, but actually I have to go home for a family emergency, and Wilma looks so sympathetic I feel ashamed. She's saying, Oh, Marah, I'm sorry, I hope it's not too bad, and how disappointing for you as well. She asks if my head of programme is being supportive and I say I haven't told him yet and would she mind because really what I'd like to do is just have a hot shower because by now my teeth are practically chattering and I think I might knock something off the shelves I'm shaking so much. The way Wilma is standing there, just in her towel, you'd think it was a sauna, or the tropics.

I lock both doors once Wilma's left. It may seem silly to lock the door through to my room, but I do *actually* know of girls who have had intruders in their own dorms. It can happen any time of night or day. It doesn't cost me anything to lock the door and it might cost me a lot if I don't. Steam fills the triangle room and my skin starts to turn pink from the heat. I draw shapes on the wall, making lines in the condensation. Not writing words, just patterns. When the water starts to run cold, I turn the taps off and lean my head against the wall. Trying to breathe the steam into my chest, into my lungs. Although there's barely any point keeping my voice tip-top if I'm not doing *Dido*. And there's a chance, I know there is, that they'll never let me do another lead. It doesn't matter, though, because you have to be there for your family, that's important. Because they'll always be there for you.

Elisabeth will have barely any time to get a decent rehearsal in. Three weeks is nothing, not when you think of all the time I've had to work on each piece. The decent thing is for me to get down to Stoeckel as soon as I'm dressed and fill Lenherr in. Instead of throwing on the nearest thing, brushing my hair, running out the door without sit-ups or stretches or breakfast, though, I start pulling all my clothes out from the wardrobe. Thinking about what I'll need to take and what I'll leave behind. Everything gets laid down on the bed, alongside each other and some things folded in a pile. Above the window, from the curtain rail, I hang my three suits. I'm not sure whether it's best to pack now or later. Mother and I decided it was best that I just came straight away, otherwise I'll be hanging around here, doing what? Nothing, that's what. Packing and unpacking and repacking and you can't do that for three solid weeks when you should be rehearsing the lead in the first opera of the year. When I've got all my clothes out, I brush them with the WonderBrush which I bought in New York. Two dollars, fifty cents, and it really does collect fluff from almost any sort of fabric. Small enough to travel with as well, which is what I was after. My plan is to travel quite light, because I've got plenty of clothes at home which are perfectly adequate. It'll be nice to be part of the preparations, to be around long enough to be a help. After minutes and minutes standing in the room just looking at my entire wardrobe spread about my room, I decide on the grey suit, my black skirt, two blouses and my jeans. I'll carry my green dress in my overnight case, on the plane. In case anything happens. It's always good to have a change of clothes and fresh underwear with you.

Even after I do my sit-ups and stretches, I'm still cold. Even with my thickest sweater on. It's so thick that it rubs my back while I'm doing my crunches, but I'm shivering too much to consider taking it off. What I'd love would be a kettle in my room, so that I could have coffee in here whenever I wanted. Some people do have that, I don't know why I never bothered. Couldn't really imagine myself sitting in my room drinking coffee, I suppose. So today, when I really need it, I have nothing. If I go into the dining hall, I know that the smell of the grease will make me sick, because I feel dangerously close to it now. Saliva is clustering in the top of my mouth and I've got those flushes that come when you're ready to vomit. So it's best to avoid the dining hall and head straight for Lenherr. Which doesn't exactly fill me with the joy of spring, either. When I think about my choices, though, telling him first wins easily. I'm tempted to hold out, to give myself one more day of being the star, of being part of it. It wouldn't be impossible, I could pretend I got the phone call after rehearsals. But I can't do that, I'm too honest for my own good, if the truth be told.

Lenherr's office is downstairs and I'm half-hoping he won't be in. It's too early for him to be teaching, but he could be in one of the studios or, I don't know, something. I can't work out where other people are all the time, he just might not be in, that's the point. He could be anywhere. Having breakfast, for instance. When I tap on the door I'm gentle with my knuckles, I don't want any loud noises, even coming from my own hand. Lenherr says, Come, from inside. Always that one word, Come, a command. Never, Come in, or, Hello? Questions aren't really Lenherr's style. Commands are. Which is why it takes me ages to open the door and even longer to edge myself into his long, narrow office.

Ah, Marah, he says, my favourite Dido – and then he smiles, sits back in his chair and puts his hands up over his head so that his belly sticks out. Ready to talk about your control problems with that final aria? I know that you believe it's breath, but you have to believe me, the breath will take care of itself. All these young singers always saying Breath, breath, breath, as if it can't do it on its own. You're breathing now and you didn't even notice. It sounds like breath is the problem there, but I guarantee for you that it is not breath. No, it's control and placement. You have to think solid and get your placement here – he bangs the top of his head – and then you will soar. Is there anything else?

So he did notice my demi-croak. How could he not? It's his job to notice the smallest lack in a singer, but I didn't realize it was such a huge deal. It didn't occur to me, for instance, that he would have been sitting here for two weeks waiting for me to admit the problem. Which is obviously what has been going on. Stop. I know I'm getting out of control, that my head is running away somewhere that I don't want to go and I don't need to go there. I don't. So I won't. Lenherr is still waiting for me to say, Yes, thank you, you've solved the problem. Or something. So I open my mouth, I have to tell him.

He says, Yes, is there something else, Marah?

Air rushes into me, cold and fast and I push the words out on the hot breath coming out of my mouth. I'm sorry, I say, I'm very disappointed.

Lenherr sits forward and asks what on earth is the disappointment and tells me not to be so upset about necessary critical work. My mouth is talking before I get a chance to put the words in from my brain, so I stand and listen to my mouth telling Lenherr that there's been a family emergency, it's my mother, and I have to fly back immediately and I'll be back for next term.

My body must be shivering still because he takes his hands off his head and says, Oh, I'm so sorry, in a very soft voice. Oh, dear, he says. Oh, you poor girl, being so far away, I do hope you get there in time.

His office is cold too, as cold as my room, and the shaking seems to be getting worse. Also, tears are coming out from my eyes, although I don't feel remotely like crying. It must be Lenherr's sympathy for me, his soft, kind voice, like a father. He picks up a blanket and puts it around my shoulders and says, You must have a cup of sweet tea, I'll get it for you.

The door bangs behind him and I'm completely ashamed of myself, I really am. I know Lenherr thinks my mother is dying and I know I have to tell him the truth. But the truth is, he might not let me go if it's a wedding not a funeral. Which I think is plain wrong.

The other thing is, I can't seem to stop crying, it's as if my mother *is* dying, I'm crying as if she really is. Which is plain stupid, because she's not dying, she's getting married. Which is a happy thing, really. It really is, I love weddings. And it would be impossible to miss it, especially after she's bought the ticket for me. The thing is, with weddings, you have to take what dates you can get. You can't just get a reception at the Hilton any time you want. There are only fifty-two Saturdays in a year, that's the problem, really. And it's fantastic that they've booked the Hilton, amazing that they managed to get it at all. So it's silly to wish they'd held off, waited until next year, when I'd finished. Breathe, breathe, breathe. Breath and control. Breath and control. By the time Lenherr comes back in, I've got them both back. My face must be puffed up like a bumble-bee, but I'm water free and I seem not to be shaking.

Lenherr gives me a warm cup with a picture of a daisy on it. Without the stem, just the flower and a few leaves. I find myself staring at the daisy and wondering whether a daisy could survive without the stem, whether it would still be able to get light and food and water. Probably not, is what I decide. Which is also stupid, I mean it's a stupid thing to even think about. Obviously I know that if you pick a daisy it dies, it can't survive without the roots, let alone the stem. When I was a kid, there used to be frangipani flowers floating in a bowl, a blue bowl. They didn't have stems and they survived sometimes for a week, just the

120

flowers, floating in the blue bowl. There must have been a frangipani tree somewhere in the neighbourhood. I suppose Mum picked the flowers. Or Dingo, or something. I don't know. But it's a daisy on the cup, not a frangipani. There are no frangipani in America, not as far as I know. Sweet tea runs down the inside of my body, it's hot and milky and it must have two teaspoons of sugar in at least. I drink it anyway, with Lenherr sitting in silence, waiting for me to finish.

When I put the cup down, Lenherr says, Don't worry about the administrative problems, I'll take care of that. You may need to fill in a release form, do you think you could do that before you leave? I'll slip it into your pigeon-hole and you could perhaps pick it up this afternoon. Good. Also, we'll need to get over and let Leisha know, would you like to do that, or would you prefer if I did it? Elisabeth will have to be informed, certainly – oh, but, this is all nothing and you don't need to be concerned with it. Certainly you don't. I'll let Leisha know, shall I? And I'll inform the school, if you'll just remember to pick up the release form and drop it back to me. Slip it under the door if I'm not in. There's only the few weeks of term left, so we don't need to be too concerned anyway. Now, let me know if there's anything we can do. And, Marah – your Dido really was shaping up to be spectacular, it's a great loss to the production.

All I can squeeze out of my throat is, Thanks, thanks for everything, and then I shut the door behind me. My footsteps sound empty in the corridor.

Grass has been mowed outside the hall, I can smell it, although I can't see it. Amazing, really, that my nose could be stronger than my eyes, or sometimes even my voice. Fresh mowed grass is supposed to be a happy smell, but it doesn't make me feel happy. Today, nothing will make me feel happy, that's the truth. I'm sure that's a selfish and mean thing to think. Because, as Mother said, this is a time of celebration, of the whole family being together. It's also a time for Elisabeth to get to play Dido, and perhaps I should feel happy and celebratory for her. But I don't, I just don't. Heavy and full, from the sugar, is what I feel. There's still my room to be tidied and packed away, I've left my clothes just lying on the bed and hanging on the walls. Mother wants me to go for a fitting almost as soon as I get off the plane, it will all be a bit rushed. Strange to be walking away from Stoeckel, away from Sprague, and towards the hall. So early, when I know there's a rehearsal due to start any minute now. Hot flushes run up my cheeks when I imagine running into Alex or Gerald or – I feel sick when I think of this – Elisabeth. Having to say, No, I'm not on my way to rehearsal, I'm actually dropping the part. Family emergency. Yes, family comes first. So, it looks like you're Dido, Elisabeth. The whole speech goes through my head, just like that. And I imagine Elisabeth nodding her head, looking sympathetic but secretly really pleased. Of course she would be, why shouldn't she?

Without even noticing myself doing it, I'm heading for the green, looking around me like a thief. Trying to spot Elisabeth before she spots me. She'll be on her way now, I know she will. I know I'm a coward, I know I am. I could walk across the green and, if I see her, I could wish her the best of luck and say, Sorry, I won't be able to come to Quebec. Wish her all the best, that sort of thing. Instead, I notice that the door of the white church is open and I go up the steps and in the door, into the dark and cool and quiet. There are chairs instead of pews, and I sit on one at the back. After a minute, I get up and pull the door shut, because I think maybe you can see me from the outside. If you were walking past and turned your head just at the moment you got to the door. After I pull the door shut, I go closer to the front. It's simple: a white cloth across a long table, a huge vase of flowers. The floor is cool and hard and I slide down, off the chair, so that my back is resting against the legs. Quietness in a church feels wrong. We did a concert in the cathedral, when I was at the Con. Beautiful acoustics. Churches usually have great sound.

I tip my head back and let out the first line of the final lament. *Thy hand, Belinda, darkness shades me.* My voice hits the ceiling and echoes, wraps me up. I'm ready to fly into the rest, but I think: what will happen if Elisabeth's walking past? She'll know my voice and come in, and then what? Then the whole scene, all over again. Elisabeth's sympathy and celebration. I shut my mouth and my eyes. Light dots in front of me and I get a sudden picture of large hands, a man's hands, driving. All I see are the hands and then, what? Slapping? Something, the hands off the wheel. Then the dots again. Someone beside me is breathing with little gasps, cries almost. And for some reason, the shaking has come back. The gasping is me, I realize that when I open my eyes.

Above the table, hanging high, there's a blue banner. Gold fabric has been sewn into it, to make a river running down from the top of the banner to the bottom. At the bottom, in the corner, there's a pair of hands, open-palmed. Red shiny fabric, maybe satin, has been cut into words. GOD HEALS. That's all it says, running diagonally across the river. It must have been the hands from the banner that I saw, when I closed my eyes. Like with dreams. All sorts of pictures that you just pick up from around you stay in your head and get churned up in dreams, or when you close your eyes and drift off, just relaxing. Funny, how I must have looked and not even noticed the banner, the hands.

The door opens at the back. It's a heavy, deep sound. Louder than you'd expect – it's all the echo. Elisabeth must be at rehearsals by now, they must all be hearing about why I'm not there, and making soft sympathy noises to each other. Even so, even though I know that, I shrink down so that I'm practically lying on the floor, with my neck cricked into a curve. Footsteps clump down the aisle, two sets, and there's some whispering.

A woman's voice says, Oh yes, look at the brass, and the footsteps move closer.

Cold tiles are numbing my back but I lie myself flat and keep even my breathing quiet. There's a camera flash and the sound of something dropping. A man's voice says, Oh dear, and then another flash.

The woman says, Very nice, shall we look at Nathan Hall's statue now?

The two pairs of footsteps go clump clump, softer and softer, until the door squeaks. Light runs down through the church, slips across the flowers on the cloth-covered table. The door thuds shut and it's dim again.

After the footsteps have died away outside, I stay where I am, lying on the floor, looking up at the hands. Waiting at the foot of the golden river.

*The Vows*

# All that I have

Jethro's cries wake the whole house and everyone in it, and probably the ghosts of the dead as well. Moonstripes are sifting in through Charis's window. She is woken by the cries, but for a moment is unsure – perhaps it is the light which has woken her after all? Later, she will swear it is the light, that the sudden parting of a cloud and a breath of wind shifting the curtains meant that the force of pure light was turned on her face. Of course it would wake her, just on its own. It is only after she is awake – this is her story – that she hears Jethro's cries. Really, it is unlikely that this is true, for the noise of Jethro is cutting through even the moon. Marah is already pulling on her dressing gown, not bothering with slippers, running to the door like a warrior, right now, while Charis is deciding which – moon, or cries – pulled her from sleep. Charis stays in bed, doesn't bother even sitting up, sure that the cries are a long nightmare. Although they keep going; it's not one cry, one waking-up-from-a-horror yell. No, it's moaning and groaning and calling 'Mum, Mum.' Noeline is in Jethro's room when Marah gets there. She has put his small blue lamp on and she's sitting on his bed, stroking his forehead. In the half-light from the lamp, Noeline looks golden, angelic.

'Go back to bed, Marah. Jethro's got a toothache. He'll be fine.' Noeline whispers, even though the noise has already driven sleep far, far away.

'I'm already awake. Will I get him a drink?'

'No, darling. Please. Go back to sleep. I've given him some paracetamol and he can chew on a clove. We'll go to the dentist in the morning.'

127

Marah pads back to her room, climbs beneath the covers still in her dressing gown, and tucks herself up as small and safe as a snail. Jethro's cries slowly die down, quieter and quieter until the ghosts and the dead and the whole house and everyone in it can all go back to the softness of sleep.

When Marah wakes up, there is busyness in the house. Noeline is in her blue track suit in the kitchen, poaching eggs. Soft, for Jethro's teeth, she says. Something soothing before the dentist. She drops the slotted spoon on her foot and says, 'Oh, bugger.' Shaving noises are coming from what is now Noeline and Dingo's room instead of Noeline and Joe's room, and Charis is on the phone. Trying to find a frigging dentist, is what she says, and Noeline says that Charis will need a dentist if she insists on speaking like that, because Noeline will knock her teeth out, and would Charis like a poached egg or not? Not, actually, and nor does Marah. The thought of poached eggs, their soft, runny yolks, the wobbling white blurring the edges of the plate – it's enough to make you sick, really it is. Charis says yes to sausages, though, even though the smell is cutting through the morning, making Marah say that she wants to go back and lie down some more. Grumpy from lack of sleep, that's what Noeline suggests – and, who knows? – she could be right.

'Right.' Charis slams the phone down. 'I said it was an emergency and they still can't fit him in until Tuesday. She said he'll have to go to the dental hospital.'

'Damn, damn, damn. Did you try Dr Wilson?' Noeline piles eggs on to a red plate for Jethro. Red to cheer him on.

'I'm not stupid, Mum. I've tried everyone. They're all busy. But you can try if you want, I'm not bothered.'

'I can't do everything, Charis. In case you haven't noticed, I only have one pair of hands, unfortunately. Phone the dental hospital, then.'

'She said you don't make appointments, you just go into Emergencies and wait in line.'

'Bugger. We'll be there all day.' Noeline plonks two plates on the table and hands one to Marah. 'Go and take this to Jethro. And tell Dingo I need him.'

'Can't you just call him yourself?' Marah takes the plate, rubs her foot on the floor.

'Just get him, Marah. For goodness sakes, I don't know what's got into you. You behave as if Dingo is going to bite your head off. He's done so many things for you as well – running you around, installing your stereo. The least you can do is give him a chance. Here, give this orange juice to Jethro as well.'

And what is there to say to that? That Dingo is not her dad, should not be in the house at all, should never have pushed and shoved Joe and started a big fight? That if she was going to call anyone, she'd rather call Joe, except where was he these days, and that was another thing, why did the phone keep ringing and Noeline or Dingo jumping to answer it and saying, 'Oh no, no one there,' and then hanging up? As if Marah didn't know who that Mr Nobody was, as if anyone couldn't tell. None of this passes Marah's lips, though, it barely even swims to her surface. No, she just takes the orange juice and the plate and patters carefully down the hall.

Marah pushes Jethro's door open without knocking. She knows it's rude, she's been told often enough, but it's hard to carry a plate and a cup and knock on a door, all at the same time. Jethro has his back to her, lying on his side.

'Jethro.' Marah keeps her voice soft, in case he's asleep. Finally dozing after the painkillers have had a chance to jump in and do their work.

'Owww.' Jethro rolls over, holding his jaw, like a cartoon character who's been beaten-up. 'Whaddaya want?'

'I brought you some soft eggs and some orange juice. You have to go to the dental hospital. There's no appointments at Dr Wilson's or anywhere else.'

Jethro nods, indifferent. Touches the egg with his finger and watches it wobble softly. 'When?'

'Whenever yer up.' She backs herself to the door, watching Jethro poke and prod at the dead egg on his plate. The red doesn't seem to cheer, or not very much. She taps on the door of Noeline and Dingo's room, doesn't poke her head in even to check if Dingo's in there. 'Mum says can you come down a second, she wants you.'

There's a grunting kind of 'yes' from inside the room and Marah walks quickly down the hall. Doesn't run, she's not being silly, not running away or anything like that. Just wanting to be spared the embarrassment of having to talk to Dingo all the way to the kitchen. When there's nothing, absolutely nothing, to say.

When Dingo shuffles into the kitchen, newly shaved and ready for his eggs, Noeline gives him a kiss on the lips. Turns around and kisses him, right there in the kitchen. Which never happened with Joe, not that anyone can remember. She kisses Dingo like Joe has never been here, never lived here, never been the dad of the house. 'I have to take Jethro to the dental hospital. I'm likely to be all day – the waiting time there is atrocious, almost as bad as Casualty. Will you keep an eye on the girls?'

'Course I will, darlin. No worries. I'll take them in to the beach, or somethin.'

'I don't want to go the beach.' Charis glares Dingo down. 'I hate the beach.'

'OK. We won't go to the beach, then. We'll think of somethin. Don't worry, Noel, just go.'

Noel says she will, she won't worry and she'll trust the girls to behave themselves, to be grateful for what they get and to think themselves lucky. Really, it is Jethro who is lucky, even with his face swollen up and his breath smelling of cloves. After the dentist, for being so brave, Noeline promises him a treat. Perhaps some comics, or a balsa-wood plane. Anything he likes, from Toytell. Maybe even Donkey Kong, if he keeps being so brave. Marah says she's always brave, even when she's really, really hurting, and no one ever buys her special treats.

After Noeline leaves, with Jethro a small mute bundle beside her in the car, Dingo says, 'Right, girls, what would you like to do?'

'I don't want to do anything.' Charis flicks on the TV. *Countdown*. Molly Meldrum is babbling on about some new band being the best, the absolute best. And this time he really means it. The phone rings through it and Charis jumps up, says, 'I'll get it,' but Dingo, as always, is aleady there. Already listening, saying nothing and then hanging up.

He stays standing by the phone. 'Mr bloody Nobody again.

130

We'll have to get our number changed again, we can't have these nuisance calls all the time. Anyway. I was thinkin of goin down to the sailing club. I thought you might want to come out sailing. On the VJ, not the sixteen-footer. Whaddaya reckon? Wanna learn how to sail?'

Molly Meldrum is interviewing Madonna, who sings 'Burnin' Up'. She's got a high, squeaky voice. Charis stares hard at the TV, keeps her tongue and sprawls along the lounge. She swings one leg up so that it rests on the back of the lounge. Noeline says she looks insolent when she does that.

Dingo sits on the floor, blocking the screen. 'The only thing is, you'd have to not tell yer mum. She wanted me to take Jethro out first, so we'd have to keep it quiet. It's a good day for it. But we'll leave it, if you don't wanna do it. Stay here, watch telly.'

They have heard these promises to Jethro. Promises to take him out sailing, to take him camping, to teach him how to use a welding rod. Always Noeline who offers these promises, but they are always Jethro-and-Dingo. Jethro-and-Dingo should do this together, should do that together. Noeline has been heard telling Dingo that Jethro needs a father figure. Marah pokes Charis, squeezes her arm.

Charis sits up, stops sprawling. 'Yair, OK. There's nothin better to do.'

'Marah, what about you?' Dingo doesn't move an inch, not a millimetre.

'Yair, righto.' Marah is careful to stare ahead, at *Countdown*.

It is only later, on the way to the sailing club, that Marah stops staring straight ahead. Turns her head to the right to look at the river swanning past. Her view is interrupted by the rush of Sunday traffic. Dingo says something about Sunday drivers and people who don't do anything except drive for fun when they could be out sailing. Australians list driving as their number two hobbie, that's what he says. Gardening is third and television is first. Charis cheers for television, says that it's her number one. Dingo grins at her, reaches out and ruffles her hair before she has a chance to cringe away. His hands are big and brown, hairy around the knuckles. The river is grey and flat, even the trees

131

crowding the edges look somehow washed out, somehow can't be bothered.

White walls come into view, and a blue sign: LOWER HAWKES-BURY SAILING CLUB (AMATEUR). Other words get clearer as the car gets closer: 'NEW MEMBERS WELCOME. Enquire within.' In smaller writing, there's a list of names – treasurer, secretary, president. Dingo was president, once. Before, when Joe used to sail with him, when Joe was his mate, when Noeline loved Joe and hadn't traded him in for the president. Joe was never president, never even treasurer. Never even sailed, not properly. Could barely remember to save himself from drowning – that's what Noeline says. Could barely remember to screw his head on straight – she used to say that about him, too. Now she says Dingo wouldn't remember to eat if she wasn't around, what on earth would he do without her? It's like having another kid in the house, honestly. She said the same for Joe, so maybe it's Noeline who wants everyone to be useless, headless, foodless, motherless. Maybe, who knows, who can ever tell? Dingo was also treasurer of the sixteen-footers club, half a mile up the road. He says he tries to take turns, spend time on each boat, but really he's mostly on the sixteen-footer, he gets bored with the VJ. He's quick to add that it's not boring, though, that the girls will love it, and anyway it's just a first taste, isn't it?

Gravel scatters beneath the wheels, Dingo keeping the speed up too high and skidding as he steers the car into the brown dirt car-park. Skids to be cool, to be tough and young, it's obvious that's his game, because he laughs as he does it and looks across at Charis in the front seat, says, 'All right?' As if he is still the president. He leans over and pushes the door open for Charis, as if she is a baby and can't open it herself, then asks Marah if she's OK, if she's ready for a day on the open sea, if she thinks she's forward-hand material. From the boot he collects two brown sports bags, gives one to Charis to carry and slings the other one over his shoulder. Charis and Marah have to run along beside Dingo, his strides are long and they are like poodles yapping at his heels.

Lower Hawkesbury Sailing Club (Amateur) club-house is rambling and stained white. Paint peels from the walls, leaving big gaps of exposed brown wood beneath, like scabs dotted all over the building. At first, it looks like it's two storeys high, but you see the secret when you get closer. It's not a ground floor, of course not, it's a boat shed. The doors of the shed are up and Dingo says to go on and have a look. Dinghies and small craft are laid in the shed like coffins, each of them with a special rack, a shelf to lie on. Charis says the names one after the other: sabots, herons, lasers, skates, VJs. She knows them all from reading Jethro's *Australian Small Boats* book. Noeline gave it to him, not for any reason, just so he could find out about it before he went sailing with Dingo. But it's not Jethro who's here, ready to go out on Dingo's VJ, it's Marah and Charis, breathless and cold with the river wind biting through the door. The club-house is right on the shore, so close it would tip in if the shore shifted in a storm, and there are small ramps down into the water. Dingo points to a VJ half-way up the wall. *Ladybait* is written in gold writing on its side.

'Reckon you girls are strong enough to get it down?' He unties the ropes which criss-cross the boat. Then laughs as if he's told a joke. 'Nah. Course ya don't need to get it down on ya own. I'm strong enough for that. Anyway, come up and register first, let em know it's me who's got her and not some boat thief. Not that they'll check.'

Charis squeezes Marah's hand on the way up the steps, following behind Dingo, watching his Reeboks go thump thump on the old wood. Marah screws her face up at Charis, rolls her eyes about as if she is dying. Charis keeps hold of her hand and says, 'Don't worry about it. It's just sailing, it'll be fun. We don't even have to speak to him. Jethro'll spew if he finds out.'

Upstairs and inside, there are four tables with metal legs and plastic table-cloths on them. The room is long, with a whole wall of windows looking out on to the river. There's a counter with a till; a short man stands behind it. He calls out to Dingo, calls him a manky scrounger who spends all his time at the sixteen-footers. Dingo slaps the man on the back and says 'Gidday' to the only two other people in the room – a woman in a yellow floral dress with grey hair pulled back from her face, and a man in a blue tracksuit. Above the till, there's a blackboard with FOOD AND

BEVERAGES written on it in green chalk. Below that a list of chips, chocolates, tea or coffee.

'We'll grab some chocolate to take out. Emergency rations, eh? We can slip em down our sprayproofs. Orright, Bridie, giss a couple of Crunchies and a Pollywaffle.'

The short man opens a new box of Crunchies specially. Looks at Charis and Marah. 'Who are these two, then? Bit young, ain't they, Dingo?'

'Daughters of the new missus. Thanks, Bridie. Register us will ya?'

'Need their names.'

'Marah Dell. And Charis Dell,' Marah pipes up, offers her hand to the man as if he is already a friend.

'Just whack the names down, willya, Bridie? I don't wanna miss the wind while it's good.' Dingo is already walking to the door, hauling himself down the steps so that Marah and Charis have to follow.

In the shed, they pull the boat from the rack. Really it is Dingo who pulls. Marah holds on to the back – the *stern* – and tries to put some muscle into it, but Dingo is taking most of the weight. Charis does nothing, just stands at the side with her hands out, as if the boat will fall. From the sports bags Dingo pulls out two life-jackets with TAFT written across the front and hands one to each of them. Then red sprayproof jackets, shiny and light. Charis pulls her hood up, laces the whole thing tight over her life-jacket so that she looks round and bobbing. The centreboard is lying flat and Dingo says they have to rig up before they get her on to the river but it'll only take a second. Marah sits on the gravel, watching the river, while Dingo pulls the mast up, tightens the stays. Charis helps, she wants to learn the whole thing, wants to have a boat, go racing around the world. She's told Noeline, she's told everyone, that's what she'll do, go off around the world. All on her own in a boat and no one will catch her. She reads the books about sabots and herons and skates and looks at the magazines about bigger boats.

*Ladybait* is in the water before Marah even notices, before she's pulled back from some dream she's in, some dream of somewhere else. Charis is on the small deck, calling to her to come on.

134

Marah wades in, seaweed wrapping around her ankles, her trainers slippery and icy. Dingo slaps her on the back, and says, 'Good girl,' as he pulls her on to the flat deck. There are two planks on either side of the deck, instead of a gunwhale. Marah tries to sit on one, but Dingo pulls her back, says, 'Not yet.' It's Dingo who jumps back in the water, pushes them further out, then jumps on, yanks at the sail rope and slips the centreboard in. The wind rises quickly, fills the sails and pushes them out, further into the river. The club-house shrinks behind them and salt rises up in small fountains, covering them with spray and coolness, like mint, like celebration. Even Marah is smiling in the face of it, not noticing or minding the wind making matted knots of her hair.

Dingo gives the rope to Charis, and tells her to pull tighter, then looser. He zigs and zags with the tiller, so that Marah has to jump from side to side, ducking low to avoid the swinging boom. Charis is half-lying in the centre of the deck, flattening herself down when the boom crosses. Dingo pushes Charis aside and lets the jib out. It unfolds itself, red and orange and as round as a stomach, and the boat shoots forward, tilts to the side with the speed. Charis pulls tighter on the rope and Dingo calls out, 'No, looser, looser,' and yells for Marah to get out on the plank. She does, laying her whole body length right out, trying to bring the boat back to flat, stretching even her arms above her head. It is wonderful, delicious, there is no question of it, and the rainbows through the spray are as tiny as moths.

They stay out until they are shivering and the Crunchies and the Pollywaffle are gone, eaten as a mix of salt and sugar. Dingo rinses the boat and puts it away while Charis and Marah sit upstairs in the club-house, drinking warm sweet tea and eating salt-and-vinegar crisps. Marah's hair is a mass of wet lumps, she can't get her fingers through it at all. Charis says she'll help when they get home. When Dingo collects them, he says, 'Remember, we've been into town, to the beach.' Charis giggles and says, 'Oh, yes, wasn't the surf good,' and reaches under the table for Marah's hand. Quiet fills the car on the drive back to Windsor, and Noeline's car is in the drive when they arrive. Dingo leaves the sports bags in the boot and calls out, 'How was the dentist?' All cheery, as if Jethro had been going to a fair. Jethro's face is swollen and he can't talk properly, but he's got a Donkey Kong and he's lying on the floor, right in front of the television, playing it. Noeline says that it was a nightmare, they had to wait all day, absolutely unbelievable, but anyway, it's all sorted out now. Charis heads straight for the shower, hiding her face from Jethro, and Noeline looks up, notices the smell of salt and the wetness on them. Says, 'So you went for the beach after all, good.'

Marah nods, staring at the floor. The waste-paper bin is right near her foot and she can see an empty crisp packet, some used tissues and an envelope addressed to Noeline Dell. Familiar handwriting somehow, but other things rise up and take her away from it: Dingo smiling at her, for instance, letting his silence grow, letting the secret swell and rise up, until it fills the whole room. She knows who the envelope is from, she knows the way her father loops his letters, but she stares away, keeping mum, keeping quiet. Who knows why? Perhaps because the silence is so big now that it is filling her. Then it swells some more, until it fills the house. Marah keeps staring at the floor, making no noise, speaking no words.

# Charis

Janey starts crying before we get off the tube. Hounslow Central is some sort of cue to her. She looks at the station sign outside the window, and at my pile of luggage – two brown suitcases and one grey rucksack – tottering at my feet, then squeezes several tears out. *Squeezes* is definitely the action here; I'm convinced she thinks it's the thing to do and she's been working up to it since I dragged my cases downstairs. Humiliating that she's taken this long to get to it. She's doing better than me, though – I can't work up anything in the way of heart-rending farewell. I've got no intention of staying away, that's why. Janey's convinced, though, she's sure that I'll never come back once I get the dry soil of my homeland under my feet. Please. What I haven't reminded her of is the fact that Janey is completely indifferent to my existence unless John is having a 'distant man' day. Selective memory is what Janey does well. And if anyone should know about that – about selective memory – it's me.

Heathrow is full of couples hugging, tearfully farewelling – maybe that explains Janey's tears, maybe it makes her think of some sad parting she might have with John. She gathers a trolley for me, plonks my bags one on top of the other, and shoves me into the check-in queue.

'Passport? Wallet? Tickets?' Janey has taken it on herself to be my minder.

'Of course. I'm hardly gunna get this far without them, am I? How stupid do you think I am, exactly?' The queue is stretching for miles in front of me and making my temper unravel like stretched chewing gum, ready to snap you in the face any second. My money belt is double-knotted around my waist, I pull

137

out the passport, the wallet. The empty ticket folder. 'Bloody hell.'

'Check the money belt again. Here, let me have a look.' Janey's digging through my pouch as if she's a demented joey. 'No, not in there.'

'Bugger, bugger, bugger.' I get creative when I'm under stress. The trolley is beside me, with my rucksack just about to fall on a small child who's too curious for her own good. 'It'll be in me rucksack. Get out of the way, child.' Cardigan, wash-bag, *Marie Clare* and *Cosmo* (both pinched from Janey), bag of crisps (for emergencies), two-litre water bottle, clean knickers (grey, once were white) – I line them up on the ground next to the trolley. When my rucksack is empty, I haul the smaller suitcase off and get ready to start on that. The bloke in front of me has turned around to ask me something and is politely avoiding laughter, just as well for him.

As I open the suitcase, he squats down beside me, and now he is laughing. 'Sorry, I couldn't help overhearing. About your ticket.' An Australian accent.

'You should be careful, or your ears will drop off and you'll have to wear ear-muffs all the time to stop people asking why you haven't got any ears. Except, I suppose, they'll ask you why you're wearing ear-muffs.'

'I know. I thought of all that before I deliberately stood in front of you so that I could hear your conversation. I decided to take the consequences. I think your ticket is poking out of your pocket. When you knelt down – look, it almost fell out.'

I pull the ticket from my shorts pocket and attempt to cover my face with it, saying, 'I am the Queen of Embarrassment, the coronation shall take place at five-thirty.' The queue has moved forward three places and the happy mummy and daddy behind me are telling their two little girls that you should always check before you leave home and before you pull everything from your bag. So glad to be of assistance in today's Airport Educational. The bloke lifts the suitcase back on to the trolley while I stuff my life back into my rucksack. Janey has stopped pretending to wipe tears away and is snorting openly. Being supportive and caring.

Half an hour has passed by the time we get to the front of the queue. Friendly Bloke gives me a wave once he's checked in and says, 'See you on the plane.' I smile and nod, even though you never see people on the plane if you've seen them at check-in. Strange but true.

Janey is looking at her watch, all nervous. 'I think I'll just have time for a coffee with you before I have to go. My shift starts at five.'

'Let's not get coffee. It's too expensive and the money goes to the evil empire. Might as well say goodbye down here.' I shuffle forward, get the bags on the weigh-in, smile at the lipsticked girl and hand over my ticket and passport. The lipsticked girl gives me the nod and a boarding pass, so I stick the rucksack on me back and head for the glass doors.

'Sure? When will I see you?' Janey's arms go around me, muffling her voice.

'In six weeks. Don't let Alice get too homey.' Some waitress friend of Janey's is sub-letting my room while I'm away. Handy, considering that I am now without an income, courtesy of Fat Friendless Donny and his Fragile Ego.

'No. Have a good wedding. Oh, I'll miss you.'

'You won't even notice I'm gone.' I push her off me and start heading towards the escalators. 'Have fun. I'd send the wedding snaps, but I don't think witches come out on camera. Bye.' Solitary coffee calls me.

Some article about a woman who left her lover for another, richer lover has completely absorbed me, so that when the final boarding call comes through I have to gather myself and do that horrible rushing-pretending-not-to-rush thing. Stampeding through the farewelling couples. Rushing is a waste of time, of course, because what they mean by 'final boarding call' is 'sit in departure lounge for another half hour while we work out who's important and who's not'. Friendly Bloke isn't anywhere to be seen, and I'm not even aware that I'm looking until I've scanned the room. Curious to see if my theory holds out. It always has, so far. I've never, ever seen someone on the plane, or in the departure lounge, or getting off the plane, if I have previously seen or encountered them at check-in. My bum aches on the plastic seats, so by the time they say we can really truly board, I am ready to kiss the woman checking our passes. Manage to restrain myself somehow. Probably the thought of shocking-pink lipstick smearing across my face. Women eat more lipstick than they do vegetables. Where did I see that? Somewhere, so it must be true. Which, if you ask me, explains a whole lot about breast cancer, cervical cancer, possibly osteoporis and certainly the pathetic creatures women turn into when there are men around.

Joy of joys, they've given me a seat three rows from the video screen. The little package of blanket/toothpaste/eye-patch is tucked in the pocket of the seat in front. I pull it out, unwrap the blanket, put it at my feet, stuff my bag under the seat, look through the magazine to see what films are on (*Rainmaker* and something called *Mousetrap* – at least it's not *Titanic*). My aeroplane, my castle. This is the best bit, the anticipation, the setting everything up, the checking the buttons. Cabin doors shut, there's a mumbled, inaudible instruction from the chief steward (maybe it's not an instruction, maybe it's, 'Help, I'm stuck in the cupboard,') and out come the team of dancers to do the lovely 'clip your seat-belts' routine. Still no one sitting next to me. Three seats, all to myself. I love flying, love it more than leaving and more than arriving. It's lazy person's heaven. You don't have to move; flick a switch and someone brings you food, there are films, and by doing nothing, nothing at all, you get somewhere. I want my whole life to be like that.

After the seat-belt lights are switched off and I've got my peanuts and orange juice, I slip the arm rests up and stretch my legs across the seats. A steward leans over, taps me on the arm. 'Do you mind if we seat someone here, now?'

Not nodding, not shaking my head, I stare at him, trying to look fierce, or mad. For some reason, he takes this as a yes and trots off happily down the aisle. I don't want to share my seat with anyone else and I don't want to have to talk to a tedious woman from Leicester who wants to fill me in on all the career moves of each one of her thirteen grandchildren. Because, let's face it, that's what you usually get stuck with on these flights. Outside the window, the sun is gold, flashing against the clouds. My breath comes out in patches on the window when I press my face against it, wanting to look distant, non-communicative. *Just don't bother.*

'Hello, again. Best seat in the house, ay?' His voice booms in at me, past the gold sun. Friendly Bloke. He climbs into the aisle seat, not the middle one. 'At least there's this one free. We should make sure we order an extra meal for them.'

'You've taken my seat and you've ruined my theory.' I want to glare at him, but the thought of extra meals has got me interested.

'I was sitting at the back, squeezed between the toilet and the escape chute. Couldn't see the screen. When I came down to see if there were any better views, I saw you here with your two empty seats and perfect view and I thought – that seat is for me.'

'Well, it wasn't. It was for me.'

'Don't worry, I won't talk to you or breathe in your air and I certainly won't offer you any of my sweets.' He pulls a pack of lemon sherbets from his bag and unwraps one.

'You can offer me a sherbet. That's allowable. Everything else, you're right. No talking. Especially no making stupid comments about *Rainmaker*.'

'What's your name?'

'Charis.'

'I'm Elgin. Charis, I believe people who make any sort of comments during films should be tossed from the window. I can't believe you could look at me and think that I was someone who would consider such an action. Although I have to say, *Rainmaker* is amazingly bad.'

'That's your stupid comment. It doesn't have to be during the film. Now you have to be ejected from this seat.'

'I don't think they'll have that. They've put a feuding couple in my old seat. I'm stuck here with the grumpiest woman alive.'

'I haven't even started.'

'You can't be cross about *Rainmaker*. It doesn't need your sympathy, believe me. Pathetic woman gets rescued by burly hero who takes advantage of her perilous state to seduce her. You'd hate it.'

'How would you know what I'd hate? I might love the idea of pathetic women being rescued.'

141

'I doubt it. You don't look that sort.'

I'm tempted to ask him what that sort does look like, but he's already breaking the rules by speaking to me at all, so I smile in what I assume is a polite manner and turn my head back to the sun. It's dipped below the clouds now, and there are purple and black shadows below us, shifting on a flat plane. Could be France, could be anywhere. Geography is my weak point. Food smells are coming from the front of the plane and my mouth starts to water. Ocean appears below me and I imagine small white yachts being tossed about. We went sailing once, with Dingo. Only Marah and me, I can't think where Jethro was. He always wanted to sail, back then. So did Marah. She knew all the boats, she'd borrowed some book from the library. She knew them all: sabots, herons, skates. What else? VJs. I'm amazed I remember them, I don't know how I know that. Cats, lasers, mirrors – although a mirror is like a sabot. Marah must have told me this stuff, or Jethro, or someone. She wanted to sail off around the world. Or was that Jethro? Or was it me?

Elgin has put the tray down on the seat between us. The stewards are rattling down the aisle with food trolleys and some American family values thing is on the screen. When the stewardess gets to us, I smile blankly, collect my little tray and hold it to my nose. Airline food is fantastic, I don't understand the complaints. All those little sections, the tiny packets to unwrap, the surprise smell of something you didn't even know you wanted. Elgin twinkles at the stewardess and points to the empty seat. 'Chicken, I think.' He looks over at me. 'Was it the chicken, or the beef?'

I smell my own meal. Smells like beef. 'Chicken.'

'Thanks.' Elgin puts the tray between us and grins at the stewardess's back. 'Great. There's never enough food in these things, don't ya reckon?'

'I usually stock up on peanuts to keep me going. I bags the dessert.'

'No way, it's straight down the middle. So, are you going back home? Have you been travelling?'

I know I'm getting trapped into a conversation here that I don't want. Once you start, it's hard to stop, and if you're on a

142

plane you can't just say, 'Well, see ya,' when it gets boring. You're in it for the duration. Usually, I'm faster than this. I get the earphones on as soon as there's a sign of 'Wanna talk?' Because I don't. Not usually. Not on planes, not when there are re-runs of *Friends* to watch and little buttons to press to make people come running. But I'm going to share that extra meal with him, so I might as well share some words as well. Just a few, and then I can put my earphones on and give him the signal, the just-shut-up signal. 'I live in London. I'm going to a wedding. You can have the bread – here.'

'Why London?'

'Whaddaya mean?'

'Well.' He reaches over, scrapes a splodge of Waikiki chicken on to his plate. 'Why did you go in the first place? Any good reason?'

No one has ever asked me this question. When I left, no one, not one person, said, 'Why are you doing this?' It seemed obvious. London was bigger, brighter, better. All the books, when I was a kid, talked about Europe, England, London. All the stories I read were adventures in England, all the bands, all the clothes, all the talk – it all came from America or England. Marah always wanted to go to Yale, never Sydney, or Macquarie. And me, for no reason, no reason at all, except that it wasn't Australia and all the news and all the pictures made it seem more real than home: England. The centre of the universe. So of course that's where I wanted to be. Except it doesn't feel like the centre of anything, unless it's a grey storm. 'No good reason. Seemed like a good idea. Everyone was doing it. London is, was, the centre of something. Bigger than Sydney.'

'Not brighter, though. I was in London for three years. Same thing – no reason, but I thought everything would be happening. It's not, though, no more than it's happening at home. Don't you miss it? The water, the space, the *sky*?'

As he's speaking, the way he says 'home' and waves his hand in front of him, drawing the open sky, I do miss it. Quickly and unexpectedly, it comes from nowhere and it will go back to nowhere, it must. 'Only now, because of you saying that. Mostly,

I don't even think about it. Anyway, I wanted to be as far away as possible.'

'From?' He's leaning forward, the last bit of bread roll in his hand.

'Nothing.' I don't have to unravel here, in front of this stranger. I will not do that. 'Stuff, you know. Are you going back for good?'

'Sure am.' He leans back, slips the plastic lid from the mini-mini-cheesecake, and cuts it in half. 'Here, eat. It's good. Full of chemicals to make your hair grow. Whose wedding?'

I look at him. He's got cheesecake falling from his mouth, crumbs on his jeans. Pale red hair, brown eyes. Nice eyes, if you like that sort of thing. 'My mother's.'

'Lucky number two, ay? Take her long to find him?'

'Number three. I don't believe in luck, and I have to say I'd be totally arsed if I did.' I attempt to bung on a Somerset accent and end up sounding like I've got a muffler up me bum. 'That was supposed to be, you know, deepest Devon or something. Accents turn into one blob for me. German sounds the same as, well, Somerset. No, it didn't take her long. He was my dad's best mate, she left me dad for him, oh, years ago. Buggered if I know why the hell they bloody well insist on getting married now, dragging us all out, practically ruining my sister's career. Not that she'd give a toss, as long as she gets her man. Anyway, they've paid for me, so here I am. No bloody choice.'

Even I'm surprised by the rage in my voice. I sound like I could kill her. Like I would, like I'd burn her up, if I had the chance. Him, too, but her – I go cold when I go too far down that alley: what I would do, what I would say. I close my eyes, put my headphones on, switch on 'Soothing Sounds' and try to follow the instructions: *Imagine you are a lotus flower, white, floating.* Realize I don't know what a lotus flower is, so I switch to the screen – *Rainmaker* – and tune out.

Everyone is hauled off the plane at Singapore and Elgin waits for me at the gate. Nicely, though, asks if I mind, if I fancy checking out the thriving airport scene with him. We spray nine varieties of perfume into the air in the Duty Free shop, and walk through the spray with our arms out. There's a tasting tray of fruit fudge, so we try each one and then ask for a refund. Lights flash everywhere, the brightness waking all the tired bones. We lean against a pillar, watching the hordes stream past. From nowhere, or it seems like nowhere, Elgin asks me why I'm so angry about the wedding, or what is it I'm angry about, why am I so angry? And I tell him. I don't know why I tell him; I've never told Janey or anyone. I'll never see him again. It's just because he asks and leans in and nods and, well, same as with the being-in-London thing − I don't know if anyone has ever asked me that, either. Why I'm so angry. But then I'm not, usually. Not so you'd notice.

When I tell him, I look at the ground, waiting for him to walk away. He doesn't, he sits down, leaning against the pillar, and pulls me down with him. Puts his hand on my knee, palm up, so that I can put my hand there if I want to. After I put my hand there, after I've told him everything, I look at him. His eyes are looking right at me, brown and big. Tears are falling out of them, a small trail of tears making their way down his face. He squeezes my hand tight and says, 'I'm sorry, Charis. Oh, how horrible.' My face is dry, but I nod and say, 'Yes, it is.'

Strange, but I'm not embarrassed to get back on the plane with him. He keeps talking, slides into the seat next to me. Asks me questions, tells me his mother died last year, while he was in London. Not fair, he says, so much isn't fair, we have to do the best we can. It's only when the lights flash, when the voice says we're finally heading into Sydney, that I stop scratching at my palm. Landing is a bump so hard I think I'll throw up. I know I'll never see him again and I certainly don't want to, so I grab my rucksack from underneath the seat and bolt while he's still got his head in the overhead locker. Passport control is smooth, the first time I've been the first through. Even my bags come out early and I've got a trolley without a wonkey wheel. I keep my head down, head to the barriers and collide with a grey-haired man. His bags fall on the floor. Desperate though I am to zoom off, or maybe to run and hide in the toilets, I kneel down and start helping the old bloke gather the bits together. One of the bags has fallen open and notebooks are dribbling out. Elgin calls out to me while I'm scrabbling on the ground, collecting the man's spilt papers.

'Here. If you want to call me, do. I'd like it if you did. I'm around. I'll be around if you want to talk at all. It might be hard, you know, being there. You don't have to, it's just –' he stops talking, steps forward and hugs me so tight I lose my breath – 'it'd be good, you know, if you did. I'd like to hear from you. If you want.' I nod, take the piece of paper from his hand and put it in my pocket. When I get through to the Arrival Gate, where I can see Marah waving, her big grin covering her face, I'm still breathless.

# *Marah*

Mother's got a new step machine, she's working out for the wedding. Not that she hasn't always kept in shape, she's quite good like that, quite careful. Obviously, though, she wants to work a little bit harder for her wedding day. I've had a couple of work-outs on it, it's not bad, although I'd rather go for a run, if the truth be told. If I had a choice in the matter, which of course I usually do. The morning I arrived, I felt too tired to run, so I worked out on the stepper then. Took my time, didn't go too fast or too hard. Actually, although most people get off a plane and go straight to bed or to eat, the best thing you can do is to exercise. Get blood moving through your body again and work off some of the stodge which they insist on feeding you on planes. Every five minutes they're back with another tray of food. Worst thing is, I get so bored that I eat the meals, even though I know I don't need it, because it's not as if I'm using any energy up or anything like that. Daniel's only been around twice since I got back four days ago. Partly because I was so tired the first couple of days, I didn't want to see anyone, that's the truth. Shock, too, I suppose; it's always a shock, coming back here. Not for any reason, I think that's just normal, when you've been away, when you come back. It's strange, that's all. Lying in the bed I used to sleep in, looking out through my window. As if I've never been away, that's what the strangeness is.

Daniel was going to come with me to the airport, to pick Charis up. That was the plan, but he phoned this morning. Forgotten that he was on call, the silly thing. Actually, when he called, I was using the stepper. Seemed quicker than going for a run, somehow. Mother is going to stay here, get things organized, while I collect Charis. No point in overwhelming Charis. Mother says that and I agree. Usually, I would plan to be at the airport a good hour before the plane was due, I mean I'd leave in time to get there an hour before. Because that way, you're allowing for traffic jams and hold-ups and flat tyres. Mother says an hour is ridiculous and just to give it half an hour, so I'm settling on forty minutes. Charis makes me nervous sometimes, I don't know why. I get twitchy, keep smoothing my dress down when I know she'll be around. Partly, probably, because she always makes such a fuss about everything, nothing is ever easy with her, she's never happy-go-lucky. Never lets things lie. Which can be quite tiring to be around.

Jethro stomps into the kitchen while I'm making a cup of decaff. Caffeine makes the vocal cords tighten and tense, so it's best to avoid it. In the six months I've been away, Jethro has let his hair grow long and straggly. Going for the hippy, layabout look. He asks me if I want juice, which is at least polite of him, because to be honest he has been known to help himself to the last of the orange juice without thinking about whether anyone else would want it or not. Frangipanis are floating in a blue bowl on the kitchen table. What on earth the frangipani are doing flowering at this time, I have no idea. Sweet smell, though, a little bit overwhelming, but nice. Jethro scrapes a chair out and says, Where's Mum?

I suggest he looks in the garden but he stays sitting at the table, staring into his glass. Asks if I want to go with him to pick up Charis, he's just got to check that he can take the car. Of course I explain that he doesn't need to collect her because the plan all the time has been for Daniel and me to go and collect her. Before I get a chance to add that Daniel can't come after all, Jethro's saying, Do you really think that's a good idea? Charis has got so many chips on her shoulder she might not want to be met by someone who isn't family, it's bad enough when it is family.

Now this, I think, is offensive. Because Daniel is practically family, we are practically engaged and he helped Dingo mend his boat *and* he offered to coach Jethro through his exams. Before Jethro decided to drop out. Which isn't Daniel's fault, or mine.

Most of that I do get a chance to say before Jethro says, Oh, chill out, Marah – as if I'm the uptight one, the one with the numerous chips on my shoulder. Sometimes, Jethro makes me want to smack him. When Mother comes in from the garden, carrying an armful of white miniature roses and some purple stocks, Jethro straight away asks for the car. Mother, quite rightly, says that I had already arranged to drive, so why doesn't Jethro come with me? She can't go, because she and Dingo have to go and talk to the florist, and they've already left it quite late. Actually, I think it's better if Mother and Dingo don't go out to the airport, even if it weren't for the florist. Charis gets so jumpy with Dingo, she's liable to say anything. Honestly, I do think it's time that she grew up and moved on, stopped blaming everyone else for all her problems. It gets a little bit tiresome, to tell you the truth.

Finally Jethro says, OK, you drive to the airport and I'll drive back.

I'm perfectly happy with that, because at least I'll get to talk to Charis, and to tell you the truth, I really don't think it's worth an argument over who exactly is going to be behind the wheel.

Parramatta Road is swarming with vintage cars. Must be some sort of rally. Women sit in the passenger seats bundled up in big hats and scarves and long dresses and gloves. The men, who are driving, wear caps and goggles. Even if I weren't stuck behind them, I'd want to slow down just to watch, it all looks so elegant. Jethro is humphing and puffing beside me, looking at his Swatch and glaring at anyone who makes eye-contact with him. I'm not smug, but I like smiling at him and saying, Chill out, Jethro. That makes him huff even more, squirming and saying we'll miss the plane. No, don't worry, I tell him, we've got plenty of time – I told you it arrived at twelve to get you out of the house. She doesn't arrive until one. Come on, lighten up, Jethro.

Jethro doesn't lighten up, he calls me a witch and a control freak. Not that I'm bothered. At least I get myself out of bed in the morning. I don't say that to him, though, because I'm not stupid, I know it would go downhill from there. Anyway, it's true, even if I don't say it. The vintage cars are slow, and by the time we get to the turn-off, I'm starting to wonder whether I left enough time for every possible problem. They do turn off, though, with lots of horn tooting and waving and calling out to each other, and the road is clear the rest of the way. Heat comes in through the windows, it's like summer is still hanging on. Jethro is dozing with his mouth open when I pull into the airport car-park. He only wakes up when I slap him on the leg. Honestly, he doesn't get up until practically midday, so I can't see why he should need a cat-nap.

He grins at me and wipes the spit from his chin. Says, Sun makes me dozy. Are we here already?

As if we've had to drive through the whole state instead of just into the city. Trains only take forty-five minutes to get into Central, if you can get a direct one, so it's not like we're out in the sticks. Jethro carries on sometimes as if we are, though, gives the impression that we live way out, nowhere near Sydney. Surrounded by bush. Hardly. Trees, yes, there are smatterings here and there, but certainly not enough to make up the wild scrubland that he'd like it to be. Still, if you asked Jethro, he might tell you a whole different story, he might not see it like that at all.

Somehow I always expect Mascot to be small and quiet after JFK. It amazes me when there are crowds, when there's proper airport security, all of that. I tell Jethro it's bigger than I remember, that I got a shock when I arrived back and Mother took me to one of the bars to celebrate. Shocked at the size of it, because I'd shrunk it to something small and town-like in my head, in my memory.

Jethro says, You're *full* of it, Marah, it's not like you've been away for years, and what's with this *Mother* business? She was *Mum* when you left.

That's not true, I say, I've called her Mother since I started at the Con., and anyway, people are allowed to change and grow and develop ways of speaking which are more appropriate to their new environment, and also time can seem very long if you're in a very different situation, which I have been. He groans as if I am a headache and I tell him he'll understand when he grows up. Which, to be honest, I doubt.

Charis's plane is coming in fifteen minutes early, so we only

150

have ten minutes to stand around in the newsagents. Jethro picks up *Simple Living, Free Spirit* and *GQ* and gets so absorbed that when I tap him on the arm and tell him we should go out and be ready for Charis, he tells me he'll be out in a second and just keeps reading. Fine, I say, meet me at Gate Four when you can drag yourself away. People are swarming off the plane when I get to the gate, most of them all crumpled and messy-looking. Really, it doesn't take a huge effort to have a wash, put on a bit of make-up before you actually get off the plane. People forget what they look like after twenty hours flying. Daniel said I looked as fresh as a daisy and just as pretty when I got off the plane. Those were his exact words: fresh as a daisy. I'm looking out for Charis, and also trying to keep an eye out for Jethro, because to be honest, he's likely to wander off to completely the wrong gate and set us all off on an afternoon of chaos. Which nobody wants and especially not me.

Charis comes through in the first swarm. Her trolley seems to be wandering all over the place, she's pulling at it with one hand and trying to hold her luggage on with the other. She sees me waving almost straight away and grins at me. She looks tired, but she's lost a little bit of weight. At least I think she has, she looks well, anyway. The trolley collides with my foot when I push forward to hug her and say things like, Here you are at last, and, How was the flight? Charis's arms are around me before I've got a chance to say any of them properly. Her voice is muffled in my hair, but I can hear her saying something like, Oh, you poor darling. For a while, I hug her back, and then I step away so that she has to let go of me. Jethro still hasn't turned up, so I tell her we'll have to go and find him.

When I say, You know, same old Jethro, Charis laughs and says, Same old Marah, and hugs me again. Jethro comes running up, completely out of breath, so that you'd swear he'd run a marathon instead of a few yards. He smashes straight into Charis in what I suppose is a version of a hug. When a tall, red-haired man comes out through the gate, Charis stops hugging Jethro and says, Come on, then. Let's go. The red-haired man waves at Charis and calls out, Hopefully, Charis. Whatever that means, I'm about to ask her who he is and what he's talking about –

because, actually, he's quite good-looking in a not very athletic sort of way – but she's bustling us along as if we're pieces of her luggage and giving me the very strong impression that she's desperate to get home. Which I have to say surprises me. Given the way Charis is.

Jethro drives us home and I sit in the back, leaning forward so I can ask Charis what the flight was like and who the red-haired man was. She doesn't answer, not to either question, and instead says, just out of the blue, What about your show, Marah? Weren't you supposed to be the lead?

Jethro says, Oh, what happened about that? I'd forgotten that.

The truth is, no one has really mentioned it since I got home, everyone has been so full of the wedding. Obviously, it isn't really a priority at the moment, with everything else going on. I'm here now and Yale is there and Elisabeth is doing Dido and I'm sure she's doing a fine job. Elisabeth comes into my head most mornings, I wake up and hear her voice running through the lament. Reedy on the lower end, she really is, I hope she gets that sorted out before the performance. It doesn't make me feel good, hearing her voice, particularly if I imagine it soaring through the lament. Which is possible, because if she works on that lower register, she actually has quite a magnificent voice. But there you go. She's there and I'm not. I'm here, for my mother's wedding, where it's right for me to be. Where else would I be? It would be ridiculous for me to be on the other side of the world while everyone went through the wedding here. And it definitely wasn't feasible for them to change the date. How could they? I say some of this to Charis – nothing about Elisabeth being Dido and good luck to her or even about her being weaker on the low notes. Only about the wedding and how I don't even think about Yale at the moment, because I'm here, not there.

After a while of being silent Charis turns around in her seat – to be honest, I don't know how she can do that, it makes me sick if I can't see the road unravelling in front of me – and looks right at me. Well, she says, Why the hell couldn't they get married later, after you'd done your show?

152

Jethro pats her leg and says, Who knows? Don't start getting uptight about it, Charis.

She smacks his hand away and spits out, Selfish cow.

Jethro's uptight now, I can see that, anxious about whether Charis is going to do her usual trick of having a big tantrum scene and spoiling everything. He doesn't want to be bothered, though, he never does, so he says, You're tired, don't start a scene when you get home, just have a sleep, OK? As if he's ten years older than her, instead of the baby of the family. It's unusual for him to even open his mouth, actually, and it seems to shut Charis up, at least until we pull up the drive.

We leave Charis's bags in the car and go out the back, into the garden. Mother grabs Charis in a huge hug before anyone has a chance to speak and says, Oh, darling, *how* exciting. Charis says she's very tired and whatever happened to cups of tea and cakes? When Charis pulls away, I can see that Mother's hands are shaking, just a little bit, and her lips are pulled in tight in that very anxious way she has. Relieved, though, by the looks of her, that Charis appears to be on her best behaviour. Naturally, with a wedding coming up and Mother wanting to look as trim as possible, there's no cake in the house. Charis scrounges around in the cupboards as if she's never been away. Squatting down with her head in the cupboard, she's muttering things like, Bloody typical, and, Just what I need, a house full of diet obsessives. Which, to be honest, I think is a little bit uncalled for. Just because people want to look their best doest not make them obsessives, it definitely does not. Eventually she digs out some Milk Arrowroot.

Jethro makes a pot of tea, brings the tray in and says, Anyway, welcome home, sis, I've got to practise my guitar.

He does a lot of that, hiding in his room, practising. Or whatever. Charis waves him off like she's the Queen of Sheba and he's come to pay her court, or homage, or whatever it is that they paid queens back then.

Let me hear what you're working on later, she calls after him, but I don't think he's heard – the door has slammed shut behind him.

Mother sits forward, pours tea for each of us and tells Charis

153

that she'll be wanting to see the invitations and the dress before anything else, she supposes. Charis sighs and says, No, and, Why are you getting married now, Mum? Why now?

Mother giggles, and I have to say she does look like a girl. Highlights have been put through her hair, nothing obtrusive, just enough to give a delicate touch, and she's been putting in time getting the sun in the garden. She looks exactly like a bride-to-be, that's the truth. She touches Charis's arm and says, Well, it's all very romantic, isn't it, Marah?

I say that I don't know, because she hasn't actually told me why now, or why at all. She breaks off a tiny corner of an Arrowroot biscuit and bites it so that the crumbs fall on to the lounge. Couch. There's some television programme, that's what she tells us, where you go on as a couple, and if you win, the prize is to get married.

Charis drops her biscuit on the floor and says, How revolting.

Mother picks the biscuit up, dusts it off and says, Oh, don't worry, it's fine, you're tired.

When Charis rolls her eyes at me and mouths, Not the biscuit, I pretend I can't see her. Because I'm more interested in the rest of the story.

Mother dusts the crumbs from herself, stirs her tea about fifty times, in a way which makes me think she must have seen Charis mouthing at me. Finally she says, Well, anyway, Dingo and I watched it every week and thought it was just brilliant, just a laugh and great fun, and for no special reason, I decided to enter us, to see what would happen. Secretly, I had been waiting for ages for him to ask me and of course I wasn't going to ask him, and I kept missing leap years. Anyway, the prizes are marvellous – trips up north, wedding rings, the works. I forgot about it, of course, and then a few weeks later, I got a letter inviting us to an interview, for the producer to decide whether we really were in love enough and a proper couple to be on the show. Too old, as it turned out. Never mind. For the best really, because then Dingo got down on one knee – he did it all properly – and asked me to marry him anyway. And I said yes. Incredibly lucky for us that we got the Hilton for the reception. It was only because some other reception had been cancelled – cold feet, I think, poor things. First marriage. But it's all worked out marvellously, the timing, because Dingo's just finished the big race. Came in ninth, did I tell you? Not bad for an old man, ay? So, well, a bit of an accident, I suppose. But a lucky one. And I'm so glad all my chickens could be here.

Charis clucks as if she's a hen and Mother laughs, but Charis doesn't. Charis takes a sip of tea and, as if it's any of her business, says, It's a big shame about Marah's show, I think that sucks, I think you could have been a bit more bloody considerate in your timing.

I tell her to shut up and mind her own business and also that she hasn't got a clue what she's talking about, because I'm starting to feel as if it's me who's jet-lagged. As if I've been dragged through a hedge, or a dream. If I could, I'd like to faint, I wish that I could do it on demand, but I'm far too robust for my own good.

Eventually, Charis does shut up and Mother says, Well, I think you're just a bit tired.

Truthfully, I could slap Charis, I could slap her so hard across the face that she wouldn't know what she had coming. I'd knock her teeth right through her head and knock her on to the floor, so that she was lying there for hours, not knowing what had happened, while I stamped on her hands again and again. I don't, though. I don't stamp or hit. Very quietly, I say, I'm going to go over to see Daniel, I hope you have a good sleep, Charis. I say it as if she isn't my sister, but just some stranger who is a bit of a nuisance. And when I look at her, round and heavy and hunched over her teacup looking red in the face, I honestly don't know who she is at all.

*The Giving*
*of the Ring*

# With This Ring

Sun is beating down in the back yard, burning the cement, flaming up the frangipani tree. Heat travels up the path, you can see it, everything bending and swaying before it. Across the back fence, the Ellroy's house is buckling, wobbling as if it's a mirage. Marah screws the plastic sprinkler into the green hose, calls out, 'Get ready,' and runs back to the tap, shoves at it hard with both hands. Rusted and ancient, last used no one knows when, it doesn't budge, the sprinkler stays unsprinkling, the heat stays fast. Charis is straddling the sprinkler already. Her school uniform is tucked high into her knickers, so that it looks like an all-in-one baby bloomers set. 'Hurry up.' Her voice has got an overheated whine in it. 'I'm boiling over here.'

'It's stuck. Give me a hand. Jethro, get off the ground and help.' Marah pushes at the tap.

Jethro lies flat, his arms making wide shadows on the grass. 'Can't. Too hot.'

'Lazy bugger.' Charis stands deliberately on his hand, stomps over to the wall and pits all her strength against the tap. 'It's giving. Get out of the way. Move.'

The sprinkler splutters as if it's a living thing, and then whirs into action, spraying water across the yard, covering the house, the grape-vine, the half-trodden miniature rose bushes. Jethro lifts his arms up and lets the water rain down on him, but doesn't move the rest of his body. Water pelts down, faster and harder as Charis turns the valve.

'Shove off, Jethro. I'm gunna jump across there and I'll land on yer fat head if ya don't move.' Marah hoiks her uniform up and lines herself up for the great running leap across the sprinkler. Jethro rolls over and over, the wet grass catching on his school shirt and covering his legs. Dirt is smearing across his face. Marah jumps across the twirl of wetness just as he rolls away. She skids across the lawn, slithering up a slice of mud as she goes. Charis dances around the water, laughing like a madwoman, or a baby.

It is Charis who says that what they need is the plastic sheet from the shed and the washing-up liquid from the kitchen. She stands in the middle of the yard, pointing arms, giving orders. Sending Marah to the kitchen for detergent, Jethro to the shed for the long strip of greenish thick plastic covering Dingo's old kayak. They spread the plastic across the lawn – Jethro weighting it with two white stones from the flower border – and squeeze a line of detergent in a snake shape. Not much of a slope, but Charis says it's better than nothing. She does the first slide, running from the back wall, pelting harder and faster until she gets to a leap before the plastic slide. Her legs fly out in front of her, her tunic swings up over her bum, and she pounds on to the slide. Slips down sideways, covered in foam and with bubbles in her mouth. Jethro leaps on top of Charis before Marah has a chance to say it's her turn. Instead of leaping, Marah gets Charis to give her a push off. She stands back in the sprinkler, washing the foam off. Says she doesn't like being covered in the sliminess of it. The side gate clicks open while she's squeezing the bubbles out from her uniform.

'What on earth are you doing? Marah, do you intend to wash that uniform yourself?' Noeline drops two bags on to the cement path. 'Look at the three of you, didn't it occur to anyone to change into swimmers? Honestly, if you had a brain between you, you'd be dangerous.'

'I already am dangerous.' Jethro dives across the plastic, skidding into the mud.

'You certainly are, my boy. Come over here and let me look at you.'

Jethro trots over to path, holds his hands out for inspection. 'It was too hot. Anyway –' he points to the mud-covered sheet – 'we made a slide.'

'I can see that. I can also see that you're completely filthy. You

160

too, Charis. And what are you doing with your skirt hitched up like that, showing off your knickers? Pull it down.'

Charis yanks at the skirt of her uniform. 'What are you doin home so early, anyway?'

'Doing home, not doin. I got an early mark.'

'Fibber. Why really?'

'It's not that early. You lot have probably been out here for hours. Do you want some watermelon?' Noeline points at a plastic bag at her feet. 'I got some from Froot 'n' Toot on the way home.'

'Excellent.' Jethro wipes at his shorts, trying to scrape away the thick clod of wet grass which has attached itself to him.

Noeline clumps up the back steps with the three bags. The back door bounces shut behind her. When she comes back out, bearing a dinner plate teetering with thick watermelon slices, her shoes are off and she's got shorts on instead of her grey head-teacher's skirt. She sits down on the back steps and waits for the leaping, wringing-out and mud-rolling to end. Charis has stripped off to her blouse and knickers, has left her skirt lying in the flower-bed.

'Watermelon's here when you're ready.' Noeline has the voice, temporarily, of *Brady Bunch* land, where golden-haired mothers bake cookies and romp with their adorably mischievous children. 'Leave the sprinkler on, the lawn could do with some water.'

'Yum. Watch yer head, Jethro.' Charis spits a line of watermelon seeds at Jethro's head. Perfect aim.

'Well, it looks like you've ruined your uniforms and I'm going to have to wash a load for Monday, doesn't it?' Noeline wipes her fingers on the cement step.

Jethro grabs at the plate. 'Yair, but you'd have to do that anyway. Can I have that piece as well?'

'Actually, I had a thought about tomorrow. Although I'm not sure that you deserve it, given the state of your clothes and this garden.'

'What? What is it?'

'Dingo's got more work this weekend at the boat-builders in

Newcastle and there's a fair on in Newcastle which I want to go to as well.'

'A fair – excellent.' Small chunks of watermelon pop out of Jethro's mouth as he speaks.

'Not with your mouth full, please, Jethro. Not that sort of fair. It's a Computing in Schools fair. Displays and information about getting computers into schools. I'm thinking abut getting a computer for the school.'

'We've got six at school.' Charis is smug, the high-school representative, spitting the last of her watermelon seeds on to the grass. 'Anyway, does this involve us?'

'Hold your horses. It struck me that, seeing as we won't get to see Dingo much on the weekend, we could all spend the day in Newcastle. He only needs to do a couple of hours tomorrow and while I have a look at the computers, he could spend some time with you lot. Maybe take you out to lunch, and then we could spend some time as a family. We don't get to do that very often.'

Later, huddled by the shed, scraping the last of the mud from the plastic sheeting, Charis says, 'Family, she keeps saying we're a family, and we're not. Dingo's not family, he'll never be my family.' It is something like that she says, or someone says. Perhaps it is about something else it is said, or perhaps spoken on another day, but the heart is there whenever or wherever these words come forth, whoever speaks them. Dingo is not family, no matter what you do or what you say. He'll never be family.

In the morning, Marah wakes up bright and sparky at seven, raring to go, eats Breakfast D-Lite, washes her face and packs her swimming costume. Noeline is in her dressing gown, drinking a cup of coffee. Marah trots out to pick up the mail from the letter-box, the grass cold against her feet. There's a pile of letters squished into the box with three catalogues, one for Toys 'R' Us. Marah plonks the letters down on the table and fans the envelopes out, reads the one which says: 'Noeline Dell, PLEASE REPLY'. She points to it, to the curvy writing, and says, 'Is that from Dad?'

Noeline slams her coffee cup down, almost as if she's been slapped. She picks up the envelope, looks at it. 'No, I don't think so. Your father hasn't been in touch since the injunction, not really. No.' She turns the envelope over, reads the postmark. 'Doesn't look like it's from your dad. I see what you mean, though, the writing is a little bit like his. What's that? Toys 'R' Us? What about we call in there on the way back this afternoon, have a look about?'

Bits of sleep are still flecking Jethro's eyes when he half-staggers out to the kitchen. He grabs at the Toys 'R' Us catalogue and says he wants a model racing set. He eats his breakfast – Coco Pops – with his eyes closed and to an accompaniment of Noeline saying she gives up on trying to get him to eat nourishing food, she really does. By the time they all pile into the car, there are complicated lists being made about who will have what.

Before they even turn on to the main road, Jethro says, 'Oh, no, I forgot me swimmers,' and Noeline doesn't say, 'My, not me,' she just nods at Dingo to turn back. There are no games played in the car. Charis says, 'Let's play I Spy or Car-plates,' but no one takes it up. Noeline and Dingo talk quietly in the front seat; with the radio on you can hardly hear what they're saying. Murmur, murmur, it will be fine, really, murmur murmur. That's about all, that's the strength of it. As the Hawkesbury starts to wind out alongside the car, Marah leans forward and asks Noeline to please turn the radio up so she doesn't have to listen to everyone blabbing away. The Hawkesbury is thick and green, heavy with eels hiding beneath the surface, where you'd never see them, not if you didn't know. Snaking and sliding near the road as if it's a twin, and then all of a sudden, gone. Disappeared, so that it seems as though the river has backed away, turned on itself, when all the time it's the road which has been quietly edging away, creeping further and further from the thick trees, the huddled banks.

When they pass the sign saying LAKE MACQUARIE: GATEWAY TO THE HUNTER VALLEY, Charis is dozing with her head on Marah's shoulder and a small line of dribble on her chin. Marah nudges her awake and says, 'We're nearly there.' Charis nods and closes her eyes again. She opens them when the car stops outside the Newcastle Workers' Club. Noeline is gathering up her cardigan and briefcase, kissing Dingo and leaning into the back seat to touch Marah and Jethro on the shoulders.

'Wish me luck with the computers.' Noeline pushes her lips down, clown-like. 'Now, I'll see you after lunch, I'm sure I'll manage to get a sandwich here. Jethro, remember not to go in the water without your sisters, please. I'll see you at two-thirty in front of the pavilion.'

'OK, we'll be fine. See you there.' Dingo pulls the door shut and starts the car before she finishes speaking. 'So.' He looks into the rear-view mirror, his eyes moving across the back seat. 'Beach or Bogey Hole?'

Jethro yells out, 'Bogey Hole,' as if he is at a footie game.

'Beach.' Marah doesn't look away from the window to speak.

'What's the Bogey Hole?' Charis smacks Jethro on the leg. 'Shut up for one second.'

'It's where the Bogey Man lives and if you hit me again, I'm dobbing when Mum picks us up and you'll be grounded, so there.'

'Wrong, mate.' Dingo pulls over, behind a yellow combi with two surfboards on top. 'The beach is just down there, so whatddaya think? I can't believe you don't know about the Bogey Hole – it's not like it's a huge trek for you guys to get here.'

'Just tell me what it is. Spare the lecture.' Charis winds her window down and glares at the passing traffic.

'It's a private bath, built by convicts for some bloke called Captain Bogey – no, seriously, that was his name. He had all the convicts build him a special bath, complete with a shelf for soap and rubber ducky. Took the convicts six months or something to build it and they reckon a load of em died, got swept out to sea. Dunno about that, though. Pretty impressive, ay? Imagine being able to snap yer fingers and get a load of blokes to do what ya wanted.'

'Seems a bit rough on the convicts.'

'I've changed my mind. I want to go there, can ya swim in it? Let's go there, come on, Charis.'

'Yair, OK, whatever.'

164

'Good-o, the Bogey Hole it is, then. Good choice.' Dingo swings the car across the road and overtakes a motorbike.

They twirl along the Beach Road, watching the dots of swimmers and surfies flicking in and out of the blue wet shine, and up past the Merewether Ocean Baths. Beyond the baths, Dingo pulls on to the side of the road and turns the ignition off. 'Well, here we are.' His seat-belt clicks undone.

'There's nothing here.' Jethro's voice is small and whiney.

'Yair, there is, it's down the steps. Carn, get outta the car ya lazy buggers.'

They pile out, hot tar burning bare feet, and ooch, ouch, ah, to the crooked steps leading down to the Bogey Hole. Metal rails, thin and rusted, travel down to the wide mouth of water at the bottom. Hands wrapped hard around the rail, Marah stands on the top step, staring down at the fenced-in pool. No bogey man or convicts swimming about in it. No one, in fact, just the strange sea-fence and the walls of stone. Charis pelts down the steps, never minding the crookedness, the slipperiness. Clothes fall from her as she runs down, so that at the bottom she is glorious in her red swimmers. She calls up for Marah and her voice is both echoed and muffled. Marah keeps her hands on the rail as she steps down, down and into the cave-like changing room at the edge of the pool.

'Here, I'll hold me towel up so ya can change. Why didn't ya just put yer swimmers on?' Charis's skin is pink from the cool air. 'This is fantastic.'

'I didn't want to have a wet bum all day.' Marah pulls her shirt over her head and squeezes into her Speedo one-piece while Charis holds the towel like a flag in front of her.

Dingo and Jethro are walking on the edge of the pool, balancing on stepping stones with stakes attached to them. Jethro has hold of Dingo's hand. When Marah and Charis jump in behind him, covering his clothes with splashes, he tells them to get off but says he doesn't want to swim. Not here. Even when Charis promises there are no bogey men here and dives down and swims the length of the pool underwater to prove it, even then Jethro says he's happy. Happy looking at the edges, happy holding Dingo's hand. Marah says 'traitor' under her breath and half under the water. Limpets floating by hear her, and the rocks, and the tiny fish, too small to be properly seen. Charis grabs at Marah's legs and tries to pull her under, and Marah kicks at her, tells her to get off. Cold and choppy, the water starts to numb their ears and they race from end to end to warm themselves and keep from yelling at Jethro, who is too young to know any better anyway.

When they get out of the water, Marah's lips are pale, almost white, and the skin on her fingers is shrivelled. Dingo is waiting in the stone changing room, by the rough-hewn ledge for rubber duckies, with their towels held up for them. Warm and dry. They run up the stairs and get into the car with the towels wrapped around them, letting the heat of the car dry them off. When Dingo says he thinks they should go to the London Beef-Eater for a posh lunch, Charis cheers. Marah says nothing, just slips her clothes over her wet swimmers. Charis doesn't put her clothes on until Dingo pulls up in the London Beef-Eater car-park.

Waitresses wearing long velvet dresses and olde England white bonnets cut back and forth across the restaurant floor. They wait in silence at a standing sign with WAIT FOR YOUR YEOMAN written in gold letters on it. It's a yeoman-in-training who comes to show them to their table. He leads the way to a round table at the back and tells them it's his first day so they'd better be kind to him. Tells them in a non-stop voice that the specials of the day are Beef Wellington and Roast Beef with Yorkshire Pudding or they can choose from the menu. Charis doesn't even glance at the menu before saying she'll have the Beef Wellington, if it comes with chips. Marah looks through the menu, reads each page and in the end settles for fish and chips because she can't think of anything else. When Jethro asks for the Roast Beef, Dingo jumps in and asks them to make it a child serve.

The yeoman-in-training wanders off with his little leather notepad and then comes back, looking embarrassed. 'Sorry. Forgot to ask – what would you like to drink with that?'

'Two cokes – is that what you want Jethro? Marah? And a carafe of house white. Do you want wine, Charis?' Dingo is still looking at the menu, not at Charis, not at the waiter. 'Two glasses, just in case. Thanks.'

166

Charis is silent, although her face is pink.

Dingo snaps his menu shut. 'Do you want wine? I think that if you're going to drink – and I know people your age do – I'd rather you did it with me, in a responsible environment. You're fourteen now, I'm happy for you to have wine. Or would you rather have something else? Bacardi?'

Marah, who has heard Katie Wilkins say that she has Bacardi and cokes on weekends, says, 'Bacardi and coke. I'll have that.'

'You're too young, Marah. You'll have to wait until you're Charis's age.'

Charis tosses her head, tosses at Marah, but her voice is small. 'Yair, Bacardi and coke, that's what I'll have.'

Dingo raises his hand slightly, and one of the velvet-dressed waitresses rushes over. Dingo's eyes go to the gap between the line of her dress and the start of her neck. 'Could we have a Bacardi and coke, please. No, leave the wine glasses, that's fine.'

Charis drinks the Bacardi quickly, through a straw. She makes slurping sounds in the ice at the bottom of the glass and asks Dingo if she can have another one instead of wine. Dingo laughs and says, 'Like it, huh?' The second Bacardi comes with the meals. Gravy spills from Jethro's plate as the waitress plonks it down in front of him. He licks it up with one finger. Charis drinks the second Bacardi straight from the glass, no straw. She picks the ice out of the bottom and crunches it, then scoffs her chips. Doesn't touch the Beef Wellington.

'Giss one of yer chips.' Charis leans across the table, picks the chip off Marah's plate.

'Get out, greedy-guts. These are mine. It's not my fault you finished yours in two seconds.'

'Hey, settle. Charis, eat some of yer beef, garn.' Dingo taps at Charis's hand, not a slap, just knocking.

She cuts a mouthful, chews. 'Yuk. Gross. I've finished my drink, can I have another one?'

'No, you can have some wine. Marah and Jethro are still on their first coke. You need to slow down a bit. Sip this.'

Charis sips it, downs the glass in fact, and takes another chew of her beef. Gets up and goes to the toilet. By the time she comes back, Marah has eaten everything on her plate and Dingo has called for the bill. When Jethro tells her she's got gravy on her cheeks, she giggles so much that she has to lay her head on the table. Dingo says, 'Oh, no,' and makes her drink a cup of coffee before they go. Heat has stormed into the car, filled it up while they've been in the cool of the London Beef-Eater, and it hits them when they open the car doors. Charis is loose and sloppy, being shoved into the car by Marah and not slapping Jethro when he kicks her leg. She winds the window down and leans her head into the air, opens her mouth as Dingo drives and calls out 'aaaaah' on one soft, long note.

Dingo parks directly behind the pavilion. Newly painted blue cement reflects the sun, so that it's hard to see any people at all. Dingo looks at his watch and says, 'Oh, no,' again. He turns around in the front seat. 'Right, how are you feeling, Charis?'

'Rubbish.' Charis's head is still resting on the open window.

'OK. Listen, we've got to go and meet yer mum now. We could just say yer sick and go home, or we could spend some time on the beach. The beach might be good for you, sit in the shade, recover a bit, whaddaya reckon?'

'Orright.' It is more a grunt than a word, falling on to the footpath below Charis's mouth.

Noeline is sitting on a striped beach towel with her back against the pavilion wall. Ice-cream drips down the cone in her hand and on to her fingers. She waves when she sees them, but doesn't stand up. 'How was it, good lunch?'

'Fine, Charis has got a funny tummy, but apart from that, fine. How were the computers?' Dingo kisses Noeline on the lips and takes a lick of her ice-cream.

'Not sure. I'm still not decided. What's wrong, love?' Noeline puts her arm out to Charis, who is sliding down beside her.

'Nothin. Bit sick. Sick and sicker.' Charis leans her head back so that it bounces off the cement wall. Her bottom jaw is loose, so that you can see her tongue flopping about.

Noeline puts her hand on Charis's forehead and looks at her for a moment. Charis starts hiccuping and lays herself flat on the cement. For a second, or even less, Noeline looks puzzled, her face clouding over, a frown shading her eyes. After a moment, quick as water coming in, the clouds go, the sun arrives and

Noeline is bright and sparkling. She eats the last of her ice-cream. 'Who's going for a swim? Dingo and I can sit down here on the sand near Charis. She needs some shade until her belly clears up. Go on, then, you two go in, we'll wave to you from here. I'll come in, in a moment.'

Noeline lays the striped towel on the sand and flicks Dingo's giant yellow beach towel down next to it. She sits down with her back to Charis, hands Dingo the bottle of Coppertan and undoes the strap of her bikini. Her hands entwine with Dingo's as they lie face down, beneath the sun's shimmering heat. Behind them, on the cool cement of the pavilion, Charis rolls over, and groans. From the ocean, from between the flags where Marah and Jethro stand in the waves, glancing up occasionally, she is a small white shape, twisting and turning and wiping her hands over her head.

Twisting and turning and tiny. So tiny you would hardly notice her if you didn't know she was there.

# Charis

Dirt feels like it's worked its way into my pores somehow, in here while I've been sleeping. Me face feels ground down with dirt, me arms feel grainy. They're not – I rub my hands across my face to check, and no brown or black or red comes off on me palms. In the middle of the night I opened the window wide, I thought I would suffocate if I didn't. Cicadas were outside, but I like the noise even when it keeps me awake. Must have been, I dunno, midnight or something. They didn't keep me awake, as it turned out. I knelt up on the bed for a while, with my face against the fly-wire, taking gulps of air as if it was water. Being here, around the witch-mother, around Dingo – it tightens me up, knots me. There must be some kind of sandstorm going on somewhere, though, because it's not just tightness, I do feel as though I've got solid grains lodged in my throat. As if there's a bloody tap-dance going on in there. Water, orange juice, things to wash it away with, that's what I need. Breakfast, even. Food to soothe the suffering soul. Not that I'd expect to find much of interest here in the House of Diets. Surely Jethro must eat like a normal human being, though. Please God.

There's no one in the bathroom when I tap on the door, so I drop my dressing gown on the floor and jump in the shower. At last, a proper shower. Might even be worth the purgatory of being here in order to get it. Water and steam pours down over me and I open me mouth to let the water in, to wash the grains away. They've remodelled the bathroom so that it's all new and white and pseudo-antique fittings. Back in the bad old days, this was a pink bathroom with a plastic bath and a rail for old ladies. Of course, the witch-mother will never be an old lady, not in these glory days of thigh and brain replacements. I don't bother getting dressed when I get out of the shower, I wrap the very glamorous pink towelling gown – left on my bed by the ever-considerate witch – about myself and leave little wet footmarks from the hallway back to the bedroom. Big boobs and bum, tiny feet, that's me. It's amazing I don't fall over – if me bum was any smaller, I probably would topple. Which I think is a perfectly valid argument for eating more cake at every possible opportunity. I drop the pink disaster on the bed and put on the shorts and top from the flight. Wrinkled, but not too smelly.

Silence in the kitchen except for one bloody-minded fly which has managed to sneak in through a briefly opened door. If it weren't for the fact that I hate flies, I would admire the determination of this one to be inside. Stupid, but determined. There's no rich pickings in here, Madame Fly, only bloody cottage cheese and celery. After valuable minutes trying to encourage it to fly through the door when I open it, I start jumping around, swatting it with a clean tea-towel. When it lands on the bench, I manage to flick the tea-towel on top of it. Muted buzzing for a moment and then, nothing. My brains must be still in my suitcase, because I lift the towel up to see why the fly has stopped buzzing. And I'm supposed to be the smart one in this nuclear wasteland which passes for a family. Fly buzzes merrily off, smashing itself joyfully against the wall, the window and the toaster, and I quit. Start hunting for some breakfast which isn't celery. Fortunately, there's some chemical-sweetener-free jam in the cupboard, so I cut some fat slices of bread for toast.

Outside, a car door slams and keys jangle. Footsteps – two sets – come close to the door. If I was ever to be asked to describe the difference between them, which is, I admit, bloody unlikely, I would say that one set of footsteps is quite clumpy, the other is more tottering. Click click of stilettos, that sort of thing. Which means the witch-mother rather than Marah, who never wears heels designed to break her neck. At least on that front she is sensible. What I'd like to do is make myself invisible. To not have to do all the greetings and shriekings which I know will be required of me; to slip sideways from the hugging and touching. Choices: slip under the table, bolt for the door and hide in my bedroom for the next two weeks, or sit here and brazen them out. Brazen wins. The door opens and a pile of boxes is dumped on the floor. Voice off, then Dingo bending down, piling the boxes into his arms, standing up and looking straight at me. Practised look of surprise on his face.

'Hey, yer up and about at last. Howya feelin? You'd collapsed by the time I got back last night. Sorry I didn't get to see ya. Giss a hug, then.' He drops the boxes on the floor again and comes over to me, arms outstretched.

'I'm fine. Still tired. Might go back to bed, come to think of it.' I'm up in an instant, stepping into the kitchen, opening the fridge as if there's something in there I've just realized I need.

Clicking of heels and Mum comes in, *sans* broomstick, but with several plastic bags which she plonks on the table, almost on top of my interrupted breakfast. 'Lingerie for the honeymoon. We're going to Fraser Island, did I tell you? For a fortnight. Feeling better this morning, darling?' She kisses me on the cheek before I've got a chance to duck.

'Lucky you, Noel. I couldn't getter to give me a hug even with a bribe.'

'Oh, Charis, you're always so grumpy when you get off planes. Give Dingo a hug. So, I think we're on top of everything.' She pulls out a list, starts reading from it as if she's mistaken me for someone with a bit of interest. 'Flowers, yes. Cake, yes. Dresses. Now, I've had them run up with your measurements, but, mmm, I think you might have put on some more weight. We've got a fitting this afternoon, just to give her a chance to tighten or loosen. Jethro and Dingo are hiring suits, so that's not a problem. Did Jethro tell you he's giving me away?'

'Mum, I've been here for about five minutes. When would he have told me? I haven't seen anyone this morning, I don't know where Marah is, or Jethro. Why is he giving you away, anyway? You're a grown woman. Jethro is your son, he doesn't own you.'

'Well, someone has to give me away.'

'Says who?'

'Stop it, Charis. Just let everything be nice, for once. Leave things alone. We're going to unpack these things and I'm going to enjoy preparing for my wedding. The fitting's at two-thirty, try and be in a better mood by then, would you? Please? Come on, Dingo, give me a hand upstairs with these.'

Witch-mother clip-clops out of the kitchen, half-staggering under the weight of her bargains, leaving me with my cold toast and a tied-up throat and clenched first and yet again the feeling that, after everything, it's my fault. It always comes back to this, always. When I'm away, I can be clear, I know the story, I know what's true. Here, with everyone in my face saying, 'Stop causing trouble, making noise, being a problem,' I get confused. Start to think they're right, that I am a nuisance, don't know when to leave well enough alone. She – Mum – has a way of tightening her lips, bunching them up so that she looks terribly, terribly hurt. I hate it, I hate her looking like that, small and wounded. And I should be grateful. For the air fare, for anything. My toast is still untouched and I'm practically ready to go and apologize for – what? Opening my mouth when it should stay closed. I'm tired, jet-lagged. That's what I'll say. But then the door swings open again and my heart tightens up, because it's Marah and her weasel and she looks so tired, so thin, so held-in, that I forget about being a good quiet girl and remember the important things. About never shutting up, not until it's time.

Marah is clinging on to Daniel, balancing against him. Her voice is thin. 'Hi. You recovered?'

'What from? Hello, Daniel. Long time blah blah blah.' I stand up to give him a halfish sort of hug. Polite if not enthusiastic.

'Yair, good to see you, Charis. You're looking good. Flight all right? Marah said you were pretty tired when you got in last night.'

'Did she? I'm fine.' I put my hand out to grab hold of Marah, to make contact. 'Did you stay at Daniel's last night?'

'Yair.' She flicks her eyes up at him and it's all I can do to hold back from a big fat puke. 'Amazingly, no calls came through, so I got him all to myself.'

'Will I make some coffee? Daniel? Whaddaya reckon about Marah's show? Bad timing, huh?'

'You mean the college show? Well, it's not like it's open-heart surgery, is it? I mean, no one's gunna die because she's not there. And you're OK about it, aren't you, sweetie?'

173

Marah nods, looking at the floor. She takes a cup of coffee from me. 'Thanks. Yes, exactly. Stop making a fuss. Please, Charis, *please*.'

She's said *please* to me like that before, with that same staring at me from her round green eyes, and I said 'yes' then. I said anything she wanted, I would go along with. But that was ages ago, too long to remember, and I made a mistake, I said the wrong thing, made the wrong promise. So this time, I say nothing. Books are toppled on the bookcase, the bookcase Dad built. Frederick Forsyth, Steven King, Catherine Cookson. Something by Salman Rushdie. Three DIY books, a whole shelf on gardening and another on sailing. One, *Small Dinghies*, has such a battered spine you can barely read the title. 'Remember this? You used to read it all the time. Why don't you sail any more? You used to go over and over the names of the boats. You loved it.' I hold it up, offering it to her.

She takes the book out of me hands, turns it over and looks at the back. 'No, I didn't. I didn't read this, it was Jethro's.'

'I know, but you used to read it. You pinched it off him and he punched you.'

'I didn't. *You* used to read it all the time. You told me the names of boats, that's how I know them.'

'Rubbish, Marah. What about that first time we went sailing? Dingo took you and me. Dunno where Jethro was. Honestly, Daniel, she stood in the boat shed and recited the name of every boat in there. Took ages.'

Marah is shaking her head, her eyes are wide. 'That wasn't me. I hated sailing. I always hated it. First time I went sailing was with Jethro and Dingo and Mother. On a sixteen-footer.'

Daniel is laughing his head off. 'Sisters, hey? You'll have to agree to disagree.'

That boy is so revolting I want to smack his pimply face. And I am not going to agree to disagree, because I am bloody right. 'You did. You came sailing with me and with Dingo, it was on that old VJ of his. Some stupid name. Bloody hell, Marah, I was there.'

'*Ladybait*. That's what it was called. Jethro went to the doctor's or something. He was sick, or Mother was sick, was that it? But it

174

was called *Ladybait*. Definitely. You're right, I do remember that. Not long after Dingo moved in and, that's right, built the bookcase.' She gives me the book. 'But I hated sailing and I never read this book. You were the one into boats. Ask Jethro.'

'Dad built the bookcase. Before Mum kicked him out. What world were you living in?' I'm laughing now, because it's so ridiculous.

'This world, right here. Anyway, it doesn't matter, it's not a big deal, actually. Did Mother tell you we've got a fitting this afternoon?'

'Yair. Are you comin as well, Daniel?'

He shakes his head and puts his coffee-cup down. 'Nope. Gotta be at the hospital at three.'

A smatter of wind shifts in through the window, so that the curtain blows half across Marah. She pushes it out of her face, and the light from the window comes bright on her, so bright that I can't make out her features, only her shape. Blackened by the light behind her. She squints and then the curtain is back in place, but for a moment, she looked like she was on stage. Apart from school, I've only seen her perform twice. Once at drama school and once at the Con. Suddenly, out of nowhere, I want to hear her sing. Ideally, I'd see her as well, on a stage, in full Viking palaver or whatever it is that opera singers wear – all those stupid clothes. Not that I can talk, having whiled away a good deal of my supposedly enlightening/liberating/widening time overseas by traipsing about in French Maid costumes. Opera is bad, but it's better than that.

'Marah? Will you sing a bit from your show?' I'm embarrassed asking her, as if it's a dirty secret.

She laughs. Meant to be a laugh anyway, I assume. Sounds more like a cat choking on a hairball. 'What show? The one at Yale? It's not my show, I'm here, I'm not even in the show.'

'But you were. Daniel, when was the last time you heard her?'

Daniel looks at his watch. This is not unusual, he does this every few seconds. Some kind of nervous twitch. Better than nose-picking or bum-scratching. Maybe. He does a kind of grimace at Marah. 'I'll have to get going in a few minutes. Could

175

do with reading through some journals before I go to the hospital.'

I slap at his arm, to stop him looking at his bloody Rolex, or Swatch, or whatever it is. 'You can spare the time to hear the world's greatest rising young opera star. Medicine won't die without you.'

He looks straight at me, dead straight. 'Maybe not, Charis, but the thing about medicine is that if you don't take it seriously, not only do you not get anywhere, but you do stand a chance of putting someone's life at risk. It's very serious.'

I hold back from attempting to explain to him that whatever Marah is doing is at least as life and death as him and his little plastic needles and urine pots and stethoscopes. Daniel takes himself very, very seriously. Instead, I point to the kitchen clock and say, 'When the big hand is on the six, then you can go. One song. Please, Marah. Otherwise, I'll sing a telegram song and make you both crawl around on the floor. I mean it.'

Marah is finally laughing, loose, not as if she's a cat but as if she's herself. 'OK. I have to warm up first. Go into the lounge room. I'll go and warm up in the bathroom with some steam. Why did they get rid of the piano?' She dumps her cup on the sink and rinses it, then heads for the bathroom.

'Will I go up and get Mum?' I poke my head into the hall.

She stops at the bathroom, her hand on the door. 'No.'

Daniel and I stay sitting at the kitchen table, Daniel desperately trying not to look at his watch, me desperately trying to keep from telling him that he's a wanker. Although he must know that already. Marah's voice bounces around in the bathroom, ooh and aah sounds which slip me right back into living in this house, with Marah's voice floating through from all corners, all the time. And me, I was silent, shut-up, hushed-up. Though Jethro says I was the Noise. He was too young to know where my noise came from, and how I shut up at school so that Marah would shine. Not that I care about that – I'd do it that way again, any second, any day.

Daniel is looking down at the table, and he looks small and weak, as well as merely stupid. He doesn't have a clue and I don't understand at all how Marah shuts herself down to be with

176

him. But then, that's Marah's thing, that shutting down. She's good at it and sometimes, only sometimes, I wish I was as well. He gives up restraining himself and looks at his watch, then smiles at me. 'Looking forward to the wedding?'

'No. I'd be very happy if it was called off and we had a party at Burger King instead. You?'

He shakes his head at me, but doesn't bother asking why, or who, or how. He's not that sort of boy. 'Let's go and sit in the lounge and wait. So, Charis –' he stands up and holds his arm out in front of him, directing me through to the lounge room as if he's a traffic cop – 'what are you thinking of doing with yourself?'

'Sorry?'

'Doing with yourself.' He smiles again as if he's ten years older than me instead of one year younger.

'Listening to Marah, and then getting through the next two weeks without killing anybody and then, back to my mad, busy, social whirl in London.'

Marah calls out from the hallway, her voice slapping the doors. 'OK, I'm ready.'

'I'll do the introduction. Wait for the applause.' I jump up, nearly trip on Daniel's feet, and put on my party voice. 'Ladies and gentlemen, straight from her sell-out American tour, please welcome the one, the only, the truly marvellous, Marah Dell. Yaaaaaaay.'

She stands in front of the bookcase and I can see that she's embarrassed. Her hand is at her throat and she looks at Daniel before she opens her mouth. She doesn't speak, just closes her eyes, takes breath and lets out the first note. I look at Daniel. He's staring out of the window, tapping a finger on his leg, another nervous tic. Marah keeps her eyes closed, it's something about a papa, *O, papà*, she's singing. None of the words mean anything to me – I think it's Italian – but it makes me full and empty at the same time. Marah's face is tilted up, her hands clenched below her throat, and she's got a single tear running down her cheek. *Papà, o, papà*, and her voice is as hard and solid as metal, or – dunno – it's something real, not airy, not invisible. There's one note held for ever and then she goes soft, softer and softer so that the last line is almost a whisper. She could be singing, 'Oh, papa, I need some breakfast right now, anything at all but not those disgusting scrambled eggs you're in the habit of making lately' – in fact, knowing opera, it's likely to be exactly that – but, even so, it makes me want to curl up and weep. On Daniel's lap, if necessary. When she finishes, she sits down at Daniel's feet, quickly and without looking at me. She takes his hand and puts it on her shoulder.

'Thanks. That was beautiful. I wish you were in the show.' I'm whispering, not wanting any other noise to come in. Wanting to say, but not wanting to say: I wish you knew how much you're worth, I wish you knew that.

'That wasn't from *Dido and Aeneas*. I decided to do something else.'

'Why?'

'I wanted to. No reason.'

Daniel claps his hands together, the way dads used to in old American sitcoms. 'Well. She's good, isn't she, Charis? Very good, Marah. Lovely. I'd better get going, get some reading in, still just time.' He stands up and brushes himself down, holds his hand out to help Marah up. 'Have a good fitting, Charis.'

Marah walks with him to the door and I hear the little crisp kiss and the shutting of the door. She comes back in, sits on the floor again. 'We should start getting ready.'

'That was beautiful, Marah.'

She looks up at me, says nothing.

'Do you remember the concerts we used to do as kids?'

She leans forward, rubs at her feet. 'Did we? No, I don't remember that.' She couldn't sound more interested if I'd introduced the subject of Lesser Bills of Parliament 1850–60.

I'm quiet for a second, my head full of Daniel and watch-checking. 'Do you think Daniel appreciates what you do?'

'What do you mean?' Her voice has got her tight little growl in it; I should be warned, but I'm not.

'He never seems very interested in anything but medicine. He never seems very interested in, well, you. When I'm around, anyway.'

She stands up, crackling like bloody starch. 'For God's sake,

Charis, you're always looking for problems, always digging around. Why can't it be *nice*, for once?'

'I'm not looking for problems. I'm only saying what I've noticed. That he doesn't seem to listen. Don't stomp out on me like that. Marah.' I run after her, into the kitchen. 'You don't always have to have a bloke around.'

She turns, looks me fair in the face, says really quietly: 'And you don't have to fix things that are none of your business, and you don't have to hate all men. Whatever it is with you, just drop it. Leave Daniel alone. He's fine. I'm fine. You're the one with the chip on your shoulder. I'm going to have a shower and get changed.' She bristles past me, into the hallway. The bathroom door slams behind her.

Everything I say here is wrong, every syllable from my mouth clutters things up. Not one person in this house thinks I'm sane, not remotely. And I do not hate all men. Only Dingo. I put my hand in my pocket and feel for the scrap of paper. Crumpled and warm, it nestles in my hand, makes a nice rustle. I take it out, smooth it on my lap. Underneath the number, he's written: 'Call for sane talk!!!' I fold the paper, so that only the number is showing. No noise from upstairs, so I go into the lounge and shut the door. I have to sit down on the floor, and I feel like an idiot, but even so I pick up the phone and dial. My breathing mingles with the ringing until they're one. Echoing with possibility.

# Marah

There are three women in blue bridesmaid's dresses, each of them standing on a box. One of them is very fat, in fact I would say obese. I'm surprised, if you want to know the truth, that the bride has asked her to be a bridesmaid, because it just doesn't look good. However much you might want it to, the truth is, it doesn't. An obese bridesmaid is embarrassing, especially in midnight blue puff sleeves and gathered skirt. Poor girl. Someone should tell her. When the bride comes out of the changing room – in what looks like a crinoline skirt – she looks at the three bridesmaids and says, Oh, lovely, the sleeves match exactly, don't they?

The obese bridesmaid looks very uncomfortable, I have to give her that, and the assistant – who is *very* pretty, brown skin and long red nails – says, The blue is a lovely contrast, if you're having blue in your flowers, that would match up and probably pass as your Something Blue.

Charis, sitting next to me on an orange leatherette seat just like mine, says, Oh, bloody hell, spare me the bridal closet, and I slap her on the leg. She has this thing about weddings, Charis. Sometimes I wonder if she's a lesbian.

Mother has been in the alterations room for ages, and the other assistant – the not so pretty one – comes over and asks if we'd like a drink or anything while we wait, and would we like to have a look at some bridal magazines while we're here, because, you never know, it could be our turn next.

Actually, I say, Yes, I would, because you do never know, and of course Charis groans again beside me and says, Why do you get sucked into this, Marah, this whole thing?

There's no point even bothering to reply, not to Charis, not when she's in this rabid mood she gets into, which could be any time. Erratic, that is definitely a word I would use about Charis. Unpredictable is another one. Because she can be perfectly nice, not making any fuss or trouble, going along with whatever is happening. She often is like that, I've seen it. But not at the moment.

There are lovely dresses in *Beautiful Bride*, all the brides look lovely, wrapped up like lovely presents. Beautiful. And what's wrong with that? With wanting to be wrapped up, presented and lovely? There's a special section on Wedding Etiquette and it says that in the case of a second marriage, the Bride may be given away by the son or a close male friend. So that's all right, because Jethro is giving Mother away. It tells you all about the reception as well, who's supposed to speak in what order. Father of the Bride, Best Man, Groom. Charis looks over my shoulder at the etiquette article and points to the bit where it says it's not usual for women to speak at weddings.

Bloody hell, she says, why don't they just put a gag over her mouth and handcuffs on her wrists and be bloody well done with it?

See? Always making a fuss, about silly things. It's not that I don't love Charis, because I do, it's just that I think she needs to be a bit more sensible sometimes. Move on with things. Stop looking for problems.

Charis takes the magazine off my lap and puts it on the little round table between us. Even though I tell her I was reading it and that it's extremely rude to take something off someone's lap just like that.

She leans across, stretches her hand across the little table and grabs my hand. Looks right at me, looks hard at me, and says, She can't marry Dingo, you know she can't.

You would think Charis would have got it through her head by now that I am not the person to have these conversations with. Perhaps Jethro is, I don't know. If she could ever drag him out of his bedroom, maybe he would be interested. But he won't come out of there, hardly ever anyway. Even this afternoon, with us all expecting him to come as well, he stays in his room. Saying no, he can't come, he wants to practise his guitar. The truth is, he'll never get to Indonesia or Thailand, or wherever it is he thinks he wants to go, if he doesn't start applying himself and getting out of his bedroom. Actually, if I think about it, he's been like that since high school. Staying in his room, no friends, no games. Not even football, which he loved as a kid. So, maybe he's not such a good person to talk to either.

Charis is tugging at my hand, putting a bit of strain on it as well, almost hurting. She squeezes it and says, You haven't told her, have you? She's putting quite a lot of pressure on my hand now and I have to ask her to let go.

While I'm trying to rub some life back into my hand, I say, Told her what?

Charis rolls her eyes as if I'm supposed to be some kind of mind-reader and know what she's talking about all the time, and says, Oh, please, Marah.

That's all, just that. So I say, Can I have my magazine back now, please?

And she says, Only if you promise not to fill out the chart of Your Perfect Wedding at the back.

She's lying, of course, because when I pick up the magazine again, I check at the back and there is no chart of Your Perfect Wedding.

Charis is looking down now, not at me, and biting her lip like she's worried or making up her mind. Then she looks at me and says, OK, do you remember when I got drunk for the first time – when we went to the Bogey Hole with Dingo? Do you remember? Mum and Dingo took us to some café place afterwards, Mum must have gone off shopping for a while or something and then, I suppose, she came back, but anyway, Dingo bought me a load of Benedictine and coke, and I was drunk. Remember?

Well, I don't remember at all – why should I? It's Charis's story, not mine, it doesn't sound like it's got anything to do with me and, to tell you the truth, I can't think why she's telling me. So I tell her I don't remember at all, although something in me wants to say, Bacardi, not Benedictine – just like that: Bacardi, not Benedictine. But then, I think that's because I know there's no way anyone would ever order a Benedictine and coke, and where on earth would Charis have heard of Benedictine anyway? She's hardly the most sophisticated person, even now. Obviously, I don't say all of that to Charis, only the bit about I don't remember.

She says, Marah, stop it, stop forgetting.

I honestly don't know what she's talking about, but I have to say that I really don't like it when Charis speaks to me like that. As if she's older than me, wiser. She always did that, before, when we were kids. Played it up, being older, right until I got to high school, and then she stopped. Started being all nicey with me, like she couldn't be bothered being the eldest any more. She kept doing it to Jethro, though. Not that he'd even notice, if you ask me. If you ask me, Jethro doesn't notice anything that goes on around him at all. Before Charis has a chance to go on any more about whatever it is she's going on about, Mother comes out of the alterations room.

Lace falls down from her shoulders in two long strips, falling down her back. She's half-holding her dress up, because she's got no shoes on, but even so, she looks like a proper bride. She's kept her tan and it shows up against the white of the dress. She does a twirl and asks what we think.

Charis says, Why white for the third time?

And Mother says, If you're going to have a wedding, why not do it properly?

Which I have to say I agree with, because I wouldn't see the point in doing it in some old shed dressed in a pair of pyjamas. People do, people do all kinds of strange things. Lots of people get married at the top of the Empire State Building, even though it's nothing much, it's not the best building on the block. But I can see why they'd do that, there's a reason for it. There's not a reason for getting married in a shed, not that I can see. Mother wants to get married in a church this time, because she didn't before – not to Charis's father and not to mine. Who, according to Mother, couldn't even be bothered to turn up in court for the divorce hearing. That's what Mother and Dingo both say – he didn't even bother. It doesn't make sense to me, that, how he could say how much he cared about us, how he could turn up at our door yelling about wanting to see us and then: nothing. There was an injunction against him, quite rightly, too, because he came around once and got all violent for no reason at all and what was Mother supposed to do? Charis always says that he used to phone and write, only we were never told, but that's Charis for you, full of big conspiracy theories. Anyway, you can't blame Mother for wanting to get it right this time, the wedding, everything. I can see why she wants to, that's what I mean.

Mother is twirling around and holding her hair up on top of her head, the way she's going to have it done, still standing on tiptoes. She drops her hair and says, Oh, Marah, I did ask you to sing, didn't I?

I say, NO, you didn't, and I almost yell the no, though I don't mean to, it's just that she hasn't mentioned it and the wedding is so close and I don't think she understands about practice and focus and clarity and intention. I say, Well, I suppose I could do something from, say, *The Marriage of Figaro*, and Mother says, Oh, no, we want 'Ave Maria', of course, you've sung it before, at school. What I don't say is that of course I've sung it, everyone on this side of a piano has sung it, she might as well ask me to sing 'Twinkle Twinkle'. But I don't say that, I smile like I'm so pleased, and I say, Well, of course I will.

And out of nowhere, out of nothing, I'm looking at her and she starts to look faded in front of me, like I'm losing my sight, or it's gone dark. She's saying how Dingo has waited far too long to ask her and isn't it about time, and my throat is getting tighter and tighter, for no reason. Maybe the air-conditioning is on; that can play havoc with sensitive throats.

Charis puts on a quiet, it-just-occurred-to-me kind of voice and says, Why did you leave Dad, anyway?

Mother stops twirling and I stop rubbing at my throat, because it really is silly, Charis bringing things like this up right now, today. Charis keeps talking, as if she hasn't said anything out of place, saying, What makes you think the same thing won't happen with Dingo once you marry him?

Mother speaks very softly, not wanting to draw attention, because the blue bridesmaids are wandering in and out, looking at garters and shoes and little baskets. Mother says, Charis, I don't know what the problem you have with Dingo is, but you'd better get over it, it's really time you got on with things and stopped blaming everyone else for all your problems. I for one have had enough.

Charis raises her voice – I would say she does it deliberately – saying, I'm not talking about blame, I'm talking about you for once answering my questions or, shock, horror, actually listening to me.

Mother says, If you were going to be like this, why did you even bother coming home?

And Charis says, Because you didn't give me any choice, the same way you didn't give Marah any choice, the same way you never gave us any choices, because all that matters is you getting what you want.

Mother has pulled her lips in and the assistant is looking over in an embarrassed way. I suppose you could say that Mother hisses at Charis – it's certainly a whisper but very, very sharp and piercing – she hisses, As far as I can see there is only one person here who is behaving like a spoilt brat, and for the record, I left Joe because he had us constantly in debt. Every time I came home from work, he had bought another hi-fi, CD player or video camera on hire purchase. I left him, Charis, because if I didn't, I would no longer have been able to feed you children. Happy? And I fell in love with Dingo because he was responsible, an adult, and he was prepared to help me be responsible for all of you. Not that it is any of your business *at all* and I think the best thing is for you and Marah to sort out the fitting for your own dresses because I'm going to get very angry if I stay here with you. I'll see you at home. You can get the bus, you're both big girls.

By the time she finishes, her voice has risen above a hiss and both of the assistants have edged closer, trying to get in on the gossip. Mother has tears trickling down her face and I feel so sorry for her, I can't bear it. I put my hand out to her and she says, Leave it alone, Marah, all our nerves are frayed. She holds the dress up and marches back into the fitting room and Charis and I sit on the orange chairs for ages not looking at or talking to each other. After a while, Mother comes out of the dressing

185

room wearing her jeans and carrying a shopping bag. She doesn't look at either of us, but stops and talks super-brightly to the assistant. I can't hear most of what she says, although I'm trying, but I do catch some words: jet-lag, busy, time, children.

The red-nailed assistant comes over after Mother has gone and asks if we're ready to be fitted. We go through to a large cubicle, more like a small room. There are two deep red dresses hanging up, a solid satin with chiffon overskirts. They look lovely. My throat is still tight and I'm embarrassed about Mother walking out like that, worried that the assistant might think we have public fights and things all the time. Not that this was like a fight, but Charis was definitely raising her voice, there's no getting around that. I smile at the assistant and try to think of something light to say. As it turns out, I don't really need to because she's just lovely. She tells us her name is Karen and that Mother had to guess at the sizing of the dresses but chose a colour which she thought would complement us both and Karen can see that she made the right choice. She asks us to slip the dresses on while she pops out and gets the seamstress to do the final pinning. Charis starts undressing before the assistant has even closed the curtain, just dropping her top on the floor as if she doesn't care. She looks at me and says, I'm sorry about Mum walking out, are you OK? I tell her I am, of course I am, but that I think she should stop making a fuss all the time, can't she try harder? It's upsetting, I want a quiet time, that's all. Really I expect her to start an argument with me, but she doesn't, she just says, Oh, I know you do, I know it's hard for you. Anyway, my throat is feeling like I've swallowed dust, so I don't really want to keep talking about something which has already happened and doesn't need such a big fuss made of it, not if you ask me. So I take off my dress and hang it on the coat-hanger and pull the chiffon dress over my head.

Karen the assistant is right – the colour is good for both of us. We stand next to each other in the mirror and I can see that our cheeks look bright. My dress is too long and Charis's is too tight. The seamstress taps on the wall outside the curtains and says, May I? She's got a Greek accent and when she comes in I can see that she is Greek, dark hair, white teeth, all of that.

Yes, she says, I will nip this up, no problem at all. She looks at Charis's dress and says, It's too tight under the arms, that's all, you need a size sixteen, which will be too big, but I will nip it in.

Charis doesn't seem at all fazed by having to wear a size sixteen, she just says, OK, no problem, will it take long, though? I hate standing around in dressing rooms. Then she smiles at me as if nothing has happened and says, The dress looks lovely on you, Marah, but I'm going to find this hard going, I don't know if I can do it.

Oh, I say. Not knowing what else to say; how would I? Not really knowing why she's saying it, what she's saying it about and anyway getting distracted by Karen the assistant coming back in with a size sixteen for Charis, and the seamstress sticking a pin in my leg. When Charis puts the sixteen on, it looks lovely, although it really is a bit baggy.

One strange thing is that the seamstress, when she's pinning the seam on Charis's dress, says, Such a lovely figure. As if she means it, too, not as if she's just being polite. Which is a nice thing for Charis, I suppose, although if I were her, I would think that it was just to make me feel better for wearing a size sixteen.

After we change back into our clothes and Karen puts the dresses in their plastic covers, Charis asks if I want to walk with her to the train station. I tell her I don't, that I'll get a bus and see her at Mother's house. She hugs me outside the shop – SOFIA'S BRIDAL WALTZ it says above the window; I didn't notice that when I came in, even though it's neon – and she says, Take care on the way home, I love you, Marah. Playing the big sister again, but I'm sure it's out of guilt for making Mother walk out like that. I don't watch her walk around the corner, although I have to stop myself turning around. I walk up to the main road, and cross over without pressing the button at the lights. Knots are in my stomach, thinking about Mother, about the tears on her face, about her walking out like that, leaving. And at the same time, even while I'm hating thinking about all of that, I'm thinking about when I marry Daniel, what I'll wear. Long and simple and elegant, like the new Caroline Kennedy, who is, I think, the epitome of elegance. I'd have my hair tied back like hers as well. What I realize then is that I want to get married in America,

187

where I know who I am, not here in this no-history place of disappearing. That's what I realize. Even thinking all that, though, about America and no-history and Caroline Kennedy, I can't get the picture of Mother walking out with her shopping bag to go away.

There's no sign of a bus, not as far as I can see down the road, and there's a newsagent's a block down the road. I start thinking that maybe if I take Mother a copy of *Homes Beautiful* or *Your Wedding*, she'll calm down, cheer up. There's an old woman behind the counter in the shop and I kneel down to look through *Your Wedding*. There's a *She* there as well, and I open that too, start flicking through, just to pass the time. 'Best Friend Jealousy', with pictures of two girls with their backs to each other; 'Quick-Fix Beauty – Three Minutes to the Perfect You', all about using lip-liner and eye-liner to look like blush, eye-shadow and foundation, quite clever really. 'He Stole my Innocence: The Teacher Who Went Too Far', a photo of a man getting into a car with his face blacked out, on the next page a picture of a school playground. I think it's a bit much, all this making people scared. I snap the magazine shut and stand up to buy just *Your Wedding*. The old woman smiles at me and says, Anything else? Before I know what I'm about, I'm saying, Yes, please, a family block of chocolate. Then, in case she thinks it's all for me, I buy three cans of lemonade as well. I put them all in my bag except the lemonade. Outside, away from the shop, I throw the lemonade in the bin.

When the bus comes, I sit up the back like a schoolgirl. On the back seat, but wedged against the window, staring out. My fingers feel into my bag, to the chocolate block, and I think, Maybe I'll have one piece, or maybe one row. So I open it, still with my hands in my bag, still staring out the window, and I break off what feels like one row. It's gone in a second and everyone on the bus is looking straight ahead, not looking at me. The second row goes too fast as well, and I pull the whole block out of my bag and unwrap it completely. I keep my face pressed to the window, holding the whole chocolate block up to my mouth and eating it like a banana. All the time I'm eating it, I'm thinking how maybe I'll get another block when I get off the bus

188

and maybe I'll get a hamburger after that, who knows? There's nothing else in my head, nothing else anywhere except me and my mouth and this big chocolate block which is gone way too soon, way before I finish the bus ride. Gone so soon that I have to sit until the Windsor Heights stop with an empty wrapper in my hands and a pit of disgust in my stomach and, I'm sure, a brown streak around my mouth, even though I wipe and wipe and wipe at it, and tears, tears, tears are running down my face. Just like Mother.

# The Yale Daily News, Spring Term

## Review: Dido and Aeneas

Yale School of Music, dir. Leisha Degrant
Reviewed by Shona-Marie Holt

From the moment the audience is ushered into the auditorium it is clear that we are in for a special experience. Rather than the expected closed curtain and hushed audience, we are greeted by a bustling stage – stage right, someone lies eating grapes, whilst on the left, three men are in deep counsel. Servants wander about, courtiers read and chat and play a strange kind of board game – perhaps a game of fate. For it is fate which is the central theme of this opera of Purcell's. It tells the story of Dido, Queen of Carthage, who falls in love with the man destined to found Rome – Aeneas. Her own destiny is for ever changed by her love for him, and it is the tragedy of this that the opera explores. This production is visually sumptuous and quite modern, directed by the internationally renowned Leisha Degrant. The students have obviously blossomed under her experience.

When the audience are settled and the house lights dimmed, Queen Dido enters, and we are entirely in the hands of the highly polished cast. Dido, played with stunning colour by Elisabeth Rhose, enters sorrowfully, with her assistant Belinda (Janie James) behind her. The palace springs to action, servants begin to look as if they've been busy all along and the courtiers rush to get a little attention from the queen. The lighting is rich and luscious, as are the voices, although this reviewer found Janie James's vocal flourishes a little overbearing. Elisabeth Rhose does deserve special mention, as she stood in at the last minute for Marah Dell, who had to leave the country for a family emergency.

To some extent, the real stars are the witches. Rather than a cave, Degrant has set the witches' lair in a bedroom, covered with pop posters and lit with brightly coloured candles – perhaps a comment on supposed 'sisterhood'? Collette Kane is marvellous as the head witch, dancing about with joy at the thought of bringing Dido down. Her voice is rich and fruity, and she hints at an enormous range. Gerald Cotes as the first sailor is predictably confident, although lacking his famed mother's delicate control.

As the action begins to draw to a climax – Aeneas's fate calling him to Rome, Dido's despair leading to her death – the lighting changes to suggest flames. This is masterfully done, so that the entire auditorium becomes lit with a flickering gold and red light, until the audience seems to be part of the tragedy, engulfed in the mock-bonfire. It is with this background, this lighting, that Aeneas attempts a reconciliation with Dido. But no, she tells him he is right to pursue his fate, for she could not live with him knowing he had ever thought of leaving her. How many women could echo her sentiments! As Aeneas leaves the stage, the flames get higher and the chorus flick strips of gold silk across the stage, a beautiful and moving effect.

This is a marvellous evening's entertainment, and it is well worth supporting fellow students. For those who are not naturally fans of opera, remember it's very short, leaving plenty of time for coffee afterwards, or a night of revelling at Moray's, where you can choose to remember Dido, 'but ah! forget (her) fate'.

*The Kiss*

# You May Kiss the Bride

The truth is that it's been ages, ages and ages, with Charis in the bathroom, not even the sound of a shower going. Charis, who normally leaves the door unlocked and wanders in and out with her blue towel around her. Marah has been banging on the door for minutes, seconds, hours, and still no noise from Charis. You would think she had climbed out of the bathroom window, if you didn't know better, if you didn't know how much Charis hates to be uncomfortable. Charis would never climb anywhere. This is the first morning, the first morning ever, when Marah has not been able to saunter into the bathroom while Charis is in there. Although it's quiet, as if no one is even in the bathroom, it's obvious Charis hasn't left, hasn't slipped out somehow, because the toilet has flushed and taps have been turned on and off. Now, though, there is no noise at all from beyond the door.

'Charis. Let me in. I'm busting. Whaddaya doing anyway?' Marah kicks at the door, not hard enough to dent or damage, only a sulky bash which would make no difference to anyone.

There is the sound of a cabinet door slamming and a muffled 'Go away.'

'Carn. I'm gunna wee on the floor.'

Jethro shambles out of his bedroom, stops and gazes at Marah. 'What's wrong?'

'Charis won't let me in the bathroom. She's locked it. I have to wee.'

Jethro snorts, a small and deliberate noise. 'Yer gunna have to wee in the garden. Water the flowers.'

'Get lost, ya pig.'

'At least I'm a dry pig. Oink.'

'Not if I wee on ya.' Marah runs towards him, making rushing water sounds.

'Err, get out, ya gross-pants.' Jethro backs away, heading back to his bedroom.

Marah leaves her post and, legs half-crossed, hobbles into the kitchen. 'Mum, Charis won't let me in the bathroom. She's been in there for ages and I have to wee and she's locked the door and everything.'

Noeline looks at Dingo, tosses her head. 'Looks like Charis has finally turned into a teenager. It's all downhill from here.'

Dingo laughs and tilts a glass of orange juice to his mouth, holds it there, sucking the last of the liquid out. When the glass is dry, he pulls his chair back and picks up Noeline's breakfast bowl. 'She'll come out in her own time, doncha reckon? Anyway, love –' he kisses Noeline on the head – 'I gotta go.' He picks up his jumper, lying across the back of the chair. As he opens the door, he calls back over his shoulder, 'Ya might have to kick the door down, Marah. I'm sure Jethro will help ya.' The door slams loudly behind him.

Marah prods at Noeline. 'Mum, go and tell her to get out of there.'

'Give her another five minutes, and then if she's not out, I'll come and give her a boot. OK? I just need a chance to get everything together for school.'

Marah stomps back to her post outside the bathroom door. Bangs on the wall. 'You've got one minute to let me in or Mum's coming.'

'Who just left then? Was that Dingo? Has he gone to work?' Charis's voice is masked, but close, as if her head is against the wall, listening closely. Let's say her head is there, leaning against the wall inside the bathroom. Her face is red and wet and her ear is pressed so tight to the wall that perhaps it hurts. It might be like this, or it might be that she is on the other side of the bathroom, maybe even sitting on the toilet seat, picking at her toe-nails the way she does. Throwing her voice. Making herself sound big.

'Yair. He's just left. What's it got to do with anything anyway? Let me in, Charis, Oh.'

The door swings open and Charis is standing with one hand on the handle, the other clutching at her nightie. She's got her towel across her shoulders as if it's a cape and her hair is wet, so there's no doubt that she's showered. Yet somehow, newly cleaned and pinked up, she has changed back into her nightie, which she is clutching tightly around her self, her arms crossed across her chest. Marah, hopping up and down with desperation though she is, has to ask, 'Why have you got yer nightie on?'

'Forgot to take me dressing gown into the shower.'

'So? What's wrong with yer towel?' Marah has almost forgotten her need to wee.

Charis peers around her as though she is a super-spy. 'I'll tell ya later.'

There is, of course, nothing to say to that except, 'Get out so I can wee.'

Later, walking to school, with Jethro tailing behind, kicking his bag from side to side and dawdling like mad, Charis takes hold of Marah's hand. Walks along like that for about three blocks, swinging Marah's hand as if that is nothing strange or babyish. Jethro stops kicking his bag about and calls out, 'Are you two lezzos?' which is a new word he's learnt that week from Shaun Watson. Charis drops Marah's hand and runs back down the street after him, getting as far as the piano-shaped house on the corner of Buckingham Avenue before she tackles him. Holding his hands over his head, Charis calls for Marah to come and tickle him and Jethro laughs so much he nearly wets himself. When they get to the primary-school gates, Jethro bolts inside as if he's a feral cat, calling out that he doesn't want to be seen with his lezzo sisters. Charis says she'll get him later, he'd just better look out, and it is only then, as Charis is turning away to head off to the high school, that Marah remembers. 'Why did you have your nightie on? You were gunna tell me later.'

Charis crosses her arms over herself so that her rucksack puckers up at the back. 'Nothin. It was no reason. Forget it. I'll see ya this arvo.'

'But you said there was somethin to tell me later.'

'It was just to shut ya up. I've gotta go. See ya.'

At lunchtime, in the playground, when Jethro calls out,

'You're a lezzo,' to Marah, she runs over and punches him fair in the face. After lunch, Mrs Bland has a special meeting with Class Six and announces that they are to have a dance, just for them, as they are the seniors of the school and this will be their last year as South Windsor Heights Primary students. They will be expected to behave like young ladies and gentlemen and refreshments will be provided, as will a DJ. When Jethro and Marah walk home together – without Charis, because the high school finishes way later than South Windsor Heights Primary – Jethro says he's sorry for calling her a lezzo. When they get home, Marah puts a pack of frozen peas on his nose, still swollen from where she punched him, and tells him about the dance and how they are to behave like ladies and gentlemen. Jethro wiggles about the lounge room going, 'Oooh, how dooo yoooo doooo, young lady? May I have this dance?'

When Charis gets home, Marah is dancing to Culture Club, twirling around with her arms out. She yells over Boy George, 'We're having a blue-light disco. Only Class Six is allowed to go.'

Charis turns the record down. 'When's it gunna be? We never had a dance in Class Six. We didn't get anything, not even a muck-up day. Got a lecture about responsibility and trying our hardest, that was all.'

'It's next Friday night. We've gotta bring a permission slip home tommorra.'

Jethro mock-waltzes into the lounge, holding an invisible partner in his arms. 'Ooo, darling, yoou dance divinely.'

Marah sticks her foot in his path. 'Get out, Moronoid.'

'Don't have to. I live here just as much as you.'

'Well, get out anyway.'

'I'm dobbing when Mum gets home.'

'Good.'

But when Noeline gets home, Jethro doesn't dob at all. It is clear from the way Noeline drops her briefcase in the hallway and then drops herself on to the lounge that she is in no mood for dobbing – not from anybody. She says that they are to have a new phone number – again – as of next week, because of all the Mr Nobody calls and that, for the time being, they are to keep doing the usual, letting only Dingo or Noeline answer the phone.

This is for everybody's protection. Dingo comes in half an hour after Noeline and she asks him to get her a gin and massage her feet, and announces to everyone that there will be take-away Chinese for dinner unless anyone can be bothered to cook, because she certainly can't. No one else can, either, but the lure of Chinese take-away is greater than anything which could be offered at home.

'Sweet-and-sour pork and honey prawns and prawn crackers, carn, Mum, sweet-and-sour pork.' Jethro has forgotten his dancing lady, is dancing up and down himself now, so that Marah is forced to tell him to go to the toilet if he needs a wee so badly.

'Not honey prawns, Mum. We always get what Jethro wants. 'Cashews and braised beef. *Please*. And sweet-and-sour chicken not pork.' Charis raises her face to Noeline. 'I'm the eldest and I never get to choose.'

'Liar. You always choose. You always get what you want and stay out. We don't get anything, any rights or anything, just cause we're younger.' Marah shuffles closer to Jethro, joining his team.

'You got to have a watch when you were ten. I had to wait until I was twelve. You both get it easy. You do. They do, Mum.'

Noeline puts her hands over her ears. 'Quiet, the lot of you. For goodness sakes. I've had to listen to screaming children all day. The last thing I want to do is continue the torture at home. Right: everyone can choose one, *one*, dish. OK?'

'Someone will have to choose fried rice and I bet it ends up being me.' Charis screws up her face at Marah.

Noeline's face creases and for a moment looks pale. She half-closes her eyes and her body droops. When she speaks again, it is barely a whisper, as if the words – any words – are an effort to squeeze out through the exhaustion. 'No one will have to choose fried rice. We'll get fried rice as an extra dish and we'll eat left-overs for the rest of the week.' She tips her drink back and sighs. 'Please don't go on any more. Just once, just this once, can't you make it a bit easy for me?' She has never looked so tired.

After Dingo heads off to the Chinese with Jethro, Noeline asks Marah for a pillow and lays back on the lounge with her arm dangling on the floor. Marah sits on the floor waiting for her to open her eyes and move again. Minutes and minutes go by and Noeline still hasn't moved, her breathing is slow and deep. Marah pulls at her hand. 'Mum, we're havin a dance. Next week. You have to sign a petition form.'

Noeline shifts a little and says, 'How nice,' as if she is having a dream.

'I've got nothin to wear, not really.'

'Borrow something from Charis. Go and ask her now. Call me when tea's ready. Go on.' Noeline's hand twitches, as if a fly has landed there.

Charis's door is shut. Marah taps, first as soft as a whisper, to which there is no response. She puts her mouth next to the door and calls: 'Charis? Can I come in?'

'Whaffor?' Charis's voice sounds as if it is coming through a pillow.

Marah pushes the door open. 'I want to borrow somethin to wear to the dance. Mum said I can. Whaddaya doin?'

Charis is lying on her back, cuddling her pillow. 'Nothin. Whaddaya wanna wear?'

'Maybe yer leather skirt? And that white puffy top.'

'No way. Ya can't wear me leather skirt.'

'The puffy top?'

'Here.' Charis is pulling hangers from her wardrobe: the puffy top, a red gypsy blouse, a ra-ra skirt, her special buffalo-girl hat. 'What about the white top with me ra-ra skirt? Or –' she opens a drawer, scuffles around in it – 'me velvet straight skirt. Garn, try it on.'

Marah slips the ra-ra skirt on under her school uniform, which for once Noeline hasn't asked her to change out of. Attempting to squeeze the top on by putting her arms inside the tunic and wriggling herself around gets her knotted up inside the blue gingham. She pulls the tunic off and crosses her arms in front of her chest, then makes a grab for the top. Tries to ease it on in one go, without uncrossing her arms.

'You're gunna need a trainer bra soon Marah. And that top doesn't go with that skirt at all. I dunno. Try it with the black straight skirt.'

'As long as you don't tell me I need trainer knickers.' Marah's face is pink, although her voice is light.

'It's nothin to worry about. It's nice. Don't get thingy about it.'

'I'm not.'

'Good. Put the skirt on.'

Marah gives up the wriggling-hiding method and pulls the ra-ra skirt off, drops it on the floor. The straight skirt is loose on her, leaving wrinkles around the hips and thighs. 'I look like the saggy-baggy elephant.'

'OK – I've got it.' Charis jumps from the bed in a superwoman leap and lands at the wardrobe door. 'Me white dress. Go on, try it.'

The white ruffles and the saggy-baggy skirt fall to the ground. It is while Marah is holding the dress up, turning it round in front of her, that the bedroom door creaks softly open. Dingo comes right in, right into the bedroom, right near Marah in her knickers and nothing else. He looks straight at her, but not at her face. She pulls the dress close to herself.

'Sorry, girls, I just wanted to let you know we had the dinner. When you're ready.' He is still looking at Marah.

Charis does the superwoman leap again, so that she is standing in front of Dingo. 'Knock. Knock on the door. Don't ever come in here without knocking. No, just don't ever come in here. You are never allowed in my room. Go away. Go on, get out. Get.' Louder and louder, until she's yelling so hard that Noeline calls out from the living room to ask what all the fuss is. Dingo calls back that he forgot to knock on Charis's door and has accidentally invaded her privacy.

'Sorry, girls. I'll put yer dinner out.' The door closes behind him.

Leaving the dress, Marah pulls her tunic back on. She looks at Charis perched on the end of the bed. 'Ya didn't have to yell so hard, Charis. Mum'll be in a foul mood now.'

'I don't care. It's the second time today.'

'Whaddaya mean?'

Standing up almost as if she will creak or break, Charis starts hanging her clothes back up. 'Nothin. Ya can wear me leather

201

skirt, if it fits ya. With your black off-the-shoulder top it'd look good.'

'Thanks.' Marah folds up the saggy-baggy straight skirt and hesitates for a moment. 'Are you all right? Are ya comin for dinner?'

'Spose.'

Tin-foil trays clutter up the middle of the table. Noeline is piling up the plates, one by one. She doesn't look up when Marah and Charis sit down. 'That noise was a bit uncalled for, Charis. Dingo was just calling you to dinner. I appreciate – we both appreciate – the fact that you need your privacy, but I think it's a bit much biting Dingo's head off when he's asking you to come to dinner. You can hardly expect to him to skulk around in the hallway.'

'Marah was getting changed.'

'Was she? That's still no reason to start yelling like a common fishwife.' Common is bad, a dirty word to Noeline.

Jethro has already started eating, stuffing his prawn crackers down without bothering to chew. He pours extra sweet-and-sour sauce on his rice, until there is a pink-red sea on the edges of his plate. Charis eats quickly, gulping down honey prawns and satay, keeping her eyes on her plate and her mouth full of food.

'So, Marah, what about this dance?'

'Nothing. I'm wearing Charis's leather skirt.'

'Did you hear about this, Dingo? Marah's class are having a blue-light disco. No juniors allowed, apparently.'

'Blue-light, hey? Will they have cops to keep an eye on you lot?'

Marah shakes her head. 'Only teachers.'

'Anyway –' Noeline strokes Dingo's hand – 'how did you go today? Did you manage to get hold of the gear for re-wiring?'

'Yep. Give me twenty-four hours and we'll have piped music through the whole house, and the yard as well. Great for barbies. I'll tell ya what it made me start thinkin, though.' He reaches across for more chow-mien. 'We should stick a pool in. I could do the landscaping and the design, get it all laid. Whaddaya reckon?'

Jethro spits a prawn cracker on to his plate. 'That'd be excellent. We could have pool parties.'

'I don't know, I'm not sure about suburban pools. Lots of work and, well, I'm not sure. Pass the sweet-and-sour sauce, Jethro.'

'Carn, Mum, a pool would be great.' Jethro grabs at the sauce, almost throws it at Noeline. Big slurps of it land on Marah, spreading across the top of her tunic.

'Thanks, dumb-boy. That's the only uniform I've got clean for tomorrow.'

'I've got it.' Dingo is up, wringing the Chux-wipe at the sink. 'Sit back.' He pushes Marah back in her chair and dabs at her chest with the cloth. 'Yair, no worries, it's comin off.'

His hand wipes at the top of the uniform while Marah stares at the table. Small traces of pink sauce remain and even though Marah says, 'No, leave it,' Dingo keeps rubbing at the stain. Noeline says she'll get some soda water, that might do it, and goes to the fridge. Marah keeps looking down at the table, not making a sound, not looking at Charis, not looking at anyone. Even when Dingo's hand stops wiping the stain and wipes down, right across her breasts, right across where she is newly budding out, where Charis tells her she needs a training bra. Even when his hand opens, so that his palm instead of the cloth skims where the trainer bra should be, even then Marah makes no sound. When Noeline brings the soda water back, the stain is almost gone. Except for a small, pinkish streak. Which matches exactly the flame which is shooting across Marah's face. Deep and red, like a sunset just that moment before everything goes dark.

# Charis

Once again, I've managed to avoid having to speak to anyone over breakfast. I'm not good at early morning chit-chat at the best of times, but surrounded by wedding-mad lunatics, I run out of words. Bloody wish they'd run out of words. How long can one grown woman talk about the relative value of white stockings and blue garters? My mother didn't have enough dolls to play with as a little girl, or maybe she had too many. Perhaps some mad aunt gave her a lifetime supply of bloody bride dolls and she got the habit. You would think that by now, the third time, she'd think there was just a little bit of irony in the old till-death-do-us-part routine, but no. She has no sense of irony. Witches don't. They have to sign a statement when they join the wicked-witches-of-the-West clan swearing to trade in their irony for something more useful, like a pointy hat. Hence the witch-mother last night, spending at least an hour talking about signing the register, will the organist play properly, blah blah blah. No wonder Jethro never comes out of his room. No wonder Dad gave up.

I'm rinsing my breakfast bowl when Marah whistles past me with a towel around her, sun-screen in her hand, sun-glasses perched on her head. Although it's obvious where she's going, what she's doing, I ask her anyway. Trying to be friendly, to be easy, to be *nice*. Because I don't like being the ogre, the problem, the loud-mouth. And I didn't ask for the job, I was handed it on a rusty platter. I've decided to make an effort, for the sake of something or other. Make an effort to be peaceful, to make chit-chat, to not raise nasty subjects, to keep my mouth shut. After all, I don't have to stay here. I can divorce them when I get home. Home. That confuses me, thinking of London as home, when all the time away I've thought: Australia equals home, home equals Australia. Not specifying where in Australia, or what. Not that I've seen outside of New South glorious Wales. Now, here I am, here, wanting to be away, wanting home. Not knowing, suddenly, where home is. It isn't here, I know that.

Saint Charis is here, and I've got wings. Jethro is, as usual, in his room. Supposedly practising guitar, but he never plays it to anyone, and I never hear any noise of any kind coming from his room. When I tap on his door, he grunts, which I take as a 'come in' rather than a 'get away'. It's a friendly sort of grunt. Dark mouldiness swims up from inside his room when I open it. Jethro is lying on the bed, staring at the ceiling. The sickly sweet smell of a just-finished joint hangs in the air. Air being an overstatement.

'I just wondered if you wanted a coffee or anything? I'm making some, that's all.' I have to squint to see his shape on the bed.

'Nah. I'll come out in a sec.' He doesn't move, not even a twitch. When did that boy disappear? As if I don't know.

So. Stage one of Saint Charis: poor results, but not disastrous. There's iced water in the fridge, so I pour it into a nice glass jug and cut up some lemon slices. Put it on a tray with two glasses and nearly fly bum over boob when I shove the back door with my foot. Marah is lying on a bath-sheet, her arm above her face and the straps of her one-piece pulled down to under her arms. She looks up when I kick the door. Ice clinks against the jug and I feel as if I've turned into Alice in the *Brady Bunch*. Have to restrain myself from calling out, 'Cookies, kids!'

'Brought you some iced water. Here.' I sit down on the grass beside her, pour her some water and hand her the glass.

'Thanks.' She sits up and takes a sip. 'Mother's going in to pick up the dresses and have a preliminary hair appointment today. She asked if we wanted to have a meeting with the stylist as well.'

'I'll just brush me hair on the day.'

'You can't.' The sun has got to her, making her voice slow and lazy. 'So do you want a meeting first, or not?'

'I'm meeting someone in the city.'

'Who?'

'Umm, someone I met on the plane and got chatting to. Anyway, what are you gunna do?'

She wipes her hand on the glass, then across her face. 'Don't know. This heat is amazing, isn't it? It's not even summer.' She looks over at the garden bed. 'They should have put a pool in here, there's plenty of room.'

'Dad was going to, once. He tried to talk Mum into it and she wasn't having any of it. Got as far as having the pool guys come round and do measurements. We should have insisted.'

Marah's eyes have got the glazed look she gets when I start talking about way back when, before. 'Don't know. I don't remember it ever being discussed. I don't think I do. Dad might have done that, I just don't remember. It mustn't have been important. I'd remember if it was important.'

'Ya reckon? I'm not convinced.'

The door bangs again and the witch-mother herself appears with an armful of magazines – *Best Wedding Looks for You and Your Broomstick*, no doubt – a towel over her shoulder, a teensy eensy bikini and her endlessly brown skin. 'Is this the sun-worshippers meeting?' She does a little hopwalk across the lawn, as if there are bindis, but there aren't, they'd never survive the weed-killer. She plonks herself down on the other side of Marah. 'Never too late to catch some last-minute tan. Can't be too thin or too brown.'

I'm still working on niceness, so I don't tell her she should try telling that to a starving Somali teenager. Instead, I pour her some water. 'What happened about having a pool in here. Wasn't there a plan for it, years ago? Pool guys measuring up and stuff.'

'Thanks. Oh, that's lovely and cold, just what I need. Well, I don't know, Dingo wanted to put one in and I thought it would just be too much work. Who would have looked after it when you all disappeared? I'd be stuck now cleaning out slime.'

'Dad wanted to do it, didn't he? Not Dingo.'

She looks straight at me. 'Joe wouldn't have been able to

organize a pool rep to come here or anywhere else. Sorry, love, definitely Dingo.'

Marah gives a little half-jump, the kind you do when you're drifting off to sleep and dream you're falling down a hole. You do a little jump and it wakes you up.

'You all right?' Mum shifts so that she's on her side.

'Yes. Nothing. I'm fine.'

'Anyway, Jethro would clean it. If you got one now, he could clean it. He doesn't look like he's ever going to leave the house and it would at least get him out of his room.' I don't really care who did or didn't plan to put the pool in, but I'm starting to think it would be nice to have one here. In case I do come back to visit. Also, I do wonder about Jethro. 'Do you think he's depressed?'

'Who? Jethro? Of course not. Pass me the sunscreen, Marah.'

'He never leaves his room.'

'He's practising. For goodness sakes, Charis, don't start.'

'I'm not starting anything. The boy never leaves his room and I don't hear any practising going on.'

'Leave it alone. He's got no reason to be depressed, he's fine.' Witch-mother lets out a huge groan which, I know, translates as, Bloody hell, what did I do to deserve this? Which, if she said those words, would be great, because I could tell exactly what she's done to deserve this.

But because it's just a groan, all I can do is say, 'Have you got a train timetable? I've got to go into Central.'

'They're every hour on the hour. Forty minutes to get there. You're not coming to the stylist, then?' She manages to make everything she says sound like an accusation. Which I thought was pretty much my speciality.

'I'm happy with whatever you decide, or to brush my hair and go as I am. Whatever. It's your wedding.' I've gone into dangerous territory on the 'Jethro-is-depressed' front, so I'm trying to swing things back to Mr-Nice-Charis.

'Yes. It is.'

The station is smaller than I remember it, but then all of Windsor seems small. Strange, too, a strange coupling of spread-out gum trees and little English bungalows. All the streets are named after places in the home counties: Surrey Road, Reigate Place, Richmond Drive. Even this train station somehow looks like a model of an English village station, complete with pub planted across the road. On the train there's a *Sydney Morning Herald* on the seat near me, and I try to read it. All about people whose names I don't know, and endless articles about the Olympics. There's a train-line map above my seat, with pictures of the all-new, all-shining Olympic railway. I've only been away three years, but it feels like a whole different country. After I read the Arts section and the comics, I chuck it on the floor and spend the time staring out of the window instead. Trying not to think of my sad-mad family, or to think of Elgin and whether meeting up with him really is such a good idea after all. Whether he really can offer me sane talk, and whether I really want it. Having someone to say 'I think Jethro's depressed' to without them jumping down my throat, that would be good. That's all.

It's not supposed to be summer, but the heat is rising off the road so that once I've got off the train, manoeuvred my way through the ticket barriers, passed the taxi rank and crossed the road, my hair is already sticking to my face and my back feels wet. I have to ask someone where Glebe Road is and they look at me like I'm a country-bumpkin, or a Westie. Which, technically speaking, I am. Somehow, I manage not to put on a fake London accent and say, 'I've just got back from London.' Looking around, at the swarms of people absorbed in their worlds, I don't think it would impress anyone. It would have impressed me, once. Sad but true.

The café is at the bottom of the road. I'm walking practically sideways so that I don't miss the sign, but trying to look casual at the same time. It's there in eighties' neon: Lolita's. Elgin is out the back, in the courtyard, exactly where he said he would be. Seeing him stand up as I walk in, I realize that I'm surprised he's here at all. I expected him to stand me up, and I didn't even know I expected it until now. He waves, as if I haven't already seen him, and smiles – and it looks as if he expected the same thing too, because what I think I see on his face is relief. He leans over and kisses me on the cheek, or tries to. Actually ends up kissing my sweat-covered hair, because I'm not sure what he's about to do and I turn my head out of some reflex. At least I don't punch him, that's my other reflex reaction.

'I half-expected you to change your mind. You sounded like you were in a state on the phone, but I thought, you know, when the moment has passed and all of that. I've ordered a smoothie – do you want one?' His eyes crinkle up when he grins. He looks different to the way he was on the plane. At least, I remember him differently.

'I'll have, I dunno, I need to see the menu. Yair, thanks for meeting up. They are truly driving me mad.' I realize I'm about to launch into a tirade about my family without a courtesy enough-about-me-what-about-you. So I shut me gob for a moment. Pause, think, breathe. Not necessarily in that order. 'Has it been OK for you? Are you recovered from the flight?' It comes out sounding all polite and try-hard. Eat your heart out, Eliza Dolittle. Hoo kind of yoo to let me come.

He smiles at a waitress and she comes over straight away. 'Can we have a glass of water, and, Charis? Do you know yet?'

'Smoothie's fine. Strawberry. Thanks.'

He waits till she's written it down – which, considering it is only one item with no difficult words in it, seems to take a ridiculously long time – then turns the smile on me. There's no doubt about it, it is a good smile. 'Fine, it's all been fine. Thanks for asking. I think I've got it really good with my dad; he's, I dunno, he's a fantastic guy. He could have lost it when me mum died but he put a lot of energy into making sure me and my brother were OK. It's great seeing him again, makes me realize I've missed him. And he's offered to help set me up.'

'Set you up how?' I'm feeling dazzled – I've never heard anyone praise a parent like that before. I don't know any people who like their families and I'm surprised that any exist.

He looks up at the ceiling and then back at me. 'One of the reasons I've come back is to open a café. I've saved enough, but if Dad didn't help me out, I'd have no leeway at all. Do you think it's mad to try and open yet one more café?' He droops and I'm inclined to pour water on him, as if he's a prize flower. 'It's not as if there's a shortage.'

It's true, even without knowing the city as it is now, I can see that cafés have sprung up everywhere. 'I don't know. There are other cities, though, would you have to do it in Sydney?'

'Maybe not. That might be worth thinking about. Anyway, I'm bored with that. So, did things settle down after you called? It sounded like the whole world was storming out on you.'

'They were. I've turned over a new leaf and I'm keeping my mouth shut. If it kills me. Which I'm sure it will. I'm ready to scream at the lot of them. No, that's not true. Only her. And him. Bloody weddings.'

'Why are you going? Do you want something to eat, by the way? I'm thinking we could walk up to the markets and get some food in a bit.'

'Yair, that'd be good.' I'm shy to go on with the saga-of-my-life now that the subject's changed. 'Let's go up now, before we get squeezed in here.'

Outside, the street is crowded with people milling up to the markets. They seem to have come from nowhere – when I went into Lolita's, there was hardly anyone about. I'm expecting Elgin to leave it there, the whole wedding conversation thing, even though that's supposed to be why we're here, why we met up. To remind me of the real world, real perspective. But I don't feel like I'm getting any perspective, not at all. Almost the opposite, in fact, I feel like I'm losing ground, losing focus. Shifting around, grabbing for something. And I feel stupid and shy, which I have to say is unusual for me. I don't know what I'm doing here, what I thought I was doing ringing him up in the first place. This man is a total stranger to me, and I ring him up as if he's a friend, so that I can unload my own version of Family Feud on to him. So my instinct now is to grab the money and run. Except there isn't any money and it would be too rude to run right now. Not without a visit to the markets.

'Where did you get Elgin from?' Now I'm here, I might as well make small talk, in keeping with my new leaf of Saint Charis the chit-chat queen.

'What do you mean? I've always had it.' He puts a look of mock outrage on his face. 'Madam, are you suggesting I acquired Elgin through improper means? Are you suggesting theft? Because there are very strict libel laws in this country and I could have you deported. In fact, I think I shall.' He waves at an oldish man on the other side of the road. 'Gendarme – deport this woman immediately.'

The gendarme turtle-tucks his head into his shoulders and I have to lean against a street lamp. 'So we have a linguist in our midst. Who named you Elgin and why? Do you know in some countries it is actually illegal to name your child a name which isn't on the national register?'

'Well, Charis would hardly be legal, then. My parents emigrated from Scotland in the fifties on the ten-pound ship crossings. They were trying to get nice Brits to come and populate the place. Mum was desperately homesick and named me after her home town. So I suppose it's the same reason that we've got Newcastle and all that mob. What a legacy, hey? Anyway, what about this wedding? Why are you going?'

Spicy smells hit me in the nostrils as we get to the market. Food and sweat mixed together, but mostly food. Someone standing near me has bathed in patchouli oil. 'Because I have to. That's why they bought my ticket. I've got no choice.'

'I dunno, there's always a choice, I reckon. About everything. Even a crap choice is a choice. What would happen if you told the truth? Are you interested in this curry?'

There's a stall with a low brick fence behind it. Two women are sitting on the fence eating yellow curry and rice from a paper plate. My mouth is watering and for the first time I notice my stomach growling and because I don't want to think about that thing, about what would happen if I told the truth, I think about that instead, my stomach.

We get saggy plates of curry and sit on the brick wall, next to the two women. I'm not even aware I'm making 'mmmm, yum, oh, yes' noises until Elgin laughs and says, 'It's really nice to meet a woman who's not terrified of food.' He takes a mouthful, chews, and then says: 'I've got a confession to make to you.'

My head goes, Oh God. Because I don't know what confession means. It could mean anything, so I say nothing, just nod.

'On the plane, I wasn't stuck up the back. I was a few rows behind you and I asked the steward if I could sit next to you.' He's gone pink on his ears.

There's a weight in my stomach. I hate that, I hate the idea of someone watching me, spying on me and, yuk, creepiness, asking to be sat next to me. Even someone nice and twinkly, like him. 'Why?'

'I thought you'd be more entertaining than the sales rep I was stuck next to.' He must notice me looking squelchy, because he suddenly sits up straight and shakes his head. 'Oh, god, it wasn't anything slimy. I didn't want to come on to you or anything. Don't think that. You seemed chatty and funny at check-in and it's a long trip and I wanted to talk to someone chatty and funny.'

So now what I want to say is: why didn't you want to come on to me? Relieved that he wasn't, but wanting to ask, 'Why not?' Both at the same time. I'm not sure which one to go with, so I say, 'That's OK. I think. If it wasn't slimy.'

'It definitely wasn't. Please. Trust me.'

And even though I barely know him, I decide that I will. Just like that, as if it's the easiest thing in the world. Like falling off a log, like riding a bike. Like telling the truth.

# Marah

Steam makes patterns on the tiles and I run my finger through it, drawing stripes, crosses, small stars. The water is so hot that my skin is turning pink, and I love it, truthfully. It's one of my favourite things: hot, hot shower water powering down on me. Yale Graduate Halls of Residence have a lot of things, a lot of things I like very much, but they do not have powerful showers. Only Australians know how to make showers properly. I will give them that. They haven't managed to be an independent country or get rich or rule the world, but they make good showers. My eyes close and my throat opens and I let the steam in. Because I've been having the tightness, that rawness in my throat for days now and it doesn't seem to be getting better. Also, I've come out in hives. All down my arms. Deep red blotches which itch and look like infected pimples. Marvellous, because of course the dress Mother has chosen for me is sleeveless. Which, really, is a mistake anyway, because Charis isn't thin enough to wear sleeveless dresses. Neither am I frankly, the way I'm going. I've probably put on three pounds since I've been here. Obviously I've been eating only salads for lunch the last few days, because I did go overboard with the chocolate after the fitting, but even so. A moment on the lips, a lifetime on the hips.

Steam still fills the bathroom when I turn the shower off. When I step out of the shower, I can barely see the toilet, let alone the mirror. I switch the fan on and sit on the toilet to dry myself. Maybe I should have put the fan on first, before I even got into the shower, but I thought my throat needed it. My throat isn't good, and being madly busy doesn't help. Elisabeth sent me a review of the show, but of course I haven't had time to

213

read it. What does she think I'm doing here? Having a holiday? Anyway, the steam is good. I like sitting here drying myself and hardly being able to see my legs. Still feeling the heat of the shower. Somehow – and I know this is strange, there's no reason for it at all – it makes me feel cooler. Having a really hot shower and sitting in the heat of it afterwards. When I go outside, the air feels lovely and cool.

After the steam clears, I wipe the mist from the mirror with my towel and put my dressing gown on. Personally – and perhaps this is something which Mother has taught me, I'm not sure – I always think it's best to get dressed *after* you've put on your make-up. Because then none gets dropped on to your nice clean clothes. Of course, there's always the possibility that you could smudge the make-up when you pull a dress or a shirt over your head, but if you put a scarf over your head and hold the ends in your mouth, it keeps both hair and make-up in place. I've got a scarf I use specially. Charis gave it to me for my birthday when I was fourteen. Maybe fifteen.

Dingo bangs on the door and calls out, See you later, Jethro and I are off. I call out, Bye, Dingo, bye, Jethro. I'm a bit surprised, actually, that Dingo managed to get Jethro to go off to his buck's night. Actually, I'll be amazed to see Jethro at the wedding, dressed up and giving Mother away and not huddling in his bedroom like a wombat. Charis starts banging on the door before I've even got my concealer on. She taps softly at first, and then when I ignore her, she bangs as if I'm deaf, and yells out, Can I borrow your blusher? I tell her she can borrow it when I finish and that she'll have to wait until I've finished in the bathroom.

After a moment, she says, But Marah, I have to wash my face first. Can I come in? Please?

She hugs me when I open the door, as if she's been away in Siberia instead of outside the door. She can be overly dramatic, Charis. Which is strange, because you would think it would be me, who would be operatic and hysterical. But I'm absolutely not and I don't like it when people are. It's unnecessary, that's what I think. She helps herself to my face-powder before the blush and when I remind her that she only asked if she could use the blush,

214

she hugs me again and says, You're so funny, Marah. Which I don't mind, actually, because she says it as if it's funny-nice rather than funny-peculiar or even funny-haha. She hasn't got foundation on and when I ask her if she's going out without it on she says that she absolutely is. After she's used my powder, my blusher and my eye-liner, she lifts up the toilet seat and sits straight down, as if she's in the bathroom on her own, and starts going to the toilet. I finish doing my eye-shadow and say, Do you have to do that while I'm here? She laughs and says, It's only a wee. As if that makes any difference.

I show her my face, ask, How do I look?

She kisses the air and says, Bellissimo. Then she says, Marah, do you think it's fair that I should have to stick to a promise I made twelve years ago?

For some reason, even with the heat from the shower still clogging up the bathroom, I go cold. My skin prickles, but I say, It depends.

She says, Listen, I have to talk to Mum, I have to tell her. You know I do. It's only fair.

Although I don't know what she's talking about, I say, You can't spoil the wedding. If you want to talk about fair, that wouldn't be fair.

She looks at me for a moment and then shakes her head. Whispers, Come on, Marah, you know that doesn't come into it. She has to know before the wedding. We have to tell her about him. We do.

My voice is very calm, although I'm shaking inside, because Charis always does this, has this chip that she wants to drag out all the time. Always wants to get some attention or sympathy or something and I wish she wouldn't, I wish she would just shut up.

All I say, though, is, *We* don't have to do anything. I haven't got a clue what your hang-up is, Charis, but can't you let it go for now? All I want to do is get to Mother's doe's night without spoiling everything. And I think you should keep your promises.

I really don't know what makes me say that, about the promises. Just trying to suggest that she's a bit flighty, I suppose.

Really, she's two years older than me and she has no sense of responsibility.

Charis says, very quietly, Marah you are the most important person in the world to me but I don't understand you at all. And then she puts my eye-liner back on the sink and walks out. I can hear her calling out to Mother that we'll both be ready in three minutes, and then Mother sticks her head in the door and says, Taxi will be here in five minutes, better get a wriggle on.

Charis and Mother jump into the back of the taxi and when I get ready to slide in beside them, Mother says, Jump in the front, darling, it'll be less crowded. The meter ticks over and over and I look at the taxi driver's hands. Big, with hairy knuckles and an onyx ring on his finger. He screeches around a corner and I get that picture in my head again: a man's hands, large hands, on the steering wheel, then, something, the hands not on the wheel any more but – what? waving? hitting? Like it's an image from a recurring dream. Mother is asking me something in the back, or telling the taxi driver something, but I'm only half-listening because I'm suddenly remembering the dream I had about Daniel. I'd forgotten it totally until now. In the dream, we're getting married and I walk down the aisle towards him. When he turns around, I realize that not only do I have no clothes on – only a white veil – but I also have a man attached to me. By the penis. The man is in the process of making love to me while I walk down the aisle, but only his penis is attached, nothing else, no arms, no mouth, no legs. Daniel keeps smiling and smiling as if he doesn't even notice.

Mother says, Here, thanks, just here, the Greek restaurant.

The driver nearly runs over a drunk stumbling into the gutter and says, Damn, would have got five points if I'd hit him. He laughs as if he's incredibly funny and the three of us climb out of the taxi.

Mother says, Good, we're early, I wanted to be here before the others, so I could welcome them. Some of them don't know each other. I asked Karen from back at Saint Wildred's and she won't know anyone from Hampshire Heights.

The restaurant is dark inside, with carpets on the walls and a huge dance floor. The head waiter gives Mother a rose, so she

216

must have told them it was her doe's night. Our table is covered with candles and small bowls of yoghurt and dips and bread and olives and little filo parcels. Charis grabs a piece of bread as soon as she sits down. Mother orders daiquiris for us all, which I have to say is not a very Greek drink, but she doesn't seem to mind. I'm looking for something to do with my hands, so I tear at a piece of bread and put little bits, one by one, into my mouth. It's dry, so I pick at the olives, and then have a filo pie as well. By the time Mother's colleagues arrive, and we're ready to get the menus, I feel like I've munched through a whole meal.

There are ten of us at the round table: three teachers and the secretary from Mum's school, and two from her last school, and Karen, from way back when Mother was just a regular teacher. All teachers, actually, except for the one secretary, and me, and Charis. Mother suggests that we each order something and share, which worries me a bit, because I've already eaten three olives, two chunks of pitta bread and dip and one filo parcel. Although they're only finger-size, they're loaded with cheese and oil and I wouldn't even try to estimate the calories in each one.

The waiter comes over and says, Who is the lovely lady getting married?

Mother calls out, Me, I'm the sucker.

Karen, who's got a soft little pink dress on and looks like a little girl, calls out, Yet again – some people never learn.

The waiter laughs and the three teachers from Mother's school do what sounds like a shriek from a song. After he's taken our orders – I just ask for a Greek salad, because I can at least pick at that without doing too much damage – the waiter goes out the back. Mother pours us all some wine and the secretary declares a toast. She stands up and says, Order, everyone – I'd like to declare a toast: to Noel, and to new beginnings. We all raise our glasses and say, New beginnings.

Someone is asking Mother about why she's marrying Dingo and she's telling them about the television programme and they're saying they'd love to go on that if they could find a damned groom and both of them shriek again. The woman next to me is called Esther, and she asks me if I've got any plans to get married. I tell her yes, of course I do, and that my boyfriend is a first-year doctor and perhaps when he stops being a junior doctor and when I finish at Yale, maybe then we'll get married. But as I say it, I know it's wrong. The truth is, I can't imagine living here again, in this country. Everything looks like a copy of America to me. And I know Daniel can't imagine living anywhere else. But maybe that's because he hasn't been anywhere else, maybe he just needs to be convinced.

A waitress brings out two bottles of retsina and Esther says, So, how do you feel about your mum getting married? Before I get a chance to say that I feel fine about it, why wouldn't I, the waiter comes back with another man. Both of them have their shirts unbuttoned to their waists and the waiter has a classical guitar in the shape of a lute.

He kneels down at Mother's feet and says, We are going to sing you the song of the lovely bride. In the song, the bride hides away in the mountains, hiding from her lover until one morning, he comes to get her. Then there is rejoicing in the village, and a great wedding feast.

Mother laughs and says, Yes, that's exactly the way it happened for me.

The waiter starts what sounds like an almost flamenco strum, but with a triple metre. The other man kneels as well, and starts singing to Mother. All the words are Greek, but the singer beats his chest and even, at one point, unbuttons his shirt right to the bottom and tears it off. Obviously, all the grown women at our table call out, Get it off. The singer doesn't look especially bothered by it, he seems to enjoy it actually. He's not bad – his voice has got quite a reasonable timbre and he has good control, although I have to say that he overuses his vibrato ridiculously. Anyway, when the song finishes, he kisses Mother on the cheek and says, Good wedding.

Esther pours retsina for us all and says, Doesn't it taste disgusting? It does, too, but we all sip, even Charis, who says that it smells more like sick than sick does. Charis is sitting at the other end of the table talking to one of the teachers from Mother's old school. Talking quite intensely, by the look of them. By the time the endless dishes full of food arrive, everyone seems to be talking extra loudly and punctuating everything they say

218

with a big shrieking laugh. I couldn't drink the retsina, so I've just had one glass of wine and the daiquiri. All the others are half under the table already.

I manage to make some Greek salad and tzatziki last while everyone else scoffs all the fat-covered dishes. There's a plate of plain tomato and onion, so I have some of that as well, even though I know it will make me stink later. And I am planning on going over to Daniel's, as long as I can get away early enough.

Esther says, Marah, you've eaten like a bird, why don't you eat something else?

I say that I'm fine, which I am, and she shuts up. About half-way through the meal, a five-piece band shuffle on to the stage and start playing slow smoochy Greek music. After we've eaten most of the meal – although there are still plates of food left on the table and my mouth is watering, because actually they do look good – the band changes the music to fast dance music.

The waiter comes over and says, Ladies, please, for the bride you must all join me in the dance. Afterwards, you have your desserts.

We're all pushed up on to the dance floor and everyone else in the restaurant starts looking at us as if we're the floor show. Which Mother seems to be loving, judging by the way she's draped herself across the waiter. He arranges us in a circle, holding hands, and grabs some men who are sitting at other tables. Fortunately, it's quite dark, so you can't see how much my face is burning. When he's arranged all the men between us, he nods to the band and they start playing something slow but with a solid two-four beat. He's at the front of the line, holding hands with Mother, and showing us the steps. They get more complicated after each round, and the music gets faster. The man next to me smells of beer and he keeps putting his hand on my shoulder, stroking the top of my arm. I'm trying to follow the steps and shrug my shoulder at the same time, and we're all tripping over each other. The women have to lift their hands up, and do a twirl – I can see that it would look very pretty if it were done properly, but it's not. As I twirl back to the man, he puts his arm out for me and his hand touches my breast. Really, I don't know if it's deliberate or not, but it makes me feel sick in my stomach. I cross my hands over my chest and go and sit down.

After the dance has finished, Mother comes over to my seat and says, What's wrong – why did you sit down? I tell her I feel giddy and also that I need to leave, that I'm going to Daniel's and I don't want to be too late. She looks disappointed, even though I've already told her that I'm staying at Daniel's tonight, but says she'll see me later and to let the waiter call me a cab. When I stand up to leave, Charis looks up from her seat and raises her eyebrows at me. Literally raises her eyebrows. As if I'm supposed to have any idea of what she's trying to tell me. As if I'm supposed to think about something, her stupid promises, or threats, or something. Things I don't have to think about.

The cab is waiting outside and I jump in, tell the driver to take me to South Windsor. Halfway down the road, there's a big neon sign, with a picture of an ice-cream flashing on and off. What I think is, that I could pick up something nice for Daniel, some chocolate or something, and take it home to him. Because he'll have been working all night and he'd appreciate it. So I call out to the driver to stop and I jump out right there.

I'm half-dazed when I walk into the shop, and really I know what I'm going to do, I know because I've already started to feel like I'm wrapped in a blanket. Even before I open my mouth and start pointing to things, even before I check how much money I've got, I know why I'm here. I can hear my heart banging in my chest, I can hear it as if somehow my heart has moved right up my body, right into my ears. There's nothing to think about except this: the rows and rows of chocolate, the bags and bags of crisps, all the things I never eat. Because I can't decide which one I will allow myself, I get five chocolate bars and three bags of crisps. Then I see the shelf with cakes and muffins and I get a blueberry muffin and a packet of biscuits as well. The woman behind the counter asks if I'm having a party and I say, Yes, I am, sort of. She puts everything in a blue plastic bag and tells me to enjoy the party.

Taxis are lined up in a row just a little way down the road and I don't know what else to do so I get in one and tell them to take me to Windsor. Thinking: I'll phone Daniel and get him to come

220

over and get me, then it will be all right. I'll give him the muffin and the biscuits and tell him the crisps and the chocolate are to keep him going when he's studying. I've forgotten my wash things, anyway, so I need to go back to the house first. When the taxi stops at the front door, I freeze for a moment when I see the kitchen light on, but I think and I think and in the end I'm sure that I remember Mother leaving it on deliberately. And I must be right, because when I go inside, there's no one around. Of course.

My wash things are in my room, so I go in and shut the door behind me. I get into the bed with my clothes still on, and, first of all, open one of the chocolate bars. As soon as I tear the wrapper, I feel myself go, feel myself disappear. As if someone has come and given me a lovely injection of something which makes me sleepy and warm. If I touched myself, I wouldn't feel it, I wouldn't notice the contact. Even if I pinched or slapped myself, even then I wouldn't feel it, I'm sure I wouldn't. My mouth keeps eating, I keep going, one by one by one, through everything in the bag. Opening the biscuits is the worst, because I know then that I won't take them to Daniel and that this is it, I'm going to eat them all, every single one. Although I do start off going: just one, just one more, just one more after that.

When I've eaten everything, my stomach is swollen and I can't sit or lie or anything and all I can think of now is how many calories there are in a packet of biscuits. My stomach is too swollen to move properly, so I practically waddle to the bathroom. My hairband is in the cabinet, so I tie my hair back and bend down over the toilet bowl. It's hard, I can barely make myself do it, but I know if I don't, I'm going to have all that food in my stomach and that's worse than having to stick my fingers down my throat, even if it does hurt. My stomach must be strong, because in the end I have to stick two fingers down there and wriggle them around until I can feel the back of my throat. I gag about three times before I finally manage to be sick, and even then it's only twice, and small amounts. Nothing like the amount that I've eaten.

I rinse my mouth and clean my teeth. Get into bed and lie there in the dark, with my hands on my stomach. There are

221

three days to the wedding; if I drink only fruit juice until then, it will have evened out. For ages, I lie there doing the sums in my head, working out how many calories I've just eaten and how it would even out over three days to a reasonable amount, if I'm careful. Fruit juice and maybe steamed vegetables, then I'll be OK. And I can think about that all night, and all day tomorrow and every day until the wedding and then I won't have to think about Charis and her promise.

*The Sermon*

# And It Will Be

Rain is pouring down outside and although Charis says it's just a summer shower, it feels cold if you go and stand out in it. Which is exactly what Jethro does. Goes right out into the yard, takes his footie with him and starts kicking the ball against the shed until he's soaked right through. Soaked to the skin and shivering as well. The sky has a strange green to it, almost luminous, and if it weren't so cold and also so wet, you would want to stand outside and look at it, wondering about the colour. Jethro isn't looking, though, he's merely bashing the ball, kick-bash, kick-bash, kick-bash. Like that, on and on so that the sound mixes with the pelting down sound of the rain and makes a rhythm. Pelt-pelt-pour/kick-bash/pelt-pelt-pour/kick-bash. You could put a song over the top of it and it would make sense, it would sound like music.

Charis looks out the back window at Jethro kicking, kicking, bashing; looks at his small shivering self and grabs the big umbrella, the one Noeline calls the family umbrella. While Marah stays sitting in the warm, watching *Scooby Doo*, Charis marches outside to collect her little brother, as if she is a hen, or a mother. Brings him in with water dripping off him and his hair sticking to his face so that both Charis and Marah fuss over him as if he is a baby. He is wrapped in a towel and sent to change while Marah makes him milky hot chocolate. When he emerges from his room, changed into his track suit, Marah asks him why he stayed outside for so long anyway.

'Bored. There's nothin to do here and I can't go over to Wylkie's cause he's grounded.'

'Why's he grounded?' Charis tosses herself on the lounge, hogs the whole thing, with her legs stretched right along it.

'He blew up a cat.' Jethro lowers his voice. 'That's what he says anyway.'

'Yuk. Here's your chocolate.' Marah hands him the mug, specially sprinkled with extra bits of Ovaltine. 'Why don't ya watch telly if yer bored?'

'Don't wanna. When's Mum comin home?'

Charis shifts position on the lounge. 'Not till late today, she said. She's got some assessment thing to do.'

'Shove up.' Jethro pushed Charis's legs up, so that she is curled up and there is room for him. She puts her legs over his lap.

'Do you wanna play a game, then?' Charis reaches down and rubs Jethro's hair. Small and wet like this, he looks like a pet puppy, endearing and soft. She has put on the special sympathy-soft voice she keeps for when she is being elder-sister-who-loves-her-brother.

'What sort of game?' Marah sits on the floor, looks around the room for inspiration. 'Blind Man's Bluff?'

'It's not dark enough. Hideys. Bags not being in.' Jethro swallows the last of his chocolate and jumps up, ready to seek his hiding place immediately.

'Wait. We have to do eeny-meeny first. Yes, we do, Jethro. That's the only fair way.'

'But I don't want to be in. I got wet.'

Marah prods him, but gently. 'That's got nothing to do with it. You should have come inside.'

Charis does eeny-meeny because it was her idea to have a game in the first place and it's as obvious as anything that she cheats. Her finger moves fast, and taps at her own foot several times, so that it is no surprise at all when she is in. Perhaps she doesn't, perhaps it isn't cheating at all and double taps here and there are added in later. Some of these things are hazy, the voices are indistinct. But this is sure: Jethro leaps in the air as if he has scored a goal and he has to be held back by Marah until Charis starts counting.

Charis finds Marah, hiding in the bath, almost straightaway, but it takes both of them to find Jethro. Neither of them could be

226

sure whether this is deliberate or not, for surely his hiding place in Marah's wardrobe isn't difficult to discover. Jethro vibrates with delight, as if he is his long-gone five or six-year old self. Marah counts as slowly as she can and then spends ages looking in the lounge room in the places no one would ever hide: under the lounge, behind the curtains, behind the armchair. She marches straight to Charis's wardrobe, sure that Charis has tucked herself in there, but it is Jethro, squashed beneath her dresses and trying not to breathe. The front door opens just as Charis is discovered beneath Noeline's bed and Dingo yells out a loud 'hello', so it is just as well no one is hiding or the whole thing could have been given away.

'What are you blokes up to, then?' Dingo shakes the water off his umbrella and turns it upside down against the door.

'Playing Hideys. Do ya wanna play? I'm in this time, but Marah only found me because the wardrobe tipped a bit.' Jethro grins up at Dingo.

'Yair, orright. A game of Hideys'd be good. Just let me get me bags down. So you're in, Jethro. Anywhere out of bounds?'

'My room.' Charis glares at Dingo. 'Are you sure you wanna play? Mum'll be home soon anyway. In fact, I don't really want to play any more.'

'Come on, Charis, please. One more round.' Jethro is already in place, hands over his eyes ready to start counting.

'No. I said I don't want to.'

'Please.' Jethro turns his face up to her, so small he looks like a cat.

'OK, just one more round. Cause I've got homework to do and stuff.'

While Jethro rattles through counting to one hundred as quickly as he can speak the words, Charis runs for the long wardrobe in Noeline's room and stands right at the back of the coats. She piles shoes around her feet so that you would have to really check to know that she was there. She's barely been in there a minute when the door opens and a strip of light passes on to the shoes. She can hear Jethro in the living room still counting, rushing through from eight-eight. Dingo pushes the coats back and Charis whispers, 'Get away, sssh.' Jethro is right at ninety-three, so Dingo says, 'There's no time,' and gets into the wardrobe, pushing himself to the back, and shoving Charis forward so that she is barely covered by the coats.

Charis tries to make herself thin and Dingo puts his arms across her and pulls her back, so that his whole body is in contact with hers. Jethro's footsteps come closer and she stops breathing until the footsteps pass, echoing off up the hall. Dingo whispers something in her ear which sounds like, 'Stay still and he'll never find us,' but she is tempted to kick the wardrobe door, it's so hot in there. There are footsteps running, and giggling from both Marah and Jethro. Dingo keeps his arm across her chest, but his hand goes limp, maybe from the heat. It goes limp and just rests on her breast. Jethro is outside calling, 'I'm gunna get you, Charis,' and Dingo's hand presses, just for a moment, hard on to Charis's breast, right where her nipples are. He presses and his thumb and finger squeeze together, it only takes a second and then his hand is limp again, just resting against her chest. Dingo's breath is getting louder in her ear; she is sure that Jethro can hear it. This is not hazy, this is as clear and as sharp as the glass which cuts and when she speaks of this later, every word falls clear and formed and makes a thump on the ground. Charis shifts her weight and kicks at the pile of shoes so that there is a loud thump.

'Someone's in Mum's room, in the wardrobe. Quick, go and look.' Marah's voice is loud and commanding. 'Quick.'

Jethro runs to the wardrobe and yanks the door open. Air floods in and Charis gulps it down. She pushes the coats on to the floor and climbs out. Jethro says, 'Hey, two in one,' and Charis stomps past him, saying, 'I'm not playing any more, you can do what you want.' She spends the rest of the night in her room, because she's got a terrible head-pain. Jethro is allowed to take her dinner to her on a tray and he puts it down on the table beside her while she keeps her face turned away to the wall.

The three of them walk to school together in the morning, with Jethro in the middle, his hair still sticking up from sleep. He is so quiet, his feet barely making a sound on the tarmac, you would almost forget he is there. Marah says, 'Are you all right from yesterday?'

'Yep. I'm better now.' Charis swings her arms and doesn't slow down a bit.

'Was it the game?'

Charis looks straight at Marah and stops swinging her arms, stops walking and stands in the middle of the road and tells her everything, how Dingo said, 'There's no time,' how his breath got loud in her ears, how she gulped down the fresh air when the door finally opened. She says Marah is too young to know so she doesn't know why she's even telling her, then she says: 'I don't know whether it was an accident or not. He got in the wardrobe with me and I'm sure it was an accident. But he's a creep.'

'I'm sorry I made you play the game, Charis.' Jethro grabs her hand for a moment. 'I didn't mean for Dingo to be horrible.'

'You didn't do anything. It was nothing, it doesn't matter. Just shut up about it.' Charis starts walking again and then stops, sits right down on the verge. 'I have to tell Mum. I do, Marah. She would want to know. She would. Because he came into the bathroom once when I was in there and looked at me, and he's always touching and horrible. He is.' Charis looks up at Marah. 'I have to tell her tonight. I wish Dad was still here. I wish he'd call, or I could write to him. Anyway, I'm telling her.'

'You can't. She'll be angry and she'll, well, what if she just goes away like Dad did, what if she just goes off and never comes back and leaves us with Dingo?'

'She won't. That won't happen.'

'Come on. Get up.'

They walk in silence the rest of the way to school and at playtime Mrs Nobel asks Jethro if he is all right, because he's been so quiet all morning. He buys a Sunny Boy at the tuck shop and takes it over to Marah, sitting underneath the dead gum tree. She says thanks but no thanks and asks him just to go away. When he says sorry about the game again, she tells him not to worry and it's Charis he should tell, not her, and anyway to go and play with his friends. He kicks his footie around with Wylkie for a bit and then spends the rest of playtime sitting at the goal posts, doing nothing, nothing much. Lunchtime is the same and Marah stays inside, working on her cars and buses project. They walk home, just the two of them, in silence, with Jethro occasionally bouncing his footie on the road. Once, just before they cross Main Road, he says, 'It's my fault,' but his voice is drowned by a red car zooming past.

When Noeline gets home from work, Charis is sitting on the lounge with Marah beside her. They are sitting up straight, as if for an exam, and Marah is biting her nails. Noeline tosses her jacket on to the armchair and flops herself into it, her legs reaching on to the footstool in front of her.

'Where's Jethro?' She rolls her neck so that the muscles creak.

'Outside playin footie. Do ya wanna drink, Mum?' Marah is on her feet, ready to play hostess.

'Oh, thank you, darling. What have I done to deserve this? Will you make me a cup of tea?' When Marah pads into the kitchen, walking softly softly, Noeline stretches her arms above her head. 'Why isn't the telly on? Have you girls developed a sudden allergy?'

'We have to talk to you. About important things.' Charis twitches in her seat, leaning forward and nodding at Marah to hurry up, get a move on.

'Oh. OK. What's up?'

'Wait for Marah.'

Noeline waits obediently until Marah brings her too-weak-but-never-mind cup of tea and then starts again: 'So, what's up with my girls?'

Marah, knotting her hands together, looks at the floor and then at Charis. She makes a sound as if she is about to speak and then turns it into a small cough.

'Umm. It's Dingo.' Charis, too, sounds as if she is ready to cough or splutter.

'Are you still finding it strange without your dad? I'm sorry he hasn't been in touch, girls, but that isn't Dingo's fault. You know it isn't.'

'But you made the courts send him away, you had a law put on him that said he couldn't come here any more. Anyway that's not the thing.' Marah has her voice back, not spluttering but

230

speaking suddenly and sharply words which have lain waiting all this time, this two years.

Noeline puts her cup down. 'God, is that what you think? Darling, I'm sorry if I never explained to you, but your dad didn't turn up at either of the access hearings. We rescheduled three more times and each time he didn't turn up. I'm sorry, sweetheart. The door is open to him any time.' Her voice is tight and she doesn't look at either of them.

Charis puts her hand out and squeezes Marah's. Later, she will say what she knows, that this doesn't matter, these words of Noeline's, because they are lies, all lies, not one word is true. 'It's not that anyway. It's nothing to do with Dad, only to do with Dingo.'

'I'm waiting.' There is a slight snap in Noeline's voice, a bristle of impatience, or perhaps only tiredness.

'Dingo came into the shower when I was in there and, he came in and, well, he didn't go straight out. He looked at me. And then he came into my room when Marah was getting changed and looked at her.'

'Oh, sweetheart, I know it feels strange to have your body changing, but Dingo's not watching. You just feel self-conscious. All teenage girls do. I did. He was very embarrassed about walking into your room that time, and about the bathroom as well. The poor man wanted to go and use the toilet and you hadn't even locked the door. Anyone could have walked in then, Charis.'

'But it wasn't anyone, it was Dingo. And no one ever locks the door, you're supposed to knock. That's what we used to do.'

'Well, darling, when there's a man in the house who isn't your father, it really is up to you to lock the door. Fair enough, you hadn't worked that out then, but you know now, so it's all to the good.'

Charis has red blotches marking her neck, her face is creased. 'And he touched my boobs.'

Noeline takes a breath in, sudden and sharp. 'When? What do you mean? That's a very serious thing to say, Charis. Tell me what you think happened.'

Charis is getting more and more of the same pink on her face, small burning spots travelling down her cheek. 'He touched Marah as well.'

'Marah?'

'Maybe it was an accident. It was when we had Chinese one night and Jethro spilt something on me and Dingo was wiping but he wiped in my boobs. And then, yesterday when we were playing Hideys, Dingo was in the same hiding place with Charis and he did it to her.'

'How?'

Charis lifts her head up and tries to let air into herself. 'When Jethro was coming to find us, Dingo pulled me back and he put his hand on my boobs.'

There is a ringing silence for long seconds. Noeline takes her feet off the foot-rest and sits up straight. 'Look, it's very difficult when you start developing, I remember how strange it was to discover my breasts. Now, I was in the room when Dingo wiped that stain off and I know what I saw, Marah. I'm not suggesting you're being deliberately malicious, but the sorts of things you're both trying to suggest are very dangerous. Now, I'm sure Dingo would be mortified to discover he'd accidentally touched your breasts, and I'm sure that you're much more conscious of it than he is, sweetheart. And I'm sure you miss your dad, but Dingo is trying his hardest, you have to give him a go. Listen, I've got a good book at school called *Your Teenage Body*, I'll bring it home for you tomorrow. And in the meantime, I'll tell Dingo to be more sensitive. OK?' Everything in Noeline's body – the way she brings her hands together on her lap, the straightening of her shoulders and smoothing of her skirt – says the interview is over.

Katie Ryan at school goes to the Catholic church on the hill with her mum and she says that she can ask God or Mary or Jesus for anything, anything at all. Later, lying on her back in bed, Marah whispers to God or Hail Mary or Jesus Meek and Mild – she's not sure who, which one, she's speaking to, so she tries them all. She whispers and asks please please please for Noeline not to get angry and go away and never come back, asks for her not to do what Joe did, disappearing like that, not bothering to turn up, not calling. She says that she will be good, very very good, if God

232

will promise this one thing and also if God will protect and look after Charis and she asks God or Jesus or Mary to show her a sign that they've heard. Please make me good, she says. I'll be good, I will. Please speak to me. She whispers for hours, asking and asking. And all night the darkness covers her face and silence answers her prayers.

# Charis

My body seems to be adjusting to this hemisphere at last. Waking up before noon is usually a good sign. Not that I'm remotely bothered by not waking up till noon, I'd be happy to sleep all day if it means avoiding the palaver in this house, avoiding the new niceness with which I've decided to face them all. When I say 'all', obviously what I mean is Dingo and the witch-mother. Although, technically, under my new 'make-an-effort' contract, I shouldn't call her the witch-mother any more, I should give her a chance to defend herself, to make her case, stake her claim. But I can't help what goes on in my head. Can I? Anyway, I'd be happy to lie here in bed, listening to the noise of them rushing about with juicers and hair-dryers. I'd be happy to lie here all day, if my stomach weren't so insistent on rumbling and demanding food, food, food.

Dingo is in the kitchen whirring up some revolting-looking concoction in the juicer. Celery seems to be a major factor, so I assume it's for Mum, rather than him. Celery, watermelon and parsley. People drink this stuff. Mum thinks if she wees enough before the wedding she'll be stick-insect thin, and that will be marvellous because then no one will be able to see her and she will have wasted all that money on the dress.

Dingo does a mock double-take. His eyes are bloodshot. 'Bloody hell, what's happened? Charis has risen before lunch-time. Call out the guard. Make pronouncements across the land.'

'Ha bloody ha. I couldn't sleep through the noise of the juicer. Where's Mum?'

'She's getting dressed. We're going into the Hilton to check the reception details. Wanna come?' Dingo puts on this we're-best-mates-and-I'm-such-a-good-bloke voice with me, he does it all the time.

'No, thanks. When will you be back?'

'Around lunchtime. Just when you should be getting out of bed. And I would have thought that the lot of you would be walking hangovers this morning. You look bright as a sparrow and yer mum's barely queasy.' He drinks the juice in one go. 'That'll fix me.'

'Yuk. I thought that was for Mum.'

'Best hangover cure this side of the black stump. Noel doesn't need it, she's got a cast-iron stomach.'

Witch-mother comes into the kitchen in a green linen suit and matching green shoes. Clippety-clop like a pony. 'Yep, that's me. Right. Are you ready, Dingo? It'll take us an hour to get in there with the traffic, so we'd better move.' She air-kisses me, her cheek barely brushing mine. 'Are you all right after last night? Dingo could barely move when I woke him up.'

'Lies, all lies. Come on then, woman, let's sort these bastards out.' He grabs his keys from the 'Our Sweet Home' key rack and heads for the door.

'See you around lunch. Will you be here?' Witchy-pants trots behind Dingo, calling to me over her shoulder.

'Yair, probably. I'm goin into Sydney later though.'

After they've gone, I sit at the kitchen table for ages, thinking about the conversation I have to have with my mother. Some time. Some time soon, before Saturday. Today would be good, would be the best time, I know that, but the thought of it puts me off moving. Let alone eating. The grumbling in me stomach seems to have gone, so I make some coffee and go and sit on the back steps. Feel the sun washing over me. The warmth of it is soothing at least. My head is resting against the brick wall and I'm thinking that I could make lunch and be gentle and raise the topic then. Thinking about how I'll say it, how careful I'll be, when the doorbell rings and I have to pull myself away from the sun.

The lounge room is dark after the brightness, small red and yellow spots float about in front of my eyes. When I open the door, I have to squint out as if I'm ready for me colostomy bag and zimmer frame and I'm tempted to croak, 'Who is it, dear, is that Little Red Riding-Hood come to see her grandmama?' As it turns out, I don't need to say anything, because the shadow-shape steps into the doorway and straight past me. It's only when he is on my level that the brightness clears and I can see Daniel's face.

'Marah up yet? Howya doin, Charis?' He asks it in that hurry-hurry way which makes it clear that under no circumstances does he want a reply.

I step aside to let him in. 'I thought she was at your place. Wasn't she going over last night after Mum's doe's night?'

'If it finished early enough. I finished studying at about midnight and she certainly hadn't shown up by then.'

Cold water runs down my back, but I keep my voice flat. 'Oh, she must have come back here. Do you wanna go and check?'

While Daniel marches off to Marah's room, I sit on the lounge, tapping my foot on the floor. Marah wasn't around when we got in last night, and we only left the restaurant maybe forty or fifty minutes after her. Daniel doesn't rush back out to the lounge room calling for a mobilization of emergency services, so after about ten minutes, I assume she's safe in her warm little bed. If I had a boyfriend like Daniel, I would do everything in my power to avoid ever having to spend time with him, in case I died of boredom. Which would be marvellous for him, having to make a spot diagnosis. He could tell all his little medical friends about it. But then, I'm not Marah and Daniel's not my boyfriend.

My stomach starts grumbling again, so I make some toast and sit down with a book of photographs. *A Day in the Life of Australia*. Crumbs and smears of Vegemite are getting spattered across the pages, but it's a beautiful book, glossy pages. I don't know where all the books on these shelves come from – I'm sure they never get read here. Always too busy doing DIY and weddings, as far as I can tell. There's a wall chart in the kitchen which has colour-coded stickers on it: fittings, flowers, rehearsal, meeting with minister. When I asked her why she wanted to get married in a church – I mean, she never goes near one any other time – she says she wants to do it right this time. Getting married. She married my dad in a registry office, and had a reception in her

236

mum's garden. Her mum had been run over by a truck by the time she married Joe, so they only got the registry office and a schooner of Fosters in the local pub. So this time, she says, it will be done the proper way. She could start with marrying the right person for once.

Even if I spent all day looking at their wall charts and shelving systems and paint samples – and, believe me, these things are endlessly, oh, endlessly fascinating and there's nothing I would rather do – I would still have no clue what they do, how they spend their time. Certainly they have even less clue about me. Also, I have no interest in them and I don't know why I'm here, why I didn't say no in the first place. But I am here and I have to do something with it, make the most of it and all that, and I think that making the most of it means that I have to open my mouth, make an effort. Take the risk. Do my duty. All that. Lunchtime, I'll do it at lunchtime.

Jethro wanders in eventually, smelling like a brewery. He grabs at some milk from the fridge and, when I ask, says he'll be around for lunch. Because I think I need this to be a whole family thing, although I don't say anything like that to him. To Jethro, I say that maybe we could all have lunch together and he looks at me as if fire has come out of my nose and says, 'Why? You want to look for some more problems or tell us how badly done-by you are?' Fair enough, I suppose, given that I hardly have a history of initiating cosy family get-togethers.

Daniel comes into the kitchen, all brisk business, while Jethro is loading a plate with toast. He shakes Jethro's hand as if he's at a business meeting and then pulls out the celery from the fridge. 'Marah's feeling a bit under the weather, bit of a poor tummy. She wants some celery juice. Doesn't seem to think she could manage any food, but I'm starving.' He takes a piece of bread from the bread-bin and pops it in the toaster. That bread-bin was a new discovery to me yesterday. Daniel knows the workings of this kitchen better, much better, than me.

'Is she staying in bed? I thought I might make lunch for everyone.'

'I'm sure she'll be up in time.' Daniel stands at the toaster awkwardly; I can almost see his little brain trying to come up with an appropriate bit of small talk. After a while, he goes: 'So you're going to make lunch? That'll be nice for your mother.

'Mmmm.'

Daniel sticks the celery in the juicer and says something I can't catch: 'Blah blah later, then.' I only hear the 'later, then' because he switches the juicer off and starts pouring.

'Bang on me door when it's ready, then. I'm goin to practise.' Jethro picks up his plate, stuffs a piece of toast in his mouth so that crumbs gather on his chin.

'Jethro?' I look at Daniel, waiting for him to exit with his toast and juice. 'Can I talk to you?'

'Whaddaya mean?'

Daniel finally gathers his goodies and squishes past me. 'OK? Nice toast.' Small talk is obviously not his strong point either.

I wait until Daniel's footsteps have padded away. 'I just wondered how you're going, that's all. You seem to be a bit, I'm not sure, quiet, or low, or something.'

'Nah. I'm fine. No worries. Leave it alone, Charis. You're the one with the problems, don't try and put it on everyone else. I'm practising, I'm on holidays, that's all. God's sake, give it a break.'

'OK. Fine. I just wondered, that's all.'

I'm cooking mince and onions and garlic when Marah comes out, looking fairly green. The smell is fantastic, but she screws up her face as if I'm forcing her to take a big sniff of pigswill. Lasagne is the only meal I know how to make, so obviously that's what they get. My thinking is that if I provide the food, I get to decide the talk. Optimistic, I know, but it's the best I can go on.

'Lasagne for lunch, OK? I thought we could all have lunch together.'

Marah knows me too well, knows what I'm thinking. She folds her arms, Madam Suspicious. 'Why? Anyway, I'm not hungry, I don't want any lunch, I'll have some juice. Daniel will have some, I suppose. But we might want to go into Bankstown and do some shopping, it's his only day off. We have to get a wedding present.'

'You being here, I mean, giving up your show is a present. You have to eat, even if it's a little bit.'

'Give my share to Daniel.'

'I was hoping it would be only family.'

'Daniel is family. What's the big deal, Charis? Why do you suddenly want to feed everyone and have us all together?'

'For God's sake, Marah. I have to tell her the truth, it's not fair if I don't. And I don't want to be carrying it around any more, I'm fed up with it, it should have occurred to me years ago to open me mouth, but it didn't, so this is the only chance I get.'

Marah stares at me as if I have started speaking Turkish and she needs a translator. 'You should just go and sort out whatever this thing is that you've got such a problem with, and you should have thought about it before. You shouldn't have come if all you wanted to do was make trouble. Anyway, I absolutely don't want any lunch, so I won't be here. You do what you like.'

So I finish making the lasagne and lay the table and wait for Dingo and witch-mother to get back and when they do, I tell them there's lunch in the oven but that Marah's gone out with Daniel and I've got to go into Sydney, meeting someone later for tea, blah blah blah. Mum flutters in the kitchen, going, 'How sweet of you to make us lunch, Charis, but what about you, darling? You have to eat something. Oh, it smells delicious, doesn't it, Dingo?' I tell them I'll get a sandwich later and that I've only just had breakfast. Because, for the first time in a long time, I've lost my appetite and the last thing I want is food. The lasagne might as well be pigswill, as it turns out. Maybe I should sit and pick and be polite, but I can't do it. Now that I've made up my mind, until I've said my bit, I can't keep pretending it's all hunky-dory. Dingo says he'll ask Jethro to drive me to the station and I back out the door as fast as my fat little legs will carry me, going 'No, no that's fine, Jethro's probably starving anyway, I'll see you later.'

Just for the sake of it, I walk down the middle of the road, watching my shadow stretch out in front of me. There are no cars and the road is as wide as an English town. I forget how wide and expansive it all is, even in the suburbs. Flame trees dot along the road to the station, evenly planted, which looks wrong somehow, having them so ordered. Behind the trees, near the station, there are wide patches of land with brown grass and small patches of scrub. Waiting to be bought up, I suppose, and built into another series of brick bungalows surrounded by super-neat-could-be-anywhere gardens and the obligatory pools. It still counts as Sydney, but when I get off the train forty minutes later, Windsor could be another world. Another planet. Which it might as well be, for all the common ground I have there.

Not surprisingly, I'm hungry when I get off the train. The sick tightness has left my stomach, and that leaves room for food, praise to the great god of cakes. I'm still a bit early, so I buy a kebab and a slice of carrot cake from the station shop and sit on one of the orange plastic benches, munching away. Elgin gave me directions for the bus, but I walk half-way up Glebe Road before I bother jumping on one. He's drawn a mud map on the back of a 'Lolita's' serviette, and told me to phone if I'm lost. It's only ten minutes, if that, from the bus stop, and the directions are perfect. Once again, I have no idea what I'm doing here – I seem to be spending my days being zombied into places I don't recall choosing to be in. But I did choose to be here, I did say, 'Yes, I'd love to come to dinner, anything to get out of the house, yair, a break would be great.'

The house is as un-Windsor red-brick bungalow as I can imagine. Leadlight doors and windows, a wooden verandah with some old bits of furniture piled up. Elgin opens the door about one and a half seconds after I ring the bell and hugs me before I get a chance to say anything.

'It's really good to see ya. Come through and I'll make a drink.'

In the kitchen, I can see out into the small garden. A grey-haired man is bent over, pulling up weeds. Elgin fills the kettle and points out at him. 'Dad likes to imagine that he has an acreage to fill with exotic plants.' Elgin taps on the window and, when the man looks up, lifts a mug in the air. His dad nods and waves at me. Nice face from what I can tell. Elgin hands me a coffee and picks up the other two cups. 'Do ya wanna come outside and say hello to Dad?'

'Sure.' I follow behind him, puppy-like, my ears pricked up, my tail wagging.

The garden barely fits the two deckchairs which are leaning

240

against the fence. Elgin kicks his dad on the bum. 'Dad, here's yer drink. This is Charis. Charis, this is Jim.'

Jim stands up, wipes his hands on his shorts and gives me a big grin. His face is small, somehow reminds me of a monkey, – although I don't think I've ever seen a monkey close up – but he's got the same eyes as Elgin, deep and wide and brown. 'It's a delight to meet you, Charis. It's great that you could come over. Elgin tells me you're in the midst of wedding-fever – how's it going?'

'Madness. Utter madness. It's a relief to get away.'

'You're probably supposed to feel guilty for not arranging some flowers or place-mats or something, but I wouldn't let them get to you. Guilt isn't good work.'

Elgin sits down on the grass and pulls me down beside him. 'Guilt is the last thing Charis needs to feel, by the sounds of her family.'

I shift away from him slightly, not sure that I'm happy about the idea of him merrily discussing my family and me with anyone who'll listen. 'You haven't got a Scottish accent, Jim.'

He laughs. 'I've lived here for forty years and I was a twenty-two-year-old baby when I came out. It's definitely home now, I wouldn't know what to do if I left. Mind you, Elgin tells me I sound like a right Scot if I'm angry.'

'Which is whenever you read the bloody newspapers.' Elgin jabs at his dad's foot. 'Siddown, yer making us feel uncomfortable.'

Jim stares around the little plot. 'I'm just wondering whether I could fit an apple tree in here.'

'Dad, you couldn't fit a rose bush in here. Get real.'

Jim sits down on the path and asks me how I feel about the wedding, whether I have contact with me dad, what's my family like, why on earth I want to live in London. All I can say to that is: it's not here. By which I mean: it's not there, not South Bloody Windsor. But then, neither is this, so I end up confusing myself. Jim stretches out on the grass and keeps asking me questions, all sorts, until I'm dizzy with answering. When the sun starts turning cold, Elgin says he'll make dinner, and Jim says he'll take a walk up to the bottle-o. Elgin grinds seeds and pods with a mortar and pestle while I sit on a wooden fold-up chair watching him, drinking way too many cups of coffee. He gives me a sharp knife and a garlic clove, tells me to start slicing. While I'm peeling it – slowly, because I want to smell the garlic on my skin – he slits a red chilli and nearly chokes on the fumes. He swallows some water and then goes: 'So have you worked out how you're gunna cope with the wedding?'

'I don't think I can go. I'm not going to, I'm just going to not turn up. I'll go out the night before and not turn up. I'll be sick if I have to sit through it.' Until I say it, I don't know that this is true, but as soon as the words are out of my mouth, I know that I can't go.

Elgin watches the garlic sizzle, stirring it with a flat wooden spoon. He stares into the pot for a moment, quiet. 'Are you sure?'

'Absolutely.'

'What about yer sister? Isn't she, I dunno, the important one to you in all this?'

'Yair, but she's not gettin married.'

'She's singing, isn't she? Might be tough for her to carry all the flack of you not being there. You know. I'm not suggesting you should go, maybe just think about it. It's a big decision. Do ya want more coffee?'

When Jim comes back from the bottle-o, the coffee changes to wine and by the time Elgin lays the table with dishes of rice and dhal and vegetable curry and pickle and yoghurt and poppadams, I'm not only ready to eat the chair, but also quite close to falling off it.

Candles reflect on the windows and Jim pours wine and wine and more wine and gets up every so often to change the music, and they both make me laugh so much that my eyes are wet and I can barely talk. Eventually, Jim says he's going to bed – 'I'm away to me bed' is what he says – and he rubs Elgin on the head, says, 'Great dinner, mate. Night.' Then, as an afterthought, or an automatic response, he calls, 'I love you,' over his shoulder. Elgin says it back and it makes me want to hug them both. Probably the wine, and it's probably the wine as well which makes me think it's a good idea when Elgin offers to make up the sofa-bed

242

for me. The thought of dashing for the last train fills me with lethargy.

We pile the dishes into the sink and Elgin pulls out the insides of the lounge so that it turns into a nifty bed. Very impressive. As soon as it's made, I collapse on to it, and he sits down beside me. Says: 'I meant to ask – have you said anything yet?' I plop my head back on the pillow and say no, there hasn't been time, or it hasn't been the moment, or, or, some such thing. He flops down beside me and watches me. In a sleepy-sleepy voice, he goes: 'You've got to, though, doncha think?' My eyes are closing and I sort of murmur a yes sound and he murmurs something back and we go on like that for ages, little grunty murmurings drifting between us. Eventually, in slippery warm semi-sleep, I pull the covers up over us both and lie there next to him, breathing in time, but keeping myself on the far side of the bed, my body as stiff as it can be, given that I'm so tired I wouldn't be able to sit up straight in an electric chair.

When the sun burns me awake in the morning, Elgin is still next to me, lying close, with his hands resting on my shoulders. His eyes flicker and I watch him for a moment, think about pushing his hands off me and rolling further away, right to the edge of the bed. But it all seems like too much effort, so I close my eyes and drift back to sleep. His breath is warm beside me and I don't ever want to wake up.

# Marah

Daniel is still asleep when I open my eyes. His mouth has flopped open and a trace of spit is on his chin. Also, if I want to be truthful, his breath doesn't smell very good. Although this is a three-quarter width bed, there isn't actually room for us both, so I am squashed with my face against the wall and my shoulder jammed under my chin. It feels strange, having him sleeping here, somehow, even though I know he stays over when I'm not here. When he goes out sailing with Dingo. Even that feels strange. He doesn't trust me to turn up at his place now, that's what he says; just because I didn't make it over after Mother's doe's night. I'm sure he's joking. He must be.

To climb over him, I have to squeeze myself up sideways and breathe in. As soon as I lift myself up and start to climb over, though, his eyes open and he grabs my arm. Asks where I'm going in a sleepy voice and I get a gust of his breath, which really isn't good at all. I tell him I'm going to get some water and, fortunately, he doesn't try to kiss me, so I tie my dressing gown on and open the door. Voices are coming from the kitchen and the smell of coffee. After I go to the toilet, I go into the kitchen for some water and coffee to take back to Daniel. Lying about in bed isn't normally something I would want to do, and neither would Daniel, but the coffee smells so good, and it will be easier than having to explain to them all why I don't want any toast or cereal. Mother would be fine about it, I'm sure, and Daniel hasn't seemed to notice that I'm not eating – or if he has, he quite rightly assumes it's none of his business and has kept his mouth shut. Unlike Charis, of course, who practically tried to force lasagne down my throat yesterday *and* tried to insist that we all gather for some problem-solving or something like that. Honestly, I never have half a clue what she's on about, but she does seem to think you will die if you don't eat. Which is ridiculous, because you can fast perfectly safely for up to three weeks. It's been proven.

Mother is in the kitchen chopping celery and watermelon and carrot into pieces and putting them into a plastic Tupperware container. She points to the percolator and says, Have some coffee, I'm just storing up some extra veggies for juicing, so we don't have to chop them all the time.

Dingo is sitting at the table reading the *Windsor Chronicle*. He says, Hi, sweetheart. All right this morning? Want some juice? I tell you, this paper is a rip-off even if it's free, it's full of adverts. They should pay me to read it.

Mother laughs and says, Oh, get off your high horse, you're just grumpy because you slept in. Ignore him, Marah.

I do ignore him, and help myself to some of the celery and watermelon which Mother has cut up, because I think I might as well have my juice now as later. Forgetting that the coffee will go cold while I'm juicing, or at least have some of the heat taken off it. Daniel comes out while I'm putting the cups in the microwave. Completely washed and dressed. He doesn't like to dawdle over things like washing or showering. Likes to get up and get on with the day, which is what I like about him. One of the things I like about him, obviously. There are lots of things I like about him. All sorts of things. For instance, I like his commitment to his work, I think that's important in a man. That's only two things, but there are others. Lots of others.

Daniel takes the coffee-cups from the microwave and sits down next to Dingo, says, Anything interesting going on in the world?

Dingo says he wouldn't know, because it wouldn't be reported in the *Windsor Chronicle*, unless there was an advertising campaign to go with it. I make Daniel some toast and sit down with my juice, which Daniel has a sip of and says that it's disgusting.

Dingo says, Women are always on diets, mate, just let em get on with it. Mother slaps him on the head. Not really a slap, actually, more a playful little tap.

The bathroom door shuts and I can hear the sound of the toilet seat being dropped down or put up, I'm not sure which. The shower is turned on and it makes a pumping sound which goes through the whole house. Good showers here, but noisy.

Mother takes the paper away from Dingo and says, Stop being so anti-social. Oh, the shower's on. Goodness, something must be wrong with Jethro if he's up already.

I do wonder why she assumes it's Jethro and not Charis in the shower, especially when, as far as I can tell, Jethro doesn't even like to be clean particularly. What I mean is, he wouldn't rush to get to the shower every day. Actually, I'm sure there have been days since I've been here when he doesn't bother having a wash at all. I can't remember whether he's always been like that. Probably. He seems to spend ages in the shower once he does decide to have one, though. Not that I'm counting, or keeping check or anything, but I do notice that Daniel has made another pot of coffee and I've had time to peel and eat an orange before the shower is turned off. So that must be at least eighteen minutes. Given that the percolator takes twelve minutes and we had time to finish the first pot – which I think would take six or seven minutes. And that is a conservative estimate, definitely.

Jethro comes straight into the kitchen, doesn't bother going into his room to get dressed or anything, and he's only got a towel wrapped around his waist. Drips of water trail behind him across the floor, but he doesn't seem to notice at all. Jethro doesn't notice much, if you ask me. He helps himself to coffee and sticks three pieces of toast in the toaster. Mother tells him to go and get dressed for once before he has his breakfast, particularly given that Daniel's here. Jethro says that if Daniel hasn't seen anything that Jethro's likely to flash at him, then Daniel has a lot of problems. Daniel doesn't bother responding, he's absorbed in the private ads in the *Chronicle*. There's a one-page wedding feature next to it, with an ad for a horse-drawn carriage to take you to the church and the reception. Daniel flicks his eyes across to it and says, Let's have one of those when we get married, Marah.

Everything feels over-quiet for a minute. Dingo takes a loud sip at his coffee and Mother says, You'd better ask her first, Daniel.

Jethro half-chews a piece of toast and opens his mouth so that you can see everything in there and says something about more bloody weddings, but it's almost impossible to understand him. Actually, I feel a bit cross with Daniel, because I think he should say that sort of thing to me privately, not in front of people who can then say, Well, why don't you ask her? As for me, I keep silent, because I'm not sure what I think. Obviously I want Daniel to ask me to marry him, I mean, I think I do. Charis would roll her eyes in that way she has and say, Why don't you ask him? And I'll tell you why. Because it's not appropriate. A man should be able to feel like a man and it's his job to make those decisions. It would make me feel unfeminine if I had to ask him, it really would. As if I was planning his life. But – and this is the bit which feels strange – I'm not sure, I'm really not, that I want to be married to Daniel. What would I do? Sing here for ever, in Sydney? And as soon as I think that, I feel like I'm the most selfish person on earth.

Dingo gets up and says that he'd better make a booking for the restaurant tonight, and does Daniel want to come for the family pre-wedding meal. Daniel's working, which is why I never invited him, but I'm sure Dingo's only being polite anyway. Daniel asks why we're not having the do after the rehearsal tomorrow night, but Mother jumps in and lists the people who will be around: organist, minister, choir. Not even mentioning Brian, Dingo's best man. So, there's only tonight. If I'm honest, I dread the thought of another restaurant, but this one is the local Beef-Eater, so I can order salad and make sure they don't bring me bread. Jethro skulks off to his room without saying a word. Leaving his dirty plate on the table for someone else to clean up, which, again, is fairly typical of Jethro these days. It's not until after lunch that anyone asks where Charis is. And it's not until late afternoon, when we're starting to wonder whether she'll be around for the Last Night Out before the wedding, that she actually turns up, as if she's just popped back from the local shops.

Mother says, Oh, did you stay over at your friend's house?

247

And that makes me cross because Charis doesn't tell me anything these days, not like she used to, not unless it's to complain or nag or threaten or force, and that's not talking, not actually.

One problem is that I have barely practised 'Ave Maria', and I haven't even been doing my vocal exercises. Getting lazy. For some reason, Mother sold the piano, which means that I have to practise with a tuning fork to start me off, and that's not ideal. She says it was in the way. Also, my throat still has a tightness to it which I'm not happy about, although that may be from not warming up properly. As Lenherr would say: If I were an athlete, there would be no excuse for not training every day, so there is no excuse for a singer. Lenherr has probably forgotten all about me by now, I'm sure he'll be so immersed in *Dido*. Elisabeth is doing marvellously, I'm sure. Which is good, of course. Good for her.

Daniel heads off to the hospital not long after Charis arrives. He kisses Mother on the cheek and says, The next time I see you, you'll be a blushing bride.

That gives me a shock, that it's so soon. Because it's true, although I hadn't thought of it. If he doesn't come to the rehearsal, the next time he sees Mother will be at the church. Oh, God. That makes me feel dizzy. After he goes – he hugs me at the door and says he'll see me at the church as well – I fill the bathroom with steam and do a vocal warm-up while I'm standing in the bath. It must be a week since I've done any vocal work, so it's no small wonder that I can barely reach the top notes without straining. Jethro yowls from his bedroom, which is what he always used to do when I was practising at home. It wasn't funny then and it isn't funny now. Jethro's musical appreciation begins and ends with Paul Simon. Seriously. While I'm in there, in the bathroom, I fill the sink with boiling water and steam my face, to open up the pores before the wedding. Photographs can make your pores look terribly clogged, if you're not careful, and it's best to steam one or two days beforehand.

I'm in my room doing leg-lifts when Charis taps on the door and asks if she can use my blusher again. When she sees me still in my jeans, she says, Do you know the time?

I have to jump up and throw my blue knitted dress on and I've only got about five and a half minutes to put my make-up on before Mother starts calling out, Come on, troops, let's get a move on here.

So I do get a move on and I'm ready and standing to attention, practically, in the hallway while Mother is still tying her hair back and Charis is looking for her shoe. Dingo starts hustling everyone into the car. Jethro has to be practically forced from his room – which is starting to smell, actually – and Charis has to give up on finding her shoe and put on the only other pair she's brought with her. There's talking and yelling on the way out the door and for a moment it feels like when we used to go on excursions. Like when we drove up to the Northern Territory, singing and playing I Spy. It's only after I get in the car that I remember that Dingo wasn't on that trip. Neither was Mother. It was Joe. We drove and drove playing I Spy. D. Dirt. D. Dust. D. Dead wombat. Funny how I'd forgotten that. Some lady in a truck stop said, How do you do it, drive all that way? And Joe laughed and said it was easy, you just turned the engine on, kept your hands on the wheel and you got there.

I'm sitting in the back, squashed up between Jethro and Charis, and I have to sit forward so that I can breathe. As we pull out of the driveway, Dingo's left hand drops down from the steering wheel on to Mother's knee and starts massaging it. Like a kitten has landed there on her knee and is squeezing its claws in-out-in-out. We drive towards the main road and I watch his hand, big knuckles, dark hairs on the backs of his fingers. I watch it clawing in-out-in-out and I start to feel hot and sweaty. A wave of dizziness comes down over my head and runs all the way down my body. His other hand is still on the wheel, still turning this way and that, easily, as if it's the most natural thing in the world. His hand clawing, clawing. My throat is drying up, really, actually drying. As if I couldn't speak, not to save my life. Charis is saying something to Jethro and Mother is laughing in the front seat but in my ears there a sharp sting of a sound which makes everything else far away. When we get to the Beef-Eater and Dingo jumps out and opens the door for us, my face is covered in a thin sheet of sweat.

They bring us drinks first, and after about half a jug of water, I start to feel better. Well enough to order a plain garden salad with no dressing and a freshly squeezed unsweetened orange juice.

Mother says, Oh, come on, Marah, you have to have some champagne at least. In the end, I do have champagne, because although it's loaded with calories, it is at least fat-free, and I can see that I'm not going to get a break unless I join the toasting. Everyone takes a turn making a toast during the meal. Mother says: To True Love and Real Romance. Which I think is sweet. Dingo's is: To weddings, may they come no more than three times in a lifetime. Mother hits him when he says that and Jethro makes a toast to everyone getting on with the meal. Even Charis laughs at that and then she proposes a toast to honesty, which is not really appropriate for a pre-wedding toast, but we all drink to it anyway. I'm last and I don't really know what to say. I almost drink to the bride and groom, but I think that's too obvious, so in the end I say, To all of us. Everyone says, Hear, hear. And Charis says, Good toast, sis.

There's a young waiter who brings us our food, and I notice that he keeps coming up to my end of the table. The hot dizziness is gone now, and in its place there's a kind of emptiness. Hunger, maybe. We order more champagne during the meal and the waiter comes and pours a glass for Dingo and Mother, and then one for me. He leans over as he does it and says that he has been making toasts to me all night. That's sweet, I think, and I tell him that – that I think it's sweet – and he says that he knocks off for his break in twenty minutes and do I want to meet him outside for some fresh air and a chat. Actually, I tell him, I do. I see no reason why not. Charis is watching me the whole time, I can feel her eyes on me, so I look up and poke my tongue out at her. Like I'm five, but I don't care. I'm all tingling up the inside of me, like something is rubbing against me. I cross my legs hard and the tingle gets stronger. Dingo pours me more champagne, and when they ask for the dessert menu, I see the waiter walking out the side door, with a look back at me. They're all too absorbed in the dessert menu to notice me getting up, but I say that I'm off to the toilet, in case they wonder. Not that I'm doing anything wrong, for goodness sakes, getting some fresh air and chat, that's all.

He's outside, leaning against a drain-pipe, with a cigarette in his hand. Although I hate smoking and the smell makes me ill, for some reason – maybe it's his black trousers – it looks incredibly, well, sexy on him. There isn't another word to describe it, there just isn't. He asks if I want a cigarette – ciggie is what he says – and asks my name. When I tell him, he comes over to me and puts his hand up to my hair and says, You've got beautiful hair, Moira. I'm about to tell him no, it's Marah, but the ratty tin door opens and I have to turn around. Charis pushes the door right open and comes out into the alley. I'm still standing there, a breath away from him, whatever his name is, and his hand is on my shoulder.

Charis says, Oh, there you are, Marah, we're about to order desserts and we couldn't think what you would want. She grabs hold of my hand and takes me inside, like I'm truly a little girl. She lets go before we get to the table and Mother tells me that in the end they ordered me fruit salad with no cream and is that all right? Somehow I manage to nod at her, but my head is somewhere else.

I've gone whoosh, all of a sudden, slipped back without even trying. Remembering the time when I was in my second year at the Con., when Charis came to a post-show party. I'd only been going out with Daniel for a few months, and he was studying or working or something and didn't manage to see the show at all, so Charis took the comp. ticket and came along. At the party she wandered off and then I wandered off and then she came looking for me and found me outside, against a wall with some third-year whose name I can't remember. Actually, no, it wasn't a third-year, it was a friend of a friend who'd gatecrashed the party. Charis must have been a bit drunk, because she said, Stop fucking my sister. Or something like that, and then she wandered off again and she never said another word to me about it.

Funny, isn't it, how I'd completely forgotten about that. My brain must be like a sieve. Really. Things go, just disappear from my brain and then come back at the oddest times. Even when I don't want them. Especially then.

*The Blessing*

# Go in Peace

Wylkie is banging on the door, even though it's wide open. His feet are inside the doorway, and really his whole body is as well, but he keeps knocking as if he is outside and he can't see Marah coming right for him, right for the door. Before she reaches the bookcase, she yells at him to shut up and stop banging.

'Where's Jethro? We're late for footie practice. He was supposed to come straight to my place after school.' Wylkie is jumping around as if he's got ants in his pants, hopping from foot to foot and looking ready to run any second.

Noeline calls from the kitchen, 'Hasn't he made it to your place, Michael? I thought he would have left by now. Go and get him, Marah. Give him a boot up the backside.'

Marah is obedient, working these days on being Good, keeping Noeline sweet and happy and present. Jethro, lately, has been invisible, picking quietly at meals, not going sailing, watching telly on his own. Sometimes, he tugs at Charis's arm and says he's sorry about the game and Charis shakes him off, staring into the distance as she does. Not a clue what he's talking about, she says, not a clue. The week before last, though, or maybe even the week before that, he suggested a game of Chasies and Charis said she was fed up with games and to leave her alone and go and play with his friends for once. Instead, he disappeared to his room, reading comics or playing with his models or who knows what? There are no more calls from Mr Nobody, not since they changed numbers, but Noeline is always careful to get the post and three times, maybe four, Marah has seen her throw letters straight into the bin, without even opening them. Being good, being quiet, she asks no questions.

255

'Jethro, Wylkie's here for footie practice.' Marah calls at his door but doesn't open it.

'Tell him I'm sick.' Jethro is a small, far-away voice. The Wizard of Oz.

Marah pushes the door open. 'What's wrong?'

He's lying on his side, reading an old-looking book. 'Dunno. I'm just sick.'

Wylkie is sitting on the step when Marah comes back out. He jumps up when he hears her behind him. 'Is he comin?'

'He can't go. He's sick. He said for you to apologize to Mr Bullock.' She adds the apology in herself, softening the blow.

'He was all right at school. Anyway, he should have called me, now I'm gunna be late as well. Tell him to ring me up tomorrow if he wants to come over and hang out on the weekend. If he's better.' Wylkie stomps off down the path to his mum's waiting car.

'What's wrong with Jethro, love? Did you say he was sick?' Noeline comes out from the kitchen with a plastic lunch-box packed full of sandwiches and carrot slices.

'Yair, he says he's sick. Too sick for practice, anyway. He's in bed.'

'I'll take him some lemonade in a sec. Where's Charis, do you know?'

'Dunno.'

'Sorry?'

'I don't know. I don't think she's home from school yet.'

'OK. Now, I want you all to behave yourselves this weekend while I'm away, all right? You can keep an eye on Jethro if he's sick, and I don't want any of you to give Dingo any trouble.'

'Where are ya going? Why can't we come with you instead of staying here?'

'Sweetheart, you know I've got a conference this weekend. Don't shake your head at me like that, I've been telling you all for weeks. Ask Charis when she gets home. Anyway, it's not for long. I'll need to leave after breakfast, but I'll be back just after lunch on Sunday. Dingo's talking about taking you all out sailing, if you behave yourselves.'

'Can't we come to the conference as well? We'll stay out of your way.'

Noeline strokes Marah's hair. 'Don't be a baby. Anyway, even if you could, Jethro's sick, and it's the last thing he needs.'

It is almost tea-time when Charis gets home. The street lights have just been turned on and Noeline is starting to say that they'll have to do a run up to the high school to find out what's happened. Charis is full of herself when she comes in, throwing her bag across the room and singing, 'There's no business like show business,' loudly enough to shake the windows and knock down the half-dying tree outside. Noeline asks where she's been so long and Charis says that she was auditioning for the school musical. *Annie Get Your Gun*. She makes a gun from her fingers and shoots at the bookcase. Perhaps – although this could be a blur in the memory, could be a glitch from somewhere else – she breaks into the Indian dance and proclaims that it is inevitable that she be given the lead. Certainly, she insists that Noeline knew all about it, that she signed a note weeks ago giving permission for Charis to stay back. That is definitely not an invention, not a glitch. Noeline says to never mind and gives Charis the same speech about being good all weekend and looking after Jethro who's sick and not giving Dingo any trouble.

Charis stops shooting at the walls, stops humming. 'You never told us you were going away.'

Noeline slaps her hand to her head, as if she's an opera singer dying on stage. 'Why does no one in this house listen? I told you weeks ago, and I've told you several times since. And, as I told Marah, I'll only be gone one night, so stop making such a fuss. Anyway, I'll bring you all back some presents.'

'Do we have to stay here? Can't someone else look after us?'

'Oh, for goodness sakes, Charis, do you think I've got baby-sitters coming out of my ears? Stop being silly, and you can stop this behaviour with Dingo, because it's getting quite boring.'

'Can I ring up Jenny and see if I can stay at her place? Because she wanted me to anyway, I forgot to tell you.'

'Oh, go on, then. But only if her mother says yes. Marah, you'll have to look after Jethro, all right?'

Marah stares at the telephone as Charis picks it up, trying to get Charis to look at her see the big fat *no* which she is concentrating on getting on to her face. But Charis doesn't look and the phone seems to ring and answer, because Charis curves herself over the receiver and whispers and giggles into it and then comes back and says that it's fine, Jenny's mum said yes and could Noeline drop her off on the way to the conference in the morning. Noeline says, 'You girls will be the death of me. Honestly.'

In the morning, Marah and Dingo and Jethro stand at the door waving off Noeline and Charis. Although he insists that he is still sick, Jethro has been forced up to say goodbye and do his share of the waving. Charis's face can barely be seen as the car zooms off down towards the main road, it is only her hand which is visible, waving fast and joyous and victorious. The three of them stand for ages on the step, until they can't hear Noeline tooting the horn any more. Jethro says he is, he really is, still sick and he wants to go back to bed.

'Well.' Dingo claps his hands together, as if it's him who is the head-teacher. You would almost expect him to say, Boys and girls. He doesn't, though. He says: 'So, it's just us. Now listen, I've gotta take a run to the dump today and I'm gunna need some help unloading the trailer. If you blokes come out with me, I'll take ya sailing later on, OK?'

'I'm sick, I can't go to the dump and I don't wanna go sailing.' Jethro is still in his pyjamas, his face still crumpled and sulky.

'OK, mate. Ya must be sick if ya don't want to come sailing. Looks like you'll have to be me labourer, then, Marah. Get yourself into some old clothes and I'll hitch up the trailer, OK.' It is not a question.

Marah kicks Jethro on the shin as she passes him. She changes into last year's shorts, small and denim, and a tank-top from two years ago. Both the shorts and the top are too tight and not completely comfortable, but the top has a rip in the back and the shorts have ink stains which will never come out, and they're the only old clothes which haven't already been thrown out. When she comes out to the car-port, Dingo has hitched up the trailer and is piling bags and boxes next to it. He looks up when Marah comes out and takes ages to look back down again.

He's business-like when he speaks. 'OK, you bring out the pile from next to the shed, there's two big bags and the old planks. The chair comes as well. I'll get the stuff from inside.'

Marah doesn't even screw up her face, doesn't even say, 'This sucks.' Marah is Good. She drags the planks, the chair, the bags of rubbish, one by one until they're beside the trailer and she's hot under her arms and on her face. It takes an hour for the trailer to be loaded, and then Dingo says, 'Right, let's go,' and jumps in the car. The trailer rubs against the hedge as he reverses out, and the letter-box makes a loud clunk as they go past. Marah sits close to the door, with the window wound right down and her face pointing into the fresh air. When they drive past the end of the main road and turn on to the freeway, the wind smashes into her face so she can hardly breathe, and knots her hair up into small bunches.

They turn off the freeway on to the road marked Mingin Creek. There's a sign at the side of the road with a picture of a winding road going up a hill. Underneath it's written 'For three miles'. Thick clumps of trees line either side of the road and after several turns and twists – enough for Marah to be opening her mouth to the wind, trying to calm her belly – there is a small shining glimpse of Mingin Creek. Only for a moment and then it is gone, and there are only trees crowding in and road winding ahead. Now and then, a track turns off to the right or left. Marah counts nine tracks before they reach the wide dirt track with a gate and another sign: Mingin Landfill Site. Marah jumps out to open the gate and waits for Dingo to drive through. He pretends to drive off and she stands waiting for him to reverse. It's an old trick. Noeline does it sometimes, and Joe used to, and it's always supposed to be funny and it never ever is.

Dust flies up through the open window when she gets back in the car and Dingo drives off. Marah has to wind the window up to stop from choking on the dust, and also to stop the smell from coming in. Her hands are over her mouth and Dingo is saying, 'Just breathe through yer mouth and ya won't even notice.' But she does notice. When she gets out of the car, a swarm of flies land on her arm. She slaps at the flies with one hand while she's holding her nose with the other. Dingo is already unloading, calling, 'Come on, then, the sooner we're unloaded, the sooner we can go.' He pulls a hanky from his pocket and gives it to Marah to tie around her nose, so that she looks like a gangster or a surgeon. She pulls the bags from the trailer and drags them on to one of the huge mounds of bin-bags, old beds, washing machines, bits of cars, everything. Her sandshoes rub at her feet and, standing on the highest pile, she bends down to rub at her ankle. It's only when she comes up that she realizes, first, that her breasts have half-popped out of the neck of her tank-top and, second, that Dingo has stopped hauling the last of the rubbish and is standing watching her. She turns around, so that she faces away from him, and kicks the bags to the bottom of the pile.

'Right, that's the lot of it. Let's go. Carn, Marah, ya don't wanna dig up more junk, do ya?' Dingo stands at the open door of the car, half-in, half-out.

Marah picks up an old bicycle, completely OK except for the lack of wheels. 'Nah, but this isn't junk. Check it out.'

'Stick it on the back, if ya want. I'll dig up some wheels and fix it up for ya. Here ya go.' He lifts it from Marah and chucks it in the trailer. 'Give us the rope in the back seat, will ya, love? It'll get bumped out if we don't tie it on.'

Marah finds the rope on the floor in the back of the car. She stands on one side of the trailer, Dingo the other, tossing the rope back and forth and slipping it under the trailer rails. Dingo ties it with three different knots. The bike clatters and bumps in the trailer all along the dirt road and Marah keeps twisting her head to watch it. Dingo tells her a watched pot never boils, but that doesn't seem to mean anything, and anyway she doesn't want the bike to boil, or fall, or anything. So she keeps watching. Once they get through the gates, Dingo swings out sharp and fast on to the bitumen road and speeds up along the winding road. He swerves faster and faster around each bend, so that Marah is holding on to the sides of her seat and Dingo is laughing at her, telling her he's a perfectly safe driver. After the third big swing, the bike makes a loud clatter and Dingo says, 'Bugger, we'd better check it out, tighten it up again so that we get it home in one piece.'

He slows down and swerves into a lane on the left. It's a soft

260

dirt road and the trees stay close and dark on either side. A little way down the track, Dingo pulls over and tells Marah to stay in the car while he checks the bike. She sits and picks at the red skin where the sandshoe has rubbed her ankle. Blood is on her fingers and on the grubby-white of her shoe when Dingo gets back into the car.

'All fixed.' He doesn't turn the ignition on, or even put his seat-belt on. Instead, he turns in his seat so that he is facing Marah. His hand closest to Marah is resting on the gear-stick, his other hand has dropped to his lap. 'While we've stopped, sweetheart, I think we need to have a talk. You're old enough to know a bit now about things like how you should dress.'

Marah pulls at her shorts. 'Whaddaya mean?'

Dingo lets out a long breath. 'For instance, what yer wearing today. You're growing up now, you need to be careful.'

'But it's only because it's me old clothes.'

'Even so.' Dingo pauses, as if deciding something, then reaches over for her hand. Maybe these words, the exact nature of them, is hazy, a little clouded over, but not the taking of the hand, not the parking of the car. These are the sharp lines around which the haze clusters. 'Look.' He pulls her hand to him, right to him, right to the place in his jeans where he has undone his zip. He puts her hand on to a hot hard something. Marah knows what it is. It is a penis, a dick, a willy, a prick, a cock, a todger, a plonker, a wee-stick. She has seen pictures in Sex Ed., and talked in the playground, and seen Jethro's lots of times when he was younger. But not burning like this, solid and immovable. 'Men can't help this, you see. When they see a young girl dressed in very tight clothes, this is what happens. So you have to be very careful. You see?' He pushes on her hand so that it is half around the slightly wet penis, and he holds her wrist, pushing her hand up and down, up and down. 'You see?' He says, 'You see?'

Marah doesn't see, not at all, and her hand stays loose while he pushes on her. After a moment, he lets go of her wrist and pushes his willypenisdickcockprick back into his jeans, where it makes a bulge against his fly. He puts his seat-belt on and says, 'You're almost a teenager now, so just be careful what you wear and where you go, because that's what men have got.' As he switches on the ignition and does a U-turn back on to the track, he adds, 'It's important for you to know that. OK? Now, the best thing is for you to throw out those clothes and go shopping with yer mother and get some decent ones and we'll say no more about it.' Marah says nothing, because only this is clear: that she must work harder to be decent, to be good, to be better.

Silence rides with them all the way back to Windsor, and when they get home, Dingo goes straight into the shower, where he stays for half an hour, easily, and Marah goes straight to her room. Later that day, when Jethro knocks on Marah's door and asks her if she's got any comics he can read, she tells him to get right away, to never come near her again, because she hates him, he can be sure of that. Jethro is never to knock on Marah's door, he is never to ask for her sympathy when he is supposedly sick but really is just too lazy to make a trip to the dump or any other place, he is never to play with her or come near her in any way at all, because if he does, she will kick his head in. Jethro goes back to his room and stays there till tea-time.

They have tea in front of the telly. *Perfect Match* is on. No one speaks, and Marah eats only a couple of spoonfuls of her baked beans, then sits silently, watching the contestants come back from their dates with their perfect match. After tea she says she's tired and goes to her room. With the sound of cheers and theme music from the lounge room, she shuts herself in the bathroom and puts her fingers down her throat. Red vomit fills the bowl and Marah kneels on the tiles staring at it before she flushes it away.

When Noeline comes back, she brings a new football for Jethro and a red miniskirt for Marah. The bike stays in the shed, turning brown with rust.

# Charis

The kitchen is full of people, most of whom I wouldn't know from Adam's dog. Brian, Dingo's best man, wants to picks up his suit except it's not here yet and he has the loudest voice I've ever heard. Booming doesn't begin to describe it; this man is a bloody railway address system. Karen has dropped some secret giggly gift off to Mum and she's brought her husband with her. Nameless husband apparently, because no one bothers to introduce me. He's leaning on the bench, booming away with Dingo and Brian. The three of them booming on about being trapped, haha, isn't that what women are for, haha, stuck in a suit, ha ha, and the outrageous cost of spirits. Somehow, I manage to squeeze past them and start making myself a coffee without too much interruption – might as well be invisible as it turns out – and the doorbell rings just as the kettle starts whistling.

'It's a mad-house here at the moment.' Witch-mother shakes her head, she thinks she's an extra for *Neighbours*, playing the exasperated-but-endlessly-patient-working-housewife-with-a-heart. She comes back with an armful of boxes. 'I asked the florist to deliver the corsages in the morning but they got it wrong. Brian, do you want to take yours with you? Make sure you stick it in the fridge. Oh, honestly. I'm starting to remember why I put off getting married for so long. It's hectic here at the best of times, between school and sailing and Jethro's plans. More coffee, Kaz?'

Karen shakes her head and says she'd better be getting a move on, try and recover from the mayhem. Ha ha. Oh, yes, it's all bloody go go go here. Mum says she'll go out with her, cause she's got to go and pick up the suits and dresses. She smacks Dingo on the bum and tells him not get into any mischief while she's away and says to Karen, 'It's like leaving a great kid in charge of the house.' Karen laughs and says hers is the same, then grabs the Booming Man's arm and hauls him away. To be serviced, presumably.

Dingo and his little friend go outside to play in the shed – rattling on about ladders and dovetails or something – and there's a burst of quiet which smacks into the kitchen with the sun. The corsages are sitting on the table, so I take a peek – red carnations, very original – and put them in the fridge. It's not the flowers' fault that they've ended up in the House of Hell, so I might as well be kind to them. Specks of dust are drifting in and out of the line of sun pouring in through the curtain, and I'm watching them, thinking about bits of human body and dead skin floating about in my face. They could belong to anyone, all those specks, when you think about it. They don't come only from yourself, they pile up and mount up and are gathered through neighbourhoods and towns, so that what I end up with, here, floating on to my own skin, is bits of good people, bad people, messy people, dead people. And they end up with bits of me. Scary. I'm starting to think about investing in some sort of plastic shield for myself, because I'm not sure I want to be that close to that many people, when the phone rings and cracks open the quiet.

'Hello?' 'Gidday. Wedding House.' Dingo crackles on the shed-extension, crossing over me and my succinct yet elegant greeting.

I'm about to hang up and leave him to it, but I can hear Elgin trying to make sense of the multiple voices. 'Hello? Is Charis there, please?'/ 'It's all right, Dingo, I've got it.'/ 'Is that you, Charis? Have ya got it?'/'It's fine, Dingo, I'm here.'/ 'Hello?'

Dingo clicks the phone down and Elgin's voice is suddenly loud without the cross-overs. 'Charis? What was that?'

'Doesn't matter. Hi.'

'Hi. Just wondered how it was goin. Is this phone tapped?'

'Oh, God, probably. It's OK, I'm trying not to get bothered by it all. Hey, why don't you come tomorrow?'

264

'To the wedding? I haven't been invited.'

'Come to the church and we'll work something out for the reception. Ya can share my meal and sit on me lap. Or just come for the sherry. It'd be easier if you were there.'

'I dunno, it'll feel pretty strange meeting them, you know, but, you think it'll be OK?'

'Yair. Carn. Free food.'

'Done. Do I need a suit?'

'Wear whatever, I'm not fussy. Get the West Sydney line out to Windsor and then, umm, it might be best if you get a taxi to Saint Peter's Anglican Church, Kensington Road. Be there by twelve. But I'll phone ya if I decide not to go. Or if the whole thing's called off.'

'Great. I'll go and press my best frock. See you tomorrow.'

After he hangs up, I go back to look at the skin and dry bones floating in the air, but the sun-stripe has gone. This is like labour, this whole thing, this waiting and waiting. There's nothing for me to do – at least Marah can go off and practise, but all I can do is think about To Speak or Not To Speak and make lists of jobs I can apply for when I get back to London. Singing Telegrams and waitressing. That's the total of my work experience, which doesn't offer me a whole lot of options. London seems far away and dark and I'm starting to doubt its presence at all. Being away does that; I doubt Australia when I'm over there, I think I've made the whole thing up. My flight is supposed to go next week and, maybe it's inertia, but part of me is thinking of staying. Not here in little suburbia, obviously, but in maybe Melbourne or Brisbane or Perth. There's a whole country I haven't tried, and it seems to have grown up while I've been away. Seems to be shaking its shackles off a bit. And I could go anywhere, do anything. I don't have to be shackled to anything.

Marah comes in the front door while I'm making a list of pros and cons for each city. She looks over my shoulder and goes: 'Why would you come back here?'

'Why not? What's England got that Australia hasn't got?'

'History. Culture.'

'Bollocks. Where have you been, anyway?'

'At the church, practising. I'm fed up with trying to practise

265

without an instrument. And I won't get a chance with the organist until an hour before the rehearsal tonight. I think they could have organized it a bit better, or at least asked me what a singer requires. It just shows a lack of consideration.'

This is the first time I've heard Marah give a word of complaint about Mum, or the wedding, or herself, and it leaves me with my mouth half-open and tongue hanging over it as if I'm a dog. Trying to think of something to say, trying to make my tongue work, do its job. Not that a dog would try to think of something to say. As far as I know. Eventually, I mutter, 'Well, it's not really her priority at the moment, is it?'

'She should have thought about priorities before she dumped "Ave Maria" on me. My voice has had it, anyway. I feel like I'm about to come down with a cold.'

'Stress, maybe.'

Her head snaps around as if I'm trying to catch her out. 'I'm not stressed. There's nothing be stressed about. It's a wedding, for goodness sakes. It's a reason to be cheerful, not a reason to be stressed.'

Great. So now I know the rules. Number One: I have no right to open my mouth, so just shut up. Number Two: I have no right to be stressed, so get happy. Marah stomps off to make some anorexic juice or whatever it is that she seems to be living on at the moment, and I flop on the lounge. Families. Can't live with them and you can't legally kill them. Choices, choices, choices. Divorce my family? Run away? Right now, I want nothing to do with them. And I don't want to be the one to open my mouth and shoot off and be responsible. Why should I?

As far as I recall, I never asked for the bloody job of Family Conscience, and I don't want it. If I had the guts, I'd catch a train into the city and get a bus to the airport right now. Have nothing more to do with them for the rest of my life, and I mean the whole bloody lot of them. They're all as bad as each other. But if I had guts, I would have walked out years ago, or opened my mouth instead of holding on to a stupid promise. Made when I was a kid. That shouldn't count. It doesn't count. If you promised to marry someone when you were fourteen, no one would hold you to it. So why should this be any different? Except I can't be arsed. Can't be arsed breaking the promise, can't be arsed walking out. Can't be arsed anything.

I doze off thinking about the origins of the phrase 'to be arsed' or 'to not be arsed' and wondering whether anyone has ever stood up in that bit in the wedding service where they ask you to stand up and object. I'm not really sure if I sleep or not, or if I'm in a half-dream, half-awake stage. Don't know how long I lie there either, dozing, thinking about arses and their attachments. The door clicks shut, and I hear that, but as if it's far away, and then I feel my toes being tickled and hear Dingo sliming on about sleeping beauties. I kick him and keep my eyes closed so that I don't have to see his ugly face.

'Have a nice nap, darling?' Mum is laughing at Dingo's merry little tickling trick. Oh, yes, he's such a character. Such a card. 'Is Jethro around? I've got his suit.'

What is amazing about my mother is her ability to put a bright voice on even when she wishes you weren't around. After every argument we have, she does this bright brittle thing, as if nothing has been said. You can only tell she's upset because she pulls her mouth tight, into a little bunched-up knot, so that lines gather at the edges. And her voice gets over-bright, as if it's toffee, sharp and sweet and might break into pieces any second. She's got that voice on now, which could indicate a fight with Dingo, or wariness towards me, or anything in fact. How should I know? And I don't bloody care, either. When I tell her that I would expect Jethro to be in his room, because he seems to live in there, she bunches up even tighter and says, 'Would you go and have a look, Dingo? He needs to check his suit again. Just to be sure.'

'Here. I made you some apple juice.' Marah hands me a tall glass, with a slice of green apple floating on the top, and a drinking straw propped against the side. The glass is cold, with small beads of water sliding down the outside. I rub the glass against my forehead and Marah grins, looking like a child.

'I chilled the glass in the freezer. I thought it would be nice to wake up to.'

'I feel like I'm at the Hilton.' I am caught in a fast, fierce rush of love for my sister and I know that I can't walk away, just like that, just keeping my tongue, keeping my own counsel. It takes so little to please me. A chilled glass of juice with a bit of apple, and you have won my love for ever. I'm sure I used to be harder to win over than this. Maybe not for Marah, though, maybe I was always easy for her. After all, I owe her. I owe her big time.

Later, we're all gathered around the table as if it's Happy Families at the Walton's, and Dingo is thanking us – Marah, Jethro and even me – for our support. Telling us how grateful they both are and thanking us in advance for the rehearsal, for everything we're about to do. Witch-mother is nodding, smiling, the brittleness slowly easing away and I swallow and swallow until the words rise up to my throat. They sit there for a while, heavy and thick on my tongue, while I'm nodding along with whatever it is they are saying. Something about needing to stick to times quite tightly. It's only because I have to that I open my mouth, only because it's all my fault anyway, at least partly, and only because Marah gave me an iced apple juice to wake me up and I don't know what I ever did to deserve a sister like her. Except put her in danger. Blah blah, goes the witch-mother, blah blah blah goes Dingo, and, finally, I clear my throat and announce that I need to say something important. Jethro sighs and mutters that I always have something important to say, it just isn't important to the rest of them.

'This is important. It's important to everyone.' Suddenly I realize that I have no idea, not really, of what it is I want to say. I should have rehearsed. People do that. Spend years rehearsing, practising, reading the right books, writing down the right words. Not me, I just launch in. Launch in and then notice the ringing quietness in the kitchen, the big heaviness of the air, the 'Oh, yes?' on the faces. When I've started and can't stop.

'Well?' Mum has the brittleness back, but with an edge of patience. It's the I'm-actually-a-saint-but-I-have-a-very-difficult-daughter voice. 'We need to leave in about half an hour, Charis.'

'Marah?' I nudge her with my leg.

'What?' The gentle sister of iced apple juice has gone the way of the witch-mother and in her place is the oh-for-God's-sakes-what-now face of this more familiar version of my sister.

268

'I'm sorry, I promised you years ago that I'd never say anything, but I can't. You have to tell her.'

'Tell who what? I thought this was about everyone?' Jethro stuffs half a bread roll into his gob so that crumbs spray everywhere as he speaks.

'It is. I think it is.' Suddenly I'm unsure, especially with Marah glaring at me as if I'm Number One Madwoman. 'Oh, God. OK. I'm saying this now because, I dunno, I can't go to the wedding unless I do. In fact, I don't think I can go to the wedding anyway.'

'What? Why do you have to do this, Charis? Why, every time, do you have to wait until the best possible time to cause me the most possible distress and then pull these stunts on me? I have absolutely done my best by you and you seem to constantly need to undermine this whole family.' The witch-mother is actually crying, and as far as I can tell, they're real tears. 'It was never easy for me to keep this family going, but I stuck with it.'

'It's OK, Noel.' Dingo's hand goes out, and I'm ready to slap him, hard.

'Oh, God. Maybe it was hard for you to protect us, I'm not saying you didn't try.'

'What?' Mum looks dazed, as if I'm speaking another language.

I breathe in and look down from the diving board I seem to be standing on. Scary. Turns out not to be a diving board but a whopping great bloody cliff. With rocks below. Yippee, here goes. 'Dingo, umm. When we were kids, when I was in high school, well, really this is Marah's story.'

Marah glares at me. 'Apparently not. I'm in the dark.'

'Right. Fine. When Marah was twelve, Dingo touched her. Or made her touch him. Actually touch him. I should have said years ago, but I couldn't.'

'What on earth are you talking about?' Dingo has let go of Mum's hand and has both of his fists on the table.

'When Mum went away to that first teacher's conference. Somewhere, I can't remember where.'

'Gold Coast. And I was here the whole weekend. I can remember.' Jethro looks at Marah, not at me.

'How can you, Jethro? It was bloody years ago.' I don't mean to be angry at him, but I am. As angry as I am with Marah for sitting there with her mouth shut.

'Oh, my God. Are you saying, are you attempting to say, that Dingo interfered with your sister?' Noeline has dropped her head forward, but she's still sitting close to Dingo.

I realize that I don't know the words, have never learnt the language. Interfered with. Touched. Performed cunnilingus. Made to perform fellatio. Raped. You read them in the papers, the reports, naming everything as if it's easy, but it's not, not when you don't know the names.

'Marah?' Mum is dropping even further and she's leaning right over to Marah, as if she's prompting her in a play, reminding her of the lines. 'Marah?'

Marah is shaking her head. 'Is that what you've thought all along? I don't remember that at all, I really don't. I don't know where this comes from, Charis, but it's not me. Definitely not.'

'But you told me. You told me never to tell.' It comes out in a shout and in a stream, the words making one sound.

'No. I told you I had a dream like that, maybe I told you that. Because, I dunno, maybe I did have a dream like that, once, about Dingo, and I was too embarrassed to tell. Maybe I made it sound like it was real, I don't know. I was just a kid. It wasn't real, it definitely wasn't real. I'm sorry if I told you that, and you made it real. Because it's not true, it never was true.'

'You didn't tell me it was a dream. You told me it happened. I can remember where we were sitting when you told me and you said to never say it out loud again. I can remember, Marah.'

Her voice is quiet. 'Well, I can't. And if I told you that, I must have made it up, because it never happened.'

The ringing quiet and the heavy air come back, only now heavier and thicker than before I started speaking. They're all staring at the table, at their feet, at anywhere but me, and I can feel the big fat 'I'm sorry' that I'm supposed to drop into the silence. But my mouth won't make the words, I can't say sorry for all of that, all those years thinking that, knowing that about Dingo, and then knowing something else, knowing that it was all wrong and never true. Except I don't know that, I don't know

270

anything now, what's true or right or wrong. They wait and wait for me to say something and after a while Marah says that we really should go to rehearsals and that she assumes that I will be coming to the wedding. Nod nod goes my head, but I still don't know, I still can't make sense of what it is I'm supposed to say or do. Because I don't know, now, of course I don't. Anything. But it's true what I said: where we sat, what she said, her hands grabbing at her pink denim shorts – I blink for a second, any time of any day, and I remember. Whatever she says, however hard she says it, I know this, I do. I know what I remember.

# *Marah*

The doorbell rings about five times before anyone bothers to go and open the door. Jethro is in his room, just for a change, and Mother calls out for someone else to get it. Obviously I would, I would go and open the door, particularly as I know it will be Daniel, even though he wasn't supposed to come over before the wedding. I just know the way he rings the bell. Short and sharp and definite. But I'm stuck on the toilet and I can't move. Huge knots are travelling right down my body and I'm literally doubled over on the toilet seat, holding my hands across my stomach. Ding-dong, ding-dong, ding-dong. You would think that Dingo would be able to tear himself away from whatever it is he is doing, or that Jethro could think of someone else for once and actually leave his room. Thinking of other people is definitely not Jethro's strong point. Obviously I wouldn't expect Charis to stop moaning and complaining and harping on about things that are best left buried, not even for a moment, not even just for the few seconds it would take for her to go and open the door.

Although I definitely did need to take some laxatives – because my stomach was so tied up and there was a big bulge instead of a flat belly and the dress is really tight and, after all, the wedding is tomorrow – I may have taken one too many. Not that I went overboard, I'm not silly with them or anything. In fact, I've only used them a few times before. Four times, if I'm being truthful. Maybe five. Usually, they take longer to have an effect, and I deliberately took them just before we needed to leave so that they wouldn't have an effect until later. Also because I need to feel empty, instead of heavy and sicked-up, the way I do now.

Thanks to Charis. Never leaving anything be, never shutting up, not even for one minute, and she always makes it sound like it's my fault, my idea. Even when we were kids she did that, or went off and had her own good time while I – what? While I what? That was strange, just then, my mind went whoosh, away, for a split of a split of a second, and now it's back and I don't know where I was. Away.

Eventually the doorbell stops ringing, so I assume that someone's let Daniel in. Either that or he's gone off again, disappeared into the wild blue yonder never to be seen again. Should fill me with horror, even the thought of that, even the idea, but it doesn't. Secretly – and I'm ashamed even to know this – it fills me with relief. If I went into the lounge room and Daniel wasn't there and he never did turn up again, I'm not sure I'd care at all. Now that's silly, of course it is, all this is silly. Because I do care, and I would, I couldn't bear it, I'd want to die. Really, the only reason I'm even thinking like this is because I'm so doubled over with the whole of my insides falling out in one stream, swearing to myself that this is the last time, really the last time that I take laxatives. They always seem like such a good idea at the time and then I wind up feeling horrible and more empty than I wanted to feel in the first place. Emptiness isn't necessarily the feeling that I want, it's only that I don't want fullness as a feeling, don't want the feeling of being clogged up, overloaded and weighed down with everything.

After I've flushed, I put the lid of the toilet seat down and stay sitting on it for a while, my head resting on my hands. Noise travels in this house, but even so I can't hear any voices out in the lounge room, so I've got no idea whether Daniel has been let in, or gone away, or whether he's sitting outside on the front step with his head in his hands. Just like me. Except not on a toilet seat, obviously. There isn't a toilet on the front step. Actually, what he's doing is sitting on the lounge reading a medical textbook. When I come out of the bathroom, with my stomach still hurting, he's hunched over like a question mark, huddled over a thick book. You would think that once you'd got your degree, graduated, worn the robes and actually started

273

telling people what was wrong with them, you could stop studying. Daniel will never stop. He's very ambitious.

He doesn't look up until I tap him on the arm, and then he smiles at me, but in the distracted way he has. I would definitely change that about him, if I had the choice. He says, I thought I could give you a ride to the rehearsal. Are you wearing that?

My dress is fairly crumpled, but I didn't think it looked especially bad, so I say, Yes, why, what's wrong with it?

Nothing, he says, and goes back to his book as if I haven't even come into the room.

Liquid is filling my stomach again, but even so I know I have to get out of here, and to get him to put his stupid book down for once. So I start gathering up the plastic carrier bags full of Orders of Service for the wedding and grab the folder with my score in it. Mother comes out just as I'm telling Daniel to get a move on, that we haven't got all day. Her face looks a bit puffy, even though I can see that she's put concealer and foundation on and probably used skin colorant to even out the tones, but even so. It's in her eyes, mostly. Red around the edges. Not that you'd pick anything up from her, not the way she smiles at Daniel and says, Oh, hello, Daniel, have you had a cup of tea?

I jump in before Daniel has a chance and say, No, he hasn't, but that's because we have to go. Don't you think so? We'll be late if we hang about any longer and that wouldn't look very good at all.

Mother smiles at Daniel and says, Aren't I lucky to have such an organized daughter? She keeps us all in line, Daniel. Has she given you your buttonhole? It might be best if you take it now, put it in the fridge when you get home, though. No, don't move – I'll get it. Marah, you stay here and keep Daniel company.

While Mother goes off to the kitchen to pick up the buttonhole from the fridge, I sit down next to Daniel and give him a kiss. He shuts his book and puts it on the floor, asks if I'm excited about the wedding. Before I really get to say anything apart from yes, Mother comes back in with the buttonhole held out in front of her as if it is a precious object. Which I suppose it is, if you want to see it that way. So I don't get a chance to say that I'm a little bit worried about 'Ave Maria', not because it's remotely difficult

274

– I mean, as a piece it doesn't stretch me at all – but because I haven't been working my voice and I feel the strain from even talking so much. All I've done is talk talk talk since I got here, and I'm a bit tired of it, if the truth be told. Very tired. And I would think it was obvious that I'm tired, obvious that my voice is tight. Even I can see the blotches in my skin from not getting enough sleep. For some reason I can't seem to sleep here, in this house – I've been lying awake at night the whole time I've been back – and it shows, it definitely shows on my skin and in my eyes and in my voice. Obviously not as much as I think, though, because Daniel doesn't ask me at all what the problem is, or if there is a problem. He just takes the buttonhole and puts it on his T-shirt as a joke, and then when I say we'd really all better get a move on, he says, OK, let's go.

Mother says, You two go on ahead, I'll just grab my notes and then we'll be along. We'll bring Jethro and Charis. If we can drag her out of whatever great misery she's in now. But the organist will be there any second. The church should be open – I think the vicar was going to get there first and open up. What's his name again? God, I must try and remember before we see him.

When we're in the car, Daniel puts a CD on – *Great Sounds of the Sixties*, Daniel likes old pop music – and lets the engine warm up for a while before he pulls out. He does that a lot, says it's better for the long-term future of the car, doesn't shock the engine so much. Which surprises me, because I have to confess that I didn't realize that engines could be shocked. People can be shocked, obviously, and pets and children, I suppose, but I would never have thought it of an engine. But there you go, there are all sorts of things in the world which I've never thought of. We can't all think the same things, and actually one of the reasons I love Daniel is because he is different to me. For instance, the fact that he doesn't like opera, not at all. Now that could be a problem, but it's not, because I respect it, I respect his opinion. Perhaps later on, when we're married, then it might be a problem, but not now, not at all.

'Surfer Joe' has played right through by the time the engine's warm enough for us to go, and by that time I can see Mother opening the front door.

Hurry up, I say to Daniel, we have to get there before them.

He lets the hand-brake off and reaches over to ruffle my hair. He likes doing that, but it isn't my favourite thing of his. Sometimes I feel like I'm a puppy when he does it. He only means well, though, so I don't say anything about not liking it. Instead, I put my hand on his knee and he turns the music up – he likes it to be quite loud, but only for some songs. He bops along behind the wheel, singing deliberately out of tune to 'Little Red Rooster'. Daniel really can be very funny sometimes. When the song finishes, he suddenly turns the CD down so low that I can barely hear it and says, All this wedding business is making me think about us.

I don't look at him, because I'm waiting to hear what he comes up with, so I just sort of go, Uh-huh.

Uh-huh, he says straight back at me. He goes quiet while he gets through an intersection, then says, What I'm thinking is that we should get married as soon as you finish your course. We should get engaged now, I mean.

Number one, I do not like it when he calls my training a course, it makes it seem much smaller than it is. And number two, I always wanted someone – a man – to go down on his knee and propose to me, or even to whisk me off somewhere where he'd already arranged the wedding and everything and all I had to do was walk down the aisle. Dingo would have to give me away, I suppose, but I don't like the thought of that somehow, it feels creepy. Maybe Jethro. Worse. Maybe no one, that's a better idea. Anyway, the point is, I'm not too happy about Daniel's method of proposing, although obviously I want to be engaged before I go back to Yale because it really would make everything a whole lot easier. So I don't say yes, just like that. What I do is, I go, Mmmm, do you? Daniel says, My sunglasses are in the glove box, would you get them out?

When I open the glove compartment, a small box falls out on to the floor. A ring box. Daniel is grinning at the windscreen, so I double over and pick it up. One lovely solitaire is inside, very simple, gold with a platinum cradle. Really I can hardly open my mouth, I feel so pleased. And it fits.

Well? Daniel looks at me for the first time. What do you think?

I say, It's beautiful, really beautiful. Daniel indicates and pulls into the church car-park, saying, Good, I'll take that to be a yes, then. I say, Don't say anything yet, though. I say that because I think we might steal the thunder from Mother, and also because I'm feeling liquid and burning in my stomach again and I don't want to have to run to the toilet just as we announce to everyone the happy news. That would be too embarrassing for words. Also, in spite of the ring sitting pretty on my finger, it's suddenly all I can think about – the sharp ache inside me, the fire. We sit in the car for a moment and Daniel kisses me. Although it's not what I had in mind for a proposal – something a little bit more romantic would be nice – the ring is lovely on my finger. I could take it off, but I won't, I'll leave it on but not flash it about or make a big deal about it or anything. Frankly, I don't think anyone's likely to notice at the moment anyway. Not really, not honestly.

Although the church doors seem to be open, I can't see any cars parked either in the car-park or on the street in front of the church. It's a huge church, lovely, almost cathedral-like. Apparently the minster invited Dingo and Mother to come to some services here. When she told me about it, Mother said, Can you imagine me and Dingo in a Sunday church service, what a laugh. Not that I did laugh, and I'm not laughing now either. Daniel spends ages putting the steering-wheel lock on and the car alarm, which I do think is a little bit excessive given that this is a church. Still, it's good that he's careful, I'll be grateful for that one day, I'm sure. Cold darkness hits us when we walk in. Maybe it's not really cold and dark, it just seems that way after the warm sun. After a moment or two, my eyes start to adjust and I peer around me. Red carpet down the aisle. Flowers stuck on the end of each pew and huge bunches at the front – the florist has done a lovely job, really lovely. Mother has gone for mostly miniature red roses and ivy, that sort of look, and I must say it's very elegant.

Daniel takes my hand and hums the Wedding March in my ear, starts walking me down the aisle. When we get to the front of the church, a voice calls out, Hello? and a fattish man comes out of a little room.

He says, You must be with the wedding party, is that right? I'm Michael Redmond, the minister here. I'm afraid I've had a call from the organist to say that she won't be able to make it tonight, but I'm sure that won't be a problem. Are you alone?

Daniel answers him, because I can't think about anything except that the organist isn't turning up and how am I supposed to do this without ever getting a decent run-through? Singing with an organ requires very specific vocal projection, I need to listen to the instrument to know its measure. There isn't really anyone to be angry with, but I'm fuming anyway. I'd be ready to hit someone if I were a different sort of person. Daniel is explaining that we're waiting for the others who should be here any second now and the vicar says that he'll just be in the vestry and to call him when we're ready. He goes back into the little room and Daniel whispers, He doesn't look very much like a vicar, does he?

Three stained-glass windows are lined up next to each other above the altar. The one in the middle has Jesus – at least I assume it's Jesus, because he's got a beard and a long white robe on and he's lying back on the grass surrounded by lambs. Above the windows, running the whole length of the wall, there's a wooden strip with black painted writing on it. The words are painted in a fake olde worlde style, but you can tell that it's been put up there recently, maybe in the last few years. The words say, You Shall Know the Truth And the Truth Shall Set You Free. It mustn't have been such a great artist who painted it, because the last three words – Set You Free – are sort of squashed together with hardly any space between them. I have to squint to read the words properly.

Daniel and I sit down on a pew in the front row and I say, How am I supposed to sing tomorrow when I've had minus fifty in terms of practice? Daniel points out that minus fifty is actually impossible in the context of practice and I thank him for pointing that out. Sometimes – and I really do have to admit this – Daniel can actually be a pain in the bottom. Really. He shuts up for a moment and then asks me if I can practise without the organ and I say no, of course I can't, not properly and not to be so silly. Then I say this wouldn't have happened if it weren't for bloody

278

Charis, because I could have checked, I could have been more rigorous if I had more time, if I wasn't constantly having to listen to her harping. Everything is her fault, I say. And then I shut up because I feel embarrassed and Daniel is quiet for a moment.

After a while, Daniel says, What has Charis done? I didn't realize you hated her so much.

With my eyes closed, I can see Charis driving off in Mother's car. Can't see her face, only her hand waving fast and joyous and victorious. Disappearing to Jenny's house, fat boring Jenny, and leaving me. There in that house. And I can see this too: driving from the dump, a bicycle bumping in the back of the ute, and turning down the road marked Mingin Creek, and that's all I want to see because that sign up there, above the windows, that's a lie if ever I saw one, because there's no such thing as truth or untruth, and I will not see this any more, I cannot hear the bumping bike, the gravel beneath the wheels, the car stopping. Shut-up, shut-up, shut-up.

I look at Daniel and I say, No reason, no reason at all.

# Dido's Lament

They all have an opinion, don't they? All think they know, each of them. They don't, of course. They barely know themselves, how can they know me? But I'll tell you this much: it isn't the way they think it is. He does love me, he always did, that much is obvious. Surely, even to you, that is obvious? It always was, well, fiery. Magic. Sparks everywhere, even in the beginning, even before this, even before the flames. Always sparks. What I'd waited for. Without even knowing it. Breathlessness. Adventure. Fire.

We all want to be burnt, we all want to know it, the feeling of combustion. So no one need pity me, not at all. It's envy really, because I have felt it, have known it, that madness. I would choose that you would remember me and remember my fate, because it is glorious. Who doesn't want to give themselves over? Tell me that. Before Him, there was silence. Waiting, and the endless babble of women. Women waiting for men. And when he stepped ashore, how could I help it? Glistening and gold and with sand caked at his heels. His hair was matted and his breath smelt of the sea and of desperation. I loved it, how could I not? His eagerness melted into my own desperation and lifted me. He was always eager, always planning, dreaming.

This city is dull. It has always been dull. Was, until this. These flames, this ravishing fire. Nothing is dull now, all is bright. My children growing. Growing up and away, and not seeing me at all. Not looking. Their own madness is ahead of them, I wish them well in it. Before Him, they asked for cosiness and it suffocated us all. I have been thrown about by mad love. Have you seen Aeneas when he is angry? No? It is true, not many have. I have had the power to make him angry, what do you think of that? Screaming 'deserter' at him, for his leaving. And yet he has given me this, my glory, my fate, as much as he has sought his own. So I don't hate him, how could I?

Three days it took me to build this. Do you like it? Hard work, both for the head and for the hands. Good for the heart, work. I have always known that to be true. My heart is awake and singing now, where before it slept. Of course I didn't gather the wood myself. Others did that for me. You will see them, wandering, puzzled. Of course I didn't tell them what it was for. Very few understand passion, the wonder of it, the giving in to it. And not only that, but what would happen after? If I stayed, if I didn't do this? Old Dido, I would become. Old Dido with the once broken heart, with the once mad love behind her. Old alone Dido. Even my children, my own children, would pity me. Would stay at home tending me and hating me and my loneliness. So this is better, in all ways. And he can see me, as he sails. If he looks back, even once, he will see me, and burn, and regret.

It is solid, workable. As these things go. These planks are well cut, well tied together. The building up and the tying together I did myself. Who would believe that I have never built as much as a small bonfire before? All things have been thought of. Climbing up and up is not hard, as long as I take my time. Some in the crowd are crying and that does not disappoint me. There are correct moments for these things, and I carry the taper high with me, careful not to let it ash or burn. Careful to keep it from the wind. Only when I'm high, and lying back against the pyre, do I drop it down. On to the leaves and dry grass, which catch. Perhaps there are more sobs from the crowd, I would think so, although I am not looking at them, only looking out, out to the sea. Crackling and hissing fill my ears as heat begins to rise up to me, gently at first. He was gentle at first, and I begged him not to be. Begged him to be harder, to bring the roughness of the sea with him, and he did.

Screaming is louder now, in my ears. Perhaps it is my own? No, my mouth is closed, melting tightly closed. Through the flames, down below, I see them. Smaller than they ever were, smaller than pets. My children. The three of them, each running to the flames. Running in with arms out and faces up. Up at me and mouths crying out to me. They should be pulled back, someone should pull them back. Flames are at them, my flames, higher than their bodies and I cannot keep looking down like this, looking down at them, when he is sailing out to sea. When his ship is dotting smaller and smaller and who can see if he is looking back?

My mouth will not open for me to call to him, or to them. Someone will pull them back, someone will save them from my flames. Still, I cannot look down now, for I will lose sight of him. There he is, I know that's him, the brown smudge, waving. My arms wave too, wave in the flames. Sparks scatter from my arms, drop down to the shapes below me, make more flames, make more dancing sparks. Yes, yes, this is glorious. Glorious.

# The Wedding
Procession

# Smile at the Birdie

Although Jethro has begged to be allowed to stay in the sickroom all day, there he is, on the sidelines, sulking away. Mr Moone, sports master, yells at Jethro to get a move on, get himself over to sign up for tunnel ball. 'Now, Jethro. You're no sicker than I am, and I want to see you competing in at least one event today. Come on, boy, this is your last chance.' Mr Moone glares across the sports field and then says, 'He used to be a decent young sportsman. He's turned into a pansy just lately.' It's not said to anyone in particular, although the sixth-class girls lining up for the four hundred metres race all hear him, because he says it loud enough to hear, loud enough to carry. Marah doesn't raise an eyebrow or twitch even one muscle, as if it is not her brother he is calling a pansy, just some stranger, someone she doesn't care about, never has cared about. Anyway, all there is time to think of is the line-up, the race ahead, the determination to win. Because you can't win if you aren't determined. It's not just Mr Moone who says that, it's everyone.

'Year six girls who have registered for the four hundred, line up, please.' Mr Moone has forgotten about Jethro now, who is sitting, doubled over, on the edges of the field. 'On your marks – Alison D'Arcy, are you in this race or not? Good, then get in line and get on your mark. Thank you. Now. On your marks, get set. Go.' Mr Moone, last of the Western heroes, lifts the starter gun into the air, waves it for a moment, fires, and then slips the gun into his pocket.

Marah pushes herself out, diving forward so hard that she might almost fall. Her body leans nearly parallel with the ground and her legs push and pound at the earth beneath her. Some shape is beside her, a running shape and there isn't time to figure out who it might be, that shape, there is only time to push forward harder because she will not be beaten, she will not. There is wind and the dim sound of cheers and her own breathing, and then the snap of the tape across her waist. Mr Moone is mouthing words at her and Miss Kelly calls out, 'Oh, well done, Marah. Champion.' And Marah would have been champion, sports champion of the whole day, if only she had won the eight hundred metres as well. Natalie Cox won that, spurred on by the calls of her mother on the sidelines.

Marah doubles over and watches her sweat dripping on to the ground, forming shapes like clouds and then dribbling away, swallowed by the dry ground. People slap her on the back, and all the members of the Kipling team, lined up in their blue T-shirts, cheer loudly. When Marah unbends herself, still panting and red-faced, Charis is there, standing right next to Miss Kelly. Chatting away as if she has any right to be there. Charis looks over and yells out, 'Hey there, winner.' Marah looks down again, looking at the patterns of sweat in the dirt.

Charis comes over and touches her on the back. 'Hi. Do you want some juice?'

'What're you doing here?' Marah's breath is back now and the words come out in one stream, steady and strong.

'I skipped Maths so I could get here in time. What a sacrifice, hey?'

'Bit of a waste really. Where's Jethro?' Marah raises her voice, calling past Miss Kelly, who is still smiling beatifically at Charis. 'Jethro? Jethro. Come here. You've gotta get yer stuff.'

'When's the presentation?'

'Dunno. Later.'

'So is there more stuff happening?'

'I said I don't know. Why don't you just listen for once?'

Charis backs away, as if stung. 'Sorry. Do ya want me to go over and get yer bags?'

'No. I'll get them in a bit. I'll see ya at home.'

'Don't be silly, I'll wait for you.'

'I don't want you to. I want to walk home with Jethro.'

'What's wrong?'

286

'Nothing.' Marah tugs at her sports skirt, tucks her blue T-shirt in. 'Oh, all right, then. Please yourself. But you'll have to wait while I get changed.'

Marah runs over to the square classroom block across the field, her pony-tail jumping up and down. Jethro is lying on the grass, surrounded by winners. This is the way it must be. Firstly, he groans when Charis prods at him with her foot.

'Don't. I'm sick.' His hand goes up to his head, as if he's dying.

'You're always sick lately. What races did ya go in?' Charis keeps prodding him.

'Nothin. I'm too sick.'

'Get up then, carn, we're goin home.'

Jethro rolls on to his side and then on to his feet, suddenly brisk and active. Perhaps Charis offers him a hand to get up, but he doesn't take it. By the time Marah has trotted back across the field, he is dancing about, ready to be off. Mr Moone calls out, 'Feeling better now, Jethro?' and Jethro suddenly stops jiggling, starts moaning again, putting his hands to his stomach, his head, anywhere.

'Carn, then. Hurry up.' Marah is sulky-voiced and duck-footed, worn out from winning her race. Her new knee-length denim shorts have a grass stain on the bum.

Jethro drags himself behind Marah and Charis, now and then letting out a little moan or saying, 'I wasn't just putting it on, I'm really sick.'

Half-way home, before they pass the train station, Marah speaks up, out of nowhere. Whispers to Charis: 'I've got a secret.'

'Tell me,' Charis whispers back, stepping up her pace to keep Jethro out of earshot.

'No, I haven't really.'

'You have. Tell me.'

Jethro catches up with them and grabs at Charis's skirt. 'Stop going off without me.'

Charis slaps at him. 'Get out. We're having a private conversation, Jethro. If you don't mind.'

'I do mind.' He keeps up with them, forgetting to put his hand to his belly.

'Too bad. You're too young.' Charis softens for a moment. 'I'll buy you a Sunny Boy later if you shut up and go away.'

Jethro immediately slows down, keeps himself a foot or two behind them. But if you looked, you would see his ears flapping.

'Promise not to tell.' Marah keeps her voice low.

'Course.'

'And to never ever mention it again.'

'Why?'

'I'm not telling if you don't promise.'

'OK.'

'You have to say it.'

'I promise to never ever tell.'

'Or mention it to me or anyone else ever again.'

'Or mention it to you or anyone else ever again.'

'And you have to promise to forget it as soon as I tell you.'

Charis is quiet for a moment, staring at her sister. 'I can't promise that.'

'Then I can't tell you.'

Charis stops where she is and drops her bag on the footpath. Or perhaps holds it to her, hugging it tightly, hugging the promise of a secret to her. This is one of the edges which is less sharp, less clear and sure. Something like a promise passes though her lips, something like: 'OK, I promise.'

'For ever? For true?'

'For ever and for true.'

Although the shadow of Jethro is lurking, Marah takes a breath and says out loud, almost as if she is reciting a poem she's had to learn: 'When you went to Jenny's, Dingo took me to the dump and I touched his thing. He put my hand on it.'

And then what? Then everything collapses in on itself and the words run together, stop making sense. Things get faster, so fast that they blur. Charis says things, things like: You must tell Mum, she should know, and Marah says no she shouldn't, she'll only go away like Dad. Charis knows that's true, so she shuts up finally, doesn't even say sorry for taking off to fat, boring Jenny's and leaving Marah in that house. Not a word of that, and from Marah, not a word of hate, although it's bubbling all right, bubbling away. The truth is that everything keeps blurring then. At home, Dingo is calm and ordinary, relaxed.

Months and years condense, shrink into one moment. Days of sailing, of practice at home, of Jethro hiding in his room forgetting what he did or did not hear, days of family footie games, of arguments over the TV: years of this, all blurring and muffled and softly softly. Days and years of Dingo's ordinariness, such ordinariness that it's clear that Marah must have dreamt it, the whole thing, her blurred-up memory. When Marah is fourteen, Dingo and Noeline give her a new bicycle, a ten-speed, and she loves it so much she could die. That's what she says, and she means it, she really does. There is no picture in her mind of an earlier, rusty bicycle, not that she can recall, not that she can access.

A curtain comes down, thick, thick and heavy as the earth's crust. Behind it, there is Marah. Long, long after the sports day, there she is, feet pounding, breath coming in gasps. Running, running, running.

# *Charis*

This morning I hate everybody in the whole world and everybody hates me. Zippadedoodah, what a glorious day. Evil eyes are being cast against me everywhere. Make no mistake: I am the bad guy. Marah spent the whole of last night's rehearsal getting herself as far from me as was possible, and the witch-mother kept wiping tears of hurt and disappointment away. Afterwards, I lay in bed staring at the ceiling, with a chug of thoughts running about: What's true? What's true? When the sun comes up, I'm still lying rigid, still counting truths or lies, depending on which way you look at it, and still no closer to bloody sleep or bloody sense. Today, though, today I will be sweet, I will be silent, because I've said my piece and done my bit and now I've had enough. More than enough.

What I'd like to do is sneak out of here and jump on a train, or in a car, and go somewhere else. Some other city, or the beach, or anywhere. That's not really an option as it turns out. No, no, there are jobs to do, corsages to be pinned, nails to be painted and, of course, the big event: Marah, the witch-mother and I have a cosy hairdresser's appointment together. If only we had matching Peter Pan collars. Marah drives Mum's car to the hairdresser's because, wait for it, Mum has got fake nails on and can't do anything with her hands. She sits in the front seat next to Marah telling us both that she doesn't know how she'll get the ring on over the acrylic nails and saying that next time she won't bother with a proper wedding, it's too much trouble. This is a joke, of course, because there won't be a next time. She explains that to us as well. Mostly, though, she is explaining to Marah, not to me. Because they don't quite know what to do with me and I don't know what to do with them. Everything has shifted and we are all wary. I'm happy – more or less – to sit in the back and be silent. Thinking: I don't know anything any more and I don't care.

Strangely enough, having opened my big trap and made it all so uncomfortable, I feel as if I'm lighter than I was yesterday. More free. Marah parks outside Headmaster's and says, 'So. Let's get beautiful.' Inside, someone called Shannon introduces herself to me as my stylist for the day and I say, 'Oooh, lovely. I'm your head for the day.' While she tweaks and turns at my hair she asks me whether I'm excited about the wedding. Rather than go into the whole sorry saga, I tell her I'm very tired and close my eyes. Not least because I don't especially want to see myself turned into a poodle. There are some things I just can't cope with, and seeing my hair cascading-in-a-delicate-abundance-of-curls (I think that's the look Shannon's after) is somewhere on that list.

Shannon plays with my hair and starts a half-whispered conversation with the hairdresser next to her. Something about Michael and Nikki and her not knowing what was good for her. Their voices are high-pitched and soft, so that they almost send me to sleep. Sounds of shampooing and snipping mingle in with them and, on the far side of the salon, the voices of my mother and my sister: blah blah blah. Not that I remotely want to be part of any cosy little huddle – not with my mother. But Marah is an expert at freezing me out, she's been doing it for years now. Ever since what she did or didn't tell me did or didn't happen. And I don't like that, being frozen out all the time.

After a while, Shannon's squeaky little voice cuts in on me. 'You look lovely. Roolly nice. Have a look.'

I look, and I do look lovely. If your idea of lovely is a primped-up doll. Personally, mine isn't, but I can see that the hair piled on top of my head does make my cheeks stick out in a fashionable sort of way. But it doesn't look like me, and I like looking like me. So I just smile and go, 'Mmmm,' as if I've had a nice sip of hot chocolate. The three of us – Marah, Mum and I – look like a matching set of Barbie dolls. Although I'm the only one with tits. And the only one with a body weight higher than my shoe size.

We totter out of the salon, all in a neat little row, and drive back to the house. My head feels three times as heavy as it normally does, presumably from all the hairspray. I keep bumping my hair against the seat-belt and I'm half-waiting for an invasion of birds to make me their new home.

When we get back to the house of horror, Dingo says, 'Three gorgeous birds in the hand,' and laughs as if yesterday never happened. I'm about to go and slip into something less comfortable, like a bridesmaid's dress, for instance, when he goes: 'That bloke phoned for you again, Charis. Wants ya to ring him back.'

There's a yelp in my bones when he says that, mainly because I'm kind of relying on Elgin to be there today. To be, I dunno, a bit of clarity in amongst it all. Or something. And I can't think of any reason he'd phone right now, this morning, other than to tell me he's changed his mind, he can't come, or doesn't want to come after all. The last thing I want to do is phone him back because my voice might give away too much disappointment, but I pick up the phone anyway. Elgin answers on practically the first ring.

'Hi. What's wrong?' I'm keeping my voice cool and calm, because I'm surprised by how much I've invested in this, and I don't want him to get a hint, not a hint.

'Charis? Nothing. I hope not anyway. I just wanted to check it's all OK for me to be there this afternoon.'

'Of course. Fine. Absolutely fine.' Although I haven't mentioned the new addition to the wedding meal to anyone yet. Other things on my mind. And also, until last night, I was thinking that I'd just get him there and then sort it out, but now I feel like I've got my voice back and I'm ready to stake my claim. My hand covers the phone and I call over my shoulder to the witch-mother: 'I'm bringing a friend to the wedding. And the reception.'

'Fine.' She shrugs her shoulders in a slightly not-fine way, but I'm not being swayed.

'See? Fine.' My words are rushed. There are too many people in the room and I somehow feel spied on.

'Great. I'm thinking of driving instead of getting the train. I'll feel a bit of a dork in a suit on the train. Anyway, have you thought about what yer doing next?'

'Whaddaya mean? After the wedding?'

'Yair, a bit. Next in yer life, I suppose that's what I mean. Are ya definitely going back?'

Wariness comes over me, that old feeling. 'Why?'

'I've found somewhere for the café. Not in Glebe after all.'

'Where, then?'

'Blue Mountains. Katoomba. I've had me eye on it for a while and I had a call earlier saying the guy wants to sell up.'

'Katoomba. Bloody hell, that's miles away.'

'It's a fantastic location, great community.'

'Right.' Inside my head, I'm going: why is he telling me this?

'Anyway, if ya wanted to stay, there'd be a job for you. We've got a lot to do before it's ready to go, and then, you know, I'll need someone to help me run the place. It's beautiful country there.'

'I know.'

'I'd really like ya to stay, Charis. I feel a bit attached, you know.'

I don't even take a minute to think about it. 'I don't think so, Elgin. I should get back to London. Commitments and stuff, you know.'

He goes quiet. 'Oh, OK. Right. Well. Never mind. Anyway, I'll see you at the wedding this afternoon.'

'Yair. See you.'

They're all staring at me when I put the phone down: Dingo and Mum and Marah. Drinking cups of coffee and pretending to be looking at something else. About as subtle as Ben Elton on speed, you know? Oh, no, we're not desperately being quiet so we can listen in on your bloody conversation. Absolutely not. Right. Anyway, I don't say anything to them, just go inside and lie on the bed. My turn to stare. Eyes open wide at the ceiling until the brightness makes them sting. And I don't even know why I said no, why I went cold as soon as he suggested it. London is cold and gloomy and depressed and, if I'm honest, lonely. There isn't a reason for me to be there, not one. Even if Donny hadn't fired me, I was hardly on a fast career track, was I?

Katoomba. It's true, it is beautiful, and central enough, and I have no doubt that it's crying out for some groovy café. Loads of tourists desperate to part with money. But it's not the job, it's not Katoomba, and in some ways it's not even Elgin. Ten minutes ago I was terrified that he was going to stand me up and now the thought of him fills me with terror. The moment I went cold was when he said he was attached. And I'm buggered if I know why. Everything is shifting too quickly, maybe that's it. All the things I knew, I don't know any more: Dingo made Marah touch him, my mother is a witch, all men are bastards. There's more, there's a whole whopping great list, but basically in the same vein. Also: it's my fault, what Dingo did to Marah. For years I've known that, known that if I had been around, it would have been me he'd got instead of her. But now, even that seems wrong, or not completely true. But something can be true even if you don't believe it, and it doesn't always depend on your point of view. Not always.

For ages I lie on the bed, eyes stinging, thinking around in circles. I'm on about the fifth circuit of Dingo-made-Marah-touch-him/Aren't-men-bastards?/Did-that-really-happen?/Are-men-bastards?/Elgin-isn't-a-bastard/You'll-end-up-like-your-mother/Dingo-made-Marah-touch-him, when Marah opens the door and says, 'We've got to go in twenty minutes. You'd better get dressed. Dingo's gone to the church already.' She looks pale and tired, and her voice is croaking.

'Are you OK?' My feet touch the floor and I get a rush of dizziness from sitting up so fast.

'Yes, fine. Are you?' Her hand is still on the door and she looks tiny.

'Fine.' I stop, think: I don't have to be part of this, all this silence, all this pretending. 'No, not really. Confused about lots of things. Are you happy about the song?'

'Not unhappy. But I shouldn't have had to come right now, not during my show. They should have waited. I'm going to tell her, I really am, actually, later. Let her know that it actually upset me.'

'Good idea. I'll be urging you on.'

'Not if you don't get dressed.' She smiles, tight-faced, and shuts the door behind her.

It's true: I don't have to be part of the pretending and the silence and the jolly-jolly everything-is-fineness. I know I've broken some rule by opening my mouth, by breaking my promise, but part of me feels like I've broken some enchantment as well. In fairy-tales, someone usually breaks a mirror or a twig or a chair, or anything, and then the whole kingdom is set free. Well, I broke a promise and not a whole lot seems to have changed here, not the whole world, except this: I know that these are not my rules and I don't have to play along. I've always believed certain things to be true, I decided that they were, and now I don't know any more, anything. So I'm going to have to find out. My big hunch is that the witch-mother would say that even if it is true, it's no big deal, better left in the past. But if that's true, why are we all so desperate to avoid it? Why have we spent so much time running away from it?

While I get dressed, I compose a speech in my head to Elgin. All about how I'm nervous, frightened, even, of all sorts of things. Him, for instance. Staying here. Going back to London. Lots of things. But that maybe things don't have to be the way I've always thought they are. Maybe I could give it a try, just for a trial, for a limited period only, see how it goes. Maybe I could check out the Blue Mountains, check out hanging around, see how it feels. Maybe I could do that.

The car-horn beeps outside and the three of us rustle into the back seat. Jethro, squeaky and tight-looking in his suit, slides in next to the driver. Ribbons stream out the back and a horseshoe is dangling from the windscreen. Marah sits beside me and I take hold of her hand, thinking: It's you I'm here to give my blessing to, not the wedding. I squeeze her hand hard, and for once, she squeezes back.

As we drive past the station, I start humming to myself. It's a tune from far off, far away and at first I can't place it, I just know it's stuck in my head somehow. Then I remember: driving to the Territory, Dad in the front, singing in a funny voice. I touch Marah's hand, say: 'Do you remember this? We thought it was such a funny song.' I sing the chorus for her: '*Keep your mind on the drivin' and your hands on the wheel, keep your snoopy eyes on the road ahead.'* After the first chorus, Marah joins in, adding harmony over the top and even being the bass line and the voices of the giggling girls. Mum is silent, even when we add the sound effects, but both of us are singing loud enough to fill the car: *'Keep your snoopy eyes on the road ahead. We're havin' fun, sitting in the back seat, huggin' and a-kissin' with Fred, ba DOM DOM.'*

When we stop singing, the driver applauds and I join in. Why not? I've broken a promise and I might just have broken a spell.

# *Marah*

Feet pounding, breath coming in gasps. Running, running, running. There's me, in my head, a picture of myself, as if I'm someone else, running madly across a field. It comes and goes, but all morning it's been there in the background, among everything else. Running, running, running. I did run, I used to run, I loved it. Once, I won the four hundred metres sprint and I would have been sports champion of the whole day, if only I had won the eight hundred metres as well. Natalie Cox won that. Strangely enough, my dress is digging into me, so that it almost feels tight. It certainly wasn't tight in the shop, and you would have thought that I'd be a bit thinner now than I was then. I've barely eaten anything but fruit for days and that usually does make a difference. Not always, but usually. If I remember to keep my stomach in, pulled in tight, I think it will be OK, I don't think anyone would really notice. That's what I hope. I'm trying not to think about the reception, all the food that will be there, because if I eat a big meal in this dress I know that it will show up immediately. So I have to be careful.

Two big flower pots have been set up outside the church – the florist has done a lovely job on the flowers, really lovely – and a few people are standing about, obviously looking for us. Spotters, I suppose. When we pull up, the driver lets Jethro out first, before Mother, which at first I think is a bit strange, but then I realize it's so that Jethro can be waiting to put his arm out for Mother. To walk in with her. We have to go first, Charis and me, and I know I'll have to force myself to go slow because the truth is I'm not feeling well, I'm really not. Aching throat, sick feeling in my stomach. I don't know what the problem is, it could be anything, anything at all.

The organ starts blasting out as soon as the car door closes behind us. The spotters have obviously moved fast. Everyone is standing when we walk in, all staring at us, smiling, mouths open. Charis is right next to me, then Mother on Jethro's arm behind us. I'm careful to hold myself back, walk slowly, even though I want to rush forward and get it over and done with. Right at the front in the second front row, I can see Daniel. He's on the end, leaning out, grinning at me. His arms are folded across his chest and in the second between seeing him and getting right next to him, I think: What a ridiculous position to have your arms in at a wedding. Folded across your chest like that. That's when I know, suddenly and clear as clear, that I don't want to marry Daniel and I don't want to be engaged to him, even if it means being completely on my own. Even if it means not having another boyfriend for ages, I don't care. Obviously, I can't stop on my way down the aisle and tell him that, not right now, it isn't the time, so I smile back at him and keep walking.

When we reach the front of the church, the minister stands up in all his robes and puts his arms out to the side. He says, Welcome to the wedding of Noeline and Alastair. Sniggers all round, because I don't think anyone in the church has ever heard Dingo called anything but Dingo. It wouldn't be appropriate for the minister to call him that, I suppose, not in a church. Dingo nods in an embarrassed way and steps over to hold Mother's hand. He pulls her closer to him and I start to feel cold, giddy even. It's not true, what Charis said, I know it's not, I'm sure it's not, but I suddenly feel my face burning as if it is, as if I'm ashamed. My whole body starts flaming up then, and I know that if I look down, I'll see my arms turning red and orange, flame-coloured. Even my feet feel like there are sparks flying on to them, so hot I could jump. So bright I want to stamp on them to put them out. But I don't, because it's not true, what she said, and the sparks aren't true, not really. It's just stress, just pressure.

We sit down and the minister gabbles and gabbles. Does

anyone here have any objections? Charis stares at the floor and I stare straight ahead and of course no one stands up because no one ever does, no one ever does have any objections, why would they? Dingo and Mother repeat after the minister all the words in all the right order and it seems like I can't understand them because my head is swimming. The organ is too loud and all I can think about now is 'Ave Maria'. Stupid 'Ave Maria'. To tell the truth, I don't know how it happens, because I'm trying to concentrate, I really am. I'm trying to take it all in and not think about the heat in my head and arms and feet, but it whizzes by so quickly. We sit down, we stand up, the minister says something about love and commitment, and reads a bit from the bible. Something about love is this, it is not that, it is the other. Before I can properly blink, he's whisking them off to the table at the back to sign the forms and I'm standing up and walking to the place where the minister was.

Daniel's face is big and stupid-looking in front of me, but it's Charis I really see. She's sitting forward, eyes wide on me. The organist plays through the first bar and I'm so distracted by Charis that I miss my cue. He plays through again, holding the notes long and hard and I know if I looked up, I'd see him nodding at me. My mouth opens and I turn my head to the side, just to let the organist know I'm all right. Dingo is half behind me, I can see him leaning over Mother. They're both blurred, but I can see them clearly enough to see the thumbs up Dingo gives me. My mouth opens and my eyes close and all I see is me running, running, running. Feet pounding, breath coming in gasps. Running, running, running.

The organ is loud, I can hear it, but I can't seem to make my voice come out to match it. I know if I open my eyes, I'll see Daniel looking up at me, all concerned, all embarrassed. And I know I'll see Mother looking around, grabbing on to Dingo. I have to make an effort, I have to make my voice come out, although it's true that I didn't want to be here and I shouldn't have had to come. My eyes open and I turn my head again, look straight at Mother. She's looking back at me, worried, unsure. As soon as I get outside this church I'll tell her she shouldn't have made me come, as if she doesn't know. My mouth is still opening and shutting and a thin croak is coming out, a strangled, strangling sound. Words are formed in my mouth, and maybe someone can hear them, but it's as thin as a dying frog's last sound. Croak, croak.

The organist is kind, only plays one verse through, then does a final flourish as if that's all we ever intended, and I sit down, tripping over my own feet and feeling too hot to notice anything else. Sympathy is actually tangible around me, I can feel rustlings of people in the front two rows being sympathetic and maybe even pitying and that's not what I care about. My back stays straight and my head stays up, even though I know my whole body must be nearing one hundred degrees, ready to melt, ready to burst into one big bonfire. The minister pronounces them Husband and Wife, and then Charis and I follow them out, meekly walking behind them. Confetti is thrown over us all and Dingo is loud and laughing and for some reason I have a desperate desire to punch him, hard. Mother slips herself next to me and takes my hand.

She says, What happened? Are you OK?

I look right at her and whisper, No, I'm losing my voice. But actually I never wanted to sing that song and, anyway, you should have waited until my term had finished.

Oh, she says, I'm sorry. I didn't know.

Dingo comes over and pulls me close to him, plants a kiss on my cheek and says, Never mind, love.

I pull back from him, as far as I can, and croak, Don't touch me. I'll see you at the reception.

Daniel's car is in the car-park, so I head towards it, keeping my head down so I don't have to have a conversation with anyone. Keeping my eyes on the car, I go over my little speech in my head: I don't want to marry you. That's all I need to say. Feet go one after the other and that's what I look at, not at the pictures in my head, always there, always playing through. Back, back, back. Further back than the picture of me running, further back than anything in the universe. Behind a curtain, thick and heavy as the earth's crust. All the pictures: Joe slamming Dingo against the wall, right near me, and his blood streaking near my hand; Dingo coming right in, right into the bedroom, right near me in my knickers and nothing else, looking straight at me, but not at my face; Dingo letting go of my wrist and pushing his willypenis-dickcockprick back into his jeans. All the pictures are there, I can see them all, but they're not real, they can't be real. Not everything you see is real, not everything is true.

There is no sun, but I can feel my own heat bouncing off the car, scorching my hands, probably scorching everything around. Dingo is on the footpath, being slapped on the back by the whole world, and I can see him calling Daniel over. I know it's not true, none of it, I know it's pretend, that it's come from somewhere else. The pictures are there but I don't own them, they don't belong to me and they can't be true, they can't be.

My head touches the car roof and I feel the flames lick closer. I go over it again in my head: none of this is true. Repeat after me: none of this is true. My mother is married to Dingo. She is happy. That is the truth. We are all happy. That is the truth. So why, then, why do I feel like I'm burning?

*The Honeymoon*

*Dear Charis,*

*I don't know if you've heard anything from Marah, she doesn't seem to answer my letters these days at all. I'm sure she's incredibly busy with this recital she's organizing. It sounds like all is going well with you, I'm pleased the café has opened at last. Thanks for the letter.*

*If you have heard from Marah, I assume she'll have told you about Dingo and me. If she hasn't, I'm sorry I haven't let you know earlier than this, but I've had to do a lot of thinking. Basically, Dingo and I are having what may or may not be a 'trial separation'. It's been very difficult, as I'm sure you can imagine, and I've taken my long-service leave from school so I can have some time just to make sense of it all. There was a young girl working at the boat shed part-time, I think she actually started off doing work-experience for school. Anyway, as he puts it, one thing led to another and that led to us separating. How detailed do I need to be? At least he told me before I found out from her parents; he did have the decency to do that. Her parents sound like they're quite reconciled to it all now – popping around to the flat Dingo's renting with the girl and staying in for tea and things. Easily bought. Sorry if I sound bitter. I'm sure it's all very predictable, getting frightened by commitment and so on, but still.*

*Anyway, given that the girl is quite young – I mean, she's not a child or anything like that, she is sixteen, but still – I wrote to Marah asking her to explain to me what happened when she was younger. With Dingo, I mean. She wrote back the first time and said nothing happened that there was any point in talking about and just to leave it, and since then she's not answered my letters. I know I didn't listen to you before, perhaps I should have, but I'm having to rethink everything at the moment, as you can imagine. To tell you the truth, I don't know why I need to know so badly. About what – if anything – happened. It is in the past after all – but suddenly it does matter. Marah seems certain and perhaps I should be content with that, but it does matter, for whatever reason. What do you remember, Charis? What do you know for sure? I'm sure Marah is right, that there was nothing worth talking about, but I need to know the truth.*

*Now that I've got my long-service leave, I'm thinking about taking off for a little while. Feeling inspired by Jethro finally making it to Indonesia. Maybe I'll take a coach trip around the Northern Territory! It's all been very upsetting, but I suppose the up side is that I've lost ten pounds from all the worry. Never look a 'gift horse' in the mouth!! I'd like to come down and visit you and Elgin, before I go away (if I do – it's all so up in the air at the moment), if you don't mind. Maybe just for a few days, or a week if you'll have me. We could talk then, if you'd rather do that than in a letter. If you ring me at home, I'll phone you straight back so you don't have to worry about the cost of the call.*

*I've got the sprinkler on in the garden and it's been drenching the back corner for the last hour or so – the carnations are looking very bedraggled now! I'd better go and rescue them.*

*Anyway, as always,*
*lots and lots of love,*
*Mum*

# Acknowledgements

I am thankful to both the Scottish Arts Council and the Royal Literary Fund for their generous support.

Thanks are also due to: Elizabeth and Frank Selby, for their hospitality in New York; David and Lucy Clough, for introducing me to Yale and New Haven; Dr Amy Wygant for extra information on *Dido and Aeneas*; Richard Griffiths, for the academic abstract.